FAKE EMPIRES

MARC LINDON

Matador
9 Priory Business Park,
Wistow Road, Kibworth Beauchamp,
Leicestershire. LE8 0RX
Tel: 0116 279 2299
Email: books@troubador.co.uk
Web: www.troubador.co.uk/matador
Twitter: @matadorbooks

ISBN 978 1800463 318

British Library Cataloguing in Publication Data.
A catalogue record for this book is available from the British Library.

Printed and bound in Great Britain by 4edge Limited
Typeset in 12pt Baskerville by Troubador Publishing Ltd, Leicester, UK

Matador is an imprint of Troubador Publishing Ltd

For J^3R

I have become an enigma to myself,
and herein lies my sickness and inner struggle

Saint Augustine

...even between the closest people
infinite distances exist...

R. M. Rilke

PROLOGUE

(1995)

"Carl, I hate myself for asking but I have to know. Has this ever worked?" Emma asks, waving a hand in the vague direction of the stereo.

"What?"

"This cliché-infested seduction technique of yours?"

"What?"

"This drivel, or maybe that should be dribble."

"What?"

"Oh dear, not used to the quarry having command of a polysyllabic vocabulary, are you?"

Rather than complete a monosyllabic four-timer, he opts for the visual equivalent.

"My, what an impressive array of quick-fire responses you have at your disposal."

Silence.

"You see, the part-time reluctant feminist in me just can't bear the thought that some gullible shit-for-brains fellow student may have lent some credence to your caveman logic."

"It's just a song."

"Part of a random compilation you threw together in an idle moment?"

"Something like that."

Shaun Ryder doing his best to ooze out a sexy drawl. Succeeding in little more than a constipated splurge. Bug-eyed Bez on maracas. The damning inappropriateness of it all sends a flicker of a smirk across his lips, and is the only encouragement she needs.

"Why don't I talk you through it? Let's see now. You casually slip in the conveniently rewound tape as… mmm, now what should we call her? Bimbo? No, that's unfair. After all she has made it to Exeter University and the dizzy heights of higher education. Let's just call her the unfortunate prey. So, as the unfortunate prey acclimatises to this new environment of fake leather and black furniture – by the way, one day you *will* grow out of all this *black* – but I digress; where was I? Oh yes, our unfortunate prey; making herself comfy, blissfully unaware that she is but modelling clay in the hands of a master craftsman who is revving up his potter's wheel as…"

"Careful. Metaphor-out-of-control alert."

"Shut up. There she is, being lulled into a false sense of security with fifteen minutes of classical 'pop' – what was it? Oh yes, 'Four Seasons', how original – and a lucky dip from that 'Best of Opera' compilation; the onslaught starting to dismantle her defences. Okay, she may still get groped, but at least it'll be a cultured grope. Then we move seamlessly into the twilight world of *easy listening*…"

"Sod off."

"Fleetwood Mac?"

"The Mac were cutting edge at the time; before the women ruined it all."

The words hang between them.

"Tell me you didn't just call them *The Mac*."

"Er, okay. I didn't just call them *The Mac*."

"Mmm. I'll let that one go. And as for your cutting edge, I'd forgotten the Carpenters and their much-underrated carnal catalyst, 'Yesterday Once More'.

Then you hit her with a couple off your 'Jazz Greatest Hits' album. More scattergun than targeted, but you don't care, because by now there you are beside her on the sofa, finding whatever she says either fascinating or hilarious; both, if you can muster the effort. And all the time this soundtrack of *lurrve* is subliminally nudging her towards coitus. But she's not quite there yet. She just needs a gentle push. So, what do you do? You bring out John Lee Hooker and… what's her name?"

"Bonnie Raitt."

"That's the one. Just what you need to incite coital union: an octogenarian blues singer and an ageing American country singer. But the logic is irrefutably and fiendishly brilliant: the unfortunate prey hears 'I'm in the Mood for Love' and bingo, she's in the mood for love. QED. You make your move, she responds of course, and…"

"Bob's yer uncle?"

"What? If you say so. Don't interrupt. Where was I? Ah yes. Tonsil hockey time. But who should be serenading this saliva confluence? Why of course. Enter big Barry White for some real *luuuurve. Oh yeah*, there's nothing like a sweaty, obese, warbling walrus on heat to get a girl gagging for it. And that last one was about as subtle as a sledgehammer. He sounded like he was in pain."

"He probably was."

"I'm trying to work you out," she says, eyes narrowing. "On the one hand we have this swaggering tart of a bloke, and all credit to you, you play the part with great aplomb."

"Cheers."

"But that can't be the real you. You're no two-dimensional prick on legs. There's no way you'd ever expect the tape to work by itself. Yet still you made it, and I'm having a few problems working out why. And you're the only bloke I've met here who's got a photo of himself and his dad taking pride of place on his wall instead of the ubiquitous Joy Division poster. I suppose the famous mum took it?"

"No chance. She always hated north Wales. Dad used to say that while he escaped from crowds, she escaped into them."

"A bit of a philosopher then, your dad."

"He had his moments."

With the exertions of the climb still reverberating in chests and ears, two pairs of stinging eyes drink in the Mawddach Estuary below. One allows the sight to work its usual cleansing magic; wash away the clogging stress, gently ease the tightness in his shoulders, rebalance disordered priorities. For the other it revives memories: 'Lemon Island'; the 'fruit pastille'; the rickety t(r)oll bridge; Penmaenpool, and the poem he'd learnt to impress his dad, under the flimsy cover of an English test at school; to the right stretch the 'Rhinos', sloping down to sip at the water in the estuary; and above them all, the chair of the mighty giant Idris, worn smooth during nights of star-gazing.

"I know I say it every year, but there's nothing like it." The boy nods in reply. "What were you looking at?"

The boy tells him, pointing out each landmark in turn; grateful for the chance to turn his back on the scary complexities of encroaching puberty and dwell a while in a comforting and familiar past.

"As I thought. Specifics. One day you'll just soak it all up. I reckon it's impossible before a certain age to really appreciate a view."

Another nod. But he's knocked out of autopilot by the follow-up.

"Thanks for coming, Carl."

No obvious reply to that one. A frantic scramble for the right words begins, but is brought to a standstill as his father's gaze turns to fix him through unnervingly watery eyes. Maybe the climb's taken it out of him. Maybe not.

"I worked out in the car yesterday that this is our seventh year in a row; just the two of us. *Lads' time,* as your mother calls it. In an ideal world – well, mine at least – we'd continue to do this every year, but I know that won't happen, so it's important to me that the times up here remain good memories for you. I couldn't bear to ever feel you resented them. This place and you… us… are far too important for that. This is the first year when I've sensed your preferences leaning elsewhere. A reluctance. Maybe enough to signal time; for now, anyway. Which is fine. I just want you to promise me that the next time we're sitting here, it's because you really want to. Forget my feelings. I'm old and ugly enough not to mind. If I were a gambling man, my money would be on fifteen years, with a grandchild or two for company." He acknowledges the anticipated look of horror. "No, it's an inevitable fact of parenthood that I'm about to lose you to a testosterone-fuelled, peer-pressured whirlwind that'll set you down, reeling, sometime in your twenties. Maybe we can have a coherent two-way conversation then, but in the meantime, I'm going to have to make do with a diet of grunts and the occasional titbit of a few words joined together into some semblance of a sentence, and only then if body language alone can't communicate the need for money or your distaste for me. I'll just be the bloke you pray doesn't embarrass you in public. And the harder I try, the more you'll resent me. No, my fate is accepted but – and here's where I'm heading – I have one last chance to convey what little wisdom I have to pass on, while you'll still listen to me."

And so it begins: the 'sermon on the mount'; a survival kit for those years of emotional separation; the words forever etched into Carl's memory. Not the kind of day you forget, when your dad gives you his considered opinion as to how to get off with as many girls as possible.

After navigating Carl through his remaining school years, he moves on to university, or as he calls it, a dress rehearsal for a reality it bears no likeness to… and an unrivalled opportunity.

A three-year hedonistic spurt, punctuated by the occasional inconvenience of a lecture or tutorial, an essay now and again, and then a spot of parroted learning and regurgitation onto A4 every June. Twenty-two weeks of holiday he won't want will be the biggest irritation. Forget the degree; that will come automatically, short of an emotional collapse, lobotomy or crass stupidity. Work, of course, but keep it in perspective. And that realisation will enable him to look up and around while many look down.

The friends he makes, the male ones that is – no such thing as a male and female being just good friends; one will always want more – are all that really matter. They'll be friends for life. As for the girls, never again will he be faced with such unhindered access to so many nubile, frequently willing, usually unattached girls; bodies at their best and minds at their naivest. Indulge or forever regret it, but don't rush in. For many, Mr Right will be the captain of the First XI, some greasy wimp, a complete thug or even the boy back home they've been going out with since nursery school. Fine. Leave them to it. Merely register an interest if there is one and move on.

Weekends home? Never. Politics? Student radio or journalism? Leave them to the socially challenged and idealists. Sport? For fun, yes, but don't specialise; that's just a dead-end. Future wife? Don't even think it. (The frown at such hypocrisy is waved away.) Otherwise, what's the point? The point is whatever takes his fancy. Drink by all means, but never to excess. Misconception: you're cooler, better looking and more likely to pull, the more you've drunk. Reality: slurring, sweaty, beer-breath blokes are only attractive to slurring, sweaty, beer-breath girls… or other slurring, sweaty, beer-breath blokes. Stay a pint or two behind the rest, keep his wits about him, and he'll be far better placed to profit from whatever opportunities present themselves.

And on it goes.

"That's your lot," he concludes. "The birds and the bees a few years too late, I suppose you could call it. Do with it as you will. Always remember that there's a chasm between the male understanding of the female mind and the reality of the female mind, and that can be exploited by the aware. Never show off. Never offer a talent. Always make it a surprise and be self-effacing and modest. And whatever happens, promise me that one day, when you've come through it all, you'll spare a few minutes, maybe up here, to sit down with your old dad and we can have a laugh about how wrong or right I was."

"I promise, Dad."

And there it ends. He looks drained, tired and yet never happier.

"Get that camera out. Let's commemorate what may well be our last first morning… for a while anyway."

The cassette clicks off.

"Time's up. Looks like I've survived the sixty-minute passion overture. Maybe you're losing your touch."

"You never bloody stopped talking."

"Well, it's been a few weeks now and you haven't had more than a couple of pecks on the cheek to show for your troubles. Your reputation, not to mention ego, must really be taking a battering. That either means you're very interested, or not interested at all."

STASIS

(APRIL 2007)

SUNDAY AFTERNOON

Carl strolls next door, reaches over the gate and eases the bolt across. The gate gives out its customary creak of complaint, triggering a salivatory onslaught on the door of the back porch. Four paws scrape, two tails vibrate vigorously, four eyes implore and two tongues messily smear lubricant over the glass.

Bertie and Willoughby in all their gormless glory.

He opens the door and they're upon him. He elbows wet snouts away, palms paws from his crotch and wades through the canine maelstrom to grab the leads that hang from a hook on the wall. By the time he's got the leads clipped on, his hands are coated in frothy saliva and he's breathing heavily. He opens the door through to the house and manages a snatched "Just taking the dogs out", before the laws of physics dictate that he too must exit. Experience has taught him that it's better to go with the chaotic flow than fight it.

Carl's CV may be overflowing with acronym-flaunting qualifications, but if pushed to list the lifetime achievement he takes most pride in, it would be training Willoughby to piss on BMWs.

What started as an idle, mischievous thought has, against all realistic expectation, culminated in crowning glory. But whilst Carl has long ago halted at smug self-congratulation, for Willoughby it has mutated into a single-minded obsession; the target-micturition of expensive German automotive produce his *raison d'être.* It's enough for Carl to forgive a name that's impossible to call out, either in full or abbreviated form, without sounding stupid.

They're in luck today as a burgundy Z4 squats smugly by the side of the lane, unable to access a driveway clogged with Chelsea tractors. Willoughby has already nearly garrotted himself, but like some crude auto-erotic asphyxiation technique it only seems to heighten the near orgasmic release as he cocks his leg and lets loose on the rear wheel. Then he catches sight of the logo on the front wheel, cuts off the flow mid-stream, staggers forward and re-cocks. Ensuring the coast is clear, Carl nudges him round to the front of the car and Willoughby deposits his bladder dregs messily over the bumper.

Job done, Carl tosses him a biscuit and they head for the woods, a contented Willoughby walking with a spring in his step.

Once through the gate he unleashes the dogs to source and select today's pick 'n' sniff assortment of excretory mementos.

Bertie is happy.

More than that; Bertie is ecstatic.

And Carl would be content to share his doggy joy, were it not for the fact that the source of the euphoria is the rankest-looking… dark red/purple/brown… glistening… slimy … *what the fuck?* The nearest parallel Carl can dredge up was last seen in some movie hanging from the jaws of a grazing zombie kneeling over a disembowelled corpse.

His shriek of anguish gets a cock of the head from Bertie, who senses that fun is afoot. Carl takes a step forward. Bertie eases back onto his haunches, eyes fixed on Carl. Carl raises a hand in a pacifying gesture he knows to be pointless. Bertie gives his treat a little jiggle. Carl shouts "*No.*" Bertie tilts his head again. Carl says "Good boy." Bertie shakes his head more vigorously, the entrails – if that's what they are – audibly smacking against each cheek in turn; his besmeared jaws, Carl could swear, fashioning a goading sneer.

Game on.

MONDAY

Pete eases himself into the day.

Pilates floor work.

Smoothie: blueberries, banana, strawberries, kale and kiwi; the vibrant colours reduced to a purple-brown slurry with a dash of spirulina and the flick of a switch.

Then out for a run.

*

The courier arrives at eight thirty on the dot, as he always does on every second Monday. Seph signs for the hefty package and lugs it through to the library, where she deposits it on the sofa. Resisting the urge to tear it open, she goes through to the kitchen and pours herself another coffee. She takes the mug out onto the narrow balcony – more an enclosed ledge – nudges Kavalier off the chair with her foot, takes his place, pulls one arm inside her jumper and hugs herself against the early morning chill.

As ever, the anticipation is all.

*

Carl is first into the accounts department as usual. Not out of keenness; he prefers a peaceful and largely unobserved start to the 'working' day. And it helps justify being one of the first out. He just needs to advertise his presence at this ungodly hour.

Computer on.

Sixty-three incoming emails since half past five on Friday. Horoscopes, penile enhancements, four product team meetings, two goodbye drinks, an emotional farewell from someone he's never heard of, a couple of 'social' – *get a life* – events, a sofa for sale… and on it goes; mind-numbing, time-wasting dross.

*

Pete gasps and shivers his way through a cold shower, before tackling breakfast: bowl of porridge oats soaked overnight and rendered palatable with probiotic yoghurt, assorted nuts and fruits, linseed and a drizzle of honey.

Then he swallows his daily dose of omega-3 and settles down at his desk with the opportunity-laden *Racing Post.*

*

Paul Simon once sang there were fifty ways to leave your lover. In my case it's the other way round and I don't feel much like singing about it. So it was no surprise that I approached that first date with Sophie full of trepidation. But even I couldn't have foreseen the sorry depths she would take me to that hot and sultry July.

Seph shakes her head wearily. Just about every rule of opening paragraphs broken. An inauspicious start. She glances ahead. Another twenty-four pages to go.

She's going to need more caffeine to get through this one.

*

Barely ten o'clock and Carl is already treading water.

Just what *does* a financial analyst do?

Tricky one, that.

Fortunately, no one else seems to know.

Time for a coffee.

*

Pete makes himself a cup of green leaf tea, smears some honey on a slice of wholemeal toast and stares down at the two circled names.

*

"It's a ring."

"Yep." Carl can't bring himself to give Paula what she craves.

"He only went and popped the question on Saturday." She lets out a piercing noise, reminiscent of nails down a blackboard; a siren call for all to come running.

"Poor sod."

"Ignore him, Paula," interjects that soft Scottish lilt, catching him unawares. "Congratulations."

"Thank *you,* Helen. At least *someone* cares."

"He's only jealous."

"*Jealous!* Of what?" Carl reacts.

"Oh, of seizing the opportunity to show a little commitment, maybe? How long *were* you going out with Emma for?" Helen teases, leaving him groping for some witticism as Paula is enveloped in a throng of excited well-wishers; moths around a pretty feeble flame, desperate for some distraction less than two hours into their working week.

*

Another day, another skirmish; Kevin, as ever, the intermediary.

"Hi, it's me," Pete says into his phone and hears the ring of the bicycle bell. It used to be the full spiel – 'ding-ding; *ladieees and gen-tlemen*; welcome to round a hundred and whatever in the pointless one-way battle between the noble David and that nasty Goliath' – but over time has shortened to a simple 'ding-ding' and is now no more than a sound effect. Kevin's refusal to be complicit in Pete's stubborn crusade beyond the demands of his employment contract.

"Is he in yet?"

"Yep. Standing right here listening in."

"*What?*"

"Of course not. You know he doesn't get in before midday. That's why you're ringing now. So what's today's weapon of choice?"

"Two actually. Can you read down the Ludlow 2.45 runners and odds for me."

Same old pantomime.

"Pete, no one gives a toss what you fancy, certainly not Ron. Believe me, we're not going to shorten the price just because of your poxy fifty quid."

Kevin plays along, throwing in a made-up 'Pyrrhic Victory' as odds-on favourite for his own amusement, but Pete doesn't bite. It's a deadly serious business for him. He gives his selection, takes the 7/2 and stakes a hundred; higher than normal, so the 'poxy fifty quid' had hit home.

Same routine for the second, but Pete baulks at the price, asks for a higher one, is refused, mutters something about not being value and the conversation ends.

Kevin shakes his head, puts down the phone and knocks half a point off the odds on both Pete's horses.

*

Surely there have to be better things eight consenting adults can get up to on a Monday morning? It would appear not, judging from the unabashed enthusiasm with which this sorry lot are embracing the prospect of dumping a chunk of metal, barely discernible from every other chunk they market, on their public.

He smiles his way through the pleasantries, handles the initial overview with ease, pretends to understand a 'joke' that has everyone else clutching their rib cages to prevent humour-induced implosion, receives an admittedly very pretty Gantt chart and then loses himself in the wallpaper pattern, searching for faces and recognisable shapes hidden in its flecks. Before long he drifts off into a pleasing fantasy involving a great deal of noisily-appreciated contact between his hands and Helen-from-IT's undulating curves as she leans across him to fiddle with the wires plugged into the back of his computer for reasons unspecified.

The sound of his name sends reality shearing through the fantasy. His subconscious rewinds and attempts to play back the question.

And fails.

"Sorry, deep in thought," he tries, with a bold stab at solemnity, parried somewhat by the fact that the speaker is sitting three seats away from the person he's chosen to address.

"Penny for it?"

"What?" he snaps, more aggressively than he'd have liked, as he fumbles irritably for his bearings.

"The thought you were deep in?"

"Oh. Er… I was just fantasising a bit."

"Fascinating. And would you like to share this fantasy with the rest of the team?"

"No, not really."

"Was it a product-based fantasy by any slim chance?"

"No," he says. "That would be perverted."

Raises a titter or two, but at a price.

"Let us return to my original question, shall we?"

"That would be very welcome."

"And?"

"I didn't hear the question, I'm afraid, Donald. As we've established, I wasn't concentrating."

Big sigh. "I asked if the accounts department, of which you are the esteemed spokesperson appointed to this project, had any comments to make on the figures Jeff has spent all this time putting together."

"Of course… yes… well, at this very early stage I do believe it's vital not to let our enthusiasm run away with us. My initial feelings on the figures are that they are fairly meaningless in isolation. Given the assumed unit gross profit margin, all this is doing is making the rather obvious statement that the more we sell, the more profit we make. They create a comfort zone that does nothing to assess the risk factors. We should be less interested in overall profit and pay more attention to the break-even point and its susceptibility to delays in the production process, costing variations, fluctuations in lead times and very importantly to forex movements and indexation, initially on a simple RPI basis but then assuming more severe variations in the time value of money, particularly given a current break-even point I would assess at being well over a year away. I suggest I liaise further with marketing to produce a revised forecast model and let you have a copy later in the week."

You lot bored now?

You lot have a fucking clue what I'm talking about?

Touché.

*

Seph's routine is borne of experience, respect and self-preservation.

She always reads the top one straight off. A thirst-quencher; although more importantly it invariably serves as a reality check that necessarily lowers expectations and renders what follows a little more digestible.

Once that first offering has been consumed, she does a rough count of the remainder and assesses the workload, spreading them evenly across the next five days, always allowing herself at least an hour between each. Saturday, she takes off – a palate cleanser – and then on Sunday she revisits anything that showed promise. More often than not, it's another day of rest. The next week she loses herself in literature of her own choice, regaining perspective.

She reads each one in a single sitting. Beside her are various marker pens, all different colours – she insists on receiving copies she can scribble over – which she uses to highlight the good, the confusing, the bad and the terrible. A green biro – red is so accusatory – is used to add any specific comments. Unlike many of her peers, she never skips sections; never gives up. Reads every word. She may snort, she may groan, she may shake her head… but she will hear what they have to say. There are dreams entwined in these words, however misplaced they may be. The commercial imperative will always rule, of course, but she will not disrespect those brave enough to try. She owes them that.

And once finished, she glances back and takes stock; then fetches her laptop and writes something – sugar-coated realism – for Emma to send on with the rejection. Seph insists, although she knows Emma hates it. In her results-driven world, why would you delude the hopeless? All that does is increase the size of an already formidable haystack. But Seph won't back down, maybe because it's these deluded literary aspirants she identifies with, not the hand that feeds her.

*

Pete heads off to the gym for an hour's strength work: chest and biceps.

*

Lunch.

Carl sits down at a table where Paula continues to hold court. Helen fires him a withering, censuring look that generates a brief flush of pleasure before he sinks into a silent trough of resentment. The others soon leave and it's just the two of them. A bit of a result… or not.

"Ahh, is little Carly-Warly having a sulk then?"

"No."

"You could have fooled me. All crabit and dour." That last word split into two syllables as her soft Scottish accent attractively slips into temporary overdrive. "You can't do it, can you?"

"What?"

"Force yourself to be happy for her. The poor girl comes to work feeling on top of the world and you have to do your petulant best to knock her down."

"You can't tell me you're not as cynical as I am about it."

"I can. And even if I was, some of us would just keep it to ourselves. It's called being an adult."

"She's the one who stuck it in my face. At least I was honest."

"Carl, you're not her father or brother or some close friend; you're just the prat who sits next to her at work. No one gives a toss what you think. Can't you see that?"

"I struggle to."

"All she wanted was a smile, maybe even a word or two of congratulations; but not a bloody lecture. Like it or not, this is her day, not yours. You could at least allow her that."

As they drift into polite small talk, he can't help but acknowledge, not for the first time, that if she does fancy him, she's doing a bloody good job of hiding it. It's hard to pin down what attracts him to her. Hair: mousey bob, usually looks in need of a wash. Face: small mouth, inconsequential nose, dominated by her eyes – usually bespectacled – and skin that appears a sweat away from a mild attack of spots. Breasts: pleasing swell. Behind: slightly too big for comfort, though presumably not hers. Not a body that would lend itself to close scrutiny in the harsh light of day, more one to get lost in.

"Anyway, I'll be off. Leave you to your own sparkling company. Oh, hang on, look who's coming. Serves you right, you miserable wee sod."

Any chance of rescuing some crumbs of comfort from the conversational wreckage disappears with an unwanted arrival at their table.

"Sorry to break up the party. Don't leave on my account, Hels. Eh, Carl? Eh?" Enter Darren. "Wotcha geezer. Good weekend, mate? Mine was *well* wicked." Fake cockney accent, bubbling acne, serious delusions of street credence and a job title that tries very hard to lend changing light bulbs and other routine maintenance work an air of strategic importance… and fails. Slimmed-down zitty version of the short bloke from East 17 who managed to run himself over with his own car.

"No," Carl replies limply, reluctantly withdrawing his gaze from the undulations of Helen's departing rear.

"Yeah man. Cushtie. Fuckin' give 'er one, would ya? Would ya? I would. Most definitely. Oh yeah." And off he lurches from one unintentional parody to the next.

*

An interesting layout grabs Seph's attention.

A glint.
A blade.
Slices down.
Goes deep.
A scream.
Muffled.
A life,
Cut short.

– – – –

The phone resumes its nagging ring.

He tries to block it out but Stacey shouts from the room next door that it's his soon-to-be-ex-wife on hold and can he please take it this ONE time because she's a personal assistant – that always makes him smile – not a bloody marriage-guidance counsellor.

He takes a covert swig – not that there's any need given no one can see him, but it always seems to taste better that way – from a hip flask, pushes the porno mag to one side, belches and picks up the receiver as if it might bite him.

"Put the bitch on, Stace love."

"The bitch is already on, you lousy shit."

"Angie. How lovely to hear your dulcet tones."

"Fuck you, Micky."

Yeah, fuck me, he thinks. Just another day in the life of Micky Johnson, 'Derby's No 1 PI', or so the flyers say.

"Mmm," Seph says to herself, kicking off her shoes and tucking her feet under a buttock. "East Midlands noir. Eat your heart out, Ellroy."

*

The discarded selection saunters home by ten lengths on the bridle; the price he rejected now looking like a bargain. Pete can't deny himself a pang of regret of course, but the negativity is soon replaced by rational and calm acceptance. It's nothing more than an inconvenient bump in the long road to redemption.

*

Carl blinks, shakes his head in disbelief and braves a re-read in ambitious pursuit of a comprehension that has so far eluded him. This hospital pass of an email. Subject – *'IC with UK for inventory'* – incomprehensible and hardly whetting of his appetite. From some bloke in the States who clearly doesn't get out enough.

Hi Carl

When we start this payment process, you need to make sure you convert an appropriate amount of the USD payment to GBP (based on your GBP cash requirement forecast) on the last business day of each month for spot conversion value within the next two business days (which will be in the next month).

You should book the payment and clear off the corresponding A/R in the following month to ensure the USD cash receipt component of what you forecasted in the USD net receivable balance actually occurs. Remember, I will let you know prior to you doing the month-end FX exposure forecast what you can expect as a USD payment from PFN so you can include this in your next month's ending net asset/liability balance forecast.

In order to facilitate forecasting PDD-UK USD receivable exposure from PFN HQ, I want the USD wire transfer payments of previous months' inventory purchases that have been processed through A/P to always occur on the same day before the last business day of each month. We will be setting up an interco aging (which maps to interco payable to PFN PDD) for Corporate's inventory purchases from PDD-UK.

Any thoughts?
Chad

Thoughts? How about *fuck me*? How about *fuck you*? And it's cc'd to the high heavens. A very public humiliation awaits, and there's more than enough rope here to hang himself with.

Are these really his 'people'?

*

Four down and Seph is fast losing the will, finding it harder going than usual. She abandons self-control and opts to cherry-pick the last for the day, glancing down the pile through the plot synopses for something to suit her mood.

Tender *coming* of age story set in a boys-only boarding school?

Social worker has her life turned upside down when she's diagnosed with breast cancer?

Diana and her book club chums go amateur sleuthing in Berkshire?

Former-SAS officer wreaks havoc on the team that once abandoned him in Iraq?

Elderly spinster ruminates on loves lost, wasted and regretted as she faces up to the gradual onset of serious illness and the recent death of her mother?

Feisty Petula leaves her cheating city-slicker husband and proves to the world she's no back number?

Depressed Trevor takes several hundred pages to twig that his marital and alcohol problems have their root in a childhood of abuse at the hands of an alcoholic father?

Witty and borderline-xenophobic recollections of Dorset couple who move to rural Spain?

It's a no-brainer, in every sense, once she discovers that our ex-SAS hero rejoices in the name of Dirk Hunter.

*

Pete sits down at his computer and updates his records. Three hundred and fifty up on the day; the thermometer now over a third full.

*

Carl arrives home to find his answering machine blinking three times.

"*Er... hello. A message for Carl. This is Mr... er, Colin McLeod calling... again. I'm the solicitor trying to tie up a few loose ends on your father's estate. I've tried you numerous times, by phone and letter, but to no avail. I can assure you that it is nothing to be concerned about. However, it is imperative we meet and I would very much appreciate your getting in touch at the earliest opportunity. My number is…"* He doesn't need to take down the number. It's been sitting on the top sheet of the pad for weeks now, but there's a voice deep inside telling him to ignore it, and it's proven easier to obey than confront.

The second message is Hopkins wanting him to open the batting for the Old Boys against the 1st XI at the summer reunion.

The third message kicks in.

"Hi Carl. Any chance you could pop over to see me when you get home. I… we've got some news we'd like you to hear first."

Makes the call.

"Okay if I leave now?"

"Now is perfect. Take it easy on the way over. This weather's got all the idiots out, so the traffic will be busy."

"I'll set off in five minutes."

Assorted ablutions later, Carl pulls the door closed behind him, crunches across the gravel, strolls up the path and pushes open the back door. Twenty yards that he and Emma always disagreed about. For him: proof of independence attained. For her: still tied to the apron strings.

"Just how you like it," says his mother, placing a mug of hot chocolate on the island – more of a continent given its vast surface area – and turning back to fetch her coffee. It isn't; hasn't been for well over a decade. Can't stand the grainy sweetness any more. But that's parents for you; you'll always be a passive constituent in a succession of fond childhood recollections that capture a world long passed when kids were cute and parents were respected and loved unconditionally. He thanks her, forces a smile and sinks his upper lip and nose into the marshmallow-coated whipped cream, only for it to plug his nostrils, necessitating a tactical withdrawal to take a breath before he dives once more for the chocolate.

"Bring it through, darling."

Smearing the back of a hand across his mouth, he follows her down into the lounge and offers a hand to the rising Kenneth. Should be Ken, but he hates it; dislikes Kenny even more; insists on Kenneth.

"Hiya *Kenny*."

"Good to see you, *Carly*," comes the reply, accompanied by a vice-like crushing of fingers.

"*Ahhhh*," he winces, pulling his hand clear and placing it into the safety of an armpit.

"Something the matter with your hand, *boy*?"

"Fine thanks. I can feel the blood returning. Did you know you've missed a few grey hairs?"

"Could be. Can I get you some Jelly Tots for your *hot-chocky-wocky*?"

"That's enough, you two," says his mother fondly. "What do you think of our new artwork?"

Carl takes in the splodge-fest adorning the wall above the fireplace and for once is stuck for words.

"We're so pleased to have picked it up," she adds. "He's an up-and-coming Bosnian artist. Poor people. They've had such a tough time recently, what with the war and all that, and he lost both his parents to a mortar attack. He's a recluse. So sad, but out of tragedy comes such beauty, so it's not all bad. It really resonates, don't you think? He's terribly trendy and is going to be huge. We're so lucky to have got in at the ground floor, so to speak. Cost a pretty penny but it should prove to be a splendid investment."

"I'll take your word for it," says Carl, suspecting that Bertie and Willoughby could probably come up with something of greater artistic merit in one of their pre-perambulatory frenzies. "What's it called?"

"*Prevarication.* Which is one thing I don't want to do any longer, so take a seat because we have news."

He unwisely chooses a Brobdingnagian armchair that virtually swallows him as he sinks into its clutches, balancing his ridiculously infantile drink on a knee and peering up at his mother and Kenneth, who couldn't possibly get any closer on that sofa and are indulging in a series of glances, smiles and touches that no child should ever have to sit through. Totally out of order and in need of swift curtailment.

"So what's the big news?" he asks, as if he doesn't already know.

Carl settles down on the toilet seat and his gaze settles on the framed magazine spread.

She's faced her share of heartache over the past few years, so it's great to see Fiona Armstrong back on our pages looking great, with a smile on her face, a new love in her life and a career retrospective packing in the crowds at the National Gallery.

We joined Fiona in the comfort of her stylish Buckinghamshire home and were delighted to hear that she's in a happier place than she can recall for a long time and is back behind a camera after a period where work was the last thing on her mind.

Fiona suffered the death of her husband over two years ago, but what followed was beyond her worst nightmares. The man she had given her adult life to left a trail of financial and emotional chaos that turned Fiona's life on its head.

'Losing someone so close is devastating in itself. He was my soul-mate.' She pauses and her eyes moisten. 'When I heard about the crash, I had no idea about the circumstances. The next minute there's a journalist on the phone asking me if I knew of some girl Stuart was involved with. I was distraught and felt so naïve… so used. I didn't know what to think.'

Fiona faced a nightmare as the press slowly uncovered the sordid truth about her husband's duplicitous life: the girlfriends half his age, the dodgy tax-avoidance schemes, the Inland Revenue investigations, the family's entire savings squandered.

'Friends have asked why I stayed; how I could live here with all those memories. But in truth this was all that was left. And it was our family home. Why should he take that from me as well? I can't say it's always been easy. But I'm glad I stayed. And having Carl, my son, living in the lodge has been a great comfort.'

The new love in Fiona's life, fusion sculptor Kenneth Gallagher, was present throughout the session. He likes to keep a low profile but has been Fiona's rock. Himself a former client of her husband, he too felt the repercussions of the tragedy, although he refuses to elaborate further.

When asked what the future holds, a twinkle comes to Fiona's eyes as she glances affectionately at Kenneth. 'No comment' they say, and then burst into laughter.

'I can honestly say I'm happy again. And I never thought I'd be able to say that. I can't forgive what happened. But I have learned to live with it and move on.'

Hooray to that, and aheart-warming story of love and hope triumphing over despair.

She may be his mother, but it never fails to generate a wince and quicken the transit of waste matter through his alimentary canal; and remind him of the dark days, setting those scars itching.

"You sure you don't mind then?" she asks, as he wanders back into the kitchen, Kenneth away to his studio.

"I'm really happy for you. It's your house and it's a big house. Why shouldn't Kenny-boy come and share it with you? You've had your fair share of crap over the last few years, we both have, so why shouldn't you do something for yourself. Put him totally behind you."

"It's not just that. I was thinking of you and Emma. That it might appear… inappropriate."

"Mum, that's history now. Don't worry about me. Anyway, you know you didn't think much of her."

"It wasn't that, dear. It was just that I didn't think the two of you were suited."

"You were right there."

"I wish I hadn't been, but she broke your heart and a mother is entitled to take her son's side. That's what we're for."

"I know," he says. "Look, I've got to go or I'll be late. Honest, Mum, I'm really happy for you both."

"Thanks." She pushes her hair back over her forehead and he doesn't think he's seen her look as happy in ages. "It means the world to hear you say that."

*

(SESSION 3)

"You feel betrayed, let down, abandoned even. It seems understandable that you are very angry."

"Thank you for allowing me to feel those things. For *validating* them for me."

Silence.

"Because I'm wondering how stating the fucking obvious… sorry… no need to swear, I know… but right now, I really don't need you telling me what I'm *entitled* to feel about that wanker."

Silence.

"I do get it. You want me to balance all my anger off with some good stuff. Some Disney moments. And then we can work together to transfer all this anger into something more… what shall we call it… *wholesome*?"

"You seem set on arguing with me rather than allowing whatever might come to your mind to be present here. It doesn't have to be good or bad. Just shared moments that have stayed with you."

He bites down on a response and takes some time to calm himself down. And soon they come.

"We were out on this walk once. Just the two of us. He liked his walks, did *dearest Daddy*. Mum off busy somewhere, as usual. The woods down the road. I must have been in my mid-teens. Bit of male bonding, he probably thought. Not for me though. Think I felt sorry for him. I just wanted to get back home as soon as possible. Anyway, we were walking along this path and suddenly he wasn't beside me anymore and when I looked around, he'd stopped a way back and was just staring up in the air. I walked back towards him, trying to work out what he was looking at. Seemed to be at these two trees growing right beside each other." He pauses for a response that doesn't come, so continues. "The bases of their trunks were a few feet apart, but about twenty feet up, the smaller one leaned into the other and from there on they were intertwined. Not round and round, just together. Then further up the smaller tree sort of fizzled out. It wasn't doing too well in all that shade." He pauses. "Anyway, what's the point in all this? It was just two trees. So what? You lot have to *interpret* everything, don't you? Just because someone looks at something doesn't mean there's a profound insight involved. Why does everything have to be so bloody complicated? Maybe he wasn't even looking at those trees."

"Did you ask him?"

"No. Why would I?"

"Something about that time has stayed with you."

"Here we go. The whole father-son dynamic in play. Trees are a bit phallic, aren't they? You and Freud can have some real fun there. If you *do* Freud, that is. Does he *do it* for you? Are you that *type*?" He pauses. "Hang on, I remember now. There was something else. It was more the sound. I can't remember how windy it was, but there was this straining and creaking sound. Like the noise abandoned old boats make in horror films. It seemed to be coming from those two trees, or maybe just one of them. I couldn't tell. We stood there a while, saying nothing, and then he just walked on."

Silence.

"As I said, it's your job to work it out. I'm sure you can read plenty into what was just a walk and two trees, can't you?"

Silence.

"I'll take that as a no, then."

Silence.

"Have it your way. There was another time. A trip up to London. Near Kings Cross it was. Probably for one of Mum's exhibitions. We were walking along when he told me to look up. The road we were on forked at a forty-five-degree angle up ahead and this building filled the gap between the two forks, like a big wedge of cheese. Must have been maybe five storeys high. Right on top, perched at the apex, was this observatory pod thing. Maybe ten, fifteen-foot high. Looked a bit like an Easter egg on stilts, or maybe an old diving machine from some Jules Verne film. Book that is. Not sure old Jules made a lot of films. Sorry, I'm digressing. Only yourself to blame if you're going to say so little. Giving me all this dead air to fill. Anyway, at the time I probably said something profound like 'wow' and I think I asked if we could go and look at it. He said we couldn't, of course. Said he preferred to imagine what it might look like inside, or who might use it. It must have stayed with me though, as I had this recurring dream off and on for years after, particularly when I was away at school. I'd step into some shop and, when no one was looking, I'd creep out the back and there would be these stairs. Up and up I'd go and at the top I'd step out onto the roof. There was a roof garden up there, and I'd walk through the plants to this observatory. A ladder was suspended from its base. I'd climb up, through a hatch, and he'd be in there."

"What was he doing?" she prompts, after a lengthy pause.

"Tinkering around. Smiling. Looking relaxed, content. The only times he ever looked that happy were when we were up in north Wales."

"Did he ever say anything?"

"No. Never. There didn't seem to be a need."

"When was the last time you visited him there?"

"Before."

*

"Good evening, gentlemen," commences Andrew, as he does every Monday night, addressing the other five seated around the oval green baize table. "The main event will now begin. The game is No-Limit Texas Hold'em. The buy-in is thirty pounds for a thousand in chips. Unlimited buy-ins available until ten forty-five when one last top-up will be permitted before we adjourn for a short break – to eat, drink, micturate, defecate and listen to Pete moan about his bad beats, while the rest of us wonder how the fuck anyone can play so few hands without falling asleep and still have so few chips. We then move into freeze-out and play to a conclusion. Sixty/thirty/ten split of the pot to the first three. First out on kitchen duty for the rest of the evening. Second out deals. Blinds start at twenty-five/fifty and rise every fifteen minutes. Good luck to one and all. Deal 'em up."

Game on.

As always, Carl spends the re-buy period winding up the competition; playing the player, the cards almost irrelevant. Steve manages the snooker club owned by Andrew and can never keep the deference out of his play, something Andrew uses to maximum advantage by raising him off pots wherever possible. Kevin is an open book as far as Carl is concerned. Pete just plays his own cards, rarely going in with the worst of it, but inevitably short-stacked and vulnerable to a bad beat. And Tommy, another of Andrew's acolytes, does whatever takes his fancy; difficult to read anyone who doesn't know why he does what he does.

Before they resume, and while an entente prevails, Andrew summarises progress on existing *projects* and then asks if anyone else has any fresh targets in mind.

Carl mentions some fly-tippers, only for it to fail the two-times-removed criteria. But it's clear that minds are elsewhere tonight. Steve recounts having had to sack Eamon at the club for fondling the arse of the new barmaid. When he says he sometimes wishes they could make things a bit more personal, the table nods as one and Kevin chips in.

"If we do, I've got someone in mind. Some bloke down the shop today. Complete fuckwit. Not you, Pete. Serial loser. Came in spouting shit to impress his mate. Backed the wrong horse after misreading the form and then I had to sit there and watch him look like some tipping guru."

"Yeah, but you're bookies," says Tommy. "You got it covered, right?"

"I was so busy laughing at the bloke's bullshit routine that I forgot to give Ron the word to bring the odds in. It was up at twenty to one and we could have shortened it a few points. Not that it would have stopped him. The moron was hooked by then and he'd only have told his mate he'd started some gamble."

"How much did he have on?" asks Pete.

"Two hundred, plus his idiot mate's twenty."

"Ouch. And it won?" Pete again, the upward intonation betraying him.

"Cut the pretend concern, Pete. It doesn't wash. Yes, you'll be delighted to hear that it merrily cantered home and all I've had echoing in my head ever since is the sound of him giving it all that from about half a mile out and the look of unabashed man-love on the face of that dopey sidekick of his."

"How did Ron take it?" asks Carl.

"How do you think?"

"Fucking tight-arsed bastard. Serves him right," spits out Pete.

"Boys," says Andrew. "You all know the rules. This has only ever worked because of them. It has to be *right* and we have to be protected. Nothing relaxes the rules, even if we run out of ideas. They'll come, but there can be no connection. Twice removed at least is essential. The moment it gets personal, we're exposed." Then, with a mischievous smile, he adds "However, that doesn't mean you can't amuse me with your more venomous flights of fancy as and when you wish. In complete confidence, of course. Get it off your chest. Let me release some of that pressure. I'm all ears for a good gripe against someone who deserves it. And who knows? We can but dream."

TUESDAY

It's the accounts department's busiest period… allegedly. But as Carl sees it, with George doing enough work for the two of them, there's little point in his getting in the way.

This morning he has successfully juggled progressing another article for the magazine with the capital expenditure budget, the daily crossword and setting up the year-end audit file. With the latter so far involving no more than opening an empty lever-arch file, legitimate work duties have comprised laughing at the emails coming in with the capital expenditure each department wishes to make in the next financial year. The official overall budget across the entire company is one hundred and fifty thousand, but Carl has accidentally on purpose omitted to mention that inconvenient detail, in effect inviting unfettered offers to spend the company's money. His largesse initially yielded tenders totalling well north of a million – they could probably reconstruct the building for less – and a follow-up request for non-essential items to be excluded has yielded a laughably inadequate forty thousand reduction. Carl is debating with himself how much of the picture to reveal: a spot of light pruning or a radical pollarding?

A rustle of papers and forced exhalation signal the departure of George to yet another important meeting. Carl parries the scowl with an inane grin and a shrug.

With the audit file now sporting some very pretty coloured dividers and the crossword completed, Carl's day is done… almost.

Hi guys,

Oops! Thanks for the revised FY08 calendar year capex requests but unfortunately, they're going to need ever such a slight trim.

Forgot to mention. The overall budget across the company is only £150k and £25k has already been earmarked for the new smokers' 'retreat' so please let me have your appropriately downgraded requests asap, by Friday if poss.

Sorry about that little misunderstanding. Mea culpa and all that. I do hope it hasn't caused any inconvenience.

Cheers, Carl

Nice balance between irritating flippancy and completely taking the piss, stopping just short of a smiley face. Too much? Emboldened by the knowledge that he has tomorrow and Thursday morning booked off as holiday, he lights the touch paper, presses *send*…

… and heads swiftly for the door.

*

Carl wouldn't normally bother on a weekday, but there has to be some payback for Sunday. Under cover of the encroaching dusk, Willoughby sprays a 5 Series from all angles and is rewarded with a biscuit. Nothing for Bertie. Willoughby gets let loose in the field. Bertie remains tightly tethered, the merest movement prompting a jerk on the lead and a curt admonition. Willoughby gets an overly enthusiastic 'good boy' in a ridiculous doggy-talk voice. Bertie gets repeatedly sworn at. Willoughby gets to choose between a star, house, bone or heart-shaped biscuit – like he gives a toss – while Bertie only gets to sniff the choice as it's wafted past his nose en route to Willoughby's slavering chops.

Then, on the way back, something rather wonderful happens. As they pass the 5 Series, and Carl takes a look around for witnesses, Bertie wanders over to the car, cocks his leg and urinates. He misses, but the intent was clear, and a gleeful Carl empties the contents of his pocket into Bertie's mouth, past digressions forgiven.

WEDNESDAY

The things I do for love, Carl tells himself as he makes the not-so-convenient detour on his way back from Cheltenham. He'd never allowed Emma near the March Festival – that annual pilgrimage sacrosanct; none of them wanting non-believers along to curtail their punting orgy – but the two-day April meeting had been different. A last fling of the jumps season for Carl, and while Emma had never been converted to the cause, she was fond of horses and the prospect of two nights in a country guest house and dropping in on Beth and Michael on the way home had swung the deal, and it had become a fixture in their diary. This year, without her, he's made a day-trip of the first day; wouldn't have bothered were it not for this hoped-for ancillary benefit.

Entering a seedier side of Reading the local tourist board – does it even have one? – probably keeps to itself, Carl pulls up under a streetlamp, throws anything that might attract unwanted attention into the boot, double-checks he's locked up and tries to look relaxed on the short journey to front door.

"Full marks for persistence."

"Always the warm welcome, Beth."

"Don't tell me you weren't a little tempted to keep on driving."

"Why would I want to miss out on such outstanding hospitality?"

"You'd better come in then. We are blessed as always, Carl, although I don't know why you bother any more. I'm not Emma."

Typical Beth. Glass always half empty. Got a point though. It's why he's here on this shitty estate, after all. To get as close as he can to her sister. It's certainly not for light relief. And she's exaggerating what remains of her Somersetian accent – littering her sentences with piratic flourishes – and he knows that she knows that it irritates him, if only because it serves as a reminder of the obvious efforts her sister has taken to disguise her own.

"Don't talk rubbish," he tries, his end justifying these means.

He's halfway through a cup of warm milk with a hint of tea when he remembers to ask after the geek.

"How's the little genius?"

"Up in his room on the bloody computer. Where else?"

"Softcore porn or chilling out in a chat room with a bunch of paedos?"

"More likely working through his games." She stares down into her mug. "He breaks my heart, Carl, he really does."

"Still the bullying?"

"I don't know anything for sure. Nothing's been mentioned for a while now. Sometimes I think maybe it's all done with, but who am I kidding? He hides it pretty well, but I can see it in his eyes when he leaves in the morning and again when he gets home. No one ever rings. He never plays with friends. Don't think he even has any. He should be kicking a ball round the street like the other kids on the estate, just being a ten-year-old; not running the gauntlet to and from school and then poring over a computer screen into the early hours. I just want him to be happy."

"Maybe he is."

"How *can* he be?"

"Who are we to tell him what should make him happy?"

"Wait until it's your son. Then you can spout that crap and see where it gets you."

"Sorry."

"Forget it," she says wearily. "Anyway, you going to pop up and say hello?"

"Yeah, sure," he says, torn between his reluctance to endure another one-way encounter and a desire to take temporary leave of this tepid drink and the depressed and depressing sister of the one woman who's ever had his number.

"Be kind, Carl," she calls after him as he climbs the stairs.

He ignores the *Radio-active*, *Go Away* and *Private* signs and knocks.

"Who is it?"

"Hi Michael, it's Carl." Nothing. "Can I come in?"

"Suppose."

The only light is that emanating from the computer screen, Michael's face bathed in bluish intent.

"Hope that's not pornography." Can you say that to a ten-year-old? Michael saves him by not reacting. "Mind if I take a look?"

Gets a perfunctory nod that feels like progress, and past experience has taught him to expect little more. He moves across the room and looks over the boy's shoulder. Chess. What else?

"You winning?"

"Yes, but he doesn't know it yet or he wouldn't be over-extending that pawn."

"Is this real-time?"

"This one's two days a move, the others vary."

"Others?"

"I normally have eighty or ninety on the go; that way there's always moves to make."

"Blimey. How do you keep that lot going?"

He makes a move, presses *submit* and the screen switches to a new game yet to begin. He's white and quickly moves his knight to f3. Another new game appears and he makes the same move. And again. Six times in all.

"An odd move?"

"That's the good thing about this. You get to try openings out loads of times. I try a new white and a new black opening each season. This year it's been the Réti for white. I've doubled up with the King's Indian Defence for black. The idea is you leave the middle to black's pawns and then…"

He pauses, unsure. Clearly even nerds have a built-in quality-control function. Carl smiles.

"It's all right. I have played chess." Michael's eyebrows arch. "Not for a long while. Just played a little at school. What were you saying?"

"Nothing really. Just that black gets to occupy the middle and then I attack it with my major pieces in the middle game. It tends to mess up black's prepared defences. I like it."

After this uncharacteristically verbose flow, the tap is switched off as he pores over an endgame. Carl is momentarily tempted to try again, but succumbs to a wave of tiredness after a long day of driving, fresh air and fruitless gambling, and calls it a day.

"Better get back to your mum. You coming down?"

"No. I'm sulking at her."

"Why's that?"

"There's the finals of a big chess tournament for schools in June. For the first time ever, we've qualified for it. Along with a load of posh private schools. They hold it at Pontins and you stay a couple of nights and it's really good fun. The head teacher said each child has to have an adult with them and Mum says she can't take the time off work."

"I'm sure she'll come round to it before then."

"Yeah, right."

"Anyway. Maybe see you later." As he moves away, there's an animated tapping on the keyboard that makes him glance back at the screen.

"That a mate?"

"My dad."

"What?"

"It's my dad."

"But…"

"I know."

Freaky kid. No point in pushing it. What can he say? He shakes his head and moves towards the door.

"I don't let on I know," Michael adds. "But it's him. Whatever anyone else says."

Back downstairs, Carl's relieved to find his mug removed.

"A long chat for you two. Or did you get lost?"

"He says he's playing his dad at chess, Beth."

"Get's better and better, doesn't it?"

"You know about it?"

"He mentioned it to me a while back. Says he's sure it's him from the comments he types in."

"What, 'Hi son, Dad here'?"

"Nothing that obvious. Michael says it's like a secret they share, but don't mention ever. But they do talk to each other, if that's what you call it, only it always seems to be about the chess from what Michael says. He's not some pervert."

"You hope."

"Even if he was, it would count as an improvement in his social life." She tries a smile but it's tired and unconvincing.

"Beth. He thinks he's playing chess with a bloke who died six years ago, someone I doubt he can really remember, and you're happy to play along? That's a little fucked up, don't you think?"

"Leave it, Carl. We get by, okay? A once-a-year visit to hear second-hand gossip on your ex and hopefully get favourable mentions in dispatches doesn't qualify you to give me a lecture on my son or how we do things. We each deal with it in our own way. He accepts Mark died, so there's no denial going on. And if it helps him, so be it. It's not doing anyone any harm."

Her voice is trembling.

He leaves it.

"How's Emma?" lobs Carl into the silence with the mock-casual air of the desperate man.

THURSDAY

Back in the office, a little later than planned.

The capex responses are in, and a common thread is establishing itself: … *Prat*… *Dickhead*… Y*our propensity for being a pain in the f***ing crack knows no bounds* (Geoff from R&D waxing impressively lyrical – good on him) … *Carl, looking at my diary I see we're at a development meeting next week. Looking forward to Ceeing yoU Next Tuesday, 'mate'.* Just the one more. Here it comes… *Pillock.*

"Sweet," Carl says to himself, then notices that a couple have cc'd in Greg. Time to nip this in the bud.

Dear all

I'm a little taken aback at the reaction, guys. I strongly believe in starting with a blank sheet of paper, giving your initial estimates a validity and an airing that would otherwise be denied. That your requests have somewhat exceeded the available funds is of course unfortunate, but my approach has given you all the opportunity to state what you believe to be your true requirements, something that would never have happened had I limited you from the outset. The quantification of the differential between 'want' and 'available' is a vital step towards alerting the US parent company to the reality of our needs. That may not help you this year but I would strongly argue that it puts us in a far better place as regards increased budgetary limits in future years. My actions throughout have been predicated on a fervent desire to strengthen our long-term position. I trust that clarifies my position and look forward to receiving your revised figures on a timely basis.

Yours as ever in finance, Carl

With rare self-censorship he deletes the *Yours as ever in finance*, cc's in Greg, ups the ante with Charles and clicks *send*. Time for a half hour craparooney to avoid any face-to-face confrontations and fill that irritating expanse of time before he can reasonably fuck off for the day.

He's about to log off when an email comes in: *Apologies, Carl. You are not a pillock. I was wrong to call you that. You are, however, a fucking arsehole. Sorry for the confusion.* There is just no pleasing some people.

*

Another snooker match, another 5-nil humiliation. But what does the league expect if it insists on a new club having to start at the very bottom and work their way up through four divisions before they meet anyone even half decent? They're just having a spot of fun along the way to relieve the tedium; the team taking it in turns to play the fool. Gizz provides the sideshow this week, leaving Carl to seek his own amusement; opening with a succession of safety shots, each with a fringe benefit of nudging a red into the open, then the big break attempt; only for it to stall when he loses position on forty-nine as a not-so-subtle comment from Wayne sees the focus of his attention stray to the backside of the P45-inducing new barmaid as she departs with their empties.

Her name is Laura and she has a certain something going on. She also gives as good as she gets in the bar afterwards, proving more than a match for Wayne at his cockiest. And just when they think an excited Gizz has overstepped the mark in suggesting they each take the new girl in town out for a night and she can pick which one gives her the best time, she surprises them all by acquiescing.

As the others battle with the emotions her agreement engenders – Gizz astonished; Wayne's self-assured smirk; Kevin's panicked expression – Carl steps in, books Sunday night and hopes he can wangle a plus one.

FRIDAY

The magazine holds a bank of prospective articles, to which Carl adds as and when the muse takes him; and sometimes when it hasn't. They have full editing rights and can choose whichever article they want; if they want. He may notionally hold an ultimate veto, but he needs them more than they need him, and they know he'll take what he's given.

And here it is: the monthly email from the features editor.

He takes a deep breath and clicks it open.

Hi Carl

It's double your money time. We loved the motoring article so much we're going to use it up front as part of a themed section we're running. Pays more as well. Hate to leave out your usual slot so we'll use that nickname article. I overlooked it last time but the more people we asked, the more said they liked it and it contrasts kind of nice against the moronic crap churned out by the ex-footballers and rugby players who for some reason we seem to be obliged to flatter. We've left them both pretty much untouched… for a change eh, lol.

Final drafts attached. See you Sunday night at the awards ceremony. Fingers crossed.

Dave

For once he can open an attachment without trepidation.

A little can go a long way…

Our law and order correspondent, Carl Armstrong, takes to the road for a day and ends up wondering if our boys and girls in blue are comfortably numb to a public who routinely flout the rules of the road and common decency.

A Wednesday. Just like any other Wednesday. Except that today I've been chauffeured. Not to or from anywhere in particular, just generally round and about; with a pen in my hand, a pad of paper on my lap and an eye for the selfish, the littering, the dangerous and the downright illegal things our fellow motorists get up to… and all with apparent impunity.

So, here's the damning roll call from a typical day on the highways and byways of the Home Counties:

Carl speed reads the article through to its culmination, and the number 1 in his top ten of worst offenders:

1. The young gentleman with the striped shirt, red braces and mobile clasped to his ear on the M25 as he weaved his red Saxo with the M… S Office Supplies logo – some tax dodge from Daddy no doubt, doubling up as an easy show of love to compensate for a largely avoided childhood – in

and out of the lanes at well over 90 mph without a care in the world, let alone a signal. I'd like to apologise on behalf of all his fellow motorists that day for getting in his way on his dash for some vital appointment; his hairdresser, or a pint with a mate or maybe Mummy had his favourite meal on the table.

Hello… are there any coppers out there?

Law and order correspondent? Since when? He's liking it though. They even let his corny Pink Floyd pun through.

The second attachment opens and it's back to the normal fare, albeit one of his favourite pieces.

Cracking the mystical nickname code

How many times have you heard team-sportsters quote a teammate's nickname and wondered how the hell the clever chaps came up with it? Just what intellectual mine shaft have they sunk in order to tap into such rich seams of precious inspiration? Well, worry no more, as Carl Armstrong is on the case.

Welcome to the wacky world of blue-sky nicknaming…

Emboldened by the adrenalin rush imminent publication always brings on, Carl takes a detour on his customary mid-afternoon meandering, pops outside, extracts a scrap of paper from the inner recesses of his wallet, takes a deep breath and makes the call.

Visiting Beth has been an annual event since way back, so there was a tenuous logic to Wednesday's visit. But this?

"Hello?"

"Hi, Steph?" Silence.

"Yes." Drawn out. Hesitant.

"Yeah… er… hi. It's Carl here. I used to go out with Emma?"

"Yes, Carl, of course. How are you?"

"Fine, thanks. Look, I was wondering if you could take a look at something. Sorry, that sounds crass. Professionally, I mean."

SATURDAY

"Hi Pete."

"Carl. How's it going?"

"I'm a financial analyst for a US-owned local networking firm. How could it possibly get any better than that?"

"A man who adores his work is a truly beautiful thing."

"Maybe you could try getting a fucking job sometime and share my deep joy."

"I'll give that the thought it deserves."

"Right. While you're doing that, fancy doing me a favour? If you can make the time in your hectic schedule, that is."

SUNDAY EVENING

The annual lads' mag award night; possessing an official name that alludes to artistic merit, only to undermine itself from the outset with the gorge-like décolletage adorning the programme; nicknamed *The Bonker Prize*.

And while all things remain possible, the 'date' with Laura proceeds swimmingly. They've put on a good, if slightly vulgar, show and Carl doubts any of the others will be able to match this for spectacle. Laura looks great and he enjoys the effect she has on the others at their table, particularly Guy, who can't keep his hungry eyes off her.

His award category is one of the earlier ones. Not hearing his name called out hits Carl hard. He thought he'd prepared himself for it, even practised his gracious loser smile, but apparently not. Maybe because it would have been some justification for what, deep down, he knows these literary dabbles to be: at best a delaying tactic; at worst a total cop-out.

But it's not to be and he does his best to style it out.

The rest of the table do their half-hearted best – "Just getting shortlisted is victory enough" deserves a mauling

– to summon up words of comfort and commiseration, and Carl spends the rest of the evening feigning delight as the table accumulates tacky 38DD *Oscarettes* and Carl is relegated to a minority of three, one of whom is Laura.

Not the evening he'd hoped for, and any libidinous urges subside under the onset of self-pity; the narcissist's refuge. He lets the evening play out, but his heart is no longer in it, increasingly embarrassed by association with this seedy world of self-congratulatory smut and triviality peddlers.

Isn't he better than this?

Apparently not.

MONDAY

Yet another project management meeting, this time with the added edge of three department managers still openly snarling from the capex budget 'fun and games'; Carl the recipient of more open hostility than if he'd crawled onto the table and crapped in the mint imperials.

The tedious preamble peters out and Roger from sales does what he does best: talks like a cunt.

"Guys. I say we hit this baby running and throw it open to ideation." The intended pause for maximum impact is filled by a splutter. "You okay, Carl?"

"Sure. Sorry. Guess I choked on my drink," he replies, only to find himself thoroughly let down by the absence of a cup to substantiate his alibi.

"What I'm looking for here," steamrollers on Roger, "is an idea shower. Come on. Bring 'em on down and let's get soaked."

If Carl presses his lips any tighter, they may split.

*

(SESSION 4)

"Did Emma give her reasons for breaking up with you?"

"Just said we were heading in different directions."

"What do you think she meant by that?"

"I don't know. I thought we were fine, I really did. She was getting on well at the publishers. I got a decent job. We were both going places, I thought. Still are." He drifts into silence and stares down at his hands. "She said she was tired of waiting for me to grow up. That I was far too judgmental and opinionated. A hypocrite. Made everything into a competition. Trivialised anything that threatened to get too serious. She didn't like some of the… er… pranks and stuff me and the poker crew get up to. Said who were we to… she never really approved of the poker. Wasting my time when I could have been writing my novel, then having to listen to me moan I never had any time to write. I seem to recall the words *unfulfilled*, *drifting* and *exasperating* making fairly regular guest appearances. You know, the usual stuff in any healthy relationship."

TUESDAY

"Hello?"

"Er… hi. Is that Steph?"

A pause. "Who is it?" A hint of impatience in her voice.

"My name's Pete. I'm a friend of Carl. He asked me to drop off a package with you."

"Come on up. I'm on the top floor. The door will be open."

He takes the four flights two steps at a time and pauses on the landing, relishing how quickly the heaving in his chest subsides. Then he pushes at the door.

"Hello?"

"Go through to the lounge," says a distant voice. "Make yourself comfortable. I'll be a couple of minutes once the feeding frenzy's over."

He moves along a short corridor towards the only door that's ajar. His eyebrows knit as his imagination works through possible scenarios that may be keeping his hostess from immediate attendance, only for them to unravel and rise as he walks into a world pitched somewhere between Hogwarts and an episode of Morse; a world that offends him to the core.

With the exception of French windows at one end and two closed doors, every inch of the wall space is taken up with fully-inhabited bookshelves. Not that the books have been confined to them. Piles of varying heights and degrees of precariousness litter the wooden floor and a coffee table like some post-earthquake cityscape, while splayed books teeter on the backs of a worn and cracked brown leather sofa and a battered, patched-up armchair that reveals glimpses of previous incarnations through frayed windows of ripped fabric. He considers a move to a small, bare patch of floor over by the window and is about to plot a potential route through the literary maze when a clatter of metal on floor from another room stops him short.

"Sorry about that," comes the disembodied voice, preluding the blustery arrival of, in ascending order, checked slippers, faded jeans, over-sized baggy jumper, smile, round-framed spectacles perched on end of nose, friendly eyes and a mass of mousey hair pinned by an unseen device into an unruly mop from which loose clumps and strands descend, requiring the occasional swipe of a hand or upward puff. This room incarnate. His order-seeking mind's attempts to pigeonhole her fail.

"No problem," he stammers, disarmed by this chaos-on-legs. "I was just admiring your… your…"

"Books?"

"Yes. Books. Just how many have you got?"

"How many? Why would I know that?"

"I just thought… sorry, I didn't mean to pry."

"You weren't."

"Anyway, it looks like you're running out of space," he says, surveying the heaps and mounds littering the room.

"I've another two rooms full of them and there's method to my untidiness. At least that's what I tell myself."

"But aren't you going to have to move everything along when you put these loose ones away?" he asks, with the fretful concern of the obsessive compulsive.

"How do you mean?"

"Well, I presume they're in some sort of order. Subject? Alphabetical?" Floundering.

"Why would I need to do that? They just go in where they feel right," she says, frowning her disapproval.

"But what happens if you need to find one?"

"I'll know where to look, don't worry about that. Anyway, it's an insurance policy. Hidden in all the mass-produced fodder are the valuable ones I really treasure and I don't want to flag them up on some trophy shelf or have to lock them up in a safe. How could I enjoy them there?"

The wilful disorder sees Pete involuntarily hugging himself.

She smiles, sensing his discomfort. "It's Seph, by the way," she says, holding out a hand.

"Hi Steph. Do you live here alone?"

"Bit of a creepy question."

"No. Sorry. It's just that the name by the buzzer said P. Wilkes, so I thought …" He falters, unsure of what he'd been thinking.

"That's me. Blame my parents' love of classics and desire to give me a casting boost and an eye-catching turn in the end credits."

A minute in and he is struggling to keep up, that last sentence leaving him trailing in its verbose wake. He musters an "oh" and she takes pity.

"My parents taught ancient history, Greek and English literature between them at various public schools, but suffered throughout from the delusion that where they truly belonged was on the stage performing to a rapt audience. Unfortunately, their talents never quite matched their ambition, so any spare time that wasn't spent devouring Homer, Eliot, Austen and the like was invested hamming it up in whatever godforsaken amateur dramatic production would have them. Guess the penny finally dropped, so when I made my belated and unplanned appearance in their lives, I became the receptacle for all those unfulfilled dreams, and what better head-start than a stupid, attention-seeking name."

"You've lost me," he admits, sensibly abandoning a losing battle.

"Sorry. Me wittering on. I'll start again. My name is the god-awful mouthful that is Persephone. As if that wasn't bad enough, I was left in my formative years to discover that my namesake, and the apparent inspiration behind my polysyllabic nomenclature, was none other than the asexually reproduced daughter of Zeus and the goddess of the harvest who was then abducted by Hades, the god of the underworld. A delightful little tale known as the *Rape of Persephone*. Go figure that out aged seven without fucking yourself up."

"Didn't they give you a middle name?" asks Pete, feeling like he's taking two steps back for every one stumble forwards and wondering how the hell a simple errand has seen him walk into some surreal nightmare with a quite possibly mad woman who's swallowed a dictionary and has an infuriatingly haphazard filing system that has him itching, literally, to impose some order.

"Yes. Shirley."

"Shit. Bum deal."

She does him the good grace to laugh. It's not a displeasing sound.

"Hence my taking what I could from Persephone."

"Not surprised, though why Steph? Seems a bit tortuous."

"It's *Seph*, not Steph."

"Shit, sorry," he stammers, adding foolishness to the alien emotions that are throwing him off balance.

"Why *would* you know?" she says kindly, unsettling him even more. "Always thought Emma had the patience of a saint putting up with all that… sorry… not my place…" She regroups. "So how do *you* know Carl?"

"I went to primary school with him. Kept in touch ever since."

"And why did he send you to do his dirty work?"

"Dirty work? It's just an envelope. He said he didn't want to risk it in the post, and with him being so busy at work and knowing I had the afternoon free, it made sense."

"*Just an envelope*? *Just*? I think not. This is literary gold that's passing through your hands, I'll have you know. The Holy Grail. Remember this moment. Bit thin, isn't it? And you call it *just an envelope*?"

Pete is drifting, more like drowning, in unchartered waters of confusion. "What is it?" he manages.

"Didn't he tell you? I never counted modesty as one of his attributes. It really is a day of surprises. I shouldn't really – client confidentiality and all that – but let me get you a cup of tea and then I'll enlighten you. You look like a green tea man?"

"Er… yes. How did you know?"

She smiles and takes her leave. He sinks into the sofa and takes a deep breath after the onslaught. A cat saunters into the room and looks at him contemptuously before springing up on to the chair, where it licks away at its crotch. Pete shivers with disgust and scratches at an itch that has sprung up behind his ear. Another follows above his hip and another on the back of his shoulder. Fingers flit from one to the next, then he jumps to his feet. Another cat enters the room and heads towards him. He intuitively takes a step back and sends a pile of books toppling. He's crouching down, one eye on the cat with the dry genitalia, trying to ignore the wet slurping of the other and restoring what little order may have existed before the intervention of his clumsy foot, when she returns nurturing two mugs.

"Don't tell me. You're allergic to cats?" she says.

"Yes… I think… probably… how…"

"You look the type."

His face contorts once more. "They must have cost you a fortune," he says with an expansive sweep of his arm, as much to distract her from his vacant discomfort.

"Not really. I've been given most of them actually. An occupational benefit."

"What do you do?"

"I read, basically. For pleasure and for money. Very occasionally both."

"How do you mean?"

"I get sent first chapters, plot synopses; sometimes, god help me, whole manuscripts. And I try and sort the occasional spikelet of wheat from the endless tonnes of chaff. I guess you'd call me a talent spotter."

"Who pays you?"

"Publishers mainly, primarily the one Emma works for." She pauses. "Carl's ex?"

"Sorry. Yes. Of course. I was just thinking about what you said. They pay you a salary to read?"

"Where would the fun be in that? No, I get a small fee for each one, but the real payday comes when I put one up and it gets the green light. If it ends up in print then there's another bigger fee and maybe a slice of the royalties."

"Any I'd have read?"

"Depends what you read."

"Factual books. I don't see the point in fiction, though I did once read the six Booker Prize shortlisted books in a fortnight, fat lot of good it did me. The one I backed lost. Unless I'm learning something new or useful, I can't be bothered with reading."

"It's a no, then."

"What?"

"The answer to your question."

He fills the void with the first thing that springs to mind. "Surely you can't have discovered all these books, or whatever it is you call what you do?"

"I wish. Of course not; precious few actually. Not even enough to fill a small shelf. I get a load of freebies from publishers, a few gifts from grateful authors and the rest are the ones I buy for myself. My guilty pleasures are second-hand bookshops and car boot sales."

Pete wrinkles his nose in mild disgust at the mention of such institutions, let alone the deeply unpleasant thought of owning anything that has passed through another's grubby hands first. Keen to leave such distasteful contemplations behind, he quickly changes subject. "Are you any good?"

"I suppose it depends who you ask. There's no right answer when it comes to books, just opinions. What do you do?"

FRIDAY

Greg's hand feels like a piece of fresh fish: damp, cool and flaccid. Carl moves it up and down and then releases it with relief. It firms and points in the general direction of a round table by the window, on which sits a laptop.

"Take a seat, Carl."

"Thank you, Greg."

"Tea? coffee?"

"Cup of tea would be nice. "

"Give me a second. I'll get Carole going on that before we begin."

Greg Smith. Financial controller. Carl's line manager. Company man through and through. Very dull. Photo of wife and two kids the only indication that there is a life beyond a head full of figures and these four walls. His wife looks… how would you put it tactfully? Sensible? Practical? Basically, you wouldn't. Ever. But Greg has; at least twice; the empirical proof sporting some serious sleeveless knitwear and facial expressions that would grace any technical accountancy magazine.

Greg returns.

"That's all sorted."

They indulge – too strong a word with its overtones of quality and enjoyment – in some chitchat until the tea arrives, complete with biscuit assortment. Carl selects a jam sandwich, gently twists the two halves until they ease apart, scoffs the creamed side, starts to lick the cream remnants off the jam on the other side; then realises that Greg has stopped talking and is staring intently at him with not a little concern.

"Who can resist a jam sandwich?" Not much of a deflection, but it's delivered with a grave expression that dares Greg not to concur.

"Indeed. Have another," he says, joining Carl on the conveyor belt of inanity.

"Don't mind if I do."

Greg takes refuge in some rapid keyboard tapping, before theatrically turning the screen in Carl's direction.

"Right. To the point. Have you ever seen one of these before?"

Carl experiences an immediate memory jolt as he takes in a screen populated by dozens of names in boxes linked by a myriad of lines, all of different colours and thicknesses, some only dotted. As he looks closer, even the dots vary in size and frequency. It's beautiful and he can't help envying a quality of presentation he had never achieved years earlier. Surely it can't be.

It isn't.

"It's a very exciting innovation we've been test-driving for the management consulting arm of the auditors. You look like you've seen it before?"

Something like it. A few years back.

Another office. Another stuffed shirt. And the end, it would appear, is nigh.

"A matter of great concern has been brought to the attention of the partners and it has fallen on me, as managing partner of the retail division, to nip it, as it were, in the bud."

"Sounds very important, Brian. Anything I can do to help, please just ask."

"Er, yes… well… it is… important. Extremely grave in fact."

"Gosh."

"I detect that you are not taking this at all seriously."

"Well, Brian, it would help if I knew what you were talking about."

"Right, yes, of course." He opens the manila folder in front of him and takes out a sheaf of papers. He then starts to place them on the table, hesitantly at first as he establishes what goes where, but then quickening until the jigsaw is complete. The process gives Carl time to consider his options.

"I take it you recognise this?" asks the now red-faced managing partner with a tremor in his voice.

"I call it an AIDS chart, though others feel that's a little over the top and have suggested calling it an STD chart instead."

"Others?" Now puce. "You mean you've shown this tosh to others."

"Yes. Quite a few actually."

"Here? At the firm?" Then senses a greater danger. "Outside the firm, for God's sake?"

"Mainly within the firm," he teases. "It's become quite popular."

Brian takes a deep breath and starts afresh.

"Enough. I have been given an indication of what this…" he waves in the direction of the papers "… this abomination is, but I am nothing if not even-handed and I am prepared to hear your side of the story before I deliver my judgment."

"Certainly. That's very decent of you, Brian. Are you sitting comfortably? Then I'll…"

"Stop playing the fool and get on with it."

"Right then. Well, from the moment this particular dewy-eyed student happened upon your stall at the careers fair at university, this firm has rammed down my throat its supposed ethical strengths. No sexual relationships whatsoever between the staff on pains of immediate assured dismissal. Great big fuss made about it, the clear inference being that this was something that set the firm ahead of its competitors. But from the moment I went on that first training course in Portugal, it's been a knocking shop. Total fucking hypocrisy; and that's a valid adjective, not a profanity. It started as a reaction to that. A bit of a laugh. Who'd slept with who? Who'd snogged who? Who'd tried it on with who? Then a colleague – don't even bother asking – came up with the brainwave of lines linking them and it evolved from there. A load of boxes with everyone's names on them, joined up by lines where something had happened, alleged or actual. All the lines were the same to begin with but then we started differentiating depending on the link. The thicker and darker the line joining up two people, the more they did and the more confirmation there was of it actually having happened. It started on pieces of paper and then another friend, who shall also remain nameless, helped me computerise it all. That's when it really took off. We came up with the idea of layering the thing by years. The core is the middle section, which features everyone in my intake. We added a section below every time there was a new intake and above for the years that preceded us. Names only appear in those other levels wherever miscegenation with our intake, actual or attempted, took place. Nearer the top it's a little more sparsely populated, being senior managers… and above. Although we do appear to be missing the top section, I note." Tactical pause. "The next genius idea was to give each type of linking line a value and this in turn gave everyone a score. I then came up with the levels, ranging from 'drunken mistake' to 'couple of pints and they're anyone's' all the way down, or up depending on your perspective, to 'office bike'."

"And that's your defence? This is preposterous. You don't see anything inappropriate with this infantile rubbish?" To his credit he's remained silent throughout Carl's spiel, but the words are now spat out with pent-up venom.

"It was just a bit of fun."

"*Fun*?"

"Of course. I've had no complaints. Quite the opposite. I'm always being asked by colleagues what their scores are. What the scores of others are. There's a league table. We even ran a cup competition last year. Then there's enquiries from audit seniors, looking to add high scorers to their teams for away jobs. One bloke even threw a party to celebrate hitting 'bike' status."

"You're lucky this is in my hands, Carl. Others see this and you could be facing serious accusations of libel. You can't damn reputations willy-nilly on idle gossip and speculation alone."

"Like I said, we corroborate our sources and we've not had any complaints so far. Contrary to what you seem to think, it's a decidedly honest venture. Quite ironic, don't you think?"

"Your flippancy does you no favours. You are delusional if you genuinely believe this childish prank to be some meritorious social crusade. And it simply cannot be countenanced. It is a piece of gross misconduct of the very highest order and it will not be tolerated by the partners. You are leaving us with no choice. Immediate and terminal disciplinary action is the preferred option. We have the power to stop you getting even a sniff of another job in the accountancy profession. But I've stuck my neck out for you, though goodness knows why I bothered, and engineered a compromise you don't deserve. We are prepared to permit you the chance to go immediately and quietly and no further word will be said of this. You resign, we pay you what you are due up to today, not a penny more, you get a clean reference and the matter will be deemed closed."

Carl surveys the triumphalism; the fake compassion; the self-assured drumming of fingers on the table.

"You're swimming with the big boys now, sonny boy," continues Brian, misreading Carl's silence as weakness. "You're out of your depth. Head for the shore, young man, before you drown."

"Natalie Saunders."

Carl is made redundant the very next day, bids the firm a two-fingered farewell and departs with a glowing reference and a tax-free twenty-grand redundancy payment.

"No," Carl replies, annoyed at himself for the penny not dropping weeks ago; and sensing trouble. "How does it work?"

"Do you recall the team who came in a while ago for a few days? Chatted with everyone?" asks Greg.

He does. Remembers not taking it seriously. Remembers answering in a manner that might feasibly have been interpreted as flippant. Remembers slagging them off as a waste of corporate funds after they'd left. And possibly while they were still there.

"Well, they identify lines of communication within a company and produce pictorial representations, like the one you see here, that highlight information and communicatory flows and dependencies. Highways of influence and impact if you will. The end product is a measurement of the relative importance of employees within an organisation. Sounds simple, I know, and one would assume it might be open to manipulation by the more astute of interviewees. But it's much cleverer than that. Anything not corroborated is ignored, but they get that corroboration from numerous sources. That's what the follow-up interviews were all about. They put it all in their software and *voilà*, here we are."

"Fascinating," is all Carl can muster, feeling exposed and vulnerable.

"I agree. And between you and me, I wasn't being completely truthful with you earlier when I said it was just a software test drive. As you may have guessed, we've been deep in talks with the US for the past few months. Hence my recent trip over there. Upshot is, we've got to make some cuts. Staff are going to have to go. They're talking about fifteen per cent across the board."

"*Fifteen?*" Carl exclaims, genuinely startled; a ticking-off morphing into the sack.

"It gets worse. You know what the Americans are like. Love their sales. Respect their marketing and technical departments. Take or leave their finance bods. We've got to lose at least two in the accounts department. That's two of twelve and believe it or not we've argued them down from three, though I reckon they might still push for another at a later date. Now let me try and find what I'm after."

As Greg taps away on the keyboard with the air of an untouchable, Carl ponders the five to one odds on retaining his job; knows them to be very generous as he casts a brief mental glance over the opposition; the fully occupied opposition. His only hope lies with the software somehow missing the blatantly obvious. That day hadn't been a complete disaster. In amongst the supercilious jibes and insouciant disdain, he'd displayed enough wherewithal to give pretty much the whole building a name-check as he took the data collector through an entirely fictional working week in the life of a financial analyst. All he needs now is a little reciprocation.

"Ah, got it. Sorry about that. The model can be set with any department at the centre and then it includes everyone else who liaises with that department's personnel. And here we are." He turns the laptop towards Carl, who takes in a screen that on first appearances looks like a game of *pick-up sticks* dropped from a height onto a map of a sparsely-populated Hebridean village. He blinks a few times and gradually it releases its secrets. "Takes a bit of getting used to, doesn't it?" Carl nods. His eyes are drawn first to one box that looks like the centre of some multicoloured supernova. He grunts his disapproval on finding George's name inhabiting it.

"You okay?"

"Fine, thanks. Bit of biscuit caught in my throat."

"Can I get you a glass of water?"

"Yes please." Buying time. Looking for his own *des res*. And finding it. Mmm. On the bright side, it's a fairly central location. Close to major communication routes. Just not… quite… actually… on any. Detached in every meaningful sense of the word.

There is one saving grace: a pink dotted (life)line – a footpath if this was an Ordnance Survey map – leaving his back door, bypassing his own department and making its way south-east to a distant and ignored corner, where it bumps into a similarly unpestered box: 'Darren Briggs'. *I'm a chartered bloody accountant employed on more than thirty grand a year to financially analyse, and the only person in the entire building who can bring me to mind when asked to detail their working week in exhaustive detail is the handyman. I am totally fucked.*

"Not good, is it?" concurs Greg, returning with two plastic cups, which he places down on the table. In need of a prop, Carl lifts the nearest to his mouth and nibbles at the rim. Although it appears his executioner has slow torture, rather than quick justice, in mind. "I presume you've spotted the same problems I have?"

"Hard not to," Carl mumbles, dragging his finger through the water ring on the table.

"So, you can see why I wanted this meeting, just the two of us, before decisions are made that are going to effect a lot of people's lives?"

"Yes. Of course." He can hear the resignation creeping into his voice.

"Can you see congestion, Carl?"

"Er."

"Can you see islands, Carl?"

"Yes," he replies unavoidably, feeling like a child and looking anywhere but at what is increasingly taking on the appearance of a burial plot, though he's saved the bother when Greg pushes the laptop aside and slaps a magazine down on the table. And not just any magazine.

"Do we bore you, Carl? Short of things to do with your day?"

"No. Not at all," lies Carl, a drip of cold sweat trickling down the side of his ribcage. "It's just a little hobby. Something I do at home."

"You've never used your computer here?"

"No… er… well, maybe very occasionally," he concedes, knowing Greg can prove as much.

"That's not all though, is it? This whole capex budget farce."

Fuck.

Greg pulls the laptop back to centre stage and Carl prepares himself for the next hammer blow.

"Right, I look at this screen and what do I see?" Carl has nothing to offer, but Greg isn't expecting an answer. He's on a roll. "I see cul-de-sacs. I see overloaded resources." *Not in this room, you don't.* "I see one-way traffic." *How's it hanging, Darren, mate?* "I see an inefficient use of resources." *Fair point.* "I see change on the horizon."

Punchline apparently delivered, Greg takes some deep breaths and a sip of water, leaning back with the smug satisfaction of a great orator who has successfully conveyed his message, seemingly unaware of the total confusion induced in his audience. And he appears to be waiting for Carl to say something.

"Er." It's all he can dredge up in his state of dazed imminent unemployment.

"I know what you do here, Carl," Greg says; the words a damning indictment, yet the tone strangely positive. "Those product meetings every week, the monthly KPI's, the currency hedging, all those ad hoc projects." *Are you taking the piss?* "You're a key cog in a complex machine." *Has George walked in?* "Yet here we have a model that suggests you are apparently divorced from the action." *Go figure.* "That makes you perfectly placed." *It does?* "A catalyst." *What the fuck are you on about?* "Ah, I can see from that look that I've lost you." *At last.* "Strange how the most valuable resources often don't realise their value. I say catalyst because you influence so much yet receive no recognition for doing so." Carl moves swiftly past the possibly incorrect definition and clings to what appears to be something of a sea change in this surreal exchange. "I... we... and by that, I mean Charles and I, with concurrence at board level, see you as management's dispassionate eyes. Involved in everything, yet detached. You have near enough open access to all areas, yet are as good as invisible. Objectivity personified." Greg playing good cop, bad cop all by himself. "We feel that makes you the ideal tool at our disposal."

Carl nods, if only to encourage a current of logic, however evasive, that appears to be flowing in a favourable direction. He may be drowning in a quagmire of management consultancy-inspired bullshit, but if playing along is his route to employment security, so be it.

He nods again.

And again, as Greg moves up yet another motivational gear.

SUNDAY

Carl grabs a bottle of lager, sticks some Mogwai on the stereo and sits down at the desk on which he has placed, more in hope than expectation, a pad of A4 paper and a biro. Staring at the pad for five minutes doesn't get him anywhere, so he picks up the pen and forces himself to write, jotting down a name and job title at the top of each consecutive page, the aim being to list the various pros and cons that will magically reveal some irrefutable logic, and leave him more translator than author of this corporate cull.

He starts with Carole, rumoured to be more than just a secretary to Charles. Possibly a career mistress. Probably a stunner twenty years ago, but now more Elaine Page than blonde bombshell and Christ knows how long it takes to cram herself into those outfits and slap on the warpaint. An attractive present under the tree, but one you wouldn't want to open. She should be the first to go – all right, maybe second – but Carl knows that probably won't happen.

He also knows Dermot is the most at risk. Left Ireland at seventeen to escape violent and abusive father. Disowned by the abuser. Ostracised by the battered remnants of the family he left behind, who chose to paint his departure as cowardly betrayal, rather than examine their own inability to do the same. Arrived with nothing and has swotted and grafted his way effort-fully through half a minority interest accountancy qualification and to one of those job titles – assistant bought ledger clerk – that damns itself. Gets his taste of home every Sunday morning in the ex-pat hurling league, each game degenerating inexorably and inevitably into a blur of fists, injuries and chaos. Monday mornings are a favourite time of Carl's week as a bruised and battered Dermot cheerfully recounts the events of that weekend's match, each recollection delivered with a smirk breaking through a facial palette of blues and purples or compromised by a fat lip or broken tooth. The fun is 'in the craic' apparently. In every sense of the word.

The problem for Dermot is that he ranks high on any objective redundancy shortlist on just about every criterion.

Imagination required.

The phone rings.

"Is that Carl?" The voice sounds faintly familiar.

"Yeah. Who's that?" he replies, his brain too occupied trying to place the caller to bother with common courtesy.

"It's Trev."

"Shit… Trev… how the devil are you?"

"Been better, mate. You're a tough bloke to track down. Your mum gave me your number. You not heard the news then?"

"No, what?"

"It's Joey, Carl. He's dead."

As he puts the phone down, Carl is transported back thirteen years… to Exeter, Exeterminate, Joey… and when it all started with Emma.

The allotted hour was fast approaching for Exeter University's premier, and only, heavy metal band to thrust its bulging crotch into the faces of a half-full student bar. A November Sunday night had brought together a disparate bunch. The converted, to a man and woman – so hard to tell for the uninitiated – in traditional blue denim garb, formed an expectant crescent directly in front of the stage. Behind them came a sporadic spread of fresher faces, most without the remotest idea what they were about to be subjected to; their grounds for being there ranging from cheap alcohol to the presence of the opposite gender to the on-off-on-allegedly off legendary pyrotechnics.

The lights dimmed and the makeshift curtain that shielded the stage slid, or rather was tugged, to one side; the intended pitch-black darkness on stage compromised by the light emanating from the bar that ran the length of the far side of the room. A few shuffling shadowy shapes… a snigger… someone kicked something… a whispered expletive… another snigger… and then a noise ripped through the air; a note delivered with resonance and assurance. Followed by five more. The sequence repeated. And again, only this time a drum echo kicked in over the held last note. Once more for maximum impact… then everything erupted.

Exeterminate.

Initially the senses were forced into chaotic, self-preservatory retreat from the sound, lights and smoke – the infamous 'effects' very much in effect – only for them to regroup and take in what proved to be a passable cavort through 'Walk all Over You'.

The set continued with an entirely competent trawl through the back catalogues of various heavy metal behemoths: Saxon, Sabbath, AC/DC – lots of AC/DC – Iron Maiden et al. Very little in the way of originality. And of course arm circles, a topless drummer, and feet resting on front speakers were a given.

A very decent, almost funky, version of 'Wishing Well' followed.

The singer was a good-looking bloke, and he knew it, with a white sleeveless vest top that gave maximum exposure to a tanned, sculpted musculature, and an oft-employed shake of the head that sent his long brown hair in choreographed cartwheels. The kind of bloke other men publically slated, but secretly envied; the kind of bloke men thought women fancied. The ideal front man.

The drummer and bass-player were solid enough, providing the heartbeat every body needs, even if this one suffered the odd tremor and they occasionally seemed to be working against, rather than with, each other.

Which just left the life force of the band, lurking at the extreme right of the stage; the hunched, angular, faceless jumble of straggly blonde hair and denim that was Joseph Haydn Philips… Joey… and his guitar. Rumour had it that he was rather good.

And rumour had it right.

Left hand sliding its way effortlessly up and down the frets; fingers scampering over strings with dizzying speed; structured chaos. This wasn't formulaic, solo-by-numbers guitar; this was edge of the precipice stuff. Man and instrument morphed into one masturbatory musical union. It was dazzling, even to Carl's informed eyes.

It wasn't flawless, improvisation occasionally flirting with entropy, his efforts disappearing up their own collective backside, swirling irrelevantly without the forward momentum the song, and the rest of the band, needed. As a consequence, the others struggled to maintain order at times. With only four members, the band was too dependent on their lead guitarist for a tune over and above the repetitious and military offerings of the rhythm section, particularly in the frequent obligatory instrumental breaks. They were helped by the material being so well known. Even when Joey strayed too far from base, the unconscious metronome within the minds of the audience gave structure where little existed, the flip side being that occasionally, in Joey's more 'artistic' passages, it served to emphasise just how far he was straying. But overall, the balance worked in their favour and Joey elevated the performance from competent to memorable.

During a dirge he didn't recognize, Carl cast an eye over the audience. First port of call was a pert and appealingly wiggling bum, only for its owner to throw back a mop of curly hair and reveal a beard. Moving rapidly on, with a shudder, his gaze fixed upon a bona fide female and attractive brunette leaning nonchalantly against the rear wall with an expression that suggested she was viewing this ridiculous posturing with similar wry amusement. At the very appealing end of the aloof spectrum. Stunning eyes, even in the half-light. If she knew he was watching her, she didn't let on, which only attracted him more.

The band finished as they always did. Band traipse off after main set. Crowd cheer. Crowd cheer a bit more. Crowd chant 'Freebird' repeatedly for a few minutes. Much stamping of feet. Band return. Band make pretence of debating what to play next. Band play 'Freebird'. The faithful greet with cheers and raised arms; then bow their heads in reverence, stretching and easing neck muscles in preparation.

A while later, Carl paused his 'they were good, but…' speech to ask Matt and Phil if they wanted another drink. He'd spied the brunette from earlier walking to the bar and the opportunist in him could not be denied. The diatribe could wait. Matt had only just brought back the last round, but as second year students, such over-indulgence was to be commended, not queried.

He reached the bar to find his quarry chatting to some old bloke sporting a quite ridiculous beard and bottle-top glasses combo, the latter nestling halfway down the bridge of his nose and over which he peered intently at her. Style: Open University lecturer, 1975. A damsel in distress in need of rescuing? No, she didn't look the type. And she was smiling contentedly back, a fondness in her eyes that told Carl such mock-gallantry would not be appreciated.

She shifted her position, turning away from him. No longer in view, he was forced to walk around them and seek alternative access within her field of vision. Adopting the casual swagger and nonchalance that only comes with practice and attention to detail, he leaned on the bar, flinching as elbow met wet bar towel, but resisting the impulse to withdraw it and mess with a tried and tested pose. Irritatingly, the barman was on him almost immediately, so he ordered three Guinness snake bites in as loud a voice as possible, twisting his body to open it up for fuller inspection.

Not a flicker.

Short of stepping between them, there was little else he could do. Maybe it was her dad, or some uncle. No, too old. More likely her grandfather, or even a tutor she was trying to charm a higher grade out of. What did it matter? He was getting nowhere. He paid for the drinks, crammed the glasses into a self-supporting triangle between his hands and trudged away feeling like an actor walking off stage after performing to an empty auditorium.

He arrived where he had left Matt and Phil to find their previously occupied patch of stained green carpet now vacated. Scanning the room, he heard Matt call his name before he saw them; and their worrying smirks. They were standing by one of the tables that lined a side of the room and were each enclosed on three sides by high-backed benches; somewhere else they might have been referred to as booths, maybe 'snugs'. Having disengaged himself from the three-glass-vice and taken back the nearly full glass he'd left with them, Carl looked up to find the eyes of the assembled members of *Exeterminate* and their female companions upon him. He nodded a catch-all greeting at a point somewhere in amongst the glasses, ashtrays and crisp packets that littered their table.

Introductions were made. The singer was called Dan, the bassist Trev and the drummer Gaz. No surprises there. And there was Joey, of course.

"As I was telling these guys while you were getting the drinks," said Matt, with feigned innocence, ignoring Carl's slow shake of the head. "You were telling me and Phil what you thought of the gig."

"Er," Carl stammered. "It was really good," he added pathetically, hoping for leniency. But none was coming his way. Live by the word, die by the word.

"Yeah, but didn't you also say something about the band not giving Joey here enough support. That some of the songs sounded a bit… what was it? Messy?"

"Thanks for that, Matt," Carl replied, before sucking in his lips and surveying a now captive audience. Trev scowled at him. Gaz looked confused. Dan nuzzled the ear of the girl around whose shoulders he'd cast an arm, taking the opportunity to look down her cleavage. Joey made no effort to hide his mirth at Carl's discomfort, sucking deep on his roll-up and nonchalantly sending a series of smoke rings across the table, thoroughly enjoying the show.

"Do *you* play, man?" asked Trev aggressively.

"He's a really good guitarist," offered Phil, trying to help, yet not.

"That's all right then," continued Trev. "The man's qualified. We would be *honoured* if you would deign to give us your considered critique, oh guitar guru."

To duck? Or to dive in? Dan leaned forward to rest his elbows on the table and cocked his head expectantly. His female companion looked miffed at no longer being the focal point of his attention, so she tugged down the front of her blouse and revealed a little lace and a lot more flesh. Gaz now looked both confused and uncomfortable. His female companion looked furtive and distant. Carl suspected her hand was in close contact with Gaz's genitals. The haze around Joey had dissipated to reveal a look of some encouragement. His female companion was undoubtedly stoned. Trev still looked angry. He didn't have a female companion. Maybe the two were connected.

Carl made up his mind.

"Look, if you really want my opinion, you can have it. But remember you asked for it. Thanks go to my so-called friends for that." He hesitated to give them this last chance to help him help himself, but both of them were settling in to enjoy the bloodbath. As of course he would be doing were the roles reversed. "Right. I enjoyed it. Honest, I did. But it was basically just your bog standard covers band. If that's all you want to be, then fine. But there are loads of bands who can do that. You tick all the boxes. Good-looking singer with a decent voice and suspiciously large lunchbox." Pause to observe reaction. The girlfriend's complicit smirk removed doubt on that score. Quick glance at nestling cleavage squeezed up by crossed arms. "Simian, topless, tattooed drummer bearing passing resemblance to Animal off *The Muppets*. Tick." Another glance at cleavage quivering gently. "Moody bassist who looks like he wants to kill everyone. Well, me at least." Pause for sniggers, one of which caused the cleavage to wobble enticingly. Trev didn't appear to enjoy the joke and glared with increased venom. "Lead guitarist. Tick. Throw in some denim, turn the volume up to eleven and hey presto you have a perfectly passable heavy metal band."

"Fuck this," spat Trev. "He's saying we're some *Spinal Tap* rip-off."

"I'm not. Well, actually I am, a little. Like I was saying, if you just want to be a covers band, great. You've got all the usual suspects in the set list, though there were a couple of tracks I didn't recognise. Christ knows why you picked *them*. They were so ponderous and dull. What were they? Obscure Saxon or Iron Maiden B-sides? Whatever, you should lose them. Though at least everyone got to go and have a piss without missing anything."

The ensuing uncomfortable silence was broken only by a loud snort from Joey, which he followed with a "Sorry". Carl suspected he'd misplaced a foot.

"They're mine," came in Trev, looking down at his knees. "I wrote them," he added, now staring straight at Carl, his jaw tightening.

"Shit. Sorry. Look…"

"Forget it. What do I know, eh? I mean, you're the fucking expert all of a sudden."

"I'm sorry. It's all down to taste. I've got no right to judge them. I've never written a thing."

"Stop it, please. You're pathetic."

A slowly expanding, claustrophobia-inducing bubble of silence, pregnant with squirming discomfort, threatened to engulf everyone. Trev on the verge of propelling his fist across the table. Joey lost in the complexities of cigarette manufacture. Gaz still confused. Phil and Matt looking guilty by association. Carl fast losing the will. Dan's companion hid her awkwardness by gazing out of a dark window, making the most of the opportunity it presented to style her hair. Carl enjoyed an extended cleavage update and found temporary refuge in their hypnotic swell.

It was Dan who finally punctured the suffocating bubble with a laugh and a head-lock and hair ruffle on Trev, who, by the time he'd shouted "fuck off" and escaped, had forgotten to grimace and was left with nowhere to go but forced levity.

Carl breathed a sigh of deep relief. At least it couldn't get any worse.

"Hey, Gemma," said Dan. "Carl here can't keep his eyes off your tits." While everyone took another opportunity to do just that, Carl froze, save for his eyebrows, which arched, dragging up his top lip.

"No I'm not," he bleated, though by then he was.

"Bollocks. And right in front of her fella. Must have a death wish or something."

"Er…" was as far as Carl had got before Dan burst out laughing again.

"Least he's not gay," said Gaz, picking up the thread and guffawing loudly.

"You need a rhythm guitarist," Carl blurted into the merriment before some other catastrophe could befall him. Though unasked for, he felt the need to justify himself. "Look. The drums and bass are fine. More than fine. But it's just not fair on the two of you to have to hold the fort while Joey here buggers off on a romp in guitar wonderland. There were just too many moments when you lost your way, chugging along waiting for Joey to climb back on board. Dan here standing around looking for a sign, any sign, of when he was to come back in. And Joey doing great things, but things that often don't sound anything like the song you're playing. There are minutes that could be any song and it's only the fact they're covers, most of them anyway, that stops the audience buggering off for a fag break. They need a tune, something they recognise, to keep them connected and to give Joey's sonic gymnastics some form of context." Pause for breath, encouraging nods and protruding bottom lips; though they may have just been mimicking him. "It's just plain logic. And it's not as if this is anything unusual. Allen Collins may get all the plaudits but it was Gary Rossington doing the unheralded donkey work that gave the songs form. And James Hetfield isn't just a droning voice that gets in the way of all the good bits. He's driving the songs as well. Who's the AC/DC main man? Angus in his shorts? No way. It's Malcolm that steers that band. Is Slash your main man? It's Izzy Stradlin who gives him the luxury of musical freedom. Get the picture? Fuck me, this sounds good. Sorry, you weren't meant to hear that bit." He got a laugh and dared to think he might be snatching a heavy defeat from the jaws of annihilation.

"What you doing Tuesday evening?" asked Dan.

"Fuck, no," said Trev.

Joey just sniggered.

And Carl got an audition to be in a band.

In the end it was a simple trade-off that won the day. Trev was told 'Die Young' – his favourite song, and one they'd abandoned after a try that had failed miserably to do justice to the original, the absence of another guitar obvious to all – might now be a plausible option. And Gaz was promised 'Hallowed Be Thy Name', another song previously dismissed for want of guitar anchor, but which gave him what he craved above all else: a cowbell… and licence to use it. With Dan exhibiting no inclination to take anything seriously, it became clear to Carl that the man who said the least held sway in this disparate group. And with Carl's insertion likely to set him free from the confines imposed by the limitations of the existing rhythm section, it was always about allowing Trev and Gaz to emerge with their egos intact.

And just two weeks later, Carl debuted for Exeterminate. Four became five, two more than the number of rehearsals they'd managed in the interim. But it didn't matter as the set list still predominantly comprised a hoary collection of staples that needed no introduction and little creative input to churn along while Joey sauntered gaily and unfettered. The added structure seemed to give the audience comfort; the knowledge that they were nodding along to the correct song, and that it hadn't mutated into another without them noticing.

Carl was stuck unmentioned and barely visible in a dark corner of the stage to one side of Gaz's kit, respectfully behind Trev and away from the show ponies. He made a conciliatory effort when it came to the Trev-penned clumsy dirges, adding his voice with gusto to the ludicrous chorus of 'Inch by Inch' and enumerating Germanically during 'Battle Cries'; loud enough for Trev to turn around and give a nod of approval, a smile being out of the question given the gravity of the subject matter. The audience may have been less appreciative, but the band would be forgiven provided all roads led to 'Freebird'. Which of course they did.

As they relaxed in the bar afterwards, Carl was informed that a probationary period he hadn't known existed had come to an end and he was officially in the band.

"It was by a majority, mind," Trev felt obliged to point out.

"You cock," laughed Joey.

Trev smiled, until he realised who the 'cock' was.

"Welcome to *Exeterminate*," said Dan, with as much seriousness as a sentence that ridiculous could warrant.

And with the news came an invite to a long weekend arranged for the rear end of the imminent holidays. The image that sprang to mind was of a three-day, snowed-in, boozy jam session in a remote cottage and he'd agreed enthusiastically before he'd heard Trev utter the worrying words 'creative brainstorm'. But *sod it*, Carl thought. He was in a band, so he'd happily put up with whatever rubbish Trev had planned.

It wasn't snowing, but it *was* a cottage and it *was* remote. A long winding track, punctuated by three gates and a succession of potholes, led to the ramshackle building that Trev had first moved into in his second year, and was still living in a third of the way through his sixth.

His current housemates were both third years: a geology student called Petra and a psychology student called Alice, both of whom had naively returned early on the vague promise of an 'interesting' few days. Various others wandered in and out during the course of the weekend, including a number of girls who latched themselves on to Dan and/or Gaz and/or Joey, but weren't averse in quieter moments to pursuing other options amongst what would have been termed a road crew, had Exeterminate warranted one. Trev seemed concerned at first that Petra and Alice would feel excluded, then even more concerned that they would dissolve into willing groupies. Given that conventional female students had largely shunned him, he had high hopes of any girls who had possessed the individuality or social imperative of selecting his hideaway as a logistically viable residential option. That neither had showed any sign of wanting to sleep with him was proving disparaging, but did not deter Trev from a protective and attentive regard for their well-being. Not that he had anything to fear from Carl. There was something alarmingly masculine about Petra, and a distracted intensity about Alice.

The first day meandered without direction. In amongst the alcohol and soft drugs, music was occasionally played and sporadically discussed, half-heartedly authenticating the weekend's supposed *raison d'être*. It was proving not so much a creative think tank as a forum for unoriginal debate on key issues of global insignificance. The perennial Bon Scott versus Brian Jones? Michael Schenker: guitar god, dickhead or both? On balance, would Metallica's back catalogue be better without singing? The nearest they came to creativity that first night was a protracted and heated debate on whether or not to add 'Die With Your Boots On' to the set list; Trev a big fan, his obvious enthusiasm enough for the others automatically to disagree. Trev only backed down when the lyrics were examined and revealed to be less the rousing military troop exhortation he'd claimed and, surprise surprise, more a splurge of confused and repetitive Armageddon-inspired waffle; Dan's refusal to sing 'The Frenchman did surmise', carrying the day.

By the time the room disassembled into bedrooms, vehicles and even a tent for those too drunk to care about freezing temperatures, Carl hadn't the energy to move. So he lay out on a sofa and lost himself in the oranges, yellows, crackles, spits and crumplings of the fire that was slowly dying in the hearth, until sleep enveloped him.

He awoke to a chorus of morning sounds: the clatter of china, the whine of a tap opened too fast, the rustle of a cereal packet, drawers sliding open and slamming shut, a whistled tune. He clamped his eyes shut and pulled a cushion over his head. It was the casual assault of coffee fumes that dragged up his eyelids and he eased himself up onto an elbow before taking the proffered mug from an unsettlingly friendly looking Trev and, worse still, a Trev who appeared keen to talk. To him. Pleasantries came and went until Trev got to the point and produced two folded pieces of paper from a back pocket, unfolded them with care and, teeth gently biting down on his lower lip, handed one to Carl.

"Recognise anything?"

Unfortunately, he did. Hadn't it been enough that he'd helped perform the dross. "Ah yes. Of course," he managed.

"Read them. Like poems though. That's how they're meant to be read."

"Right. Er…"

"Go on," Trev urged with breathy expectancy, leaving Carl no choice.

He started with 'Inch by Inch'… and was pleasantly surprised.

"Trev, I'm genuinely impressed," he said, genuinely impressed. "Bits of this are really good. You've got a talent."

"You should try telling the others that. Dan just sings it. And the music's a bit of a dirge. I know that. I gave Joey free reign and he never bothered to get out of first gear. I was so chuffed at them agreeing to let it in that I convinced myself they were just being respectful of the subject matter. Fat chance. Not a fucking clue what those trenches must have been like. Jeez. Bet not one of them could even tell a Sassoon from… er…" he trailed away, leaving a silence that wrinkled Carl's nose like a bad smell. "Buffoon," blurted Trev with Tourette's-like volume and timing that sent the word clattering about the room. "A buffoon," he repeated, unwisely, the word trailing away as it left his mouth.

But Carl wasn't listening. Because the verses were starting to look increasingly familiar. To his credit, Trev beat him to it.

"Okay, we both know I'm guilty of a spot of plagiarism. It's more a collage than an original. Bits and pieces from a few of my favourite poems. Glued together with my own stuff, but so you can't see the joins. My humble homage to our brave lads."

Unfortunately, Carl could now see nothing *but* the joins; Trev's input – *Hard yard. Hard yard. Killing the Hun* – not so much effortlessly interposed, as forcefully crowbarred into sections lifted verbatim from famous poems; infantile gibberish sullying all beauty, draining all poignancy. Not so much a tribute… as poppycock.

"Unbelievable," he muttered with an involuntary slow shake of the head; then panicked at the inference, only to see from the look of unadulterated pleasure he'd induced that there was no need to worry. He breathed a sigh of relief which sounded exactly like a sigh of relief, so he turned it into a yawn of theatric, eye-closing, elbow-lifting proportions, from which he emerged to find another piece of paper thrust towards him.

"Enjoy," said Trev, with complicit relish. "I'll get us another coffee… mate," he added, with the same casual ease with which he'd buggered the offerings of assorted First World War poets.

Carl approached 'Battle Cries' with caution.

"That one's all *mine*," Trev called from the kitchen.

Carl re-approached with dread.

Dear God. It looked worse on paper than it had ever sounded. The verses were drivel, but they shone with literary merit in comparison to the chorus:

Sieg heil, those Krauts are vile.
Ein zwei drei, they're all gonna die.
Fünf sechs sieben, you know we gotta cream 'em.
Acht neun zehn, it's Armagedehn.

Before building to its clodhopping climax:

We cannot lose, we have to win
The Hun's gonna test us, but to lose would be a sin.
Some people gonna wonder, some people gonna cry
Some people gotta ask the question why why why?

Why? Because we hate them.
Why? Because they're evil.
Why? Cos if we don't beat them.
Why? The world gonna fall.

Only Dan could have sung this shit without query or complaint. Acting required. Brain tired. Eyelids drooping. Caffeine needed. Nowhere to hide. Trev returning. Expectant.

"What do you think?"

"Er," offered Carl, desperately looking for the words to sate that pathetically needy look. Then he saw Trev's facial features slump.

"*Shit*," said Trev. "It's bollocks, isn't it?"

"I wouldn't necessarily say that."

"On a scale of excellent to total shite, where does it rank?"

"I fear it may well be towards the latter extremity."

"In English, you southern tosser."

"It's total shite."

"Aarrghh. *Fuck*," exclaimed Trev, pressing the heels of his hands into his temples. "So much for intellectualising a genre." His head dipped towards his knees. "Why can't anyone just be bloody honest?" he said from behind an overhang of fringe.

"I thought…"

"Not you. At least you said it how it is. I'm talking about the other sods who sat there and said they liked the songs and were fine with us playing them."

"Maybe they…"

"Maybe they fuck. That's what you get when you own the equipment, the van and the building we practise in." Carl's eyebrows rose. "Yeah. Blame a dad who thinks the more money he spends, the more he cares."

"Nice."

"Not really."

"So, basically you're in charge of the band?"

"Money talks."

"Permission to throw a spanner in the works?"

Breakfast comprised a midday greasy fry-up that nudged lunch into the early evening and ensured that supper never really happened. The dissipating daylight forced them all inside and it was then that Carl committed blasphemy.

Instruments were out and being fiddled with, and Carl had already resurrected from the previous night the thorny matter of potential new additions to the repertoire. Dropping it in. Leaving it for a while. Then casually interrupting an argument over the lyrics to the second verse of a UFO song.

"Guys."

No response.

"Lads."

Still nothing.

"*Oi.*" Heads turned at last. "Mind if I play you three songs?" General looks of concern. "On CD that is." Nods of relieved agreement. "I'll warn you now. They're nothing like what you've been playing and your first reaction may well be to hate them. All I ask is that you give them a listen. I think they'd be great to play live. In amongst the other stuff, of course."

"It's not fucking shoegazing indie crap is it, *gay* boy?" asked Gaz. "I fucking hate indie bollocks."

"Do you even know what indie is?"

"It's bollocks, that's what," replied Gaz, worryingly generating a smattering of smiles around the room.

"Look," persevered Carl, fast jettisoning all hope of a reasoned discussion, although Gaz's attention appeared to have been diverted by an inflamed patch of skin around the fangs of the recently tattooed sabre-toothed tiger engulfing his left breast. "I think there's a bit of something for everyone, so just give them a listen, will you, and try to keep an open mind? That's all I ask."

"Hey, let's give it a chance, guys," encouraged Trev, with all the persuasiveness of an ineffectual supply teacher attempting to quell a riot brewing in the remedial class; the accompanying right jab freezing the room in communal stupefaction for a brief moment, giving Carl the opportunity to slip in the CD and press 'play'.

Carl stared at the floor throughout the first track – 'Good Idea' by Sugar – to avoid the inevitable frowns and gurning, eye contact an inevitable catalyst for dissent. It only served to delay the inevitable.

"What was that called?" asked Gaz.

"Good Idea."

"Well, it wasn't."

"What?"

"A good idea."

"Excellent. I see what you're doing there, Gaz. Every Eric needs an Ernie and I'm glad to be yours."

"What?"

"He's being epochroful," came a muffled female voice from under a cushion, compounding choosing the wrong word by opting for an incorrect derivation. Though at least this was a welcome sign she had something to offer the group dynamic other than the nipple that Gaz was distractedly twiddling through the material of her T-shirt. Gaz nodded sagely at her offering, then paused, frowned, slowly shook his head and opted for a full breast cupping. Momentarily distracted by the public groping and the ongoing pursuit of what she might actually have been trying to say, Carl missed the chance to head off the voicing of further considered opinions.

"Tell you what it *was* though," offered Gaz. "A fucking load of bollocks. That's what. Knew it would be."

"I liked the bass intro," ventured Trev, supportively.

"Was that a bee at the beginning?" asked Dan. "Cos I ain't making no buzzing noise and we haven't got the equipment to start pissing around with fancy sound effects."

"We do the bell and wind thing off a tape on 'Hallowed Be Thy Name'." Trev hanging on in there. "Can you make your guitar do that fingernails down a blackboard noise, Joey?"

"No problemo. Hey, Carl, there's a load of guitar going on there. Reckon you could keep the ship afloat for the second half while I generally fuck around."

"No problemo."

"You taking the piss?" The faintest of smiles? Impossible to be sure.

"No problem," Carl replied, not taking any chances.

"Cool." A broad smile revealing he'd been had.

"There's not much in it vocally for me," said Dan.

"Point taken, so listen to this one. It's called 'Tame' by a band called Pixies."

"What kind of gay name is that? More fucking indie wimpy crap." Gaz coming back for more.

"Er. Rainbow? AC/DC?"

"Pixies and Sugar, for fuck's sake? What about Anthrax? Metallica? Saxon? Black Sabbath? Megadeth? Want me to go on?"

"Don't forget Exeterminate while you're at it. Sounds like a hesitant Dalek. Very *badass*."

Gaz glanced towards Trev, who muttered something about a silent 'e' and gave a sheepish shrug.

Carl came to his rescue. "I'll play the song."

"I can give you my review now, if you want. The words indie, fucking and shit may well make an appearance."

"Thanks for that, Gaz. The open mind is much appreciated."

"No probs."

The song ended less than two minutes later, time enough for Gaz's hand to leave its breast, head neckwards and slope under the T-shirt collar.

"Blimey," said Trev.

"The fuck was that?" said Dan.

"Indie shit," said Gaz.

"Better than you expected, then?" said Carl.

"What?" replied Gaz, clearly preoccupied with his ongoing mammary reconnoitre.

"Those vocals were truly fucked up. That could seriously mess my voice up," said Dan.

Joey was smiling to himself, but Carl couldn't tell whether that was good or bad.

Time for the third offering. Shit or bust – 'Freak Scene' by Dinosaur Jr – though not before the now customary debate on the band's name.

As the song cascaded to its chaotic conclusion, it was Joey who was first to comment.

"That was a car crash." *Shit*, thought Carl. If anyone was going to get this, it was him.

"Yeah, a fucking shit indie car crash," agreed Gaz, whose hand had emerged into daylight and was working its way down towards the top of headless girl's jeans, the tip of his tongue peeping between his teeth.

"The bloke can play guitar though," offered Trev, less than convincingly.

Gaz snorted.

"But what a crap voice," said Dan. "No intonation. It was out of tune, for fuck's sake. You can guarantee he must be a looker to get away with that shit."

"You're wrong, mate," said an unusually engaged Joey. "It doesn't matter how he sings, because I bet you he's the guitarist. And if you play like that, you can look and sing like you bloody well want."

"Don't tell me you thought he was good? He was all over the place."

"To your ears maybe, but the bloke's decent, really decent. And distinctive, which is rare. What's his name, Carl?"

"J Mascis."

"The singer?"

"Yep."

"Name as stupid as the band," muttered Gaz.

"Good looking or not?" asked Dan.

"Not."

"Bet you his dad's the one with all the money then," came back Dan.

An awkward silence. Inanimate objects became fascinating. The rain pattered unevenly on the windowpane. Tumbleweeds rolled across mindscapes.

"I don't mind dropping a song… maybe two… to fit them in," Trev said with a gravitas wasted on those present. Rarely had such a monumental sacrifice met with so little recognition.

The new additions to the set received their first public airing in their next gig that February.

"As you may have noticed, we have a new member: young Carlos on rhythm guitar," announced Dan, the rising intonation on the last word garnering a few half-hearted claps, reciprocated by an embarrassed nod of Carl's head. "If you're having trouble spotting him, he's the pretty indie-boy skulking around like a sore thumb at the back. You can blame him for this if it's shit."

And with that they dived into 'Good Idea'.

It worked, though it was always going to be the most accessible of the three. Carl was too busy providing the backdrop to Joey's scything and driving guitar to notice how the audience were reacting, but it sounded pretty good to his ears and the applause at the end, though initially hesitant, seemed genuine enough. Gauging anything more was impossible as Gaz could take this betrayal no longer and kicked straight on into the next song, throwing the rest of the band off kilter as not only did 'Doctor Doctor' not have a drum intro, but he was playing 'Let There Be Rock.' A few uneasy looks and random notes ensued before Joey kicked in on Gaz's drums, 'Doctor Doctor' forgotten, Tchaikovsky now creating, and fifteen million fingers learning how to play.

To Carl, standing on stage, 'Freak Scene' felt like it lived up to its name. Christ knows what it looked and sounded like – the original was hardly a model of coordinated structure – as Gaz spent half the time on the wrong beat and Trev struggled throughout. At least Joey looked to be having a great time, an infatuation with J Mascis blooming, while Dan savoured the f-word's intermittent appearance and the warm glow that stemmed from the belief that this was without doubt one song he was improving, his more conventional and tuneful voice tastefully renovating the original's grungy drawl. A dog's dinner it may have been, but to Carl it felt like a breath of fresh air in amongst the usual hackneyed fare, and he enjoyed the way the looks of confusion on the front few rows had changed to something approaching grudging appreciation by the end. It certainly seemed to energise a few further back in the crowd.

The song ended in disintegrating discordance; a broad smile on Joey's face, the like of which Carl hadn't seen before on stage. It certainly contrasted with the weariness that seemed to envelop him as the cow bell – not so much condemned prisoner hunched in his cell as the church bell marking the time of his imminent execution sounds across the mist-shrouded moors… as here comes Heidi the Swiss cowherd – tolled with the dramatic resonance of an empty baked bean can to signal the onset of 'Hallowed Be Thy Name'.

If 'Freak Scene' had come as something of a surprise to the regulars in the audience, 'Tame' blew their head-banging world apart. Rarely had their heads been so still, the front row all wide eyes and slack jaws. It was a song known by no one, and before they had a chance to get their bearings, it had ended. There were a few seconds of stunned silence as the final note reverberated into the ether before a few claps initiated surprisingly enthusiastic applause. It may have been more chaos than cohesion, a sonic car crash, but no one had got hurt and it had made for thrilling playing and viewing. For a covers band at a respected university, this was the stuff of word-of-mouth legend.

The only concern for Carl had been Trev's pathetic contribution to vocals; less sweaty-sex-act-cum-dirty-phone-call and more quarter-decent Ted Heath/Denis Healey impersonation. Surely it had been possible for him to breathe heavily into a microphone without shrugging his shoulders.

The pantomimic element of the performances increased with each gig, Dan taking every opportunity to play off the heavy metal loyalists against the growing contingent who liked the new material. Audiences were offered sides of the room to stand on, tribal allegiances were encouraged, the armies alternately cajoled and derided. Things reached their zenith/nadir with the introduction of a spinning arrow pinned on a wooden board on which a segmented circle had been painted, 'heavy' and 'light' alternating. The circus well and truly come to town; Trev's self-penned numbers dispatched like a couple of grouchy old clowns who can't move with the times.

But it was 'Tame' that fast became the star of every show, thanks largely to an unofficial sixth member of the group.

Horrified by Trev's excruciating shoulder-hunching mumble that first time, Carl had voiced his concerns with the others but received only apathy, such had been their collective enjoyment watching Trev make a twat of himself, leaving him looking for a way to ostracise Trev's vocal input without appearing to be doing so.

A cunning plan was required.

Come the night of their next gig, Dan announced that the following song would be 'Tame' but that before they commenced, he had a request.

"Those of you at the last gig will remember us playing this one for the first time and Trev guesting on vocals. I say vocals, but it was more like watching a spastic with his fingers stuck in an electric socket." The reaction was more muted than he had anticipated, as a hundred plus minds conjured up a mental image and then contemplated just how offensive that comment might have been and whether to laugh or shake their heads.

Carl threw Trev a *what the fuck* look to show where

his loyalties lay. Trev forced a smile back and Carl gave him the thumbs up, inwardly wincing at his own part in this humiliation. At least Trev didn't know. "Or a fucking embarrassment, as Carl here put it," continued Dan, leaving Carl feeling very sorry for himself and sensing the conciliatory expression he was manfully trying to maintain dissolve. Trev was fast deflating and Carl looked away in embarrassment and searched for dirt under his fingernails.

"Anyway, we thought we'd try something a little different and if there's a girl here, preferably a good-looking one, mind, who saw us last time and can remember the song, she might like to come up on stage and help us with a few 'uh-uh's' near the end. And if you're really gorgeous then fuck whether you know the song or not. Any offers, girls?" concluded Dan with a wink.

"Go on then," came a voice. The audience parted politely and necks craned. Climbing nimbly onto the stage came the same girl who Carl had pursued so miserably at that first gig months before. With visible discomfort and, it appeared, growing regret, she shuffled across the stage and tentatively approached Dan, who was doing his best to hide his disappointment at her marked lack of rock-chick credentials. The most wanton thing about her was the partially unbuttoned cardigan. Summoning up a dribble of enthusiasm, Dan pitched his opening gambit somewhere between Paleolithic and Neolithic.

"Hiya darlin'. What's your moniker?" he asked, inexplicably moving into some godawful gobbledy-cockney accent.

"No, I'm Emma," she replied, arriving by accident at the correct answer.

"Right then, luv," Dan continued, the sexual chemistry not so much effervescing as inert. "You up for this, then?" The first in an inevitable stream of clumsy sexual innuendos. You had to give it to the bloke; he had stamina.

"Why not."

"Excellent. When the time comes, all you've gotta do is lean over this and moan," the microphone in his hand lowered crotch-wards.

"Riiigght."

"You wouldn't be the first," stumbled on Dan, with the judgment of the truly self-obsessed.

"That's a lovely offer, and I'm very flattered, but I'd rather have his." And pointing at Trev – who unwittingly struck comedy gold with an instinctive look over his own shoulder – she swivelled on the ball of one foot and strolled across the stage towards him. She smiled and asked him if he minded her using his microphone stand. He nodded dumbly, disarmed by rare female attention and fast falling in love.

Gaz sounded the opening beats.

Going 'uh-uh' a dozen times wasn't a lot to work with, but she milked it for every drop. Hands clasped around the microphone stand from the moment the song started. The way they slid up and down, the speed increasing in tempo. The sway of her hips. Her hair falling over her eyes. That pout. She took Kim Deal's half-hearted, amused murmurings and turned them into pure filth.

As the song came to its abrupt end, the five band members took stock. The phrase 'I'd rather have his' was stuck on repeat in Trev's addled mind. Dan endured a rare moment of self-reflection to recognise that he may have misjudged her shaggability and prepared to recommence his charm offensive where he'd left off. Carl was intrigued. Joey was laughing. "Fuck me, I could fuck that," offered Gaz. Trev tutted and shook his head ferociously, at which Gaz said "Well, I could."

And Emma departed the stage.

They allowed Trev to approach her afterwards in deference to what Carl had referred to as the 'connection' they'd established. He arrived back sweating profusely, but beaming.

"She'll do it," he said, and 'it' might as well have been giving him head judging by the look of unabashed glee on his face.

With each subsequent gig, her stint increased in knowing length, and by the final performance that term it was a laboured two-minute orgasm that made Meg Ryan look like a novice.

Gaz knew with unerring certainty that she was 'well up for it'. Dan was equally certain that she wanted him, had expected sex and been genuinely puzzled at her polite refusal. Trev had asked her out four times and mistaken 'you're very sweet, but no' and its variants for a love that transcended the purely physical, and was walking around in a lovelorn stupor. And Carl was interested. Very interested.

It was five weeks and four gigs after her first performance that Emma and Carl broke cover and became a public item. That this proved in any way a surprise to the others owed more to their narcissism than any subterfuge on the part of the newly-courting. It was another couple of days before Trev cottoned on to the fact that *la rue d'amour* he had been travelling was now a cul-de-sac… and he was *tout seul.*

It was mid-August when Carl got the call from Trev that signalled the beginning of the end. Not only had Joey covertly sat exams during the summer term – an occurrence that had somehow escaped the notice of his bandmates – but he'd seriously let the side down by actually passing them. And showing an alarming ignorance of the accepted rules of educational engagement, he'd not automatically reached for the list of post-graduate courses on offer.

"Nothing I said seemed to make any difference," said Trev, unnecessarily. "He's adamant he's off."

And he was.

MONDAY

I wouldn't say I like the taste of blood; more that I've got used to it. They say that what doesn't kill you only makes you stronger, but I guess that in my case it's only what I kill that makes me stronger.

"Oh goody," Seph says to Kavalier, who is stretched out in a pool of sunshine on the balcony, purring contentedly, and draws deep on her cigarette. "More vampires."

She throws the depressingly thick sheaf of paper on top of a depressingly deep pile. Not that first impressions should count. Maybe that's why she hadn't politely dismissed Pete when he'd rung the day before to announce with endearingly childlike pride that he'd read the book she'd given to him and really wanted to talk about it. It had been enough to stir her evangelical urges and she hadn't the heart to turn him down. His impending intrusion is why she can't concentrate on anything this morning.

She reaches for another and frowns at an introductory note that optimistically informs her that this is to be the first in a 'quadrilogy'.

I entered Shadowbridge College a shy fourteen-year-old boy and emerged a warlock. We get a bad press but not all warlocks are evil. My name is Trent Derby but many know me as Mylani and this is my story.

Never has a bell sounded so sweet. She walks into the lounge and presses the intercom.

"Er, hi. Is that *Seph*?" Extra emphasis on the name. She can't help but smile.

"Come on up."

"Would you like me to put him in another room? Come here, Clay."

"No, he's okay," lies Pete, and surprises all three of them by reaching out a hand and stroking the animal. It's nothing but a bag of bones, but he gives them a tentative rattle and throws in a half-hearted "Who's a good boy," before instinctively withdrawing his hand. He leaves it hanging stiffly at an unnatural angle on the end of a limp arm he hangs down the side of his chair.

"Would you like to go and wash that?"

"No. No, I'm… er… I'm fine. Yes. Actually, I think I might."

"Go on. First on the left."

He scampers off, sending a couple of books spinning off a pile as he does so.

What to make of him? She's no nearer an answer when he returns and careers off on another tangent.

"I didn't take you for a boxing fan."

"A what?"

"A boxing fan. You know. The cat."

"Sorry, you've got me here."

"Mohammed Ali."

"The boxer?"

"Yep. Real name. Black. Cat." The words ebb away in the face of her confused frown, before he collects himself together and starts again. "Cassius Clay was Mohammed Ali's real name and I thought you might have named the cat after him."

"Afraid not. Named after a character in a favourite book of mine."

"Oh," he says, and bids a hasty retreat. "Talking of books, I read the one you lent me." Like he deserves a pat on the back.

"Excellent. What did you think?"

"Yeah, it was… it was… good." He stares down at his hands as if in preparation to deliver devastating news.

"But?"

"Well, to be honest, it was a little unbelievable. There's no way a boy would get in a lifeboat with a zebra, a hyena and an orangutan. And then a tiger? How does that work? Totally unrealistic."

"O… kay. Did you read right to the end?"

"Yes," he says indignantly, and in a wash of disappointment she believes him.

"Right."

"So, have you another one I can borrow?" he ploughs on, obliviously.

"Yeah, sure, I'll get you one before you go." Trying to think of a favourite book devoid of depth, allegory or symbolism. She's heading for the crime and older teenager sections of her mental library when the next curve ball is delivered.

"I've got an offer to make," Pete announces, rubbing the heels of his hands together and barely suppressing a grin.

"Go on," she replies, faintly concerned.

"I want… I mean I'd like… to offer to do something with your books."

She recoils from this assault, flinching to her very core, but body language is not one he appears to speak and he isn't for stopping.

"I was thinking… if you were okay with it… that I could get all your books in some kind of order for you. Get rid of all this clutter and help you find stuff."

Like he hasn't been listening.

*

(SESSION 5)

"It's a difficult moment to end, but it's time."

"No feedback? No interim progress report?" Carl says, as he gets up and turns to face her.

Her face betrays nothing. Simply reiterates her statement. But he can't resist a final shot.

"You know what," he says, "I can make this very easy for you. You keep banging on about my father, who totally fucked off and dumped us in the shit – and I'm over that, I really am – when the real problem, the great big fucking hole in my life, is Emma. Or rather the lack of her. That's what I'm really here for. I want her back. Can this… can *you* help me do that or not?"

*

WEDNESDAY

Joey's funeral.

Carl sits in his car down the road from the church.

Memories unearthed: the day he said goodbye to his father.

"Poor lad."

"Young to lose his dad."

"Especially in such… you know… trying circumstances."

And that's just what he overheard. There was doubtless plenty more, some a good deal less restrained. Tongues were wagging. Gossip, speculation and voyeurism legitimised by a black outfit and a smattering of insincere sympathy.

Well, fuck them.

And fuck him.

And sod protocol; they were the first into the chapel, glad to escape the whispering masses, or at least banish them from sight, turning their backs from the front pew on their shuffling, muttering entrances. "Let's just get through this, Carl," Mum had said in the car as it crawled in vain pursuit of her former husband. "Today isn't about how we feel. We have to figure that out in our own time. It's about giving everyone else the chance to say goodbye to the man they knew."

Or thought they knew.

'Bridge over Troubled Water.'

"Why this?" he whispered.

"One of his favourites."

Really? Not the man he thought he knew. Revise and redefine.

Shifting against hard wooden angles, he took refuge in the order of service. Black ink on white card; folded once. *A Celebration for the Life of…* – shouldn't that be *of*, not *for*? – it proclaimed above an awful photo of his father slouching over some working papers; forced smile and tired eyes. Calculator-tapping career desk-jockey. Accountancy caricature. Looking overworked and ill; the price he paid for keeping up all those pretences.

Aside from the name and photo, there was little else to personalise it, the order of service a predictable traipse through the tried and tested. He turned over to the back. Everyone back to some pub. Directions. Collection plate for Macmillan Cancer Relief. Where was the relevance in that? Why not a charity that looked after the victims of fraud; or adultery; or absenteeism? And who the hell were Colin McLeod and Tony Stevens?

Simon and Garfunkel made way for some organ muzak and a wooden box slid into sight before coming to rest on a raised platform, a lurid turquoise curtain the background, its ruffles uneven along the top. One of the tassels was longer than the other. A cloud moved briefly in front of the sun. Someone was trying to suppress a nagging cough. There was a scrap of paper wedged under one of the feet of his bench. The crease in his trousers went off-kilter halfway down his right shin. A ceiling light flickered. Motes of dust wafted through a beam of sunlight that lit up his left shoe. Maybe he should have polished them. Sod it.

Missing Emma more than ever.

The music abruptly stopped and a balding, elderly man eased himself to his feet and approached a cross-adorned lectern. A man of many greys, reminding Carl of the old priest from *The Exorcist*. A local vicar recommended by the crematorium. "I met him last week and he seemed nice enough," his mum had told him earlier. He fixed the room with a tight-lipped smile honed over many years and designed, presumably, to convey sympathy, comfort and serenity.

It left Carl cold.

"We are here today to celebrate the life of Stuart Evans…" he began. And beyond that, he could have been talking about anybody.

The ordeal continued outside as the attendees shuffled past them. One 'so sorry for your loss' or its variant after another, delivered in reverential tones with near theatrical concern on tilted faces. The anger that clenched his fists and jaw doubtless mistaken for barely controlled grief.

Carl parks his car around the corner from the church and strolls up the road to the pub. Tugging open the door he encounters a strangely familiar bulk.

Familiar because it's obviously Sausage: numero uno fan of pre-Carl Exeterminate; Master of Head-Banging Ceremonies; King of Denim; never really forgave Carl for the direction meander, though was occasionally observed begrudgingly enjoying himself during the songs he claimed to one and all to detest; good mate of Gaz.

Strange because he's wearing a suit. Or half a suit anyway, a jacket fighting a losing battle with the considerable mass of his torso, while the tie flung around his neck is loose enough for the loop to fall below the top two buttons of his shirt, both of which are undone, leaving the next one down taking the strain. Despite the jeans, heavy boots and unkempt brown hair circumnavigating his face, he's made more concessions to the occasion than anyone who didn't know him would ever give him credit for. He scratches his beard and takes a deep drag on his fag.

"All right, Sausage?"

"Wotcha, Ponse," the endearing nickname being the price Carl had paid for banishing from the set list so many of the heavy metal stalwarts that had fuelled the expansion of that size eighteen neck.

"The others inside?"

"Yeah."

Pulling himself away from the witty badinage, he squeezes past and into memory lane; it could be any night in one of the campus bars many years earlier, save for the expanding waistlines, thinning hair and choice of beverage. For a few seconds he suffers from crowded-room-entrance-blindness as he tries to make sense of things. If this place has locals, they're submerged or long departed. He edges through the throng – faces hard to place, but recognisable enough to warrant snatched acknowledgements and greetings – until he reaches the vantage point the bar affords over the room. He spies Gaz and Dan in separate animated conversations and Trev sipping a pint on his own in a quiet corner. Eye contacts are established, fingers are pointed and, like three iron filings moving towards a fixed magnet in a tub of treacle, *Exeterminate*, minus its talisman, for today at least, is reformed in Trev's oasis of calm.

They quickly establish it's been five years since they were last all in the same room – though Trev has flitted in and out of all their lives over the intervening years – and at least as many again before that since they last played together. Then they guiltily remember the absent and show their respect in stereotypically masculine, emotionally-stunted fashion as hands reach into pockets, lips are sucked in, heads shake slowly and someone says "yeah, Joey" to murmurs of assent.

They're rescued from being marooned in this sea of awkward mawkishness by Gaz's offer of a 'swift pint' and gratefully revert to the comfort setting of fond reminiscing and piss-taking.

A few sips in and the room starts to empty. They glance at watches and neck the remainder of their glasses before joining the straggly exodus heading across the road towards the church, the cool air and alcohol fusing to reduce their regard for passing traffic.

"Brought your girlfriend then, Carl?" shouts Gaz above the sound of a car horn.

And there she is in a forest of grey-topped black, talking intently with a tall, thin elderly man and two even older looking women.

What the hell is she doing here? Faking orgasms into a microphone a few times doesn't qualify her to stroll in here and look this much at home; while he's left feeling like a little kid slipping in with his mates when the adults aren't watching.

"No, mate," he replies through a suppressed burp. "That's history. Has been for a few years now."

"What's she doing here, then?"

"Christ knows," he answers with a casual neutrality that belies the inner turmoil.

"Let's go and ask him, if he's in that is."

Gaz has cracked a joke, an occurrence of such rarity that it is to be encouraged, so Carl throws him an audible chortle. When he looks back up, she's disappeared from view.

Inside the church the congregation has helpfully resolved itself into the departments of Joey's life. It's a big turnout; the legacy of those who die young. The Exeter contingent are eminently visible with their fusion fashion and evident discomfort. They fill a half-dozen rows just over halfway back on one side. Trev moves to lead them to the row at the front of the grouping but Carl pre-empts by cutting in earlier and calling them in after him. His wide berth offers him cover and an excuse to swivel slightly and glance about the church while pretending to listen to the others.

He's puzzled not to see her in the rows immediately ahead of them and it's a while before he finally locates her on the other side of the aisle, surprisingly near the front, looking very much at home and with her interested face on as she turns to listen to someone in the row behind her. She nods occasionally, oozing empathy, before reaching to touch whoever it is on the arm. They place their hand on hers and give it a grateful squeeze. This compassion overload has the converse effect on Carl. Irritation, nausea and jealousy battle for primacy, but it is resentment that holds sway; the conflict manifesting itself in a wrinkled nose that proves remarkably prescient as his face is engulfed in a sulphurous shroud.

"Pardon me," whispers Gaz, wafting the air and giggling.

When he looks back over, after granting Gaz far more attention than he deserves, she's almost completely hidden from his view. At least she hasn't seen him.

The organ kicks up a gear, and everyone rises to their feet and wrestles with the same decisions.

Hands? Side, front or behind?

Eyes? Stare at feet, straight ahead or coffin?

Expression? Sad, celebratory or constipated?

Carl elects for pockets, coffin and constipated.

He experiences a brief pang of pall-bearer envy as, the music building, Joey progresses down the aisle and is lowered onto his temporary place of rest. The organist manufactures a makeshift conclusion and the service starts. A vicar rises and climbs slowly to a raised pulpit.

"Here we go," whispers Carl. "The vicar probably met him once ten years ago, but now the church will step in while defences are down and claim him as their own. Swamp the real person in dogma and due process."

"Uh?" says Gaz.

"I welcome you all to this service, held to celebrate the life of Joseph Haydn Philips. I've been asked to take this service by Joseph's family and am honoured to do so. He was a young man whose talents I admired and whose company I enjoyed immensely. Was he a Christian? No. Did I try to bring him on board? Most certainly. Joseph attended an Alpha course my wife and I ran a few years ago. Over the course of several months, he came to our home each Thursday evening and shared food, conversation and ideas. Whilst the leap of faith proved too much for Joseph to take, at least he was willing to come to the edge and have a look across the ravine. There is a misconception that the church craves blind faith. Far from it. Joseph may not have believed, but he described himself as an open-minded non-believer and that was as much as I could ever ask of him. However, my involvement in Joseph's life was intermittent and transitory, so my intention is to slip into the background, guide you through the order of service and leave it to those who knew him best to do the talking. While I am more than happy to make this church available to facilitate this celebration of a life, I do not intend to hijack the service. The words and music will not be imposed. This is all about celebrating Joseph."

If the words are persuasive, what follows bears no resemblance to Joey; or his life. Passages of classical music, readings of poems and passages from books and a couple of simple prayers. Carl and the rows immediately in front of him squirm awkwardly in their seats. Things don't look like improving when the elderly man he'd seen Emma talk to earlier takes his place in the pulpit.

"Hello. Thank you all for coming. It is extremely touching to know there are so many people for whom Joseph meant something. For those who don't know, I was… I am, Joseph's father. It is said that no parent should ever have to bury their child and at my age, the odds should have been in my favour. I spent forty years of my life looking after number one and convincing myself that satisfaction could lie in music, material possessions and the secure knowledge that there is no one else whose needs take precedence over one's own.

"Then I met Joseph's mother, Alice, a fellow island, who died ten years ago, and we convinced ourselves otherwise. And having taken that gamble we compounded our recklessness by having a child. I remember saying to Alice that I was worried I wouldn't have enough love to share between two people. I really meant three, of course, as so many years of self-obsession cannot but leave their mark. But nothing prepared me for the arrival of a son and the sudden subjugation of every aspect of my life, a displacement that caused me nothing but joy. From the start I set out determined not to create a miniature version of myself. Joseph was to become whatever he wanted to be. I was adamantly vocal about that to anyone who cared to listen.

"Did I succeed? Well, I spent four decades working in investment banking but thinking about and listening to opera and classical music. Joseph's passion was the violin, he played in several orchestras and was climbing the promotional ladder at an investment bank. Go figure. The best laid plans…"

A smatter of polite laughter.

"Are we in the right church?" whispers Gaz.

"As you will know, the violin played a huge part in Joseph's life."

"Apparently not," Carl replies.

"It's lovely to see so many members of the orchestras he played in with us today. I also welcome those of you who were at Exeter University with him. A planned three-year stint that turned into more than double that. I was never sure if Joseph thought I'd fallen for the rubbish he came up with. A change in direction. A sudden love of history. A concern about the career prospects for another course. The mysterious illness that scuppered one year's finals. Those of you who were at Exeter doubtless had a laugh at the dopey old father who continued to fund his jaunt through higher education, but in truth I cared more for his happiness and it seemed to me that those years were very happy ones for him.

"To conclude the service, we have a last hymn, some closing prayers and then I would like to play some film footage on the projector of Joseph doing what he loved best. I think it encapsulates everything about Joseph. The hope is that it will strike a chord, literally, with everyone here and echo your interaction with him, whenever or however that may have been. I would ask that as it plays, you allow us oldies at the front the opportunity to take our leave and you are all cordially invited to the address on the back of the Order of Service for drinks, food and the opportunity to remember Joseph in less formal circumstances. I thank you once again for attending. I know it would have meant a great deal to Joseph.

"I'm not sure how I will cope without Joseph. There's nothing like arranging an occasion such as this for hiding from one's true feelings. I know the void awaits and it will not be easy. However, that is a small price to pay. Was it better to have loved and lost, than never to have loved at all? Of course, and I pity anyone who closes his heart to the vagaries of love. Rest in peace, Joseph. You mean the world to me and I will always love you."

A broken, yet dignified man takes his leave and shuffles back to his seat to the accompaniment of weighty silence, punctuated by sniffs and sobs. Carl is moved, though it's in part for a father who thought he knew everything about his only child, but clearly didn't. A glance along the pew reveals others who feel the same; like being introduced to a mate's new girlfriend, having seen her the previous night with another bloke. The secret weighs heavy and it'll have to be best behaviour at the reception. The reminiscences might have to wait for another day. Pity. But none of them has the right to take a grieving father's memories and redefine them.

Hymn and prayers out of the way, a hush ensues before the hum of an electric motor signals the slow descent of a large white screen. The lights dim. The front rows start to file quietly along the aisle and out of the door, shaking hands with Joseph's father who now stands tall and smiling at the rear door.

A projector whirrs into life and on the screen appears an orchestra. The cameraman is standing to the side of the stage, largely hidden from the audience by a curtain, though the front rows are visible. It's an unusual, but strangely intimate vantage point, making the viewer feel more part of the orchestra than observing it. The music starts. Some vaguely familiar classical stuff.

"No wonder he kept this bollocks secret," whispers Gaz, taking refuge from his discomfort in ridicule. As does Carl, readily agreeing and voicing the hope that it's going to be a short film.

When Joey stands and moves to the front it takes them a little time to recognise him. Suit. Hair tied back in a bunch. And a violin. Carl fears the worst, but he's good. Very good. Superb in fact. The performance concludes and the crowd applauds. Joey walks over to the far side, waits a while and then returns to another wave of enthusiastic applause. He bows, thanks the rest of the orchestra, who stand and take their bow, and then with a vague wave of his arm, he walks towards the camera.

About six feet away, he reaches behind his head, pulls off the hairband, shakes his hair loose and looks straight into the camera.

The picture freezes.

The hair.

The smirk.

A wink.

And in that moment the Joey they knew is revealed. He's never gone away.

Carl smiles.

Then the music starts.

Loud.

'Highway to Hell.' Those oh-so-familiar three-note combinations crunched out on electric guitar, before Bon comes in with that salacious, infernal wail-growl-shriek and Carl doesn't know whether to laugh or cry.

Cheers and conversations ensue; and Carl almost misses the next track making its entrance. Ethereal enough to suit the surroundings and occasion and slip in under the collective sonar; identification delayed yet further by its incongruity. All of which is odd given the number of times they'd played it years ago. And even when Carl does finally place it, there's a residual doubt that whoever's controlling the music system surely can't allow it to kick off.

But they do.

And right now, there isn't a more apt song in the world than 'Die Young'. Dan mouthing the lyrics, Trev donning his air guitar and Gaz percussing on his thighs. And each time the lead guitar comes to the fore, it's Joey they can all hear play.

And when the opening bars of 'Freebird' segue in seamlessly, bodies are swaying, tears are flowing and thumbs are edging towards belt loops in preparation for one last homage.

They do their best to treat each other as invisible, but it's a farce of averted gazes, turning on heels, backing out of rooms and sudden fascination with chattels, random mourners and whatever view of the garden is afforded by the nearest window. Common sense eventually prevails, and an entente-moderately-cordiale is attempted in a quiet corner of one of the seemingly endless reception rooms in this pseudo-mansion.

The opening exchanges are so inane and forced that he's perversely glad when she does what she always did best, and cuts to the chase.

"Go on then. You're dying to ask. All this polite talk must be driving you up the wall."

"I don't know *what* you mean."

"Oh bollocks, Carl. I know you too well. You're wondering what I'm doing here. Doubting my credentials."

"I'm not."

"Mmm. Right. Silly me. Okay then, different tack. I'm guessing that you just spent most of that service thinking he didn't have a clue about his own son, didn't you?"

"No. Rubbish." Too indignant. His bluff is weak, and she'll know it.

"Then I'm sorry to doubt you. Must be losing my touch." She knows.

"Fuck it. How the hell *did* you get an invite?"

She smiles coldly. "Don't you think I *qualify*?"

"I'm not saying that. Just surprised, I guess."

"I got to know Joseph's father, if you must know."

"Uh?" replies Carl, logic escaping him, the use of *Joseph* irritating him immensely.

"He used to come to most of the concerts, the ones at the university anyway."

"I never saw him. Joey never said anything."

"He didn't know. He w—" She stops abruptly and flashes a smile over his shoulder. For the cruellest of moments Carl thinks it's for him, but the recipient is Joey's father and a pang of envy brings forth an involuntary exhalation that he smothers with a cough.

"This must be Carl. The young man who kept house while my son gallivanted around enjoying himself."

"Sorry?"

"I do apologise. I tend to speak in metaphors. It's a fault of mine. I was merely alluding to your role as unselfish metronome in the band. But there I go again."

"I'm with you now. Bit slow. I wouldn't have had it any other way. Nice to meet you."

"I was just telling Carl how we first met, Lionel." *Lionel?*

"Ah yes. I quite enjoyed all the intrigue. More Ealing comedy than high espionage. Beard, wig, false glasses, excess of tweed. But it seemed to do the trick. That is, until Emma here came up and asked which one was mine. Threw me completely, but she promised my secret was safe with her and we always sought each other out and had a little chat. It's amazing what people can miss when they're not looking for it."

"That's alcoholically-enhanced, sexually-charged students for you," Emma adds with a fond pat on the old man's upper arm that propels out a grunt through Carl's gritted teeth.

"You were one as well, I seem to recall," tries Carl, feeling left out.

"I know that, Carl. I wasn't claiming to be any different."

"Anyway, she lent my clumsy disguise an authenticity, and for that I was grateful."

"I wouldn't have had you down as a rock fan," says Carl, bitterly.

"I'm not, but watching my son thoroughly enjoying himself was enough of a pleasure in itself. The music was irrelevant, though I must admit it had a certain quirky charm at times. We both agreed that things improved markedly after your introduction. Far more structure, even if Joseph rather abused your hospitality at times."

"Thanks. I think."

"I'll leave you two alone for a bit. It was rude of me to interrupt." And with that he turns away and heads for the next gig on his tour.

"He didn't deserve that."

"What?"

"Your prickly indifference."

"Sorry but that's the way you had me feeling when he gatecrashed."

"Hardly that. It's his house after all. And his son. And what had I done, anyway?"

"Oh, nothing."

"Carl, I know you better than…"

"There you go. That's part of it. You don't know me. At least you haven't cared to for a few years now. You gave up the right to *know* me. So don't just stand there and say you know me, because you fucking don't. And all that *Joseph* stuff. *Joseph* this and *Joseph* that. And all those caring bloody chats with the relations. Those little touches and the cow eyes. And knowing *Joey's* dad for fuck's sake – *oh Lionel* – and your private little jokes which feel somehow like they're partly at my expense. All that insufferable compassion stuff you do so bloody well." Pause for breath. Certainly not for thought, as he ignores the warning signs, crashes through the barriers and heads towards the cliff-edge. "Are you like it with *him* as well?"

"Who?"

"Biggles."

"It's Alistair, Carl, as you full well know."

"Sorry. Silly me. Not with you today? Off flying a private jet somewhere?"

"Why are you doing this?"

"Just showing an interest in your other half. Isn't that what *friends* do?"

"Have it your way. Actually, he is flying today, but it's helicopters these days."

"So, more Budgie than Biggles."

"Whatever, Carl. He wanted to come but he couldn't get out of his shift."

"Oh dear. Well, at least we can all sleep easier knowing that while we've all been burying poor old Joey, some millionaire is getting picked up from the races or dropped off on a well-manicured front lawn in time for the dinner party to begin, as opposed to maybe just getting off his fat arse and experiencing terrestrial travel with the rest of us plebs."

"Have you finished?"

"I'm just getting started."

"Well, enjoy yourself. I'm afraid you'll have to find another audience, because I've had enough and one of us is going to say something we're really going to regret if I don't walk away."

"Give Ali-boy my best," shouts Carl at her back.

Try as he might, and repeatedly does, it proves difficult to put a positive spin on his performance. Less the intended cool and aloof ex who has subsequently prospered; more the complete jerk.

He half-heartedly participates in the re-establishment of a hierarchy from a very different time; one where everyone knows their place and can relax into comfortable roles. Then forces himself to pay attention as they move onto the area of life post-Exeter.

Dan is still working for his dad's firm, explaining the apparent absence of a second suit in his life; the waistband of the patchily shiny grey number, purchased many years ago for the interviews his dad had insisted on before he reluctantly cast out the safety net, more constraining than supporting. His face is also fuller, but the mischievous spark and boyish charm are still there.

Gaz informs them with false modesty that he has been 'lucky' enough to become a department manager at a flagship store.

Trev is an assistant head of history at a large grammar school.

Carl judges them harshly… then hears his own voice telling them that he's a financial analyst at a company no one has heard of that produces computer-related technology no one cares about.

Faking interest in the lives of others soon takes its

toll, apathy turns to despair as someone remarks on the tragic absurdity of the words 'fun' and 'funeral' having the same derivation, and instead of being universally derided for talking utter bollocks, eleven heads give a nod towards the profundity of the observation and someone throws in 'how ironic'.

Now he's truly depressed and it's only from this position, supine at the bottom of a trough of despair, that having another stab at Emma can possibly appeal as a good idea.

Like a lazy, but persistent, sheepdog he pursues his quarry until at long last she tires and permits him to herd her into a corner.

"Me again."

"So it is."

"Can we try again?"

"I think our time has come and gone."

"You know what I mean."

"I *was* trying."

"I know, I know. It's me."

"No, Carl. It's *us* that's the problem," she says, her exasperation clear. "I'm afraid you bring out the worst in me."

"Just the worst? That's not entirely…"

"Carl, leave it."

"So what *can* we talk about? There has to be something."

"Well, there is one thing that's been intriguing me."

"Blimey. Go on."

"Quite the military tactician, aren't we?" His frown is genuine. "Come on. The little signals you've been sending?"

He twigs. "I haven't a clue what you're on about," he lies, the frown now false.

"Do I have to list them?"

Yes please. "Do what you want," he says with forced

nonchalance, the clamour for recognition drowning out the fear of an impending downsizing.

"Okay," says Emma, leaving her mouth open with her index finger resting on her bottom lip and head dipped forward. Basic teasing porn pose. He loves it. He hates it. He loves it really. Shit, he's losing already. He attempts a distracted stare out of the window. "Where do I start?"

"You tell me."

"*Right.* I guess that means starting with an admission. Once a month, heaven forbid, I treat myself to a copy of that lad-mag of yours." *Yes.* Mental punch of the air. "I could say I only buy it for the pictures of surgically enhanced pouting starlets, hideous injuries and not-very-convincing lesbian kisses or to share the randy thoughts of some sex-mad student called Mandy. But that would be lying, because I actually buy it to read your offering. Why? It's complicated and no longer any of your business. I'm not even sure I really know." *Emotional turmoil? That's good, isn't it?* "And I can't help noticing an improvement in the quality of output. Though I'm sure thongs, lighting farts and what you'd like to do to BMW drivers are ratings winners, they're the literary equivalent of candyfloss. But credit where it's due. Some of the stuff in recent issues has been pretty damn good. The nickname one did make me smile, especially when I tried it on a few people in the office and they all worked. And the motoring and degree pieces made their points really well and were camouflaged enough to maybe sneak into the consciousness of broadsheet-fearing *geezers*. I've been impressed. There, I said it."

"You feeling all right?" This is going better than he could have hoped. The phoenix may be rising from the charred remains of their earlier encounter.

"Hold your horses. Because then we have your latest visit to see my sister."

"I drop in every year on the way home from Cheltenham. Like *we* used to."

"That's not what had jaws drooping. It's the subsequent totally-out-of-character and apparently selfless offer to take Michael to some chess tournament. Where the hell did that come from? Last I heard, and believe me I heard it an awful lot, Michael was the King of Dorks, destined for a childhood spent at chess competitions being groomed by paedophiles. Yet suddenly I'm supposed to believe that your idea of a great weekend away is a chess-themed road trip? I think not."

"Just trying to help out." Keeping a commendable straight face.

"Sorry, but the martyr act doesn't wash. I'm smelling an ulterior motive."

"Damned if I don't and damned if I do."

"Cut the self pity. Oh yes, and James says thank you for the most generous sponsorship for the London Marathon."

"Pleasure."

"And your view of people like James asking for sponsorship?"

"Pursuing personal goals for entirely selfish reasons and dressing it up as some grand altruistic gesture. Zero social benefit. If they care that much about a good cause, maybe they could throw a chunk of their own personal fortune at it rather than getting the likes of me to fund their bloody ego trip. And not only do I get to lose money, but I then have to get bored shitless listening to them fucking crowing on about it for ages. Wankers, the lot of them. I think that just about covers it."

"And your response to that IT bloke at your office who, after years of telling you how he and his wife didn't want or even like kids, came round and asked you to sponsor them to go on a two-month sabbatical to some place in Africa to 'do our bit for the kiddies'?"

"I believe it was 'fuck off'."

"I believe it was. And you don't see any essential contradiction there?"

"Not at all. I'm just happy to do my bit for a good cause."

"*Bit? One hundred pounds*? Thanks for that, Carl. He's *my* boss and you made my twenty pounds look pathetic."

"Don't blame me. You know I'm a sucker for a begging email. Anything else to throw at me?"

The colour has all but faded from her lips, so tightly are they pursed. She slowly releases the pressure. "The last exhibit, m'lord, is the emergence, blinking into the sunlight, of what many in the publishing industry had thought to be a myth: your novel. Or at least the first chapter of it. The talk in the corridors of literary power has been of little else the past few weeks." *Does she mean that?* "You were relying on it. Why else would you give it to Seph, of all people."

"That your lot?"

"I rest my case."

"You missed one nice flourish."

"I did?"

"Rather than post it or drop it off myself, I made up some busy-at-work bollocks and got Pete to take it over to Seph." She looks puzzled. "You always said we should try pairing them up."

"That was more of a mischievous and intriguing experiment than a genuine mating suggestion, but I'll grant you it's a nice, if obscure, touch. You *have* been busy."

"Thank you. I've even been to see an analyst."

That one genuinely surprises her, but just as he allows his hopes to rise and starts to tell her more, her features soften, she raises a hand and Carl sees the pity in her eyes.

"Carl," she says. Here it comes. The door he's been

pushing at; about to be slammed in his face. "You have to move on. You do know that, don't you?"

"Of course," he says, a waver to his voice beyond his control; feeling like a little kid.

"Here's the speech, I'm afraid." Carl girds himself to reap what he's so recklessly sown. "We had our time and it's over. I did love you. I really did. In some ways… in many ways… I always will. But not like you want. You seem to be stuck on the good bits and ignoring all the bad ones. When we first met, you were the brightest light in the room. Yes, you were a cocky sod, and yes, you took the piss, but it was without cruelty and there was a charm to you that was attractive. Take the band. A bunch of misfits you had nothing in common with. Yet somehow you pulled it off. Watching you with them was a joy, and the way you dealt with Trev was brilliant. And all the while I admired the way you resisted what must have been an overwhelming pressure to get sucked into the vacuous, appearance-dictated world your mother meaninglessly wafted around in, and that was because of your dad; he earthed you and I could see enough of him in you to give me hope. And Carl, you could have done anything you wanted, been anything you wanted to be. So much *fucking* potential. But somewhere along the way, the shine that I'd found so irresistible was replaced with all this anger, envy and bitterness." He can manage no more than a pout. "Just you stagnating – it killed your writing – in a world of judgment, and you were so busy slagging off everyone else that you lost sight of what mattered and I lost the bloke I thought you were; the bloke I thought you'd become. And while I hated not being there for you when your dad died, in many ways I'm glad we split before, or else I would have felt compelled to stay together longer and that would have been a disaster and we wouldn't be speaking now. Because how you've dealt with it has been quite frankly… well… look, Carl, it's time you got real, rather than living in some dreamland. I've moved on. I'm with Alistair now and we're very happy. It's not a game the whole time. I can breathe. Life feels so much simpler and I like it that way."

"You sure?"

"Totally. And the only person who'll be losing is you until you accept it and get on with your own life."

"Suppose a shag's out of the question, just for old time's sake?"

A guarded assent to a 'drink sometime possibly, but I can't promise anything' is more than he expects, and certainly more than he deserves. He's left feeling pitiful, pitied, infantile and foolish.

"How did it go?" asks Trev, appearing at his shoulder.

"I've had better."

"Come and take your mind off it. Gaz is threatening to try and set some sausage roll-related eating record and there's nothing better to take your mind off it than the sight of a grown man making a complete tit of himself."

Knowing exactly how that feels, Carl forces a smile, and as one piece of his past slips through his fingers and walks out the door, he turns to face what's left.

"Fuck me," he mutters under his breath.

Maybe it's the bottle of lager he allows himself. Maybe it's the sight of mucus-infused sausage roll detritus exiting Gaz's nose. Maybe it's a wave of the I'd-rather-have-a-beer-than-a-bird-and-in-any-case-it's-your-mates-what-matter-innit-lads philosophy that tends to follow being told to forget it by a woman. Maybe it's that beer chaser. Maybe it's Dan hijacking the stereo and letting loose some golden oldies. Maybe it's Gaz clutching his mouth and running for the toilet at a near forty-five-degree angle, only to choose the wrong door. Or maybe it's just that emboldening feeling of superiority that inevitably burgeons during any period of sustained exposure to the rest of the band. Quite probably it's Lionel's announcement that anyone wishing to sleep over is welcome and the consequent close acquaintance with a doubtless high-quality bottle of red.

Whatever the genesis, there comes a moment when it occurs to Carl that his best course of action is to buttonhole his generous host on the presumption that he'll be well up for a spot of Biggles/Budgie-bashing.

Carl is pressing ahead with an enhanced and filterless version of his earlier spleen-venting when Lionel stops staring down at his feet, places a hand on Carl's elbow, offers a smile that says 'shut up' and then says as much.

"If I could just interject. It appears that you are under a misapprehension. Alistair doesn't fly for a commercial enterprise. Not for some time, in fact. He flies an air ambulance. His shift should have allowed him to make it here at some juncture, but there was a major pile-up on the M4 and it was all hands to the deck, so to speak. Very nasty, Emma was telling me. A number of fatalities. One a young girl. Tragic. Alistair was ferrying the injured back and forth. I can't even begin to imagine the toll that must take on him day in, day out. Takes a special type of person, in my opinion."

"Yes," manages Carl, teetering on the brink of the crevasse that has opened at his feet.

The anatomy of a flailing, failing relationship…

He presses the button. It whirrs. It flashes. Its wings beat furiously up and down. It revolves rapidly. It shoots plastic pellets into the air.

"Priceless, isn't it?"

The performance concludes, the wings fold downwards and the lights fade.

"Don't you think?" he adds.

"How… why… what is it?"

"It's a missile-firing chicken."

"Of course it is."

"Happy Birthday."

"Not *more* form studying."

"Of course. These are the most important few days of the year. I can't go under-prepared."

"But there's weeks to go."

"Gotta mop up that ante-post value."

"And to think you always say you can't find the time to write your novel."

"That's different. This only happens once a year. Don't you think Pete and the others aren't doing this?"

"Tell me, Carl. Would you rather come out of Cheltenham up a thousand but Pete up ten thousand, or be down a thousand and Pete down ten?"

"What a stupid question."

"For Christ's sake, Carl, what the hell is all this? And don't piss me around. They're definitely something and they most definitely are sitting huddled together in the corner of our freezer, nuzzling up against the apple crumbles and the ice cream." Carl shrugs his shoulders. "*Well?*"

“They’re frozen turds,” he splurts out, as if injecting the words quickly into the conversation will somehow eject them out the other side without registering on her consciousness. It doesn’t work.

“*What?*”

“They’re not mine.”

“Well hoo-fucking-ray. Every cloud and all that. My boyfriend collects shit for a hobby. Whoopee. What did you do? Hang around public toilets and hope the flush wasn’t working?”

“They’re dog turds, if you must know. They’re all in bags and they’re frozen solid. They probably don’t even…”

“Shut up, will you? Like you think that explanation is going to make it all okay. And you can wipe that bloody smirk off your face. What the hell are they doing in here?”

“Hibernating?”

“Now is not the time for humour. Oh, wait. *Now* I see. It’s another of those pathetic vigilante stunts, isn’t it? You and your pals off on another of your *little missions.*”

“Don’t call them that. You know I don’t like it. You’ve never understood them.”

“Oh, please don’t patronise me. I know exactly what they are. Juvenile stunts dressed up as moralistic revenge. Nothing more, nothing less. And this was your idea?”

“No, it was Kevin.”

“Kevin? I didn’t think he had it in him.”

“He didn’t… a load of… dogs… did.” The words trailing off as he recognises the folly of pouring more oil on the fire, though of course self-censure loses out to the need to deliver a punchline.

“Ha ha, shut up. So how come you drew the short straw?”

“I didn’t, we’re all collecting them.”

“Tell me, Carl, what gives you the right to judge?”

“It’s not about judging.”

"Yes, it is. What exactly is the heinous crime that has been committed by the intended recipient?"

"Repeatedly allowing a dog to crap away on other people's front lawns, often families with young children, without any intention of picking it up, while being in possession of a prize-winning lawn of your own and shooing off any child or dog, including your own, that goes near it."

"So basically, a bit of hypocrisy."

"It wasn't your child in tears with dog shit all over their school shoes."

"No, Carl, it wasn't. And nor was it yours."

There are few better things in life than reading *Congratulations, you have made the final table* on the screen. A field of over two hundred and he's made the final nine, well into the money and over three thousand dollars to the winner. All the better for the knowledge that Pete and Kevin, both knocked out just short of the money, will almost certainly be enviously and bitterly observing his progress.

He is aware of a consistent pinkness to the shape that lingers at the extreme periphery of his vision. He fears for his evening's plans. He can't bring himself to look, though he knows it's expected.

There is a sigh and her naked form passes before him. She needlessly alters the position of a candlestick on the mantelpiece and passes back, hips asway. He can't help but notice a slight crinkling of skin at the top of the back of her thigh. There's an angry pimple on her right buttock. With the passion-tinted spectacles removed, his gaze is almost medical. He feels duty bound to watch her progress to the door, at which point she pauses, looks back over her shoulder and, with what he presumes to be a suggestively 'come hither' smile, says, "I'm going to bed, don't be long."

Poker? Poke-her? Poker? Poke-her? Poker? Poke-her?

The first insincere *good luck one and all* appears in the chat bar.

Forty minutes later he slips under the duvet, offers a half-hearted arse-grope to test the water and finds it has turned to ice. He gives a sigh he hopes will be interpreted as disappointment, should it be heard, but it's relief he feels as he lies back, stretches out, yawns, closes his eyes and replays the deciding hand.

It's the same body that he hungrily ravages the moment she comes in the door a couple of nights later, after ten hours of mental foreplay since that merest of glimpses of a favourite pair of knickers going on that morning.

His need.

Satisfied.

Carl tempts them onto the dance floor with the opening chords of 'Dancing Queen', a promise – "I can see clouds approaching, ladies, and I think I know what it's going to be raining in a couple of songs' time…" – and a thinly-veiled threat: "… but before that we have one of the bride's favourites. It's her special day and the least you lot can do is get up here, dance your little socks off and show her you're having a great time. Come on, let's see you *boogie*."

Might have pushed it a bit far at the end there – more Smashy and Nicey than Westwood – but it seems to be working. The floor's filling up fast, arms are in the air and at the centre swirls a bride too high on alcohol and sentiment to care what music is playing, her sisters by her side: Beth on sufferance and clearly hating it, but Emma partying like there's no tomorrow. He catches her eye for a split second and she flashes him the warmest of smiles. How could she have doubted him?

Mmm… let's see now… what do we have here…? Let's just fade out this seventies' dross… and… here we go…

"*Woooooo!*"

A loud grunt.

"Ru*rrr… uh.*"

And over a hundred people are trapped in a rhythmic double bind: they can't possibly offend the bride – after all this *is* one of her favourite songs, the DJ has just said so – yet to avoid doing so they must dance to a track not known to any of them. There is enough of a repetitive, driving beat to set arms and legs intuitively in motion but what motion that should be is clearly subject to as many interpretations as there are people on the dance floor. Brows are furrowed as a slightly manic voice urges them to "*Do the manta ray*". A few dancers make like fish, one even puffing her cheeks out and opening and closing her mouth. The rest look like it's disco time at an arthritis convention. They badly need help but never fear, Black Francis is here with the instruction booklet: "*Your head can go real screw… with saucers chasing you.*" Strangely, this doesn't seem to help that much, though the '*screw*' sounds like '*slow*' and this leads to a change in gear for many, while some stop and just allow their heads to loll around on their shoulders.

Two of the longest minutes of their lives.

And two of the funniest in Carl's, capped with the gloriously nonsensical "*this don't swim – this fly, fly c'mon*" delivered in a crazed falsetto.

But all good things come to an end and, repulsed by the

tangible relief and unabashed joy that greet The Weather Girls, he looks away in disgust. His eyes meet those of Emma, now standing a few yards to his left, her arms crossed and *that* look on her face. She pouts. He goes over.

"It always has to be about you, doesn't it?"

You just can't please some people.

"First time?" Emma asks.

"White, with the little bow on the front."

"First time at your parents?"

"Red, with the dark blue trim."

"Phil and Louise's wedding?"

"Black with the lacy front."

"That time we went for a walk near your house to get away from your parents arguing?"

"White with black spots."

"That one for old time's sake just after we split up?"

"Apricot."

"Favourite?"

"Easy. That totally impractical lacy white pair I bought you."

"I'm amazed."

"Thank you."

"No, Carl. Not in a good way. I'm amazed that any of that mattered to you. Or more to the point, it's clearly what mattered to you most."

"Carl?"

He feigns sleep, something in her tone sounding an alarm.

"Carl?"

Sounding more urgent this time. He's heard that voice before. It's not help she's after. It's the need to unload. To get serious. This isn't going to be good. He deepens and lengthens his breathing… as if that's going to work.

"Carl." No longer a question. The light comes on.

"What?" he asks, not wanting to hear the answer. "You okay?" As if concern at her well-being might somehow deter her from whatever revelatory road she's travelling. The crossed arms and fixed stare tell him he's wasting his time.

"This isn't working."

"What?"

"Us. I'm going to move out. We're just not heading in the same direction."

It's like a trapdoor opening beneath him. She stays calm. He doesn't. He struggles for the words. The ones that will persuade. They have to exist, but he can't locate them, so he stutters and reels through word combinations that mean nothing and can never change her mind, but he has to try. There are tears, most of them his. She has preparation and resolve to gird her. Taken by surprise, he only has desperation.

It's almost three by the time the words and tears dry up.

The real pain comes when he wakes up to a half-empty bed and the mental fog dissipates to reveal a stark and barren reality he has no choice but to face. The depression in the mattress taunts him and there's a mocking confidence and distance – an independence, of him anyway – to the bangs, clinks and rustles of her progression around the kitchen. In the face of such wilful purposefulness he groans and curls into the foetal position. This is her script and he's left fumbling for that killer line that will slice through her resolve.

But when she does stroll in, already dressed and with a toothbrush hanging from her mouth, she's already a stranger and he feels his strength dwindle in the face of her calm assurance.

The jumbled phrases that escape his lips are pathetic. And when he does finally assemble a full sentence, it's undermined by the quaver in his voice.

She shakes her head slowly.

He turns away and buries his head in the pillow, unable to face that pity.

MONDAY

There is no obvious logic to his presence here, this strangely earnest bloke with no apparent job, who claims to play what he calls 'the markets' but offers no further explanation, who can't move beyond the factual without losing his bearings, who cannot cope with disorder, who recoils from cats… and yet doesn't recoil from her.

It's not as if Seph had knowingly lowered her defences; those protective walls constructed over the years, the books her building blocks, the cement the heroes and fantasies and parallel universes born of their pages and which no reality can ever match.

She tells herself he's only here for the book project, that he can't resist a challenge to impose order. Yet every now and then there's a shared smile, a fleeting contact or a sensed observing that suggests otherwise and unsettles her with its implied contentment at spending time in her company.

"Would you prefer your myths and legends grouped by country of origin or all together?" Pete asks with unfathomable seriousness.

*

(SESSION 6)

Silence.

"That's half an hour of nothing. Aren't you contractually obliged to say something? Lead me?"

"I'm here to follow you. You dictate where we go."

"And you have to train for this?"

"It seems you find it very difficult when I don't fill the space for you?"

More than she can possibly know.

RÉTI-CENCE

"You're only doing this to get Auntie Emma to be your girlfriend again."

An hour and a half into the car journey, and this is the kid's first tussle with the intricacies of syntax. Not a sniff of a verb until now. The chess geek may be awful company, but he's a perceptive little sod.

"Did your mum say that?" asks Carl, unable to stifle a grin.

"You're so busted." Blimey, almost a smile there; softening the angular features that serve as a pointed reminder of his hopeless, ferret-like father.

"I can't think of a better way to spend my weekend than *frapping la rue* to the delights of East Anglia."

"Yeah, right. A weekend of kids playing chess. Bet you think it'll all be nerds with glasses, goofy smiles and stammers."

"No." Not convincing. "Nooo." Not a lot better. "*No*," his voice suddenly louder and more insistent, but ringing hollow nonetheless. He gives up. "There will be nerds, won't there?"

"Plenty." A genuine smile this time.

"Glasses?"

"You bet."

"Bow ties?"

"That I can't promise." This time verging on a laugh.

Carpe momentum.

"Your mum thinks you're getting bullied." Silence. "School?"

"Nothing I can't deal with."

"Why you?"

"If you're cleverer than the rest, play chess and don't like sport, you tend to stand out. Get called names and stuff."

"And out of school?"

He pauses. A giveaway, and he knows it. "Did Mum tell you to ask me?"

"No. She just hinted at it when I dropped in last time."

"After losing all your money?"

"Guilty as charged." Ignores the diversionary tactic. "She mentioned a few kids from the estate?"

"There's a group of them, but it's two brothers mainly. They're the ones in charge. The rest just go along with whatever they say. It's not only me they go for. But a small kid in a uniform with a briefcase full of chess books kind of makes it easy for them."

"How do they know what's in your bag?"

"Tipping it upside down tends to do the trick."

"How old are they?"

"Kurt's maybe sixteen, Jimmy a year younger."

"You know them?"

"Everyone does. The Hawkins family is famous round our way."

"Why doesn't someone do something about it?" Carl asks, and receives a snort. "Stupid question?"

"You could say that."

"How bad does it get?"

Lips and fists tighten. Looking inwards; dark places. Now is not the time to push. Bring him back before he's lost for the remainder of the journey.

"What kind of music do you like?" he attempts.

"Music?"

Oh dear. Tricky business, this pseudo-parenthood.

"Hand me that CD, will you?"

"Which one?"

"The one with the monkey on it. Time we started your education."

Debaser kicks in. Might as well throw him in at the deep end.

Hello Yarmouth.

Breakfast, and they're back in the seafront hotel's Artex-ceilinged, retro-feel dining room, where last night they had partaken in an evening meal that had been a throwback to childhood holidays for Carl, with guest appearances from 'fan of melon', obviously tinned soup, stack of diagonally-sliced buttered bread, crème caramel with mottled skin on the base and a glass of house red that tasted like Ribena.

Michael is sporting a quizzical look.

"Why is she looking at you like that?"

"I believe she fancies me."

"How do you know?"

"You just do."

"Are you going to go out with her?"

"No."

"Is that because of Auntie Emma?"

"No, it's a lot simpler than that, believe me." His voice tailing off as the waitress lopes across the room and deposits two plates of full English on the table with a clatter and a glance at Carl that presumably alludes to the carnal delights that could be theirs to share should he so desire, but only serves to turn his blood cold.

Carl's detachment dissipates the moment they enter the Pontins car park and walk past an intense young man in blazer, suit trousers and a checked tie – private school; you can spot them a mile away and this one wouldn't last five minutes in the state system – in Churchillian flow, repeatedly stabbing a finger into a palm. The recipients of his oratory are a crescent of rigidly attentive public schoolboys in full school uniform; trousers creased, ties knotted neatly, black shoes gleaming. A respectful distance away stands a group of parents unaccustomed to failure and paying big money to guarantee its absence from the lives of their precious progeny and ensure another generation can stay comfortably distanced from the rest of society. Not that the teacher has an easy ride. The unspoken demands made of him by school and parents are evident in his crimson cheeks and the sweat on his forehead. This is no holiday, whatever may be said to the little loves through forced grins. The only way is down. You wouldn't find this lot within ten miles of a holiday park unless it was an unavoidable stepping stone to success.

The antithesis of this melting pot of highly-tuned and nurtured privilege is the loose, directionless assemblage they find lurking in a pool of shade thrown by the anomaly of a tree; looking lost, bewildered and afraid; and that's just the parents. You can see the confidence ebbing from them as they try not to draw negative comparisons between the assured discipline of the elite neighbours and their own offspring: one is clutching a blanket; another a teddy bear and sucking her thumb; one is crying; several display the slack-jawed appearance of dissociated zombies; two are arm-wrestling on a patch of dusty ground; and another adorable child is deep-mining a nostril and depositing the sourced snot in his mouth. If appearances count for anything at all, St Cuthbert's is truly fucked.

"Where's Mr Bridges?" Carl asks Michael, trying to keep the defeatism from his voice.

"Don't know. We'd better be going in though."

They start to move off, only to be halted by a horn hoot and an obscenely cheery wave that announce the arrival of their saviour, a set of golf clubs strapped into the passenger seat of his de-roofed convertible.

"Thank God for that," says Carl.

"I wouldn't get your hopes up," offers Michael.

They wait for Mr Bridges to park, fiddle around with his roof, secure the cherished clubs and stroll over. A perfunctory greeting and then he ushers them in the direction of the hall.

As they sidestep a fruit machine, Carl finds himself singled out.

"Michael tells me you're a chess player."

"He does? I wouldn't put it qui…"

"Excellent." Not a man to trouble himself with the trivia of other people's opinions or preferences. "Happy to take you up on his offer for you to manage one of the teams." Carl casts a glance at the sheepishly grinning young Judas strolling beside them. "Only one allowed for each team, so quite a privilege. We're there to answer any questions and help out. Parents aren't allowed in during play. I'll take the under nines, if you don't mind keeping an eye on the older kids. Here's your badge." Carl unthinkingly accepts it, and in doing so loses that split-second window of opportunity to object. "It's Dick, by the way," says the teacher formerly referred to as Mr Bridges, dispensing in one fell swoop with at least two stages of the conventional familiarisation protocol.

Carl offers his own name.

"Excellent," replies Dick, in the manner of someone who isn't really listening, before promptly removing himself to a distant corner of the room, where he sits down on a stray chair and opens a novel with the unhurried calm of a man whose attention it will take more than a raised hand or polite cough to grab.

During the introductory spiel, Carl runs an eye down a list of teams monopolised by the public-school sector and feels his hackles rise. He turns back and surveys Michael's teammates. The twins look about eight and are nervously nibbling fingernails, fiddling with earlobes and refusing to engage in eye contact with their opponents. Boards two and three, Jake and Peter, are still perspiring from their bout of arm-wrestling and are now moronically bashing their heads against the boundaries of slapstick humour with a selection of fart noises and attacks on each other's pieces. Sophie, on board six, has assembled a group of small teddy bears – a hug/cuddle/comfort? – on the table beside the board and is one-by-one substituting them for pieces. Carl wonders if that thumb ever leaves her mouth.

Across the table sits a future University Challenge quiz team squad boasting between them three England sweatshirts, a county T-shirt, a facial tic and six looks of utter disdain. The high-powered tomfoolery of Jake and Peter only serves to fuel their innate sense of superiority.

Michael, on board one, looks suddenly very vulnerable in their midst – a leader of a weak and disorganised army going into war against a vastly superior and better-armed foe – and Carl feels a softening towards him. They are way out of their league. They haven't got a chance, a realisation confirmed by the look on the face of the opposing manager, who offers his hand and wishes Carl a good game as only a guaranteed victor can. Carl almost apologises in advance for what is to follow.

Once all the parents and hangers-on have left, permission is given to commence and palms activate clocks. The resulting din demands a metaphor, particularly from an aspiring author. A batch of Chinese firecrackers set off all at once? Bubble-wrap mayhem? Dominoes clattering down a wooden staircase?

Michael is playing white and moves his knight to F6. Still persisting with the Réti.

A raised hand summons him away and he bends down to deal with his first question. The boy must be about seven and is pointing across the table at some unknown horror that Carl struggles to locate given that none of the pieces appears to have been moved. The finger jabs and he follows it across the board… and up… to a two-inch string of glutinous green, the other end of which is precariously attached to a nostril, its owner seemingly incapable of movement for fear of dislodging the stalactitic emission. Carl stifles a gag reflex, rummages around in a pocket and locates a hanky that may or may not have been used before. He pushes the ball of tissue towards the boy who, instead of taking it, offers an imploring look that sees Carl shaking his head in alarm at the implication. Eventually the boy accedes, messily gathers up the snot-fall and holds the glistening tissue out.

Jake and Peter are spraying their pieces around with expansive bravado, no squares safe from their probing, no move worthy of more than five seconds of their precious time, no stupid sacrifice beyond their imbecility. They both duly crash and burn within five minutes, before sauntering out, the minor irritant that is chess banished for a few hours. Carl resets their pieces and clocks for them, the latter requiring only the tiniest of tweaks to the left. One of the opponents gives him a glance that seeks assurance as to the reality of what has just happened.

Sophie lasts longer, but only because of the time it takes to gather up her ursine companions without disengaging her thumb.

The twins – William and Benjamin; a Home Counties dinner-party-retro-rib-tickler if ever there was – are at least paying their opponents some respect. They keep their games reasonably close, though both are fighting losing battles. Benjamin knocks his king over in the face of overwhelming force, but William clearly knows the value of a good bluff, so he offers the draw and his opponent has instinctively grabbed the hand before he realises he's been done. If he doesn't already know, he certainly does when he looks up into the seething ire that contorts the face of his manager. Board one throws in a slow shake of the head for good measure.

That just leaves Michael, his game eventually outlasting all but three in the entire hall, its imminent end first apparent when an innocuous pawn move by his opponent sees Michael sigh and run a hand through his hair, as his opponent sits back with arms placed behind his head and flashes his manager the quick glance that says *job done*. The manager's facial puckering answers *about bloody time*. Michael plugs on for a few minutes, but with his time almost expired, he has to concede. The opponent says "good game" and Carl hopes he means it. No points for effort or going close in chess. Michael gets the same duck egg for battling an England player to a close defeat over more than two hours that Jake and Peter achieved for their five minutes of retardation. Then again, Michael's opponent gets no more for his efforts than his teammates, who really lucked in when they found themselves sitting across from Beavis and Butthead. Chess is no team game. It's all about the individual and their own precious grading.

Carl stands before the brightly illuminated panels and attempts to summon digestive enthusiasm, though he fears that the menu might be over-selling its wares.

Eventually takes the plunge and plumps for the Thai chicken, ordering Michael his burger and chips.

He heads over to where Michael has lost himself in a chess book that appears to comprise page after page of tightly packed annotated moves, punctuated very occasionally with the briefest of narratives. Each to their own, of course, but Carl draws the line when Michael finds something in the dense forest of letters and digits that makes him chuckle out loud. Carl looks around the room in panic and is horrified to see a group of teenagers on a neighbouring table staring at Michael like he's shit on the soles of their shoes. Carl consoles himself by imagining what they must be making of this geek infestation landing in their laps halfway through their holiday. Consoles himself further that this *is* their holiday. But when Michael embarks on a lengthy chortle it's not enough to compensate, so he opts for a diversion.

"When did you start playing chess?"

"My dad taught me." Voice wavering. Hesitant. Lying. "I know what you're thinking, but he did." Indignant.

"*All right.* I didn't say anything." *Just thought it.*

"He used to play chess all the time. He had this brilliant chess set. He wouldn't have had it if he didn't play, would he? And he was the one who showed me how the pieces moved and stuff and that's what made me want to play. It's down to him that I can play. It really is."

Carl glances absent-mindedly at the handful of under-nine games still in progress. Something's not right. He takes a few steps back and studies a board that changes shape constantly as the pieces are near-randomly shunted around.

Something's wrong.

"Excuse me," he asks a very young board five. "Where's your king?"

"I took it," answers his opponent, after proudly extracting the captured sovereign from his mouth.

Michael's game achieves kudos the moment it becomes the last one in play. He's down material and coming under pressure from a pawn storm. His opponent is releasing each piece with an exaggerated hand flourish. Cocky sod. That England sweatshirt really starting to irritate. Predictably, a crowd is starting to form; a lot of chins resting on fingers. Michael's slow demise now a public spectacle rather than a private hell. No comfort from the clock. Carl wants to reach down, pick Michael up and take him away somewhere safe.

Then from nowhere comes a moment of sublime beauty. The opponent reaches forward to pick up a piece and confidently makes his move. He's about to lean back in his chair when his body goes rigid and his gaze fixes on the board, before flitting ever so briefly in the direction of his manager, whose eyes are now closed, the heel of his hand kneading a temple. Carl spots the error just as Michael makes the move that will force a knight-pawn swap in his favour. Level on material again, the pawn attack no longer supported by the knight and only a couple of minutes each on the clock. The draw is offered by Michael and reluctantly accepted, not because it's a tough decision, but because his opponent feels some divine right to the full point.

Carl can't resist giving Michael a pat on the back as the two players reset their pieces. The bloke who gave the introductory speech is standing a few feet back on the other side of the table in close conversation with a familiar face. Carl catches the man's eyes and holds his gaze a fraction too long.

Michael is rising to his feet as the man approaches.

"Well played, young man," he says.

"Thank you."

"Sorry to bother you, but it's Carl, isn't it?"

"Er… yes." Michael at his elbow, frowning.

"You still playing?"

"No. Not at all. I sort of drifted away."

"Pity." Carl glances down to see Michael trying to work it all out. "Are you a teacher now?"

"No. Michael's my neph… er… the son of a friend," he blunders, wondering what Emma would make of the Freudian slip. "I'm just helping out."

"This man teaching you everything he knows?" Michael very confused. Carl smiles and shakes his head, his ego enjoying it, but irritated that his cover is about to be blown. "A player with some potential when I last saw him."

"I'd hardly say that," offers Carl, gallantly.

"Player?" interjects Michael.

"Board ten, wasn't it?"

"Eight," replies Carl far too quickly, invalidating his attempted self-effacement.

"Right. Been a while, of course." The wry smile telling Carl he'd known all along. Set a trap. Amused that it's worked. "Anyway, as I said, well played, young man. I trust we'll be seeing you at the England trial in July?" Michael looks doubtful. "Of course, I'd have liked to see you at a few more of the qualifiers. But you're board one for your county, so you qualify anyway." Michael still gloomily pondering logistics.

"He'll be there," Carl says. A knee-jerk promise he has no right to make.

"Excellent. I trust we'll be seeing you both at the Blitz this evening? Brush off the mental cobwebs, eh, Carl? We can chat again then."

"I don't know what we're doing yet. We're actually stay…"

"I definitely want to play," says Michael, warming

to this public outing and taking strength from Carl's conspicuous discomfort. Emboldened, he goes in for more. "Did Carl really play chess?"

"Ah, I see. He hasn't told you. Yes, he certainly did. For his country, no less. I knew Carl when he was a little bit older than you. A promising and instinctive player who could have risen higher had he shown more predilection for theory and practice."

As they depart, the questions start.

Michael gets to play in the Blitz. And so does Carl. Not without protest, but he eventually agrees and, despite himself, even starts to enjoy it; not that he permits Michael the pleasure of seeing it as they pass between games and snatch furtive glances across the room to gauge each other's progress.

At some point in the blur of hands, pieces and battered clocks, Carl's innate competitive spirit rises to the fore and the veil of reluctant altruist is discarded long before they clash in the seventh game of nine. His alpha male status under threat, Carl draws on the full armoury of resources at his disposal as they sit down and prepare to play: the crushing handshake, the self-deprecatory asides, the inane chitchat with neighbours, the queen deliberately placed on the wrong colour and so on. But when the clock starts, he's left with nothing but the dregs of a chess-playing acumen that last saw active service at the age of thirteen, before it disappeared under a welter of more attractive and instantly rewarding leisure options and was banished to a distant cul-de-sac of his brain. Try as he might to call on them, the requisite thought processes are not immediately to hand. Moves that should be automatic take vital seconds to find, or he's haunted, and hence delayed, by the nagging knowledge that a better option has just eluded him. The game is a foreign language he learned long ago but hasn't used since. He's reacting to perceived threat the whole time without ever asking Michael questions and with no long-term strategy in mind. The game demands an instinct he no longer possesses. The seconds wasted pile up unnoticed and it's over them that he finally trips, preferring death by clock to the inevitable checkmate heading inexorably his way. Carl takes comfort from at least dragging the game out, maybe garnering a little respect.

"Why didn't you pick my mum?" asks Michael, as they drive back to the hotel.

"*What?*" No need to fake surprise there.

"My mum. Why didn't you choose her?"

"It wasn't about choosing, Michael. I met your Auntie Emma first. At university. We'd already been going out for months before I first met your mum and then she was just the sister of my girlfriend." *Plus, your dad was still alive then.*

"What about… you know… after?"

"I was still going out with Emma."

"I know. But you split up ages ago. You could go out with her now."

"It doesn't work like that."

"Cos you still fancy Auntie Emma? Mum says you do."

"Does she now?"

"She says you've got it *bad*." Then sheepishly adds "Whatever that means."

"Well, I don't."

"You could choose Mum now."

"It doesn't work like that, Michael."

"Just saying, that's all."

Approaching midnight, Carl is enduring a rom-com's mushy denouement, Michael tossing and turning in bed to his right.

A period of relative quiet and stillness has him daring to hope, but when he looks across it's to find Michael lost in thought, eyes wide open.

"They made me wet myself."

"What?" Too harsh, so he follows up more gently. "Who?"

"The boys on our estate. In my trousers. They made me wet myself." Carl can find nothing to say and Michael takes it as a cue to elaborate. "I couldn't help it. They wouldn't let me get past and they just kept teasing me and I tried not to cry but they could tell I wanted to so they teased me some more saying I was a poof and a swot and gay-boy and stuff about Mum and how she was stuff I didn't understand and they were all laughing at her and I was crying by then and that just made them laugh more and then one of them said why don't we kick his head in and I just felt all funny inside and I couldn't help myself and it went all warm and then they all saw and they just laughed and I started crying again and they just laughed more and then they said I could go but when I tried to get past them one of them tripped me up and someone kicked me and then they took my bag and chucked my things everywhere and trod on them and I got into trouble the next day at school when my exercise books were all ruined and I hadn't got the right pencils and pens and stuff and the teachers wouldn't believe me even though I had a bruise on my face and my arm and everyone knows who they are and what they do to other kids but they're as scared as we are so nothing happens."

He takes a breath and Carl, unseen, dabs at a moist eye.

"What did your mum say?"

"I didn't tell her. You *mustn't* tell her. You promise?"

"But…"

"*You promise?*"

"I promise, but you should tell someone."

"I just have."

"No one else?"

"No. And you've promised, remember."

Poor sod. *Of all the people to tell*, ponders Carl, *he's picked me*. Unworthy of such trust and out of his depth. A dull pressure builds on his chest and behind his eyes as he watches the boy sigh and turn away from a cruel world, curling in on himself. Yet in a few short hours he'll have to unfurl and open himself up to that world again and gird himself for three more tough mental battles, though in truth they'll be welcome havens for him from the real war that awaits back home.

*

"Thank you for that," says Beth from the kitchen. "I mean it. He wouldn't have made it there if it hadn't been for you."

"No problem. If I'm honest, I enjoyed it."

"See much of Michael, did you?"

"Plenty. Actually, he was a bit of a star. Almost single-handedly dragged his team into the top half." He launches into a recap of key moments, but pulls up short when she comes back into the room carrying two mugs, clearly not that interested. Suppressing his irritation, he takes a cloying mouthful. *Little bit of milk, no sugar. How fucking difficult can that be?* It's amazing the sugar found enough heat to dissolve in. Beth stares into her own mug and Carl takes the opportunity to manoeuvre his tongue and upper teeth so that the latter can scrape the syrupy-lacto-coating off the former.

"I never knew Mark was such a keen chess player," Carl mischievously throws in.

"*Chess*? Maybe draughts. But chess? What do you think? We did play scrabble once. We rented a caravan in some godawful place. Pissing down with rain one night, so we stayed in. I could see straight away in his eyes what he was after, so to buy myself some time I grabbed one of the games the owners had left. I remember the look on his face when he put down t-i-t. Then he spent the rest of the game putting down two letter words, while he planned for the next smutty innuendo. I remember him finally putting down f-a-l-a-t-o with such pride that I hadn't the heart to tell him what a witless moron he was. But chess? No chance."

"It's just that Michael said..."

"Mark couldn't play the game, but he picked up a chess set once in a house clearance. The pieces were all fancy carved wood and he liked having it set up on a coffee table in our living room. Over there in the corner. It was a bugger to keep clean."

"Where's it now?"

"Up in Michael's room. It became part – a big part – of the image he built up of his dad. I didn't help. Probably told him it was his dad's and how much he liked it and that was enough. In his young mind Mark went from being the dopey sod he really was to some kind of chess master. I didn't have the heart to tell him different. I just let it go. It was kind of nice to see some sort of bond between them, even if it was post-mortem. Sounds stupid, I know, but I had my own shit to deal with at the time and it suited me to have him lost in his own little chess world for hours on end. I came close to selling it a few times, but I hadn't the heart." She smiles weakly. "You know all that sod ever did was die on me and leave us financially tied to this bloody place, but much as I want to sometimes, I just can't bring myself to come between Michael and whatever he needs his dad to have been."

"Or be, by the sound of it."

"That as well." She sighs and pushes her fingers through her hair. "What a mess."

Indeed.

DISINTEGRATION

Pete hasn't enjoyed a book this much in ages. It's another Seph recommendation, and it would be an abuse of her hospitality not to read it, sitting up as he is against a stack of pillows piled against the headboard of her bed. She's beside him, rustling her way through a manuscript thick enough to require raised knees for support. Looks like the full thing, which is unusual, and the scoffs and tuts are rare enough to imply she's quite enjoying it.

The only blot on this blissful suburban landscape is the occasional irritation of having to turn a page, achieved as it is with just his right hand. The left hand has a perfectly reasonable excuse for not helping out, given its location: the heel of the hand resting on the elastic of her knickers, the fingers splayed across the cotton drawn taut over her crotch, his middle finger resting in its own snug groove like a snooker cue nestling on a bridge. He's exercising admirable self-control, the light prickle of hairs pushing through the material pleasant enough compensation for the time being as he resists the urge to grope and awaits an opportunity to achieve the same end result, but in a more gentlemanly and chivalrous manner. He's given up trying to conceal his erection.

Seph lets her left leg fall away to the side and an involuntary moan of pleasure-cum-pain escapes his lips before he bites it back. The terrain beneath his fingers has changed and the words on the page drift out of focus as he sizes up the new lie of the land.

He goes for the old shifting-for-a-more-comfortable-position trick that justifies an application of pressure by his left hand and a centimetre's migration south. She pushes her crotch up ever so slightly, the subtlest of movements that leaves him wondering if it was knowing or accidental. He glances to his left but there's no clue on her face as she stares intently at the manuscript, that pen between her teeth only raising more questions he can't answer.

He shifts position again.

"What are you doing, Peter?" He loves it when she uses that extra syllable.

"Nothing. Just reading my book."

"Enjoying it?"

"Very much." He can't remember a thing he's read in the last twenty minutes.

"You can put it down now."

*

"I don't see what your problem is," says Emma, mopping up the gravy on her plate with a chunk of bread and depositing it in her mouth.

"How would you like to have to make the decision? I have to pick two from twelve. Make that two from ten, given Charles and Greg are untouchable. They're my colleagues, for fuck's sake. It's a nightmare for me."

"I would have thought it was obvious. Now, why am I really here?"

"I thought you might be able to help. You've had to fire people before. And I wanted to see you, of course. Anything wrong with that?"

"Carl, we hadn't talked for ages until the funeral and then… well, the less said about that, the better."

"Yeah, sorry about that."

"Might have been the best place to start, don't you think?"

"It had been an emotional day and I'd had a drink or two and…"

"Take some responsibility for once."

"I'm sorry."

"Too little, too late, I'm afraid. And despite the farce of a performance that evening, you still seem to think it's entirely appropriate to give me a call and ask to meet up."

"Hope I didn't interrupt anything with lover boy." Unable to keep the venom from his tone.

"Firstly, he has a name. It's Alistair, as you already know. And secondly, as I told you at the time, I had just come in from a run. Exercise tends to do that to your breathing."

"Methinks the lady doth protest too much."

"Well, methinks you're a philistine. The 'methinks' comes at the end, not the beginning."

"Careful, you almost cracked there."

"And your eyebrows furrowed, which means you were trawling your A level Shakespeare for something clever to say."

"What's Shakespeare got to do with it?"

She shakes her head. "I'll give you the benefit of the doubt."

"First time for everything."

"Enough. I swore to myself I wouldn't let myself get dragged down to your level. So cut the crap and tell me the real reason why I'm here. And it better not be for a bout of self-pity. The poor dumped boyfriend routine."

"Easy for you to say. You got what you wanted."

"Did I?"

"Didn't you?"

"I don't know. You seem to know all the answers."
"You're winding me up."
"No. *You* are winding *me* up. Now persuade me you have a valid reason for my presence and do it fast, or I'm out of here. There are plenty of better things I can be doing with my lunchtime."
"I've had a call from his solicitor."
"Whose?"
"You know who… him."
"Talk sense, man."
"My father."
"No, Carl. He was your *dad*. *Daddy*. Whatever. But he was never your *father*."
"You know…"
"What I *do* know is that when anything comes to an end in your life that you did not orchestrate yourself, you have to ridicule and blame and reduce it to nothing. And I know it's a protection mechanism, but knowing that doesn't make it any easier to live with. And watching you deconstruct and destroy the best thing in your life…"
"You were the b…"
"*He* was the best thing in your life, you fool, and to dismiss him after he died without one jot of compassion or willingness to even try and understand him, to give him the benefit of one iota of doubt, would have been sad to watch if it hadn't been so *fucking* pathetic."
"Are you having a pudding?"
"Fuck the pudding and fuck you. I'm off. I've had it with all this and I've got an afternoon of appointments. Will twenty cover it?" She throws down a note, scrapes the chair back and reaches down for her bag.
"I'd like you there."
"*What*?"
"With the solicitor. I'm meeting with him in half an hour and I'd like you there. If nothing else to counteract

my inability to find a good word to say about my dear departed fa… *Dad*." He tries a smile and she fashions a weak reflection. It's a start and at least he's momentarily averted another shameful parting of ways.

"What's the meeting about?"

"I don't know, but he said it's very important and he's been chasing me a while."

"And you just ignored him? Far too boring and *adult*. Where are you meeting him?"

"Their office is just round the corner, so we've got time for that pudding after all. If you're coming, that is."

She appraises him with that withering look that never failed to arouse him. "Reluctantly, I have to admit you've got my interest." She chews on her lower lip and wrinkles her nose, him loving it.

"Excellent."

"Don't push it. I'm warning you, Carl, I'm off the moment I get a sniff of you messing me round or acting like an idiot. I'm not there as your audience or sidekick. I'm just curious."

"Thank you."

"I'm not doing it for you. And I'm taking back my twenty quid."

*

It's difficult for Pete to decide what stresses and challenges him the most.

The drawers left open, demanding to be closed. Contents dribbling over their edges, demanding to be pushed safely back in. Those uncoupled poppers on the duvet, demanding to be fastened. The fact that the poppered edge of the duvet is under his chin and not beyond his feet, demanding reversal. Those gravity-defying stacks of books, demanding to be made structurally sound. That door left ajar; a door should be open or shut, not left hanging in limbo. Those cats; not their actual presence – they're not in the room right now, or at least he hopes they aren't – just the knowledge of their existence and habits, where they might have been, what they may have left behind, hanging like a discomforting shroud over every conscious moment he spends here. That strand of cobweb hanging from the lampshade above him, demanding to be removed. In fact, it could be any one of those bloody cobwebs that have colonised this room above head height. That tub of moisturiser, with its irritatingly absent lid, that reminds him of a Petri dish, sitting there accumulating bacteria to breed and fester before Seph smears them onto the skin he has become rather partial to kissing and… note to self: less licking. And to cap it all this is not his own bed – his neat, clean, logically ordered and *known* sanctuary – but instead this alien receptacle of body detritus with a questionable laundering history. Come to think of it, it could be that he is naked. He doesn't do naked; the nagging need-to-have-a-shower feeling; the itches and vaguely sticky patches of skin.

But what it most definitely should be is this tousle-haired bundle of chaos walking towards him, wearing *his T-shirt*, kneeling on the bed and handing him a mug of dark brown tea.

He takes it, winces at the suspicious stains on lip and sides, cobbles together a half-smile of gratitude and leans down to place it on the floor, only for another onslaught of discomfort as his fingers brush against an empty foil condom wrapper, begging the bothersome question of where the impregnated contents had ended up in that heedless coital abandon. An unsettling image of a cat with mouse-substitute hanging from its mouth plays briefly in his mind's eye, until he hears her dump her own mug on the bedside table and, as he rights himself, she's noisily getting in beside him.

"You sure you didn't want any?" she mumbles through the slice of toast clasped between her teeth.

"Positive."

She messily pulls the toast clear from her mouth, sending a shower of crumbs over the duvet. She follows his panicked glance.

"Oops," she says, with a knowing smile.

And it could be that, despite everything, he doesn't want to be anywhere but right here, right now, nor with anyone but her.

All of which is more than a little disconcerting… and thrilling.

*

"Hi. Colin McLeod. We meet at long last." They shake hands. "And this is…"

"Emma Darnell. Hello." She offers her hand.

"Ah yes. Carl's girlfriend, I seem to remember?"

"Not any more," she says. "I'm just here as support. As a friend."

"Right. Support. Er…"

"Fine with me," says Carl, with a swat of a hand. "I've no problem with her being here, whatever this is about."

"It's just that it is a little unconventional… and… er… arguably in contravention of my instructions."

"Instructions?"

"Yes. I anticipate you're wondering why I've not been in contact earlier? Although I have been ringing for a while," he adds, managing to make a complaint sound like a courtesy.

"Yeah, sorry about that. Been very busy. And no, I hadn't been wondering. Mum dealt with all those matters. Thought they were done and dusted long ago. Bit like my father really." There's an exhalation of air to his right. He daren't look. Colin shifts uneasily in his seat; then comes to his rescue.

"The reason for getting you here is that the estate remains active."

"It's been almost *three years*. Talk about maximising your fees. Draw it out and chuck in a bill every few months. Nice work if you can get it." He turns to Emma for support, but she's looking out of the window; fingers tapping on the arm of her chair.

"There have been perfectly sound and professional reasons, I can assure you. That's the point of this meeting."

"Sound and professional enough for me not to be able to tell Mum?"

"If you'll just…"

"Are you charging me for this? I'll bet you are. I doubt you're much into *pro bono*, are you? Where are all your books, by the way? I mean you've got the leather-topped desk, the blotter, the fancy fountain pen, the ubiquitous green lamp. All you need to complete the stereotype are shelves of legal books and some framed certificates. Not that motley collection of books over there and some maps on the wall."

"We have a library."

"So *are* you charging me?" he asks again to hide his irritation at overlooking the obviousness of a library.

"For this meeting, no."

A self-damning "Hrmph," escapes Carl's mouth, not improving his position.

"We have, however, periodically raised occasional fee notes on the estate," offers Colin, charitably. "Settled from the estate's residual assets, such as they are."

"Some inheritance that was. A failed, debt-ridden business and a house mortgaged to the hilt. That mess almost dragged us under," snorts Carl, declining the olive branch.

"I cannot comment on that."

"How convenient."

"I'm sorry, but arguing with you was not the purpose of requesting this meeting."

"Well, tough. You asked me to come, so you should be prepared to take the consequences. And what you have here is a dissatisfied customer."

But the solicitor's attention has wandered to his own fingers. He interlocks them and twiddles his thumbs round each other. Then reverses their direction. And back again.

"He's failing, isn't he?" Emma asks. Her first words for a while. Colin looks up from his knotted hands and smiles at her with amused surprise.

"You're very perceptive. And yes, I'm afraid he is. Not what I had in mind, but I do recognise this is a difficult matter for him."

"Cooee. I am here you know," interjects Carl, "and I'd appreciate you cutting out the code and treating me like an adult."

"Then start behaving like one," Emma retorts, announces they should leave and is on her feet and shaking the solicitor's hand. He has no choice but to slouch after her. She pulls open the door but pauses a second, turns around and looks through him.

"Mr McLeod, can I have a word please? Without you, Carl. Please."

He feels like a scolded ten-year-old as he walks past her into the reception area and hears the door close behind him. Several heads turn towards him and he blushes, mutters something unintelligible and heads for the sanctuary of a free chair and a pile of year-old magazines.

He's contemplating celebrity sweat stains when the door opens.

"You can get off the naughty chair now and come in," Emma says, the trace of a smile overshadowed by the air of disapproval. He slopes towards her, head bowed, but she's not in the mood. "Just for once, shut up and listen," she hisses as he returns to his chair.

"You'll have to excuse Carl, Mr McLeod. This anger is not at you, but the father he feels very much let down by. And this flippancy and desire to belittle are just defence mechanisms. They tend to kick in when he's nervous."

"Nervous? I'm not…"

"He is nervous," she interrupts, fixing him with a glare, "because he is worried. You see, in order to cope with the death of his father he has created a reality that has suited him. One that justifies anger and protects him from more complex, challenging and inconvenient emotions. So instead of seeking answers to awkward questions, he finds it easier to denigrate and hit out at those closest to him. It all gets a bit grating after a while, as I can testify from experience. But I remain hopeful that somewhere deep inside lurks the man I fell in love with. I haven't seen that man for a while, hence our going our separate ways a while ago, but I have been asked to come. *I* have *listened*," another pointed glance at Carl, "and I for one would like to hear what you have to say. Carl, how about you?"

"Suppose so," he manages.

"Have you told your mother about this meeting?"

"You know I haven't. The only person I've told is you."

"Do we… do I… have your word that what happens here stays here?"

"You're getting me worried."

"Do I have your word, Carl?"

"Yes."

"Colin. I suggest you proceed."

"Thank you. Whatever you may think, Carl, I am sympathetic. I thought an awful lot of your father." He lifts a hand to quell any response from Carl to the contrary. "You may think differently, but I can only comment from my own experience. This meeting should have taken place a while ago, two years after his death to be precise. As you may or may not know, that is the period within which the beneficiaries of an estate are permitted to agree to a variation in the terms of the will. Should they be in agreement, they can put in place a deed of variation and divide the assets of the estate how they see fit."

"That doesn't make sense. There were only two beneficiaries, so why would we need to vary anything?"

"Your father put a number of measures into place that... er... could be deemed to lie outside the conventional confines of an estate."

"What the hell does that mean?"

"Carl."

"Sorry, but..."

"That's all right. I do tend to slip into legalese at times. One of the perils of the job, I'm afraid." He pauses for an amused response, then continues in the absence of one. "Arrangements were made during his lifetime to keep certain assets out of the estate. As your father's lawyer, I was party to putting those measures in place. I may not have impressed you to date, Carl, but there are some areas in which I do possess a modicum of expertise. However, what I know absolutely nothing about are the contents of this letter." He produces, to some theatrical effect, an envelope complete with red wax seal. "Your father left strict instructions that I was not to give you this until after the two-year variation period had come to a close, and even then, it was on the proviso that your mother was unaware of our meeting and that I felt you to be, how should I put it, receptive. Only then was I to allow you to read its contents and be prepared afterwards to make full disclosure of the arrangements put in place before his death." Silence. "So here we are. It has, of course, been longer than two years. You have given me a guarantee regarding your mother, and Miss Darnell here has assured me that the contents of this letter will receive a fair hearing. I must admit to being concerned on that point after our initial exchanges, but feel more comfortable after speaking with her."

"Does he read it here?" asks Emma.

"Here is fine. I've made alternative arrangements. Maybe I'll visit the library. My office is yours. Take as long as you want and let Cassandra outside know when you're finished and she'll call me. We can then discuss how things progress from there."

And with that, he takes his leave.

They both stare at the envelope on the desk.

"Go on."

"Suppose I'd better."

"Do you want me in here while you read it?"

"Yes. I'm actually sweating and shaking."

"I know. But there has to be more to… to everything. None of it has ever made any sense to me and I hated what it did to you. I'm just hoping I'm not mistaken."

He reaches over and picks up the envelope, breaks the seal and takes out a thin sheaf of typed papers.

And reads.

Thrown off kilter from the very start.

Hello Carl

I hope this finds you well.

I've been playing this letter (this suicide letter; there, I've said the word) through in my mind for months now and there are moments when it sounds pretty damn good in there, playing away to a moving soundtrack and effortlessly righting wrongs. Yet the moment I try and put it down on paper, it becomes a pathetic, self-pitying confessional. Then again, welcome to my world, so maybe that's exactly how this should read.

But time's running out for me now, so save for the 'spellcheck' and the stormy waters of its red admonishments, this will hit the paper as it spews forth from my brain. Why aren't I saying this to you in person right now? Hopefully what follows will explain. What am I hoping to achieve? Approval? Sympathy? Understanding? Redemption? Revenge? All of them if I'm honest, but mostly this is me getting back some control and I have never been so sure of anything as much as what I am about to do. I just need to convince you, and along the way set the record… my record, straight. It's time for some context.

Let's start with the bombshell: I'm not your biological father. I can't be. Turns out I've been shooting blanks from day one. I only found out a few months ago. All those little 'accidents' without repercussions. Other stuff. Not adding up. I had a test done on the sly and either you were an immaculate conception or… well, only your mother can fill in that particular gap for you. Sorry. I can't even begin to comprehend the void I've now opened for you.

It certainly concentrated my mind… then disintegrated it.

And it's left me needing to take stock… then take control. Let the inventory begin. Who am I? Or, as you read this, who was I?

Years ago, I went on this motivational course. Not my cup of tea, but it was a client who ran them. He was trying to get the business up and running so I agreed to take a place for 'free' in lieu of his first year's accounts fee. The course started with us having to list ten words or phrases that defined us, in descending order of importance. Whilst others struggled to whittle down to a shortlist, what did I summon up from the depths of my apathy? Father – husband – son – chartered accountant – 'author' – employer – music lover… I ran dry after four and was spent at seven. What an indictment.

In reverse order…

There was a brief period as you approached your teens when you were attracted to my records and CDs and cared what I thought. Then the hormones kicked in and what I liked – or at least what you thought I liked – defined what you couldn't. From then on you knew best. I hope my 'farewell playlist' surprised you.

I employed a total of seven people over several decades. Three of those retired, one died on me and two left with my blessing for better things. I recruited all of them. Number seven was taken on against my better judgment as a favour to a colleague of your mum's. That was Lucy. I knew she was trouble from the start: forbidden fruit served up enticingly on a plate… and an action for a sexual harassment that never happened and a pay-off I couldn't afford. I know what happened, or more to the point didn't, and if others wish to believe different… well, I'll be long gone and it might even enhance my reputation!

'Author' came a hesitant fifth, and warrants the inverted commas. A flight of fancy and an ambition never realised.

I took great pride in being a chartered accountant. I worked hard for it and even harder building up the business. And all at a cost: the holidays we never took, the ambitions never achieved, the evenings hunched over the kitchen table, the backache, the neckache… everything. So permit me to feel a tad sorry for myself as the edifice I sacrificed so much to construct is crumbling around me.

Last year, my 'friends' at the Inland Revenue's Special Compliance Office launched an enquiry into a number of my clients. Most of my biggest clients. Over half my annual fees. A coincidence? No. They all had offshore links; and more to the point they all had offshore links that I happened to initiate, or rather facilitate, years ago, when the world was a very different place. SCO has asked a lot of questions. The people with most of the answers are sitting very comfortably in Jersey. They – always 'with regret' – are unable to assist SCO. That's the point. SCO can't do anything about it. Which must be infuriating. And that frustration has to be aimed somewhere. Which is where I come in; the last point of contact before the funds disappeared into the tax-less ether. Not that I'm without blame. I knew the potential for abuse, but I didn't make anyone do anything. I just made the introductions and accounted for it all. Although I would say that, wouldn't I?

The first time I saw an invoice going through a client's books for spurious professional fees from some Jersey-based firm I would stress, with the knowing smirk and emphasised syllables an accountant adopts as if the Revenue are listening on a hidden microphone, that all expenditure needed to be 'wholly and exclusively and necessarily' for the business and that the Revenue might ask that we prove as much should the amounts stand out enough in the accounts for them to be spotted. Needing to hear myself saying the right thing. The client not really listening. Me knowing that. An implicit green light for them. My backside protected. The games we played. They tried it a second time. And a third. Too easy. Too good to be true: tax relief on the expense at this end; no tax paid at that end; the funds accumulating in whatever trust structure had been erected there. The perfect arrangement. It would have been foolish not to. And if I wasn't being seen to be 'proactive', some other firm would have stepped in to do it for them. I was damned either way.

Likewise the first time a client decided that rather than supply its customers direct, it could insert a 'middle-man'; sell the goods to an offshore company who would in turn sell them on to the UK customers. Offer that offshore company some lumpy bulk purchase discounts. And what business was it of theirs what the offshore company chose to sell it on for to the end user? There was money to be made by one and all. Family futures to be safeguarded. School fees to be paid. Tales of financial acumen to be smugly recounted at the nineteenth hole.

What could go wrong?

It was a Monday morning when I opened the first letter from the Revenue and glanced through the three pages of queries, seeing immediately where they were heading. But what really froze my blood was the sight of the other identical envelopes sitting unopened on my desk. My worst-case scenario.

That first week was spent fielding panicked phone calls, allaying fears with assurances I had little confidence in. But the first time I went with a client for a meeting with two Revenue officers, we had our best laid plans and rehearsed answers torpedoed as they lit up a projector screen on which was shown a cartwheel, my client imprisoned in one spoke segment, the remaining ones incarcerating other client names (the first inclination the client had, to my intense frustration, that he wasn't alone) and my name emboldened in the hub. I was in the dock as much as anyone; the means to the end.

That first meeting didn't end in conciliation and compromise, just terseness, ultimatums and the promise of another list of questions and demands. And no matter how well I knew the client, there was always going to be a little bit of them that needed to blame someone else. And those kind souls at SCO were more than happy to point the finger.

I had nine such meetings in all: nine embarrassments; nine confused clients; nine defensive clients; nine clients wondering about me.

When the next exchange of letters failed to shift the entrenched positions, SCO wrote direct to the clients suggesting that in light of the apparent impasse, they might consider seeking separate and independent representation. Divide and conquer.

A bigger firm boasting expertise in such areas – talk about poacher turned gamekeeper; the hypocrisy was astounding; they'd been doing the same things for decades, only on a much larger and better-remunerated scale – took on the defence for seven of the clients (two stuck with me) and I was relegated to the role of glorified gopher.

Inevitably cracks formed in a few client relationships; a creeping erosion of trust. I've hung on to most of the clients to date, although it's never been the same. The need to deflect the blame will always prevail, and who better to take the hit. Several have already said maybe it's time for a fresh start. The tremors will reach further as they have introduced other clients to me over the years. Word will get round. Others will follow.

One client has gone further and decided that I am entirely responsible for the many bogus invoices they knowingly created. I have been informed with menace by the father and his four thuggish sons that I should 'contribute'.

I no longer have the stomach for what lies ahead.

The first time I saw your mother she was on stage sometime during my second year, acting in a play (The

Homecoming?) in which she played the girlfriend of a son returning home to see his family after many years. Uproar ensued and her character seemed to end up snogging half the male cast. Just writing this has me shaking my head, mindful of that scene in The Man with Two Brains *when Steve Martin, on the brink of a new relationship, asks his dead wife's portrait to send him a sign if she disapproves in any way. But at the time maybe our needs just dove-tailed and we gave each other what we needed.*

But if you're going to see the full picture (my full picture, anyway) I have no choice but to ask a question: just how do you become one of the country's most famous photographers?

You go on holiday with your boyfriend the summer after university ends and you've just discovered you're pregnant and you're worried how he'll take it, impending fatherhood and all, but then you pluck up the courage to tell him, the day before graduation actually, and he surprises you (surprises himself, he says, but you know he never had a doubt) by saying it's brilliant news and your worry becomes relief and then happiness and you will have the baby and sod what your parents say and you decide to take a holiday but you haven't much money and it's less than two weeks to go until his job starts – you've got offers yourself but the pregnancy throws everything into the air – so you decide to keep it cheap and simple and he picks a small B&B in north Wales because that's where he grew up, and you go along with it and you say you like it once you're there though you don't really what with the wind and the rain (in August!) and all that grey and a lack of anywhere decent to eat and the absence of a social pulse but you go on the walks and you do your best because you can see how happy it makes him and one day you're sitting outside a pub in the shadows of Cadair Idris and he fills an awkward silence with a challenge and he takes out his camera and he tells you about this photography competition he's seen in a magazine and how about you both taking photos and each entering one and seeing who does best and how nice it would be to have a shared hobby and it doesn't appeal but you show willing and play his little game and you snap away half-heartedly while he tackles it so pathetically seriously and a few weeks later he excitedly produces two packets of developed photos and you spend a tedious evening sorting out who took what and then you agree the best few each, though you know you didn't take any of them.

Months later you get a letter saying you've won the competition and you get a grand of photographic equipment and your photo in a national magazine and a free place on a prestigious photography course. And you tell your fiancé, that man who so wants, so needs, this pregnancy to be a romantic journey and that fortnight to have been a shared joy, and you show him the winning photo and silently take ownership of it, daring him to wipe that glow of happiness off your face, granting him the opportunity to gift it to you and he says nothing though he knows he took it, not you, and he knows you must know but he loves you and anyway maybe you've convinced yourself you did take it and it makes sense for you to go and accept the award and do the course because he's still finding his feet at work and you never did fancy the world of marketing anyway and you've always had an artistic side though you've never shown it, never even mentioned this passion of yours that now whisks you into London for an award and a photo session that produces three photos that adorn the next month's issue and there's one of you that makes you look more like a model than a photographer and you love the attention and you love the shiny equipment you arrive home with and your fiancé spends a long evening reading the instruction booklets and many evenings explaining to you how everything works and you can tell this may well be one of his dreams but you know he loves the common ground discovered and you take photos, hundreds of the things, and you know they're nothing special but you keep taking them and they improve (they would do wouldn't they, eventually; monkeys tapping at typewriters and all that) and you go on your photography course and when you enjoy that he offers to throw the two-salary financial plan out of the window and pay your way through a three-year course at the hippest London polytechnic which starts just seven months after the birth of your son although childcare is secured through a succession of local childminders and your body is soon exercised back into shape.

So you love your course and you're mixing with the arty 'it' crowd and this excites you, though you struggle with many of the assignments because you still don't really get the technical side and you have difficulty visualising the pictures you want to take which means that when you do produce anything it's predictable and formulaic. But your male tutors will always encourage a pretty face and your husband (because that is what he is now after an understated registry office ceremony followed by two hours in the back room of a local pub and a budget weekend in Cornwall; he'd wanted north Wales for old time's sake but you told him no chance as you wanted some sun) feeds you ideas for photos, often takes them himself and helps come up with clever titles and things to say about them and your marks are good and you enjoy the company of your fellow students and they love you and you may or may not be sleeping with one or more of them but you do sleep with one tutor (though that is not uncovered for many years) and that world is as exciting as home life is not, with money short and a husband studying for his accountancy exams most evenings, so why wouldn't you prefer to spend time with them and it's not like he'll stop you because he needs to be needed by you and that gives you the power and what point is there in having that power if you don't use it and this smitten dope isn't going anywhere.

And you graduate from your course and do pretty much nothing but doors that are closed to others are opened by your looks and that smile and whatever it is you do that makes people feel special and you get this offer from an editor who is impressed by your 'CV' and offers you an apprenticeship in his pictures department and you occasionally take a photo in amongst the stream of lunches and client schmoozing for which your talents are much sought-after, but then you start complaining to your husband that you're not really going anywhere and before you know it he's doing what he always does and searching for a solution to a problem you only really brought up to drag the conversation away from accountancy and his plans and onto you and then one day on a rare night when you're watching TV together and there's a sit-com repeat on with an English tourist speaking Franglais to a bewildered local and he tells you his concept and it sounds pretty naff but he says to leave it with him and sure enough a fortnight later he excitedly parades half a dozen photos and their punning titles and you can sort of see where he's going with it but the question 'And?' has to be asked and that's another challenge to him and he says to trust him on it and give him a month and sure enough he delivers although you're still not convinced but you let him take control and you go with the flow and two months later you're one of five 'bright young artists' exhibiting over a weekend in a north London gallery and you have to admit those fifteen framed poster-sized photos look great and stand out, brilliant and accessible, amongst the bleached watercolour landscapes, the painted glassware, the piles of rusting iron and the childish modern art of your fellow exhibitors and what had seemed too simple and corny for public consumption is actually really quite good with the clean bold lines of the original black and white photos accentuated by the occasional splashes of vibrant colour creating a spectrum along the walls that screams 'collect me' with their punning titles and your name in simple italic black script in a band of white across the bottom and it's working as you shake hands and smile and flirt and generally look arty and tarty and amazingly people seem to want to buy them and you point them to Stuart and he's got it all sorted and by the end of the night more than half have been sold and pretty soon the remainder but the rights are still yours and there are signed limited edition print runs of all of them and companies pay you to use them on posters and greetings cards and suddenly you're a self-employed photographer of renown.

And whilst you'd settle for this easy money and renown he won't let up. "We need to keep reinventing," he says and you flinch at the 'we' but go with him as he suggests tapping into the hormonally-charged scholarly wank-market and if they can be titillated just shy of pornography then those randy students will fall over themselves to lie on their beds occupying their right hands while admiring the view and even more so if they know a woman took the photo and you think it sounds tacky but it's easier to agree than think of something yourself and home life is far less claustrophobic and cloying when he's busy and in any case they're all easy variations on a much strummed theme and you set to work on a series of black and white posters of faceless women lying on beds in lacy lingerie.

And meanwhile your circle of contacts and acquaintances grows and some are very wealthy and well-connected and they are surprised you don't have more irons in the fire and that your husband is managing you part-time and how can that work and even though it's wonderful that you've kept it so in-house surely you recognise that all things come to an end and if you want this to really take off then surely he's holding you back because what you need is investment and professional advice from those who know and your husband will welcome the chance to concentrate full-time on the business he's trying to set up and in any case maybe there will be work that can come his way from your new contacts so it's actually in his best interests as well and so you broach the subject and you know he's hurting and it's tearing him apart but he says he's fine with it all and can see the logic so that's what you do and it's agreed and now you have a backer and he helps you find premises and you take on employees and you have a team and the world is your oyster.

Splurge over. Her backer was an exiled Libyan called Aabid, some distant relative of the royal family deposed by Gaddafi in the late sixties. Rumour had it that the King's descendants and his supporters had far from given up on a return to power one day. And that was more than enough to get the vultures circling, the sweet smell of oil and the lure of those arms deals attracting a steady stream of sycophants and would-be-entrepreneurs willing to flatter and receive; jockeying for position at the head of the queue for that hoped-for free-for-all one day.

Aabid's name apparently meant 'worshipper'. How true. The man worshipped women; the good-looking ones anyway. He certainly charmed your mother.

By virtue of some web of promises, favours, IOUs and sheer front, he and his cronies sat chain-smoking behind vast, barren, polished desks in Knightsbridge terraced buildings worth millions they probably never had, doing who knows what; while a succession of glamorous women, the majority of whom appeared to be called Nadia, of indeterminate age and function, floated around making bad coffee and animated phone calls.

It was in the basement of one such building that your mother set up her studio. The warren of rooms was filled with the most expensive equipment someone else's money could buy and staff were recruited more to populate, appease the eye and keep your mother company than with any specific functions in mind. By rights the whole venture should have dwindled into messy liquidation, but the world she was now inhabiting didn't operate by normal rules and there was a momentum that overrode any lack of talent or direction. The punning photos and posters were still selling and the latest 'Eyes Down' range proved the doubter wrong, not that it stopped her lapping up the credit, and sold to students in their tens of thousands.

Doors opened and she hit the social circuit. Party invites flooded in and she became quite the socialite; a procession of celebrities traipsing through her now-teeming studio to be captured and flattered in black and white for public consumption. Coffee-table books, exhibitions in swanky London galleries and TV appearances were to follow… and a star was born.

Am I bitter? Oh yes.

I've since found out that her subsequent artistic output was much more of a group effort than she's had everyone believe over the years. A dozen or so of the most talented photography graduates, smitten with her blossoming reputation, fell over themselves to grab an apprenticeship with her. They'd have signed anything, and promptly did, forgoing legal title to any photos taken upon your mother's instruction the moment the shutter closed. Artistic meetings were held every Monday where concepts were aired and upcoming events discussed. I'm told your mother offered little but was credited with everything. A band of assistants would accompany her on trips and they'd all snap away. I doubt more than ten per cent of the photos that appeared in those must-have coffee-table accessories were taken by her. And as for those celebrity portraits, trust me: if you have the right equipment and take enough photos, anyone can fluke at least a couple of decent ones. And she certainly proved that.

Some large firm of accountants with an atrium and a marketing budget many times greater than my gross income charged her a small fortune for stating the obvious and once a year putting their name to a set of accounts she didn't understand or care about, while I was introduced by her and her entourage to a succession of new bright-young-thing clients (who I was expected to be grateful for, as the favour was being done to me, of course) all professing to be 'in the arts' and who sucked at my time and energy like leeches with their fragile, inflated egos, outlandish expectations completely divorced from reality and a desire to pay as little as possible on the promise of the future riches that would be mine to participate in when their self-professed potential was one day realised. Pareto's Principle held sway as the majority of my weeks disappeared satisfying and mollycoddling their self-centred, pampered needs and the ambitions of vicariously-living parents unable to accept another generation of unfulfilled dreams and the shame that would entail. The majority were headed for artistic oblivion of course. They just compounded my misery by taking so fucking long to get there.

As a consequence, I found myself with an increasing overdraft and struggling to satisfy the needs of my good clients as I fielded a succession of stupid calls from the twenty per cent.

So, when your mother introduced me to a wealthy collector of her work who lived in Jersey and had an idea for how we might 'do business together to our mutual advantage', let's just say he got me at a receptive moment.

And somewhere along the way I lost my joie de vivre, my self-esteem, and I lost your mother… if I ever had her. That's what you get when you mess with love!

Looking back, I hadn't so much learned from the mistakes of my parents, as found an alternative way to fuck it all up!

A word to summarise my feelings towards my mother? Pity. More like pitiful.

And my father? Maybe 'distance' says it best. Though ask him what he thinks of me and I'm sure 'weak' and 'disappointing' would make the shortlist.

He chose an anonymous breeding machine and forced her to inhabit the shadows cast by his own needs and desires. I married a head-turning attention-seeker and accepted whatever space that left me in our relationship. He had three children and fucked them all up (though I'm attributing intent, when in reality it felt more like disinterest) whereas I had just the one and…

I remember one evening in your bedroom, your little hand tightening on my forearm as I read those last few pages of The House at Pooh Corner*, and being overwhelmed by a wave of emotion. I paused, you looked up at me in all your helpless, hopeful innocence and I told you not to worry, Daddy would never leave you. I'd always be there for you. (Sorry, it appears I lied.) I sensed your panic and the power I held over you and the responsibility that brought. By then I'd welled up and had to hide my tears in a flurry of bedtime routine.*

Looking back, I can see only too clearly what was really going on. Because I had no power. I never did. Or at least none that mattered. Any power I did feel was sourced in the unquestioning love and trust of a child. But I had it all wrong. It's the child who's holding the winning hand all along; he just doesn't know it yet. It's that knowledge that changes everything. Mothers always get it quicker; your mother certainly did. But it's the inevitable fate of the naive, entitled father to one day be toppled from the plinth he's happily occupied.

I was never Christopher Robin, as I had assumed so needily. I was just that favourite cuddly toy, destined one day to be discarded and played with no more. I'm not blaming you, of course; it's a fact of parenthood; of healthy parenthood anyway.

But what I wasn't prepared for was the impact that letting go had on me, although it didn't help that it coincided with so many other aspects of my life stuttering and stalling. From hero to zero. It took some getting used to. If I ever did.

You can sense it happening at the time, that gradual continental drift apart. Where once my funny voices had brought laughter, now you grimaced. Where once my jokes in front of your friends were a source of pride (I'd glance over and you'd be looking nervously for their reactions and when they laughed, that squirm of delight and face-cracking smile melted me every time), now you were just horrified I was even trying. 'Silly Daddy' became 'stupid prat'. An embarrassment. Everyone else's dad had a cooler job. The pity and contempt in your eyes as I mis-kicked a football, or complained about my back, or dozed during a film, or misheard something. The hand-to-the-face dread of impending humiliation every time attention turned to me in public. Doomed to failure either way: the shame if I bombed; the resentment if I succeeded. Be honest, eventually my just breathing was enough to piss you off.

Did I take it maturely? Oh no. I came out fighting. Bombarding you with fictionally-enhanced tales from the crazy world of accountancy: "You wouldn't believe the bonus this client received last year"; "Got some great news today, I won an argument with the Revenue that saved my client tens of thousands"; "Tendered for and got a big audit today"; "One of my clients knows that actor on the TV there". Then there were the knee-jerk recollections of childhood sporting achievement, embellished wherever possible by the bringing out of dusty, battered trophies and photo albums, as if tarnished cheap metal and fading photos could in some way resurrect me in your eyes. The more I tried, the more pathetic I became. And in return I won nothing but your contempt.

I'm not claiming anything wilful on your part. I recognise the internal conflict that must have been raging within: the half of you that wanted to destroy me and assume the mantle of alpha male in a constant attritional tug of war with the half that was scared to do so. I became a constricting ceiling when what you wanted and needed was blue sky.

And if we're after a watershed moment, maybe it happened on a squash court. That was one of the few things I still had over you going into your teens. That and Misére German Whist. However much I told myself it was foolish, not having ever lost to you at either became more and more important. I protected the whist by just not playing you any more. But the squash was harder to avoid and as you got stronger and fitter and I got creakier and my speed and reactions slowed, defeat became inevitable. When it did finally happen, the initial disappointment and disgust at my own burgeoning obsolescence was soon replaced with euphoric relief. I could now start enjoying our games again without this unspoken and polluting subtext. Then I saw the look on your face.

You could have beaten me earlier of course, though I would deny that possibility each time I won by convincing myself experience had triumphed over raw youth. But it was the realisation, conscious or unconscious, of what victory represented that held you back and ceded victory to the one most in need of it. I'm sure you tried not to win on that day as well, but it's a fine line to tread, particularly when you're relying on a sweat-blinded, heaving-chested middle-aged man hitting a small object against a wall some twenty feet away.

I think you recognised the import of what had happened

on that court as a few days later, for the first time in several years, you suggested we played Misére German Whist. You didn't want to beat me of course. No thoughts of a clean sweep of my self-esteem. You just wanted to give me something to hang on to. And what did I do? Made some feeble excuse. I had everything to lose and you had nothing you wanted, or needed, to win. And with that refusal I think I lost any dregs of respect you may have held for me. It was effectively goodbye until you reached an age when maturity and life experience would grant you the enlightenment to accept me, without judgment or disappointment, as a person entitled to his faults (no better or worse for them than the next) rather than a failure. The lot of the fallen idol, I guess.

We never played either again. And hardly a day has passed when I haven't longed to. Regrets, I've had a few…

Now here I am in that greying holding zone between active parenthood and passive grandparenthood. And in those moments when I've made time for myself and sat in cafés nurturing a coffee while pondering whether the impact on the waistline is worth the short-lived pleasure of a slab of adorned chocolate, I often watch fathers and their young children. The time I can never get back. And as I watch, all I feel is the profound loss and the feeling that I never did enough. That I wasted those years with preoccupations that now mean nothing to me. The deadlines that seemed so pressing, but could easily have waited. The urgent management accounts that were forgotten within minutes of reading, if they were read at all. The clients who meant nothing to me in the scheme of things, but whose needs I put ahead of those of my family.

I know why of course. Life got in the way. I had responsibilities. I was often tired. We needed the money. Boy, did we need the money; for many years your mother's business soaked it up like a sponge, and then the school fees started. I should never have let your mother talk me into that, but she could be very persuasive. And the money came from clients so of course they often had to take priority. But I just can't shirk the feeling that I could and should have done more. And from a distance of several decades the choices I made now look so misguided. It takes so little to create a moment in time, an experience, that will always be cherished and live forever in a child's mind. So why did I not fill my days in search of such shared experiences. How did the minutiae of accountancy ever take precedence? What a sad indictment of those many years hunched over a desk. And the weight of all those never-realised moments weighs so heavy, even more so when the present feels so empty. But they never happened, and instead our lives were polluted by the mundanity, the irritability and the fundamental falling short that characterises so much parent-child interrelation.

BUT…

…I held you in my arms as you blinked at a new world and I stared into those dilated pupils as they tried to focus, your tiny hand clasping my finger. I came running when you woke in tears, held you in my arms and rocked you back to sleep. I patiently held spoonfuls of tasteless paste in front of a shaking head and a raspberry-blowing mouth. I mopped up your wee and wiped your bottom and cleaned up your sick and reassured you until your panic receded. I held your hand at the dentist and was the last face you saw as the anaesthetic took hold; the first you woke up to. I never missed an assembly or school production, watching them all through a shaky lens in order to commit each word and movement to videos that would never be watched. I dried your tears when infant school didn't go well. I spent hours kicking a ball with you in the garden. I stood shivering through every training session and match, vicariously kicking or striking or bowling every ball with

you. I rejoiced in every up; longed to share the pain of every down. I taught you and endlessly played every board game we could lay our hands on, no matter how crap or devoid of skill or pointless. I gave unconditional love and have never regretted a second of it.

I wasn't alone of course. Your mother was there. I was half a team, however much my shattered ego may wish to write her out of this narrative. But I was your father. I am your father. I will always be your father. You don't get to choose your parents and you got me.

There you go. I've put my life in a pan, stuck it on the hob, turned up the heat and let it bubble and reduce down to its very essence. And the bottom line is that death feels like my best option right now. It gives me purpose, definition and certainty. It gives me peace.

I know where (you of all people should understand the location), I know how (I'm essentially a coward and the choice between 'crash and burn' and 'fading out' was an easy one), I know when and I know why. I am in charge.

Have a great life, Carl. You're the one aspect of mine I can honestly say I'm proud of.

"Are you all right?" Her hand on his shoulder. Carl looks up and his vision blurs. He realises he's crying.

"What the *fuck* am I meant to do with *that*?" he demands of the room, smearing the back of his hand across his face and throwing the papers down on the desk.

"Do you mind if I read it?" asks Emma.

"Be my guest. I need some air." He gets to his feet and heads for the door, ricocheting off the frame as he passes through. He weaves between desks, dimly aware of something hitting the floor in his wake, then follows the signs, pushes at the horizontal metal bar of a fire escape door, staggers into the brightness, walks down an alleyway and turns right along a pavement. The anomaly of a small walled garden imprisoned between buildings stops him in his tracks. He wanders in hesitantly, as if it might be some mirage that could vanish any second, spies a bench and lies on it.

Closes his eyes. Throws a forearm across them for added insulation. Tries to flatline his mind, seeking refuge from the emotions crowding in.

But soon they come: random, inchoate fragments of a childhood he'd demolished and buried along with his father in order to survive and rebuild.

Playing football on weekend mornings, Dad prowling the touchline trying to look ambivalent, but failing; communicating with smiles and nods and clenched fists – playing Misère German Whist and Dad never losing – the impossible excitement of that first Scalextric; building the track with delicious anticipation, then never wanting it to stop, Dad responding with a wink when Mum comes in to say it's bedtime – *Ask the Family* on the TV, waiting for those close-up photos to guess as the camera pulls back; trying to beat Dad, though never sure if he's really trying – watching *The Great Egg Race*, then designing and building egg-carrying contraptions for hours on end; the resulting inertia and cracked shells seeing them dissolving into fits of giggles – Dad letting him stay up late on Wednesday to watch *Sportsnight* if Spurs have a big game and the highlights are on; sitting through a few dog races, maybe some boxing while waiting, the tension mounting; Glenn Hoddle's wonder goal in the cup replay against United – Saturday afternoons watching *World of Sport*; Dickie Davies, On the Ball, wrestling and the ITV 7 – *Big Match* on Sunday afternoons, warm-up man Jack Hargeaves back in his hutch; muddy pitches, long hair, tight shorts, crunching tackles – the Martin Gardner books that Dad bought him: building a computer with toilet rolls and pink beads that learns from its mistakes, sprouts and Brussels sprouts, the hanging that can never take place, M. C. Escher, cartoons that make sense both ways up – waking just after midnight on Christmas Eve to see a shape in the doorway silhouetted against the landing light; "Who's that?" "Go to sleep" – watching *The Saint*, the two of them singing along to the opening refrain: "na na na na na na", trying to keep up as it grows ever more shrill, the n's becoming w's, their voices cracking – snuggled warm under the duvet, Dad sat across his legs getting to the end of *Winnie the Pooh*, his speech going funny and his eyes wet; "Dad, what's wrong with your eyes?" "Nothing. Just hay fever, that's all" – bonfire in the garden on an autumn Sunday afternoon; leaves crackling, flames suddenly bursting through; pushing in sticks, leaving them a while and then pulling them out and seeing if they're alight – Top 40 countdown on the radio, then bath, game of chess with Dad, and bed; fire still glowing in the murky dusk – waking up on Monday morning and pulling back the curtains; still smoking; the smell lingering in yesterday's clothes on the bedroom floor – Dad cooking him a 'special energy-boosting Monday morning fry-up' before taking him to school on the way to work: "Go get 'em, son."

"Fancy a swig, mate?"

"You what?" slurs Carl, allowing his arm to fall from his face, squinting as he hauls himself upright.

"Fancy a swig? Looks like you could do with one."

"Thanks, but no thanks. Don't know where it's been." The last bit meant to be unspoken, but he's still punch-drunk. "Sorry, but…"

"No, fair comment. Then again, I don't know where you've been neither and the offer still stands."

There's a persuasive logic in this that sees Carl accepting the proffered bottle and taking a tentative sip while avoiding as much contact as possible with the glass. The end result is a wet chin and a tongue that feels as if it's aflame. He swallows the unknown liquid and the fire trails down his throat and alights in his stomach. He splutters.

"Shit. What the hell is that?" His voice barely more than a rasp.

"Spot of home-brew, you could say. Tends to take the edge off."

"Edge off what?" asks Carl, trying not to contemplate what might constitute *home-brew*.

"Reality."

"Here's to that," says Carl, staring down at the bottle.

"Have yourself another, fella."

Why not?

*

He walks back in to find Emma and the lawyer deep in conversation. Emma snatches a few last words, makes a slicing gesture with a hand and then turns to face him, only just remembering to fix on a smile.

"How are you feeling?" she asks.

"Never been better."

"Please be serious. Just for once. Are you okay to talk through all this now? We've got…"

"No. Not really. I just need some time. Get my head straight. I'm not up to making any decisions right now."

"You sure?"

"Yeah."

"What are you going to say when you get home?"

"Nothing. They're away. A three-month cruise to the West Indies to celebrate the forthcoming nuptials."

"Right. That's good."

"Good?"

"I just think we need to talk first. You know, before you do anything rash."

"Heaven forbid. And what's with this *we* all of a sudden? Is that what it takes to get some positive attention? A suicide and a paternity revelation? Hang on, am I in line for a sympathy fuck here?"

He regrets it immediately and is relieved she bites back an entirely justified retort. Deciding to cut his losses, he rises, bids farewell and heads for the door. Emma catches him as he reaches for the handle. She places a hand gently on his forearm.

"Sure you're going to be okay?"

"I'll be fine."

"Look after yourself. I'll ring you tomorrow… if that's all right. There's a few things we need to talk about."

"Don't worry about me. I've got a good book waiting for me that I'm going to lose myself in tonight. I've glanced through it before, but all of a sudden I fancy dipping in again."

*

Excerpts from *Fame by Frame*, the autobiography of Fiona Armstrong.

> *I've always had a fascination with cameras, right from my early years. And to my parents' eternal credit, they recognised a precocious talent and did everything possible to encourage me. Without that support I doubt I'd be where I am today. A sixth sense, my mother called it; that ability to see an image, to picture in one's mind's eye how a photo will look, to seize that opportunity to capture a moment or*

an expression that would otherwise be lost forever.

And a passion was born.

I've always loved Wales. It's where my muse sings the loudest. Such simple, charming, proud people. Those rolling and unspoiled verdant slopes are always an inspiration for me; a bottomless well of photographic potential I never tire of drawing from. Where some might see bleakness, I see mood. Where some might see poverty, I see resilience. What some might see as depressing, I see as character. Where some see the crumbling ruins of a once-mighty mining industry, I see a lost history begging to be told.

I'd noticed a competition in one of the photography magazines that regularly spilled through our letterbox to quench my thirst for this passion of mine. While in Wales on another wonderful holiday of bracing walks I determined to give it a go. Stuart thought I was wasting my time, and his, as I punctuated every activity with pauses to contemplate and frame.

I can't recall how many photos I took. Not that many; that inbuilt quality control that has served me so well had kicked in and when the photos were developed, I was spoiled for choice. Stuart picked a few, but in truth he hadn't an eye for it. I knew the one the moment I saw it. That's a lie; I knew the moment I took it. You just know.

That sixth sense again, I guess.

One of the questions I'm asked most is where I came up with the idea for the series of photos that were to propel me into the public eye. Of course, when I look back now, I wince a little at their clumsy naivety, but they certainly seemed to capture the zeitgeist.

When was the light bulb moment? Sorry, but there wasn't one. Just a gradual genesis born of a punning mind, a love of wordplay and a less-than-working knowledge of French and German. Plus a lot of hard graft on my part, of course. Because ultimately you get what you deserve in this game.

My first, and still the most famous, was of course 'Jew d'Orange'. I'd love to lay claim to true artistic integrity and say I travelled to Jerusalem for that shot. But in truth it was a bright spring day in Golders Green.

Likewise, 'Auto-bairn' was taken nowhere near Germany and hundreds of miles south of Scotland.

That said, we did treat ourselves to a weekend in Paris for 'Eye-full Tower'.

Though it might sound harsh now, it was more embarrassment that I felt when the truth started coming out. Some of his biggest clients had come from my recommendation. I'd put myself out for his benefit so yes, I felt hurt. Betrayed.

Carl frisbees the book against a wall.

"Message to self," he slurs. "Inform all bookshops of need to re-categorise from shadow-written autobiography to fiction with immediate effect."

He half rises, half falls out of the armchair and weaves his way unsteadily across the room. Throws the empty bottle at the recycling bin and watches it bounce off the rim, sending an arc of dregs across the lino, before rolling up against the leg of the table. Decides to leave it where it is. Tugs open the fridge and grabs another.

After that barrage of clichés, he might as well go the whole hog and be one.

*

"Go on then," Seph says. "Explain to me what it is you actually do, that you can be coming round here distracting me from deluded literary aspiration, dossing around in my bed on a Wednesday late morning without any apparent need to be doing anything anywhere else."

"You're not working this morning, either."

"No, but you know what I do and what it involves and where I do it. It may not seem like a proper job to you, but I'm not hiding anything. But I haven't really got a clue what it is you do. All I get is the occasional vague mention about investments and an air of smugness that might be a bit irritating if we weren't screwing each other."

Pete enquires into the well-being of the cats, but she's not having any of it, and he can sense the patient persistence of her gaze on the side of his head. He admits defeat and steps further into unchartered territory; and for a man who doesn't do venturing outside his well-fortified comfort zone, this is scary.

"Basically, I speculate."

"You *bet*?"

"That's what the uninitiated might say, but I don't see it like that. I don't bet, I invest. I know, I know," he says, in response to a raised eyebrow. "That makes me sound like every self-deluded gambler, but I've seen returns they haven't. I'm good at it. It takes study, patience and above all discipline."

"But what do you bet… sorry, *invest* on? I mean in. Horses? Fruit machines? What?"

"Not fruit machines. Waste of money. What's the point in putting money in something that tells you at the outset it's going to take near enough thirty per cent of your money? At least not unless you've watched it for hours and have seen enough people put their money in it to know the odds have shifted in your favour."

"Something tells me you have."

"Once or twice, maybe." Many more times. "Not for ages." A few weeks ago. "I only invest where I think I'm getting value." He's about to swing his leg over a favourite hobby horse and give it a ride, only to check himself on the hunch that it might be more alienating monologue than vibrant two-way discourse.

"And you do this for a living? You make enough money to live on?"

"No. Well. You could say. Yes. Basically."

"Right. That's clear then." She hesitates as if engaged in advanced mental arithmetic. "I mean *gambling*? It's just so… illogical. And everything else about you is so controlled and restrained and… logical."

"That makes me sound boring as hell."

"Not boring." Still searching for the words. "Measured." Pete fails to hide his feelings. "Don't get all sulky. I'm just searching for the right words. Okay. Got it. You're the most *rigid* person I've ever met." Pete lifts the duvet and goes for a comedic double-take. Seph sighs. "You resist doing anything that exposes you," she continues, measuring out her words slowly. Peter fails to take the hint and opts for an ill-judged second bite at the visual-gag cherry. Another sigh of exasperation, longer this time, signals she's on the point of giving up. He doesn't want that any more than he's enjoying feeling this much under attack, and in his confusion reaches for another weapon in his extensive defensive armoury: aggressive self pity.

"If that's the case, what am I doing here?"

"I sometimes wonder. Don't get me wrong, I like you here. Didn't think I'd ever say that about anyone, but I do." Pete's stomach feels like it's on a spin-dry setting. "Look, this isn't any easier for me than it is for you. You don't have a monopoly on building walls around yourself.

I think you're as scared as I am."

Pete's so far out at sea he can't see the shoreline any more, but he knows he must give her back something. Relinquish ground. Share the burden. Anything. Because if he doesn't, they'll both keep stepping back from each other, from this… whatever it is… until they're out of sight of each other. An offering is needed, however token. Fumbling for a workable compromise, he tries to buy some time.

"It's just that I'm not comfortable talking about…"

"Peter?"

"Yes," he says meekly, in response to another variant of that Swiss Army knife of a second syllable.

"It's all right. I promise."

And he knows that this is one chance he has to take. One person he can allow in.

He takes a deep breath, and lets it all out.

"My parents got married late. They'd known each other for a long time, just not in that way. Dad was a fair bit older and always used to say he'd fancied her for ages, but then had to wait for her to run out of other options. But they did get married eventually, and then I came along. No brothers or sisters. Just me. My dad worked for a local precision engineering firm. They had a big factory that turned out metal products of all sizes, mainly for the aircraft industry. It sounded really impressive when I was little and I kept begging him to take me to work with him one day. I could be a persistent little sod and he finally gave in. In hindsight I can see why he didn't want to. But I remember everyone knew him and seemed to like him. Some important looking man in a suit and glasses ruffled my hair and said that my father was the most important person in the building; that he made the whole place tick and they wouldn't know what to do without him. When I heard that, I expected him to have a big office with a shiny desk and people to bring him tea and biscuits. He was my dad and I was bursting with pride. But when I asked to see his office, he smiled to himself and took me out of the reception area and across a courtyard to a big factory building. We walked through a couple of sets of doors and I can still remember the wall of heat and noise that hit me. I clamped my hands over my ears as he led me past all the machines – health and safety would never allow it now – and through a door at the back into a large storeroom full of rack upon rack of shelves covered in trays and buckets of parts. In a corner was a small desk and some workbenches and that was where he worked. No natural light. Just that grubby corner in a dingy, stuffy room. He did his best to make it exciting for me of course, chasing me around between the racks, letting me operate some of the equipment he had there for small modifications. I got to make a cup of tea with loads of sugar and he had some Ginger Nuts, which was a real treat. Then we went outside and stood in puddles to get all the oil off our shoes, wiggling our feet and turning the water into rainbows. I'll always remember that."

He pauses reflectively and she kisses him lightly on his shoulder.

"Dad was a proud man. I just hope I never looked disappointed that day. He was so much better than that. He could have been anything he wanted. But he left school very young. That was just what his family did. All of them. Different times, I guess. Leave school as soon as you can, get a job, contribute to the household and stick at it come what may. Get out there into the big wide world. Only thing was, it wasn't so big and wide for him, just a short walk to a noisy, oily building down the road. What a waste. That fucking factory sucked him in, chewed up the best years of his life and then spat him out. You know, he'd spend hours poring over an atlas or the *Guinness Book of Records* like an excited kid, reading out weird facts or pointing to places he'd never go to. I remember this one book. A Reader's Digest book. Something like *Strange Facts and Amazing Stories*. It was purple with big gold lettering on the front, and it was full of stuff on yetis and ghosts and UFOs and I used to sit on his lap looking at the pictures while he read to me. I loved it."

Another pause. Fingers caressing the nape of his neck. Telling him it's all okay.

"The one thing he did that was in any way escapist or risky was having a bet at the weekend. Used to make a big thing of it. Lay the racing pages out on the coffee table and sit there with a pen between his lips, occasionally retrieving it to cross out or put a ring around a horse. Then, when he'd finished studying, he'd stand up and say 'patience is a virtue, son, so you know what, I'm going to reflect a while and have a brew.' He'd make a pot of tea and a glass of squash for me. He'd pour two teas. A mug for him. A cup and saucer for Mum. Then he'd disappear off to take Mum hers. He'd come back ten minutes later and say 'Right then, they say everyone's a genius at least once a year; maybe today's the day, eh son?' He'd fetch a betting slip from the pile on the sideboard, sit down on the sofa and carefully enter his selections for the day. Then we'd walk down the road to the local bookies. The same one Kev works in now. But that's a story for another time," he replies to an unspoken question. "I'd stand outside while Dad disappeared inside for a few minutes. Then we'd walk home, have some lunch and spend the afternoon watching the races on the TV, Dad cheering on his picks shouting 'go on, my son' and all that crap. He was never more animated than then. He wasn't betting much. It was the thrill of the hunt that counted. That was enough for him and I admired him for it.

"I was nine or ten when they made him redundant. They told him on the Tuesday and he arrived home twenty minutes later than usual on the Friday – some send-off – clutching a carriage clock. A bloody carriage clock. Almost forty years at that place, sitting in a grubby hole working long hours for a pittance, and all he got to show for it was a piece-of-shit clock. Looked fancy enough to a ten-year-old though and give him credit, he bluffed it out pretty well. Put a brave face on it and said it was a welcome kick up the backside. Just what he needed. Chance to try something different. A new horizon, I think he called it. It was *all good*. I actually went to bed with a smile on my face, can you believe it? But it knocked the stuffing out of him. It really did. The one thing he had was his dignity while he worked, but when they cast him out it as good as killed him. Especially when he found out he'd been replaced by some spotty school-leaver. He went for interview after interview, but no one was interested in a bloke in his fifties. He was left sitting at home with what I've since discovered was a poxy pension that barely covered living expenses and about ten grand in savings. For a while, anyway. They got rid of him during the school holidays so I was around to see it start. The Saturday betting routine became a daily one. Probably the only way he could fill his days and distract himself. I was only young, but I could see him fading by the day. It was obviously the betting. He never seemed to win and he'd just go quiet after the racing. I even found him brushing tears away a few times. We were obviously short on money. What would once have been a holiday abroad became a week in a Margate caravan park. Our telly shrank. Clothes that were obviously too small or knackered would last another term. And so on. I didn't know what to do, but I knew where the problem was.

"I used to walk back from school past the bookies

and one day I stood outside until some bloke going in asked me if I was all right. I told him I needed to see the man in charge. He laughed, but sure enough out came Ron a few minutes later. That's the main man. Still is. Kev's boss. Right shifty bastard. Anyway, he seemed to know who I was. I told him I wanted to help stop my dad betting because he was running out of money and it was making him sad. He just shook his head and smiled like I was some idiot. Told me my dad was a grown-up and more than capable of making his own decisions. Not to worry my little head about it. 'Run off home, young man, and don't worry yourself with the affairs of adults,' were his last words before he pissed off inside."

"You were too young to solve everyone's problems."

"I know that now, but it didn't stop me wanting to at the time."

"When did he die?"

"About a year or so after I'd been patronised by Ron that time. A huge heart attack one day while I was at school. I was eleven. Almost twelve. Heart attack makes it sound like bad luck, or something inevitable, but I know what it was. And I know who was to blame. Not one person from the factory turned up at the funeral, but at least there was some kind of honesty to that I could deal with. But Ron did turn up. Even had the bare-faced cheek to give my mum a hug and pat me on the head. Where was the honesty in that? My mother got drunk that night and alcohol became her new crutch. I tried to do the things Dad had done to make it better. Made her cups of tea. Tidied up everywhere. Even got the racing form out on Saturday mornings to make it like old times. But she was always so sad, no matter what I did. Then she got a letter one day. I was too young to understand anything at the time, but she just seemed to implode after that. I now know it was from the lawyers who'd dealt with

Dad's affairs after he died, saying there was no money anywhere. The savings had disappeared and money was owed to a long list of creditors. And who should be on that list but our friendly local bookie, to the tune of over twenty-five grand."

"*How much*? But I didn't think gambling debts were legally enforceable?"

"They're not. But Ron was too clever for that. Turns out he'd lent Dad the money. Formal loan agreement. Compound interest at some ridiculous rate. Unbelievable really. He lent him the money and got repaid twice, once when Dad gambled and lost and then again when he died. Talk about a perfect plan, and Dad was desperate enough to fall for it. I think that was the day I decided to get him back one day."

"Get him back? How?"

"Win back the money he took off my dad."

"What? *Twenty-five thousand*?"

"Thirty-five if you include the hard-earned savings he blew. More if you allow for inflation. I called it forty grand."

"*Forty?*"

"Yep." Enjoying the reaction.

"And?"

"And I'm getting there," he responds with a half-smile. A nudge in the ribs repeats the question. "I could give you figures, but they won't sound that impressive. You need to recognise that the odds are stacked against me."

"And?"

"The typical punter loses, so simply being up is enough."

"*And*?" Anyone else and this would be irritating him, but her repeated questioning in that increasingly mischievous and impatient tone is strangely appealing.

"I'm up about…"

"About? You don't do *about*."

He pauses, but she has his card well and truly marked, so he takes the plunge. "Thirteen thousand, eight hundred and fifty-four pounds, give or take a few pence."

"All with this Ron?"

"That's the score with him. I do have bets elsewhere now and then." Her silence hits home. "I know it doesn't sound like much, but…"

"No, it does. That takes some doing, I'm sure. But that's a long way off your target and it's taken you years to get this far and there's no guarantee you'll keep winning and… sorry."

"No, you're right, of course, but it's something I have to do. Don't you see?"

"I do. It's just that…"

"What?" Sounding defensive.

"How can you live on that if you don't work?"

"Uncle Ernest."

"Uncle Ernest."

"Well, great uncle actually. My grandad's brother. Or rather, some trust fund he set up. I never met him. Black sheep of the family who I was told made his money in the rag trade, then buggered off abroad. Anyway, he made a load of dosh and set up a trust over there. Not sure why he missed my dad out, but there must have been some clever legal or tax reasons for skipping a generation. Or maybe they'd heard about his gambling. Anyway, I got a letter on my eighteenth birthday saying there was this flat in Northwood that the trust owned and that I could live there rent-free indefinitely. They also send me an allowance."

"Who's they?"

"I don't know," he replies too abruptly, which only adds to his growing irritation at feeling irritated by this picking at an old scab he's got rather good at ignoring. "Some attorneys who act as the trustees."

"An allowance?"

"Yep. It's not a lot. Just a monthly living allowance." Playing it down. Trying hard to sound like it's the most normal thing in the world. Now wishing they were talking about the gambling, and why the hell isn't she more interested in that?

"You've never had a job?"

"Nope," he says proudly. "The rat race did for Dad but it'll never get me. Oh no."

"Nice choice to have, I suppose. How much?"

"What?"

"How much do you get?"

"It's not really important, is it?"

"No. Sorry. It's just that the way you've always talked in the past, you've given the impression you're…"

"What?"

"Nothing. Sorry, it's a lot to take in."

*

It's only as she lies in the bath several hours later, stripped of the distractions she's wilfully embraced since Pete's awkward departure, that Seph reluctantly faces up to the cocktail of negative feelings stirred up by their highly unsatisfactory earlier exchanges.

She should never have pushed him.

But she did, so maybe she deserves this shot of reality. Maybe that's what happens when you poke around in a hornet's nest.

So, gone is the mystery man; the tightrope walker perilously defying gravity with reckless abandon; he had a concealed harness all along. Not so much maverick, as spoilt layabout playing at life; accepting the plaudits for being the great risk-taker without ever having to take a real risk.

And what she really wished she'd done was grab him and shake him by the shoulders and shout "So there you are with your free accommodation and your hall pass from all the constricting financial commitments that smother and stifle everyone else's day-to-day existence, in fact a total blank slate on which to trace whatever life path you choose and be everything your parents couldn't be and yet you choose to swan around playing the big successful gambler when really it's just some petty and pointless revenge plot that in all likelihood won't be achieved and you'll take most of your life trying and even if you did manage it so fucking what? Who'll be around to give a toss? And meanwhile am I meant to sit around while you just get more bitter and all that hatred eats you up as you blame anyone other than your parents for what they did with their own lives because you need them to be perfect? Even though they were the same mix of good and bad as everyone else. No better. No worse. Just human. And humans make mistakes." Or something like that. Then hold him in her arms and tell him that he's better than his past; that his future doesn't have to be defined by it.

But then who is she to judge? Sitting here in her paper cocoon, immersing herself in fictional realities rather than face up to her own, the world speeding by outside. Convincing herself that she's surviving in spite of her parents and their smug, self-obsessed absenteeism masquerading as avant-garde parenting, while denying the inconvenient truth that it is their money – which she self-deceivingly rationalises as payback for a lonely childhood punctuated by the occasional tokenistic walk-on role in the knockabout farce of their lives – that helps fund this… this what? This hobby trade of hers? This vicarious literary existence, as if reading and judging books make her in any way an active participant. Because aren't these books her camouflage, the building blocks for the walls of the castle in which she hides?

And she's missing Pete terribly.

ENDGAMES

"Sorry about de tape, lads, but we can't be having any noise. And anyways, to be honest with yeh, which I intend to be, I couldn't give a flying feck what yeh might want to say." He can see it in their pinched, weaselly faces and dead eyes. These two are evil wee bastards.

"Da Hawkins boys, to be sure. Main men around here den, are we? Big guys? Bet day cack demselves when day see yeh two coming. Like dat? Bet yeh do. We all like a bit of respect, don't we? And yeh boys know what it takes to get some respect, eh? Yeh rule diss estate and if anyone gives any shit, yeh sort 'em out. Dat how it is?" Build them up; knock them down.

"Now the vast majority look at yeh and see scum, without caring one jot about de how or de why of it. People round here would pay serious money for yeh two to piss off and never come back. No one's interested in de causes, just the effect on dare lives. Not in my fecking backyard I tink day call it. Dat's understandable, of course, but dare are more liberal souls, admittedly ones living far away from this shithole, who would argue dat yeh shouldn't be judged for what yeh are. Dat who yeh are is far more complex. An amalgam – a gallimaufry if you like, and I very much do – of multifarious influences. Dat de fault, sorry not fault, dat'd be wrong of me; de *reason* why yeh are like yeh are lies back many generations. Dat we should be understanding yeh before we judge. Looking at the full context, and yeh can't truly *get* anyone without understanding dare past and its impact on dem now. And I've got a degree of sympatty for dat line of tinking, I really do. But, and here's the rub, it doesn't change the fact that yeh two scrotes are de only ones sitting here and youse been terrorising diss neighbourhood and I'm afraid, for your two sakes anyways, we haven't de luxury of such analytical indulgence and dare's no one else here to blame. I suggest you take it up with dem at a later date.

"But enough of diss preamble, nice as it is to chew de fat with youse two guys, tow I couldn't help but get the feeling dat yeh were struggling to keep up at times. However, I did want to do yeh de service of at least providing some context – dat word again – for what is about to follow."

He pauses for breath and a loud crack of the knuckles.

"I'll tell yeh how it is, lads. Dat psychoterapy stuff is all very well and good and admirable but we don't have de time or de inclination, let alone de training, for it so we're going for some alternative terapy; one dat won't take much time and for which we have a leaning and not inconsiderable training. It stops here. Now yeh two *big guys* may be tinking who are diss pair of sad old fat fuckers tying yeh up and waffling on when yeh could be out dare kicking stuff or selling drugs or scaring the shit out of old folks or bullying little kids, or whatever it is yeh do. Yeh may even be tinking dat once yeh get out of here yeh know some real hard guys who can come after us. But I'm afraid I'm going to have to disabuse yeh of such notions. It's like dem professional boxers. People look at dare ripped bodies and bulging muscles and one per cent body fat and tink dare de hardest guys in the world. Den I'd point yeh to a couple of pot-bellied pikeys having a bare fist fight and yeh'd laugh at dem, but I know who I'd pick to back me up. Dare's hard and den dare's really hard. And I'm telling yeh dat there's no one yeh know who we couldn't chew up and spit out and dare's nutting we haven't seen or done. So if yer not, I would be very, very afraid if I were yeh two. Because we're the real deal. We're evil motherfuckers and yer going to be seeing our ugly faces every time yeh close yer eyes for the rest of yer patetic, wasted lives."

He looks up at 'Mick', who walks over with the sports bag. It gives out a tell-tale series of metallic clinks and clanks as it passes between them. Dropping it to the floor from a height, 'Paddy' slowly draws back the zip and theatrically removes, one by one, a procession of tools and knives, which he places in a neat row. Trusts these wee shits have seen enough torture porn to fear the worst. He pauses to let their imaginations run riot. Four eyes bulging; two heads shaking; muffled protestations. The younger one has pissed himself.

"Like I said, it ends here. I won't lie now. We're gonna mess yeh up pretty bad, lads. Yer going to live, but believe me, day'll be times when yeh may doubt dat. Yeh'll be crawling out of here on your bellies and be a while in the hospital. Going to have limps for the rest of yer lives and I doubt yeh'll ever play competitive sport. And with every jolt of pain I want yeh to remember diss night and remember deese words: we'll be watching... and if we ever see or hear of yeh doing or even being involved, however remotely, in anyting, and I mean anyting, antisocial ever again, even if it's just playing yer music too loud, rest assured dat we will find yeh and we will fuck yeh up so bad yeh'll be screaming at us to cut yer throats and be done with it.

"Let's begin, shall we? And remember, what doesn't kill yeh can only make yeh stronger."

*

"What are we doing here?" Carl asks.

"Challenging your defences," replies Emma.

"What defences?"

"Hatred. Resentment. Not-so-casual indifference. All the stuff I long ago tired of. But if you're prepared to stop judging, build from scratch rather than constantly demolishing, then I'm happy to hang around a while." Carl's eyebrows give the game away. "And there we have it. I'm only really here because I want an excuse to spend some one-on-one time with you? That the flame still glows?" His silence affirms. "Well, I'm not and it doesn't. Carl, this isn't foreplay. I'm here because I liked your dad a lot and I for one am prepared to give him the benefit of the doubt. And when we're done, I'll be heading off home to Alistair for an enthusiastic resumption of conjugals. Understood?"

"I'm sensing a little frisson here."

"That'll be indigestion then, because it doesn't exist. Although…" she trails off, looking down to her lap, her lips tightening.

Carl feels his heart miss a beat. "What?" he asks as tenderly as he can manage, trying to keep the hope from his voice. Sensing vulnerability. Liking it.

"Nothing."

"No. Tell me." Just about maintains an even tone.

She looks up and their eyes meet.

"In complete confidence?"

"You have my word."

"I just wish that one time… *one time*…" Again, she trails off.

"*What*?"

"That when Alistair and I are making love, just once I'd really love it if *he* came first, not me."

And so earnest is her expression that Carl finds himself nodding empathetically for a few seconds before he realises he's walked straight into a sucker punch. He concedes defeat with a weak smile and a dip of his head.

"Right. Shall we get on, or should I just get up and go now?" she says brusquely.

"No, stay. Please."

So here they crouch, in a dusty, dank attic amongst the discarded and the forgotten.

They find it in a distant corner, still crammed behind a water tank where Carl had wedged it a few years earlier. A bulky black audit file case: his most prized, if ultimately pointless, trophy from that final week plundering of the stationery store; a not-so-little goody bag to accompany the lumpy redundancy cheque. Several days after getting *the* news, he'd found Mum standing over Dad's desk, a sheaf of papers scrunched in her hand. "What the hell am I supposed to do with all this crap?" she'd wailed at the ceiling, and Carl had placed a hand on her shoulder, eased open her fingers and shepherded her away, before fetching down the as-yet-superfluous audit case from on top of a wardrobe and filling it with the contents of various desk drawers, never for a moment dwelling on any of it. Then he'd lugged the dead weight up the rickety metal pull-down ladder. Out of sight, out of mind. All part of the healing process.

They pull it across the floor, sending up swirls of dust, and into the shifting pool of light cast by the solitary web-encased light bulb swaying gently in the draught seeping through the roof tiles.

"One thing we do know is that you… we… haven't got much idea who he really was. Agreed?" she asks. "So, we might as well start with what he left behind. And that's the letter and whatever is in this oh-so-stylish box.

You don't think it's significant that your mother wanted all this hidden away and forgotten about?"

"I'm sure she had her reasons," he says defensively. "She had a lot on her plate and it seemed to help not having reminders of him strewn about the place. Made sense at the time, so don't…"

"I was just asking. I'm sorry. Here I am telling you to start with a clean slate and I'm not much better."

"But still better, I note."

"Come on. Let's have a look and please try and give him the benefit of the doubt."

Her resolve is challenged from the outset as the first file drawn out reveals its contents.

"What the…?" she says, pausing to flick through the sheets of paper. "Oh dear. It would appear to be a worryingly comprehensive collection of *Country Life* 'Debs of the Month'. How… sweet?"

Carl can't resist a raised eyebrow.

"Say nothing," she counters, but to no avail.

"Antoinette is hoping to study fine art at Warwick. And Sophia's dearest papa is not only funding her boutique, but has also gifted her the simply marvellous surname of Hemplethwaite-Smythe; and half of Stroud no doubt."

"Carl."

"What a lovely, casual, everyday moment as Felicia – yet another Gloucestershire resident I note – stands in her ball gown by the sundial holding the reins of a horse, as one does. Probably lost her virginity to that saddle."

"*Carl.*"

"One more. Promise. Look. Lysandra Stapleton-Simpkins has five dogs, an eating disorder and in-bred buck teeth. Poor girl. Wonder which one of the dogs she lost her che…"

"*Enough*. You know you were asking why we split up?"

"*Daddy liked posh birds, Daddy liked posh birds*," Carl can't resist singing in a childish voice, and has the file snatched from his grasp.

Next to see the half-light is a weighty lever-arch file that contains a manuscript. *No Accounting for Haste* proclaims the top page. Carl winces at the wordplay, leafs through the pages and notes that unlike another draft he has more than a passing acquaintance with, this one progresses beyond chapter three and appears to boast a middle and an ending. Envy, resentment and self-loathing vie for supremacy.

"Here. One for you, I think. Do I get a finder's fee when it tops the bestseller list?" he says, unable to keep the reflexive acrimony from his voice.

She takes it from him and glances through the first few pages as Carl takes more lucky dips.

A wobbly-coiled clay pot that looks more canine faeces than functional. A vaguely bullet-shaped heft of painted and varnished papier mâché that had started out with pretensions of being a space rocket, before the end of a term curtailed artistic ambition and consigned it to being a mound of uselessness. A wobbly wooden letter rack that toppled over if it entertained anything heavier than a postcard. An even wobblier wooden pen holder that had at least served active, if rather token, desk duty. A batch of clumsily charming nursery school scrawls and paintings. Three certificate folders full of reports, certificates and cuttings pertaining to the childhood and achievements of Carl.

At the very bottom is a small white envelope, on the front of which is scribbled 'Set list and final requests' in his father's handwriting. He opens it up and takes out and unfolds a piece of file paper. Gives it a cursory glance.

"Looks like some kind of running order for his funeral. Prepare for some middle-of-the-road Radio 2 fab faves no doubt."

"Like what? Read them out."

The judgmental juggernaut stalls as he glances down the page, his readiness to assume the worst revealed for the casual betrayal it is.

"Out loud, Carl."

He swallows and reads out a list written by a man he hasn't *really* known for a long while; if at all.

Herewith the final wishes of Stuart Aled Mawddach Evans:

Reduce me to ashes.
Bruch's Violin Concerto (Uto Ughi) on loop before the service starts.

Then in no particular order:

- *'Au Fond du Temple Saint' duet from The Pearl Fishers. Don't care what they're singing about. It's beautiful.*
- *'Don't You, Parts 1 & 2' by Micah P. Hinson. If you can't be self-centred at your own funeral, when can you be? I'd like to be remembered. And just to prove it…*
- *'Remember Me' by British Sea Power.*
- *'The Road' by Portishead.*
- *if something is needed for the traditionalists, my favourite hymn is 'Lord of All Hopefulness'*
- *and as a reading: the end of chapter X of 'The House at Pooh Corner.'*
- *As the coffin slides from view: 'Farewell' by Apocalyptica.*

Then please lay my ashes to rest 155 metres in the air in a place that panders to the 10% of me that can't be sure 'he/she/it' doesn't exist, where my heart belongs and eyes can feast. A place I'm happy to die for. It's all arranged with a local solicitor called Dafydd Wells. 52043124.82113057113.9311

"You okay?"

He sniffs, smears the back of his hand across his eyes and nods.

"What do you think all those numbers mean?" he asks, attempting to distract himself from internal churnings.

"Haven't a clue."

"Which bothered you the most: the funeral songs or the manuscript?" asks Emma, as they walk to the car. It's an attempt at levity, but it hits home nonetheless. "When's your mother back from their cruise?"

"Not for another two months at least. Why?"

"I'm going to leave you be for a few weeks now. I'll be in touch as and when. Don't bother ringing me, please."

"Why?"

"Things to do. People to spend time with. Ardours to douse. Stuff like that."

"What about that redundancy thing we talked about. I gave you those papers to look at. I need your help on it. You're so much better at that sort of thing than me."

"Take a step back, get the big picture and make the logical decision that's best for everyone. It's pretty bloody obvious."

"To you, maybe. What's wrong with just meeting up briefly for a quick chat about it? It would really help me."

"Because I don't want you getting the wrong idea."

"I can change."

"Exactly. Why would that be enough? How could it ever be?"

*

Carl is surprised to find a large, muddy puddle on a warm summer day. An anomaly of nature sent to taunt him.

Because Carl is not surprised to find the puddle occupied.

By Willoughby; his useless carcass half-submerged in its centre like some smug, wallowing hippo. Eyes fixed on Carl. Mouth gaping open, its corners upturned in a deranged, mocking grin. Tongue lolling out. If this canine cunt could talk, he'd be saying "Fuck you".

Carl tells him precisely what he is.

Willoughby responds to the expletive onslaught by flopping onto his side. Loving every sodding sodden second of this.

Carl is in the process of graphically informing Willoughby just how pointless his existence is, when he senses his phone's insistent pleading for attention.

"Hello."

"Hi, it's me."

"Hello, me. Thought you'd forgotten."

"Told you I'd be a few weeks, didn't I? Anyway, what are you doing the weekend after this one?"

"Playing cricket for the old boys."

"I need you to cancel. It's important. We'll be away for a couple of days."

"Away?"

"Away."

"*Away*."

"Yes, Carl… and no, Carl."

"Sorry?"

"Don't come over the innocent with me. I recognise that tone. Let's get something straight. What is one plus one?"

"Two?"

"Wrong. It's one… and one. It's two ones. Understood? Because the moment you act like it's anything different, I'm gone. Okay?"

"Yep."

"Good. I'll pick you up at 3 a.m. next Saturday."

"In the morning?"

"That's generally what a.m. means. Problem?"

"No."

"See you then."

Carl pockets the phone, feeling like he's been handed a Christmas present, then told he's not allowed to open it. He looks around for someone to take it out on.

Finds a dripping Willoughby at his side.

And too late recognises an inevitability.

Carl is regretting the choice of white T-shirt – now more Pollock than Klein – as he attempts to style out the walk home, facial muscles aching from fixing a look of calm passivity each time he passes someone, knowing that they're inwardly laughing; the word '*fuck*' screaming on repeat inside his head.

*

The phone's ringing as Carl gets through the door.

"Hello?"

"Hi Carl. It's Beth."

"Blimey. To what do I owe this pleasure?"

"Not that music you brainwashed him with on the chess trip. Can you hear it from upstairs?"

He can. 'Gouge Away' by the sound of it.

"Good man."

"Mmm. Anyway, the reason for ringing is to pass on a thank you from Michael."

"What for?"

"For sorting it out, he said."

"What?"

"That's what I said."

"And?"

“He wouldn’t say, but he said you’d know and to thank you. What did you do?”

“Not a clue.”

“Well, whatever it was, a big *thank you* from me as well. He’s been like a different boy recently.”

*

Carl strives for the umpteenth time to achieve elusive comfort. Shifts in the seat. Rolls his neck. Fiddles with the seat belt. Desperately needs to sleep; to quiet the shrill ringing in his ears; to stifle the throbbing in his head; to dampen down the rebellious queasiness that has gripped his stomach. Two hours of fitful tossing and turning under the duvet not enough.

Taunted by the glare of oncoming headlights peeping over the central reservation, he turns and places his forehead against the window, relishing its cool consolation. Stares at the road markings flashing by, allowing them to blur hypnotically. The monotonous and repetitive beat of the music urges the slide into unconsciousness. Feels his eyelids dragged downwards. Almost there. Blessed respite awaits.

Then the car lurches to the right across two lanes and draws level with another car. Carl stares into the dashboard-lit dead eyes of a fellow early riser trying to interpret the hand signal being vigorously waved in his direction inches in front of Carl’s face. Then their car swerves violently to the left, traversing back across the two lanes.

“Not another car in sight and still he has to sit in the middle bloody lane.”

Carl summons up a noise of vague acknowledgement.

“Ah. It lives.”

He cranes his neck to check the side mirror.

"Doesn't look like he's learnt his lesson."

She snorts and silence descends once more, save for the hum of the engine, the swish of oncoming cars; and that music. What moments earlier had been pleasingly soporific, flitting about unobtrusively in his semi-consciousness, is now intensely irritating.

"Have you got something a little more anodyne you can play, by any chance?"

"He speaks. Not a Maroon 5 fan then? Too *popular* for your liking?"

"It's just so dull, that's all."

"Aren't we a bundle of fun." Her glance to the left catches him wincing in the wash of oncoming headlights. "Oh dear."

"Late night. Meant to be just a few drinks, then home, but it ended up a bit of a piss-up. Lot of a piss-up, actually. Then on for a late-night curry. Didn't get in until after midnight."

"Why? You knew I was picking you up. You've known for over a week."

"It would have been rude not to. I was guest of honour, you could say."

"What *are* you on about?"

"It was a leaving do." Pause for effect. "Mine."

"*Yours*?" She pauses, processing. "Compulsory or voluntary."

"Entirely voluntary."

"Why didn't you tell me?"

"Only decided last week. Anyway, I wasn't allowed to ring you." Realises that sounds petty. "I took your advice and applied some logic. Pretty damn obvious really, it has to be said. Can see why you said what you did now. I walked in the next morning, told them I'd completed my redundancy review and could save them over thirty grand a year and maintain staff morale. They liked that.

They didn't like hearing it required them to make me redundant and keep all the others. Clearly had their eyes on a couple of others and for some reason had great plans for me. They needed persuading so I put them right about just how little I did and bigged up the others like they were workplace heroes. They were still wavering so I came clean on a few shenanigans I'd previously denied and they saw the light. I could tell they were worried about what I wanted, but we did the deal at six grand tax free, a glowing reference and yesterday being my last day in the office. We agreed how I'd play it with the others to keep face all round, but it's not my problem now."

"Do you think the others will keep their jobs?"

"Can only hope so. Nothing else I can do. I'd be lying if I said it went against the grain not to let them know of my Christ-like sacrifice after a few drinks last night, what with all that misplaced sympathy being showered on me. But I managed to keep shtum."

"I have to admit that for the first time in ages you have both surprised and impressed me."

"Bet that hurt?"

"Not at all," she says, flashing him a smile. "So how does it feel?"

"Exhilarating at the time and I've loved the last week. Though I'm not sure how I'll feel in a few days. Now let me sleep, please."

They drive through the neon-flecked darkness and into the grey dawn. M40. M42. M6 toll. Coffee and a shared muffin at the services. M54. Past the garden centre. Turn left a few roundabouts later.

"We heading where I think we are?"

"Time to reacquaint yourself with some childhood memories."

Breakfast in Little Chef. Glass of milk. Bowl of cereal.

Round of buttered toast. Another coffee. Resurrection. Trying to keep his eyes and ears away from the full English that Emma is tucking into with exaggerated, lip-smacking relish, occasionally taking the time out from her chomping to offer him a dripping chunk of sausage or bacon. Throwing him an aggressive '*What?*' every time he flashes her a scowl.

"What's the plan?"

"Haven't got one really. Thought you could show me round."

Dolgellau hasn't changed much, Carl recognises with grudging admiration as they take a stroll down what purports to be a high street. Clinging like some camouflaged limpet to the foot of Cadair Idris, it remains the same patchwork of greys and browns he remembers. That battle still raging between the welcoming and the detesting of the tourist pound; one hand proffered out, the other giving the finger.

It's in the newsagents grabbing a paper that the past prompts him. Carl emerges with a set of brightly-coloured boules in their white plastic caging and announces they're off. More by luck than judgment – a dimly remembered landmark conveniently appearing each time he's on the point of admitting defeat – they arrive where Carl thinks they need to be, and park up. He grabs the boules and bounds into the trees and down a slope. Emma follows, the steep gradient and springiness of centuries of compacted pine needles propelling her downwards with a lolloping gait that, having initially fought and almost fallen, she has to abandon herself to and which deposits her with Carl on a small gravel 'beach' beside a calm pool of water, her ungainly arrival serenaded by an involuntary shriek.

"Nice."

"Sod off," she shouts above the clatter of the water as it escapes its temporary holding zone and cascades downwards, meandering away from them between the rocks and snagged arboreal debris.

"What colour do you want?"

"Blue, please," she says.

He wrinkles his nose.

She waits.

His forced grin is starting to crack.

She waits.

"Sure?"

"First rule of annoying Carl when playing games. Pick blue. Ever the child."

"No problem," he lies.

"Don't worry, little boy, you can have your precious blue. I'll take the green."

The four balls are hurled into the air. They land with a succession of *thwumps* in the middle of the pool, resurface and then idle, as if debating amongst themselves what to do, before some current indiscernible to the human eye grabs them and tugs them gently downstream.

It's game on as the balls bob and weave their drunken way. She doesn't tell him to shut up as the rolling commentary starts. She even reacts to it. She lets him set rules – when and how a stuck boule can be released – without protest. She pretends not to notice when he trips over a tree root. She even allows him to call this… whatever *this* is… *Aquaboule* without challenge. She lets him set yet more rules. She adheres to them. The balls approach the finish line. She celebrates her victory. She makes a half-hearted attempt to catch her ball. She misses, and Carl ends up soaking a shoe as his desperate grab sees him lose his balance. She stays quiet about his ball floating serenely behind him until it's too late. Laughs as he screams "*No*". Willingly heads back up for the rematch, the blue team now blue and yellow.

By the time they leave, only two of the eight boules remain, Carl disturbingly protective of his surviving blue. Of the remainder, three can be seen jammed in crevasses or bobbing on the edge of sheer drops further downstream that she won't allow him to go near. The others are missing in action, last seen doing *The Mission* tribute acts and destined to give someone an inapposite surprise downstream.

"What's the second rule of annoying me?" he asks as they get in the car.

"Pick the racing car."

"Very good. Any others?"

"Plenty. But they're for me to know and deploy as I see fit."

Emma indicates left out of the car park the way they came, but Carl overrules her, professing local knowledge and proclaiming that there has to be a more direct route back than the way they came. "Dolgellau's over there as the crow flies," he insists, pointing vaguely to the right. Emma gives in.

It takes twenty minutes of head scratching, barely-restrained frustration, suppressed smirking and a number of laboured turns to make it back to the car park and set off the way they came.

Emma says nothing; and in doing so, says everything.

"Where next?" Carl asks, preferring deflection to prostration; humility not one of his more accessible attributes.

"Back at university you had this photo of you and your dad in a frame. The two of you were standing with a mountain and a valley behind you. You told me he'd just delivered some long speech to you about university. How to get laid, basically. A letch-ure you called it, rather smugly if I remember. An advance warning of the painful punnery ahead I failed to heed in those giddy courting days. Anyway, I assume it was somewhere around here, so show me the way."

"All right, if you insist," he says, with a puff and a dismissive shake of the head. "Take the next left towards Barmouth."

"Are we following that pissed crow of yours?"

"Ha, fucking ha."

Carl points out a guest house where they had stayed every year, remarking that business must be good given the number of cars parked outside. Soon after, they turn right, Carl using the road off to the left to the toll bridge as his prompt.

They climb a steep and winding lane of walled gardens and blind bends, Emma's forehead inches from the windscreen and her right foot forever flitting from accelerator to brake in anticipation of oncoming traffic; the mile of claustral twists and turns feeling more like five.

There's a brief respite as the lane levels, before they cross a cattle grid and it starts to climb again, the landscape opening out into sloping, sheep-strewn fields and patchy woodland.

Ten minutes of tortuous ascent later, Emma is relieved finally to park up in a small lay-by the other side of yet another gate. A sign announces *New Precipice Walk*. They get out.

Carl's been telling her not to look to her right for a while now, but he needn't have bothered as she's not dared take her eyes off the road. Now it's the path he commands her to stare at as they walk past some ramshackle farm buildings and a white cottage set back into the hillside. A Labrador sits proudly on a patch of exposed rock at the top of the grassy slope running up by the side of the cottage. It uncrosses its paws, negotiates its way down with surprising dexterity and pads over to the barred gate, before remembering to bark.

"Shut up, Charlie," comes a disembodied voice from inside the building, its weariness suggesting little expectation of obeyance. Carl leans over the gate to pet the animal into silence, warming to its moronic appeal. Its panting enthusiasm shadows them as they follow the path that runs above head height along the front of the property.

Leaving the cottage behind, the path curves along the hillside before heading out towards the drop to the estuary below. Rounding a corner, they sit on a bench, Carl's fingers over her eyes.

The hand is withdrawn and permission is given to look.

"Woah," she exhales.

Then silence as four eyes struggle to take it all in, even the two that have seen it many times before. It's Carl who speaks first.

"He was right. Dad told me I wouldn't be able to really appreciate a view until I was older. You know I thought it wouldn't have much impact on me on the way up, but…"

"Is this where that photo was taken?"

"No. That's a little way along."

"Show me."

A few hundred yards further on they dip down towards what remains of an old cottage. Just before they reach it, they pass through a gap in a dry-stone wall to their right and follow the hint of a path winding up a large mound of rock and grass, startling sheep from their ruminations and sending them scampering off.

The path levels out and they walk along the top, pausing as the full glory of the view down the estuary and out to sea presents itself once more.

"It's just here," says Carl. He leads her round a small outcrop and sits on the nearest patch of grass, with his back against the largest expanse of exposed rock. For a few seconds it feels comfortable enough, but as he leans back more fully, he can feel his backside starting to slip, so he shuffles along and tries another position. Again, it's not quite right, so he stands and steps over to a small patch of mossy grass between a curved patch of bare rock and a couple of boulders. It's a bit of a tight fit as he lowers himself into the gap, but the curved backrest proves surprisingly accommodating, and far from getting in the way, the boulders prove ideal footrests.

"Happy?"

"Almost," he replies, twisting slightly to his left to face more inland so as to maximize support for his neck. "There," he announces, with a sigh of contentment.

"You sure now?"

"Fine, thanks."

"Excellent. Just as long as you're comfortable, Goldilocks. Maybe I'll try out a couple of the reject spots." She sits down and shifts around until buttocks, rock and grass offer something approaching passable comfort.

"All good?" Carl asks.

"It'll do."

Carl tells her that Cadair Idris, rising above them on the other side of the valley, means the Chair of Idris and he recounts the story as best he can recall it, the story that had so captivated a young and impressionable mind when his father had first told him; been the genesis of countless essays at primary school that had teachers marvelling at such imagination in someone so young, even querying at parents' evening what television he was being allowed to watch.

He points out Lemon Island ("I suppose so, though it's green, so shouldn't it be Lime Island?" "No. Maybe. Oh shut up.") and the other one that looks a bit like the Lacoste emblem, at least when the tide's on the way out ("That one's a bit more tenuous"). Far below them he directs her to the guest house they'd passed earlier, then to Dolgellau over to the left. Working back along the valley, and having to lean forward slightly, Carl points out the patch of grass that looks a bit like a fruit pastille ("I think we're getting a bit desperate, don't you?"). Keen to recover ground, he points high up above to the nipple on the ridge ("Mmm." "No, look. It's exactly like one. It's even got that little indentation thing on the middle..." "Calm down. If you need it to be a nipple, then a nipple it is"). Down comes their gaze to the rickety toll bridge across the river; he tells her he's read somewhere that a big firm accountant has bought it and upped the toll right away. Feels justified in a derogatory sneer now he's taken a tentative step outside the profession.

Proving he's learned nothing, he points back over and up to their left and attempts to communicate the uncanny likeness of a patch of forestation to a woman's bikini bottoms; not helping matters by electing to remove the article of clothing in forlorn and misguided pursuit of greater metaphorical integrity ("*That's enough,* Carl"). Moving swiftly back to their right he gestures out towards the sea on the horizon, pointing at the ridges of land jutting out into the estuary and initiating the same crocodiles/sugar mice debate he can recall – with genuine fondness, he realises, despite himself – from all those years ago.

Finally, he retraces the route of their climb along the ridged summit of Cadair Idris that time, recounting a twelve-year-old's disappointment at the marked lack of facilities and refreshments on offer from the simple stone construction they'd found at the summit; the impetuous decision taken under the heady rush of the completed ascent to take a more imaginative route down; the marked absence of any recognisable path; the following down of a dry riverbed and arrival at a steep drop; the choice between retracing their footsteps back up the slope, or the stubborn and reckless insistence that their route lay ahead; their inching down what would otherwise have been a waterfall, Dad's forced cheeriness failing to mask his apprehension; that patch of scree Carl had lost his footing on, sending him rattling in a mini-avalanche of stones towards the lip of another drop, height unknown, only for his right hand to instinctively grab at a patch of threadbare vegetation, wrenching him to an abrupt halt, the rush of adrenalin temporarily anaesthetising him to the realisation that it was a gorse bush that had saved him; looking up into his dad's blood-drained face sporting a look that was part panic, part relief and part joy; before it dissolved into a laugh that eased away the sprouting aches and pains; making it to the bottom and lying on their backs on the cool concrete of the car park, chuckling at the sheer stupidity of it all as their bruised and battered bodies began the process of recovery; the hot chocolates and banana splits they'd treated themselves to as a reward in a nearby café; his casual mention of the red line that appeared to be working its way from the scratch on his palm to his wrist and on a few inches up his arm; the drive to the hospital; the cleaning, the bandaging and the antibiotics; the getting together of their 'story' for Mum; the joyful complicity of a secret shared.

They sit, the only sounds the distant chirping of birds from the forest away to their left, the bleating of sheep – their own intruding presence a possible subject of conversation – and the distant swish and shush of passing traffic on the road winding far down below. Then there's a low, persistent, growling rumble.

"Hungry?" asks Carl.

"It appears so."

"Thought we might try down there."

They order meals and take their drinks and ticket outside, sitting at a wooden table beneath an old railway signal, serenaded by a periodic rattling as cars make their way across the toll bridge. When Emma queries the signal's authenticity, Carl tells her they're sitting on an old railway line that goes all the way to Barmouth, although there are no rails anymore; that he and his dad had walked it once, cycled it many times, before crossing the estuary bridge into Barmouth to sit on the steps eating ice creams, summoning up the energy for the return journey.

The pub is situated by a sweeping bend in the river as it meanders on its way out to sea, its passage hidden by the promontory of land that juts out into the water, deflecting its course, its crest crowned with a line of trees. The expanse of water has more of a feeling of a still pool than a moving body. She says as much.

"Hence the name, I guess. Penmaenpool. There's even quite a famous poem about it."

"Go on then."

"Not that famous."

"Anyway, it's beautiful."

"We were up there," he says, pointing at the hill opposite, directing her until she locates the white cottage and follows the line of the path along the hillside.

"No wonder it felt like the middle of nowhere."

Their number is called and they set about their meals, Carl exhibiting a customary food envy that sees him dipping into her ploughman's for the variety his whitebait and chips is lacking. She allows the first two poaches, but slaps his hand away when he returns for a third. Carl pouts and silence ensues.

"Sort of lost my virginity just along from here."

"Not while I'm eating."

"Must be the salt and vinegar on the chips that's jogged my memory."

"*Carl, pleeease*. I'm eating," she says, delaying lifting her last mouthful from the plate to authenticate the protest. He smiles, and recognising he's going to tell her anyway, she deposits the bread and cheese into her mouth, swills it down with the remainder of her drink and awaits the gruesome details.

"It wasn't sex as such, just my first intimate encounter with the female… er… ori—"

"Vagina, Carl. It's called a vagina."

"Moving swiftly on, my dad sent me up here a few times to stay with his father, who I called Grumps on account of him being a grumpy old git. But a wealthy one. Owned a farm along the road there, and much of the land on both sides of the valley. Ended up giving a load of it away, as I heard it. I know Mum got well pissed off about it at the time, then got even more annoyed that Dad didn't seem to care. He said he'd known all along he'd get nothing from him. I remember Mum calling him weak and him just getting up and walking out of the room. Anyway, a few years before then, and a year or so after the last time Dad and I came up here on holiday, he…"

"Why did that stop?"

"I was fifteen, I guess, and it was naff to go on holiday with your parents."

"And a holiday with your grandad wasn't?"

"No, it was different. I'd been going on and on about earning some money over the summer, but I'd done sod all about getting a job. Dad came up with this idea of me coming up here and working with Grumps. Probably seemed like a win-win-win solution at the time."

"How do you mean?"

"I don't think things were good even back then, with Mum and money and stuff, so it got me out of harm's way. And it got rid of a stroppy, grunting teenager and taught him a life lesson by subjecting him to a month of hard labour on a farm. I'm pretty sure it amused Dad."

"How was it?"

"Grumps got someone else to pick me up from the station, hardly said a word to me when I arrived, stuck me in a tiny room in an outhouse without heating or running water, and after one day of helping out in the fields with the sheep, announced I was 'a useless southern English softie' and told me he'd spoken to someone who owed him some back rent and agreed I could go and work there instead. Said in his best-worst English accent that it would be much more *'my cup of tea'* but that I shouldn't expect to be treated better than the others just because we were allegedly related."

"Nice. Where was it?"

"A pony-trekking place a couple of miles that way. He didn't even take me the first day. Told me it was just round the corner so I could walk." Carl stares down into the bottom of his glass and swirls the dregs around.

"How far?"

"Must have been four or five miles. And it started to rain. I got there late and the woman who ran it seemed to be under express instructions to treat me like a piece of shit. Sure enough, my first job was to follow the holidaymakers on the ponies at a discreet distance with a shovel and a wheelbarrow, scoop up the shit and take it back to dump on the huge pile of the stuff they hid out of view. What?"

"Sorry, I'm not laughing. Well, maybe a bit."

"Those first two days I seriously considered walking away and going back home, but I stuck at it. Okay, the work was crap, literally, but there I was, surrounded by a load of kids my age or a little bit older, most of them girls, and when your work is that tedious you tend to stick together. Definitely a case of work hard, play hard and at the end of the day we always did something together."

"I sense the sordid act approaching."

"It wasn't that bad. I was at an all-boys' school and pretty innocent. A load of girls walking around in T-shirts and tight trousers was like manna from heaven. All-day party in my pants, I can tell you."

"Lovely."

"There was this one girl called Mary who kept flirting with me, and then one day asked me if I wanted a feel."

"Sounds like a classy girl."

"Looking back, the word plump springs to mind, but back then I can just remember looking at that arse rolling around in those tight jeans as she led me to an empty stable. We lay down, she unzipped her jeans, took my hand and pushed it down inside. I fumbled around and then my fingers just sank into this really soft, moist…"

"Enough, I think."

"Like a hand in a velvet glove."

"A touch too much?"

"For a fifteen-year-old virgin? Definitely."

"Well, what a charming little anecdote. One I will always treasure."

Back in the car, Emma pulls down the sun visor and extracts a scrap of paper secured there. Then she reaches over, opens the glove compartment and takes out an object that Carl initially assumes is her mobile, but then thinks may be some kind of walkie-talkie. Referring repeatedly to the paper, she cautiously presses away at the buttons, sighing occasionally.

Carl is intrigued and knows she knows that. He plays it cool, affecting disinterest, but they both know he won't be able to stop himself.

"Need any help?"

"Nope."

And they move off.

"Open the gate, will you?"

A few hundred yards and a cattle grid later she gives a sigh of satisfaction, slows the car and pulls over into the nearest thing to a parking bay these lanes are going to offer; basically a grass verge wide enough to take two wheels without threatening either to scrape the side of the car against a wall or deposit them down a steep slope into a river.

"Here we are."

"Excellent. Glad I didn't get my hopes up."

She gets out, waits for him to follow suit, ignores his theatric scratching of head, locks the car and heads off down the lane. They come to a ruin, pass through a gap in the wall that may or may not have once been a gateway and find themselves at the foot of a steeply-rising small walled area of grass, dotted with half a dozen gravestones.

"I'm surprised we got a parking place," offers Carl.

Emma holds out a piece of paper, which he takes and unfolds. It's a copy of a page he recognises, the long sequence of digits ringed.

"And?"

"GPS coordinates."

"Sorry, I'm com…"

"Christ, you can be thick at times. It's here. What that means. They're coordinates. *This* is where he wanted to be buried."

Carl goes quiet.

"I'm impressed," he manages, after a while. "That's very nice of you to say so. Alistair will be so pleased to hear."

"Alistair?"

"Yes, it was him who worked it out. We wouldn't be here without him. I was *very* appreciative; I can tell you. *Very*. I'll pass on your best wishes and thanks."

Mixed emotions, none of them positive. He knows he's being played, and that he deserves it. He's annoyed that he didn't work it out. No, that's not it… he's ashamed that it never mattered enough for him to want to try. He also knows he needs to hide all this and come up with a facial expression and a few words that will save the day and show him to be something other than what he is, at least while he works things through in his own time.

But as always, she beats him to it.

"Shit, Carl. Your face. You, you, you. Always you. Is there no room in that brain of yours for anything else? I've just brought you to the place where your father wanted his ashes to be buried. Look around you, man. *Look*. It's fucking beautiful. It's stunning. And where was he buried? Some characterless patch of ground in Ruislip, right? But most definitely not here. Doesn't that piss you off? Doesn't that knock you for six? Yet all you can think about is how annoyed you are that you didn't work it out and how jealous you are that Alistair did. Talk about two steps forward and a dozen back."

"It's not as if he could have seen the views anyway," says Carl petulantly.

"The views aren't for him, you dope." She pauses, looks into the void and shakes her head. "They're for you."

Emma changes tack and lays off him for the rest of the day.

And Carl duly repays this respectful stance by wilfully acting as if nothing happened earlier and talking about everything *but* what he knows she wants him to talk about.

Old habits dying hard.

A man who can't help himself.

Maybe the choice of hotel is her idea of punishment, he ponders, as they turn their backs on all discernible activity and head inland through the gathering dusk along narrow lanes for several miles, before Emma turns into a drive that deposits them in front of a brooding hulk of a building that looks as if it's been transported straight off a Hammer film set: not another car in sight; at least thirty windows in view, only two of which are lit; one of them an attic room. Textbook horror playground. All it needs now is a couple of innocent lovebirds blissfully ignorant in the language of the genre and possessive of faulty risk-ometers to blunder from one messy climax to the next.

"We're here," says Emma, who appears to have read the script.

"Where is everybody? Are we the only guests?"

"It is a bit quiet."

"Why here?"

"Fancied somewhere a bit away from it all."

"*It all?* It's Dolgellau, for Christ's sake. We were already well away from *it all*."

An hour later, Carl is more convinced than ever that his earlier emotional illiteracy is being punished as they clutch their drinks while perching on the edge of some sofa/chaise longue style-over-practicality hybrid in a quiet corner of an even quieter lounge bar that appears to have taken its inspiration from a variety of stately homes and Laura Ashley catalogues. Bold stripes and floral patterns compete for dominance, the end result most kindly describable as *busy.* It's a visual clutter that has them looking around longingly for a plain and unadorned patch of wall, just for some visual relief. Even the ceiling offers scant respite, riddled as it is with chandeliers and elaborate plastering.

They share the cavernous room with three other guests and are the youngest by a good few decades. It's like some poorly attended World War II reunion of soldiers who fought on opposing sides. Dotted around like the points of some triangle of animosity. An awful lot of grey, tweed and disdain; and not a sound, save for the periodic flutter of broadsheet pages and the occasional geriatric splutter.

"Which one's Colonel Mustard?" Carl asks, and is pleased to see Emma snort in her drink, drawing a disapproving stare over a pair of half-moon glasses and a shake of a head.

"I was thinking more *Fawlty Tower*s."

"Or Agatha Christie. Someone's about to keel over."

"Most likely from natural causes, looking at this lot."

The eerie cast is completed by a short, mustachioed man standing behind the bar and sporting a look of such undisguised joy that they cannot but conclude that unless he's receiving a blow job under there, here is the man of the 'house' and this enclave is his fiefdom in a world where another wields the real power. Such had been his obvious pride in his well-stocked dispensary that they hadn't the heart not to give him his head.

Carl takes a swig from his pint of Randy Bishop, while Emma tentatively sips her Pink Lady, taking evasive action from an assault on her nostrils by the stalk of the cherry.

The entry of a formidably solid and sour-faced woman wipes the satisfied look off the barman's face and sees Carl and Emma sitting bolt upright.

"Your table is ready," she says to them, unleashing a

manic, forced smile that has Carl recoiling fractionally and gripping the armrest.

They rise and follow her, Emma deploying an extravagant, swinging gait and pointedly smiling and saying "hiya" to each of the military relics they pass. Initially startled, they stiffen and shake with discomfort, only for their countenances to relax as they observe her departing sway with a melancholy lamentation for distant pleasures and opportunities.

Carl finds himself empathising.

← ← ←

(EMMA... A FEW WEEKS EARLIER)

It begins with a rare appointment-free day, a horizon devoid of pressing deadlines and a nagging hunch that something isn't right.

She contemplates the base observations and suppositions on which she hopes to work a spot of alchemy. Starts with what she's amassed from various sources; some reliable, some maybe not.

Stuart had left his house that morning and driven to north Wales. He had told no one what he was doing. He had a companion along for the ride: a female student at the adult evening school where he had started teaching. Much younger than him and no good reason to be in that car. A Polish woman who some of the other students said he was clearly infatuated with and who appeared fond of him, her husband very much out of sight, out of mind, back in Poland; at least until a few weeks before, when he'd turned up and there had been something of an altercation one night in a pub.

Their bodies had been found in a burnt-out car in some woods along a rough track off the road in the middle of nowhere; any number of permutations deducible from the carnage picked at by a confused police force. End result? A lot of unanswered questions. More likely than not unnatural causes, self-inflicted.

Stuart's marriage was floundering. Had been for years. He had allegedly had a fling with a girl who had worked with him for a while, culminating in a sexual harassment case.

He was in financial trouble. Under investigation by the Inland Revenue. Haemorrhaging clients. He had been threatened repeatedly and aggressively by one particular client.

Stuart tore out and kept the *Country Life* deb page from every issue. *Move on.*

He had written a novel; kept it to himself, the water untested. The tattered manuscript making no more impact on the world's consciousness than a falling tree in the middle of the Amazonian rainforest.

That's what she knows, but what does she think?

She's scared to read the manuscript. Worried it might be rubbish.

She doesn't trust Fiona.

Stuart never struck her as the type to screw a nineteen-year-old employee.

Let alone end up where and how he did.

*

She needs to start somewhere, so why not with the man who seems to know more than anyone else. She rings him and his hesitancy and obvious discomfort confirm the accuracy of her instinct.

Colin McLeod has got his act together by the time

she walks into his office. They chat about nothing and she thanks him for his patience with Carl. He says he understands how difficult it must be. She smiles a lot and twists the course of the conversation until it is entirely natural that she be asking him what happened to all Stuart's work records and files. And rather than ask what business it is of hers, she senses a relief that she has not ventured elsewhere, that she may be an ally, not a foe; he informs her of a rented storage unit, even offers to lend her the key for a few hours if she'd like to take a look. Says he'll be back in a while as the key is in another office, and in his absence, Emma does what Emma does best: she observes.

"I see you like maps," she says breezily upon his return.

"Old ones. Yes."

Tepid.

"Of one area in particular?"

"Er… not really… well…"

Warmer.

She gets up and walks over to one of the framed maps.

"Wales?"

"Yes."

Too relaxed.

"Snowdonia mainly, by the looks of it."

"Some of them, yes."

All of them, yes, thinks Emma, but doesn't overplay her hand.

"It's a lovely area."

"You know it?"

Too concerned.

"Not that well, but I hear it's stunning."

"The key," he says, as casually as a man can who has abruptly steered a conversation off on a tangential course.

Emma takes the key. She has what she came for; possibly more.

*

The light flickers on automatically. The storage unit is bigger than she expected. It needs to be. There must be a dozen or so five-drawer filing cabinets and a load of stacked cardboard storage boxes. Everything is arranged neatly, save for one pulled-out cabinet drawer, on which sits an opened pink file. She takes a look and realises this must be the problem client Stuart mentioned, the one who got heavy with him about the tax inspection.

She glances through the paperwork and sees the pressure building. It starts with the letter to the clients from the Inland Revenue. Even as a non-accountant, Emma can sense what it must have felt like for so many of your bigger clients to get sent this all at the same time.

Like your world was falling apart.

And knowing that makes Stuart's initial letter to the client all the more poignant, as she reads between the lines and sees his desperation: to see a positive side; to paint this as bad luck, not poor planning or implementation; to allude to hidden dark forces at play beyond their control; to keep the client on side and generate a 'them and us' mentality.

There follows a succession of letters, to the client chasing a response and to the Revenue buying time. Then finally comes the killer blow from the client. Its language oozing disingenuousness; the subtext chilling. Stuart writes back to politely correct the client, but is ignored, and the subsequent correspondence turns formal, only dealing matter-of-factly with the collation of information and factual responses.

That Stuart has little to work with is abundantly clear

from his eventual full response to the Revenue. He makes a stringent defence of the offshore link, presenting it as an entirely bona fide and commercial business relationship. He justifies the sale of a forty per cent shareholding in the company to that same offshore entity for a nominal amount as *a much-needed injection of working capital* and *the best offer received after extensive investigations into all possible investment options*. But the more he waffles, the weaker he sounds.

The Revenue readily calls his bluff. They ask for proof of those *extensive investigations*. They ridicule the valuation of that forty per cent as possessing no commercial rationale; any defence fatally undermined by the paying of dividends on that holding in the next two years alone that repay the initial investment sevenfold; dividends that would be taxable in the UK on the former shareholders had they not sold their shares. They also ridicule the succession of invoices to the client that are light on detail – *consultancy services* or *architectural services* – and heavy on zeros; all of them attracting tax relief for the company as they disappear into the offshore ether, where they accumulate tax-free before filtering back into the UK to fund a lifestyle unaffordable on their declared UK income.

She skips forward across the many months and whistles at a final Revenue demand for over a hundred grand, plus penalties and interest, immediately followed by a letter from the client saying how let down they feel, that they have taken *persuasive advice* and are prepared to make a contribution as a goodwill gesture – a cheque for fifty thousand enclosed – but that they hold Stuart *personally* responsible for the balance and feel *strongly* that he should pay it on their behalf. They finish with the news that *with great reluctance* (Emma snorts derisively) they see this as an opportune moment to reappraise, that the business might benefit from a *fresh set of eyes*, and assumes that Stuart will *give every assistance* to the new accountant, who will shortly be in contact. The letter ends with the words *Trust all's well with Fiona and Carl. All the best, Barry and the boys.*

Clipped inside the front of the file she finds a batch of photos: one of a car with a scratch down the side, another of the same car with *Next?* chiselled out of the paint on the bonnet. Then a couple of Fiona and Carl, clearly taken without their knowing, each with a red cross through their faces.

Stuart paid up. Somehow found the money.

It can only have been Carl who'd left the file as she's found it. She's clearly underestimated him. She whispers him an apology in absentia and returns to why she's here.

Most of the cabinet drawers have letters on them signifying alphabetical order. She checks a few and they correspond to the client files within. Same with the boxes. There are just two exceptions: one of the filing cabinets and the box that sits on top of it.

The box on top of the cabinet contains another copy of the manuscript they'd found in the attic, though keeping this one company is a thick sheaf of rejection letters from publishers and agents. She glances through them and they don't make comfortable reading: *The world of crime fiction is always on the look-out for a different slant, a fresh voice, a new hero. It'll have to look a little longer, I'm afraid, as this is formulaic, contrived and, dare I say it, a bit dull. – An accountancy-based detective novel? Enough said. – A trial balance of a book… only without the balance. – They say you should write about what you know. In your case, I'd think about trying something you don't. Sorry. – All debit, little credit.*

Emma winces as she glances at the final sheet of paper and sees her own firm's letterhead. At least it isn't her signature at the bottom; no signature at all, actually.

Lazy. Disrespectful. The wording may be polite and non-judgmental, but she can imagine how its standardised detachment is in many ways harsher in its impact than the more overtly personal comments of others, who at least appear to have granted Stuart the basic courtesy of engaging with the manuscript. It shows how desperate he'd become that he had still sent a manuscript he'd known by then was never going to make the grade and risked it reaching her.

She hopes Carl didn't see this. It will only feed his superiority complex.

She finds the personnel files in the third drawer down and extracts the one she needs.

A quick browse through the other drawers reveals nothing until she gets to the bottom one and finds two files, the initials 'SAMEAS' on the side of one, 'SEAS' on the other. There's not much in them, just what appears to be the paperwork for the formation of a couple of limited companies. On the 'SAMEAS' file she sees a selection of pro-forma letterheads, each playing around with colours, designs and tag lines. The one with the big tick on it proclaims… *because we're the SAME AS you…* A little corny but not without legs, Emma thinks. Briefly queries the acronym before deciding it must be his initials and then Accounting Services. Neat enough.

She turns to the other file. Stuart Evans Accounting Services? No tag lines or mission statements this time, just variants of a logo that shows a river meandering through a wide valley on its way to the ocean on the horizon. This time she notices the small type at the bottom of a page and reads the words "*SEAS is the trading name of Stuart Evans and Son Limited, a company registered in Wales (and England).*"

Emma blinks away a tear.

*

Armed with the file, Emma has a name, an address and a phone number; which she rings, and discovers that Lucy still lives at home, but doesn't want to see her. Rings her doorbell one day, unannounced; the door opened by Lucy's mother, who bows her head as the expletives fly from within the house, before politely translating as "Please, just go away."

Emma seldom takes no for an answer.

She parks up the road and waits. Sees the mother leave. Walks up the path and knocks on the door again. Gets told to "Piss off" through a frosted pane of glass.

Emma is persistent, taking confidence from the continued ghostly presence of her quarry, lingering just inches away. Wavering?

Emma softens her tone. Establishes her credentials; her lack of an axe to grind. Talks of a son trying to come to terms with the father he lost so tragically; of nothing more than an off-the-record chat.

The door opens, Lucy sizes her up with something between a snarl and a pout and then turns away. Emma follows her through to the kitchen, noting that even through a sweatshirt and a pair of baggy old jeans the girl has a certain *something* going on. She accepts the offer of tea, takes a seat at a distractingly stained table and continues her observation as the girl moves around the kitchen. Because she *is* a girl. A slip of a thing. This supposed *femme fatale*.

"I scrub up well."

"Pardon?"

"What you're thinking."

"Flash a bit of cleavage, an inch or two of inner thigh, throw in a well-timed bend or suggestive wiggle and your average male is rendered fairly incapable of rational thought, in my experience."

"Miaow."

"No, I didn't mean it that way." Fails to convince. "Or maybe I did. Sorry. It appears to have come from a rather envious and bitchy place." For which she receives an ice-breaking smile. "So, it happened then, your little office *romance*."

"Not the word I'd have chosen."

"But something happened?"

"You mean did we fuck?"

"Yes."

"I'm not giving the money b…." Stops herself, too late.

"What money?"

"Nothing. Just leave it, will you?"

"What money? This is important."

Lucy scratches at her wrist distractedly.

"From his wife."

"Fiona? For what?"

"Just between you and me?"

"Yes."

Lucy debates which way to go. Makes the call.

"I'd always told my parents I wanted to get into photography, like you do when you're trying to get a bit of attention, or you're sick of them saying you don't have any passion or hobbies or stuff. My dad got me an unpaid job doing some work experience at Fiona's studios. Making the tea and running errands for a few weeks during the holidays. Let's just say I got more than my fair share of attention from some of the guys working there and Fiona took me under her wing. Looked after me. Initially, I'd thought she was a snooty cow, but then she started being all nice to me, which was cool. She even took a photo of me, all professional like. Said maybe I could get a bit of modelling work. Yeah, right," she snorts, hugging herself and staring into the distance.

"Go on," Emma encourages.

Lucy refocuses and defiantly locks eyes with Emma, trying to regain whatever ground she feels she's just given away. "I must have told her I was skint and sick of college, because one day she asked if I wanted to try some paid office work and that she could get me a job working for her husband. Accountancy." Another snort. "I wasn't that keen, but then she said there'd be an unofficial two grand bonus in it for me if I could help her out. Our little secret, she called it, and maybe we could even get a portfolio put together. Mum and Dad were at each other's throats all the time and I wanted to be anywhere but at home listening to that shit, so I thought 'why not?'. And it was nice to get some positive attention for once."

"What was the little secret?"

"I needed to get him… to be a *naughty boy*."

"What a quaint euphemism."

"I asked her what she meant, but she just gave me a wink."

"That was it?"

"To begin with. And give her some credit, she kept to her side of the bargain. Almost immediately she took those photos she'd promised. Don't think I'd ever been happier than that afternoon. She even took me out for a meal afterwards. I'd only been working for Stuart a few weeks when she upped the ante. Another two grand if I got him to screw me."

"Nice."

"She was good. Didn't sound quite so… cold and clinical at the time."

"Did she tell you why?"

"Not really. Like I said, she was good. Had me hooked with the portfolio and four thousand pounds was a hell of a lot of money."

"And?"

"Nothing."

"No sex?"

"We never laid a finger on each other, apart from shaking hands at the interview. Caught him staring at my tits and my arse a few times when he thought I wasn't looking, but I never got the feeling he was going to act on it. Guess he just wasn't the type. Christ knows what he was doing with her, though. She was the biggest prick tease of them all. Had everyone buzzing round her like flies and I don't think being married ever stopped her. In fact, I know it didn't. Bloody hypocrite."

"Was there *any* basis to that sexual harassment case?"

"None. Pissed Fiona off big time. So eventually she came up with the idea of making the complaint. Said I'd blown the four thousand but could still get something, still achieve what we… what *she* wanted by the power of suggestion and that if we threw enough mud, some might stick. She took me to see a lawyer and all I had to do was act tearful, though I don't think I needed have bothered. The two of them had it all sorted already and they came up with this document for me to sign. A load of legal stuff. I told them I wouldn't lie in court, but they just smiled and said I needn't worry. And sure enough, the lawyer convinced Stuart that ten thousand was an absolute bargain not to have his muck broadcast in court, even if he won the case."

"You got *ten thousand* for a pack of lies?"

"Not me," she hits back. "I got maybe a grand of it, no more. Fiona took the rest for legal fees and so on. Said I was lucky to get what I did, as I hadn't even done what she'd paid me for in the first place. Seemed like an odd way to get money off your husband when she could have just asked him."

"It was never about the money. What about everything you said after?"

"You mean… I didn't know he'd died until Fiona turned up one day with another plan. Not exactly the mourning widow. This time all I had to do was sign a few letters she'd typed up, dated months earlier and addressed to her, and stick to the story come what may. Money for nothing, she said. I hadn't worked for ages and really needed it." Emma does little to hide her feelings. "Well, I did. And Fiona told me what he'd done with all their money; what a mess they were in because of him. And it didn't seem that bad. I mean he was dead, after all…" She trails off.

"You said he spent his days watching internet porn. That he'd as good as molested you. Very graphic you were. Hands up your skirt. Always telling you in detail about his many sexual conquests. Insisted on sex. Threatened to sack you if you didn't oblige. Pretty much everything short of rape." Lucy shrugs her shoulders. "Was it worth it?"

"At the time, yes. Do I regret it? Yes. But it's done now and you've promised."

They play it around for a while and despite herself, Emma finds the anger draining away, to be replaced by pity for this incidental pawn in a far more complex game.

They make their way to the front door.

"Do you want to see it?"

"What?"

"The portfolio. The one Fiona put together for me."

"I don't want to put you to any trouble."

"It's no trouble. Really."

"Er… I should… sure, that would be nice."

Lucy bounds up the stairs; less honey trap, more lost little girl.

*

"So?"

"What?"

"You know what."

"Oh, that," Seph says.

"And?"

"Very odd."

"Not great?"

"Actually, I quite enjoyed it. It was like a very early draft of a book I read a year or so ago. The first in a series. I've only just read the third. You know what I'm like with my crime fiction. I'm a sucker for a maverick detective with an obscure music taste, borderline psychosis, an ex-wife and at least one addiction. The protagonist in this series is a never-married, chess-playing, obsessive-compulsive forensic accountant who likes post-Gabriel Genesis – hence the never-married, I guess – so it didn't augur well, but somehow it all works. Quite the cult following, I believe."

"What are you saying?"

"That what you gave me last week was a lengthy, clumsy, amateurish first draft that may have formed the basis of a much tighter and better written book published a couple of years ago."

"*Formed the basis*?"

"Characters, locations, plot lines, et cetera."

"So same author?"

"No chance. The style is far too different. A loose collaboration at best between two people, only one of whom could write."

"What's the name of the author?"

"Of the three published books? Philip David. I'll get them for you."

With a speed that never ceases to amaze and impress Emma, Seph plucks three books from the shelves without any perceivable hesitation and hands them to Emma.

She opens one of the books and reads the brief and obtuse biography.

Philip David lives with his memories within earshot of running water and writes when the muse takes him between games of chess and putting the world to rights. His moderate literary achievements to date are testament to the creative boost afforded by a second chance. He clings stubbornly to the belief that accountants can occasionally be moderately interesting.

"So definitely not Stuart Evans."

"Who's that?"

"The bloke who wrote the manuscript I gave you. Carl's dad."

"His dad? Didn't he…"

"Yes, a few years ago. It appears that misguided literary ambitions run in the genes… in the family."

"Thought it said Sam Evans on the manuscript?"

"His initials. S. A. M."

"That explains it then."

"What?"

"The main character in the books. The published ones. He's called Sam Snave."

Emma's struggling to keep up and can only frown, as much because she hates not being ahead.

"If I had to guess, I'd say Carl's dad sent the manuscript out to a load of agents and publishers and got rejected by one and all. I mean, it's not terrible, just not particularly good. There are some nice touches. But it's clumsily written, there's a few plot twists that aren't explained well enough and I never bought in to the love interest. Far too idealistic. In all likelihood he would have had some feedback, but most aspiring authors take any comments other than overt praise as damning criticism. I hope that they were kind and constructive. Then he dies and someone sees an opportunity and gives the manuscript to a better writer and they use the good bits as basic ingredients, add in some new stuff and hey presto, they turn water into wine. And out of respect, they named the main character after the bloke who started the ball rolling. But that's pretty much where Carl's dad's input ended, I'm afraid. And with a formula established, they'll keep them coming. Which suits me, as they've become something of a guilty pleasure for yours truly. What I call a cuddle of a book."

"But who's writing them?"

"Philip David?"

"We both know that's a pseudonym. The biog is total waffle."

"Do you know anyone at the publishers?"

Emma looks at the spine and frowns.

"Never heard of them."

*

"This is becoming something of a habit," says Colin McLeod with an empty smile. "Not that I'm complaining. It's lovely to see you again. What can I do to help?"

"I just have a few more questions." Manages to return the smile in spite of the oleaginous onslaught.

"Fire away."

Emma meanders through some well-worn ground for several minutes, before the phone console on his desk buzzes loudly and a red light starts flashing. She pauses and shoots a glance at the light that he's been trying to ignore.

"I do apologise. It's an internal call and I'm sure my secretary would only bother me if it was urgent."

"Go ahead."

Colin delivers a staccato stream of monosyllables before exclaiming, "Jesus, you've got to be kidding, I'll be right down."

He replaces the phone a touch heavily and turns to

Emma, his expression fleetingly minus the professional sheen. "I'm awfully sorry. It appears that there's a young lady in reception making absurd accusations and demanding to see me. I'll just be a couple of minutes. Make yourself at home and I'll get Cassandra to bring you a tea or coffee."

"I'm all right, thanks. Go and see to her."

Colin heads off to meet Seph. And Emma has a little nose around.

"Everything all right?" she asks as he walks back in.

"Total waste of time. Some pseudo-hippy standing in the middle of the foyer shouting her head off about what I'd done to her Keith, whoever he is, so I took her into one of our meeting rooms and asked her who she was looking for. Not me, it transpires. Not even the right firm. I hate to think what our genuine clients made of it." He takes a deep breath and Emma suppresses a smile. "Now, where were we?"

"I'll get straight to the point. I'd like to ask you about your literary interests."

"My what?"

"More to the point, these." She fetches out the first published book and places it on his desk, then drops the manuscript from a height down on top of it. She watches keenly for any reaction. He does well, but she still catches whiffs of recognition and calculation before he returns her stare.

"How can I help you?"

"Did Stuart know what you were going to do with *his* manuscript? I have contacts in the industry. Took some finding as they're hardly a big player, but I persevered and hey presto, I eventually uncovered who holds all rights to this book. That would be your firm."

"It would indeed." He pauses. Purses his lips. Thinks

things through. "I'm going to have that coffee. Are you sure you won't join me?"

She asks for a tea, encouraged by the inference that there is much to be discussed, and he takes temporary respite in making great drama of placing their order.

"You pinched his book," resumes Emma.

"Hold your horses, dear. You're dealing with half a pack."

"Enlighten me then, because it doesn't look good. And I would strongly advise against ever calling me *dear* again."

He offers up a vaguely patronising smile, hinting at a stronger hand than she has allowed for. It's troubling and she welcomes the arrival of an assortment of crockery and biscuits that wouldn't look out of place down the road at The Ritz.

"Thank you, Cassandra. That'll be all. Shall I be mother?" He pours the tea and coffee. "Sugar?" Emma shakes her head. "Ah, sweet enough already." He winces at her wordless reaction and there's a tremor in his hand that has the spoon rattling as he passes her the cup and saucer. He moves to pick up the plate of biscuits but thinks better of it, adding "Help yourself."

"Where were we?" Emma asks icily. She does *icily* very well.

"As you may be aware," he replies, "Stuart had long nurtured an ambition to get published. Before he died, he showed me the manuscript, along with a raft of rejection letters he'd amassed. They had hit him very hard and when I suggested he self-publish, he told me that would mean nothing and was the refuge of the vainly deluded, and that if he couldn't get it published conventionally then it wasn't worth bothering at all. I said I knew someone in the industry, another client who was a successful author, and could I show it to him and maybe get some ideas? He'd pretty much given up by then, poor man, so he agreed. Then a month or so after Stuart died, and unaware of the fact, this client came back to me. We met over a very pleasant lunch at his club and he told me he thought the manuscript wasn't that bad and showed some potential. He said it was a real pity Stuart had died. Had he been happy to make some fundamental changes, lose a character here and there and so on, there was some hope of getting it published. I asked him if he fancied taking it on."

"And he did?"

"Yes, but under condition that he would never be identified. His contractual commitments precluded such *off-piste* activity, but I think he fancied the challenge as this wasn't his genre of choice. He said there were a few angles in the draft that he'd taken a shine to."

"Philip David?"

"Nothing very original there I'm afraid. My middle names. As I'm sure you're aware, there's a long tradition of authors with two Christian names. Henry James. Philip Dick. George Eliot… er… oh yes, Kenneth Graham. And Dylan…"

"Very good. But let's leave that fun little game for another day and cut to the chase. What are you lot making from this piggy-backing profiteering? Plagiarism, I believe it's called. I mean is there no end to your lot's lust for money? Are you ever sated?" *Why does he look so smug?* "Not to mention the matter of a couple of sequels." *That's more like it.* "Yes, I do know about them."

He has recomposed his features into an intensely irritating equanimity that is undermining her assumed position of strength.

"A most impressive performance. I assume that the audience applauds at this point? But we both know that you are rather over-egging the metaphorical pudding.

More than anyone, I don't need to tell you the paltry level of financial returns we are talking about with genre fiction that sits way off the mainstream radar. Such royalties as have arisen to date are modest and still some way away from working off the advances received; payments I might add that were entirely reasonably passed on in the main to a writer of some note who did, after all, turn a draft that was quite evidently not publishable into a discernibly different final product that evidently *was* publishable. There comes a point when true ownership passes. If Stuart was, as you imply, the true author of that first published book, he would have written it. But he didn't, as would be clear to anyone who has read both. And he certainly hasn't written the sequels. And even should the whole affair end up turning a profit above the negligible, why on earth shouldn't the man responsible benefit?"

"Even if I agreed with all that, deep down you know what you did was deceitful and wrong and motivated by nothing more than financial greed."

"You are entitled to your opinion."

"Yes, I am. And I'm thinking Carl should hear all about it."

"That is for you to decide."

Emma is struggling and he knows it. But she has another gear to move up into. All that's stopping her is an innate aversion to supposition; to venturing out onto ice of uncertain thickness. It goes so much against the grain that he's on the verge of surviving this meeting relatively unscathed. All he has to do to dodge the bullet is to keep her finger away from the trigger.

But people seldom quit when they're ahead. "Well, this has all been jolly good fun. I take it we're finished now? It's been a pleasure, my dear, but I do have clients to attend to."

Like red rag to a bull.

And tired of all this pussy-footing around, she puts away the sniper's rifle, takes out the scatter gun, and hits him with all she's got. She hasn't a clue what it adds up to, but she knows it's something.

"So where do we go from here?" he asks, with a grudgingly respectful smile, when she finally runs out of pellets.

"I want in. To whatever it is that's going on here."

"Is that all?"

"Unless you happen to know what happened that day three years ago. I accept he wanted to die, but not like that."

"I agree, but I don't think we'll ever know the full truth."

Stuart… snapshots of a drowning man.

A little food can go a long way when you've been living in a desert, and he'd be lying if he said he hadn't occasionally nourished himself with carnal thoughts during the dragging winter months, indulging in a passing appreciation of Lucy's youthful curves pushing pleasingly and insistently against a succession of borderline-professional short skirts and tight sweaters.

The onset of spring had brought a seasonal wardrobe very much at odds with the salary he's paying her; its diminishing coverage inversely proportional to the rising temperature.

Such pleasures are but ephemeral respites from a bleak and hopeless domestic reality. His marriage in name only. Not so much the lifelong harmony of souls and bodies he signed up for, as two ships drifting slowly and irrevocably apart. From time to time, some mischievous current brings them together with a gentle bump that only serves to push them off in opposing directions once more. And worst of all, each of these brief encounters sees his hopes rise as he dares to believe that the adulterated mess of their marriage might just resolve itself into some semblance of a working union.

The more this girl flaunts herself in his face, the firmer his resolve to maintain the moral high ground. To be better than that. To be better than Fiona.

With this sanctimony comes an entirely illogical, yet deeply comforting, romantic sensibility that leaves him seeing the optimistic flip-side of every negative signal reality can throw at him. The cuckolds he reads about or sees on TV – those conjugally-dispossessed compatriots – are not just victims, they are fine and noble men; defenders of the faith.

But deep down the embers of his immolated dignity still glow and occasionally flare. And in those moments, he sees and hates what he's become: a maudlin, pitiable patsy.

They don't make love any more. They have sex. Once in a blue moon, if he's lucky. Lucky? He feels like a charity case. And what sex they do have is at best… professional. He can sense her pity. He craves the sexual act as some affirmation that hope remains. Yet each time he feels emptier, finding the physical actuality of her silently accommodating passivity far less stimulating than the visions his imagination conjures up of her trysts with assorted virile young bucks with whom he knows she dallies.

Current potential squeeze(s)? Take your pick. This latest *project* of hers, for a start; their photos splayed across the kitchen table; a montage of erotic possibility, and all of it conveniently left there to feed his imagination in her absence; to generate no end of speculative images. They call themselves *Pump It* and the website he happened to find himself looking at the other day proclaimed them to be '*thrusting at the boundaries of contemporary dance with their vibrant, visceral and downright sexy urban/tap/ballet fusion that'll have you up off your seats and unsure whether you wanna dance or go book a room*'. "Total bollocks," he'd muttered at the time, only later to find, upon inspection of a more intimate batch of Fiona's work, that his words appeared to have been less an expletive and more a factual description.

And as he lies in bed on those nights – those many nights – she's away, images come to taunt and he feels himself grow hard as she writhes and groans in various acrobatic scenarios. And with a flick of the wrist, it's over. The mental pictures dissipate in the chaos of release and the emptiness of his existence gnaws at him as he lies there spent, clutching a soggy, cold tissue with nothing for company but the sound of his own quickened heartbeat echoing in his ears, his pathetic isolation mocking him. Who'd have *him* anyway? This feeble half-man who isn't enough. Who can blame her for looking elsewhere?

But this? he asks himself as he sits at his desk. Is this all he has at his disposal for potential retaliation? A teenage girl taking an eternity to change the paper in the copier, bending away from him to reveal the pimply white expanse of skin bisected variously by the straining elastic of a dark green thong. Suggestive of what? A couple of insipid chicken fillets and three green beans. Nothing he can summon up any interest in. She just looks so young and he just feels so old.

No wonder Fiona despises him.

He despises himself no less.

*

Today has been the day.

Of reckoning.

When he totted up the scores.

And realised he's so far behind that he cannot win.

The game is over.

Time to pack in this constant struggle upriver.

Because the current is too strong.

Too insistent.

And he's too tired to fight any more.

The frenetic paddling has ceased.

A brief period of treading water, old habits and cruel hopes dying hard.

Then he'd capitulated.

Allowed his legs to rise to the surface.

Lain back.

And abandoned himself to the flow.

Four moments, on this day of days, have brought him to a state of serene clarity and release. Each of them in isolation could have been survived; overridden; rationalised. But the whole proves so much more than the sum of its parts.

The first as he drives to a client one morning for a nine o'clock meeting. One of the few decent-sized clients not tainted by, or aware of – he hopes – matters offshore. A ten-grand-a-year fee contingent on biannual visits to the director's home, usually early enough not to interrupt golfing plans and with scant regard for Stuart's commuting logistics. The director is old school. And this is how he exercises control: makes his service providers come to him so they can witness his success and compliment him on his palatial house and immaculate garden; and his dutiful, expensively-coiffured and tax-efficient wife can earn her twenty-grand salary, company car and occasional dividend by bringing in a tray of tea and biscuits before wordlessly sloping off.

And Stuart plays along. He has no choice. After all, if the client knew the full picture, he'd realise just how much control he really has. Stuart doubts he could afford to say no even if he was asked to halve the fee.

He's in a stop-and-start line of cars crawling down the hill into Rickmansworth, with little else to do but observe the intermittent clumps of schoolchildren exhibiting an entirely understandable lack of purposeful momentum, faced as they are with dragging their hormone-ravaged bodies up a long climb with nothing but a day of educational regimentation ahead of them.

Blazers are removed. Shirts are untucked. Ties are tugged at. Skirts are hitched up above parentally-approved levels. Buttons are undone. Hair is mussed. Phones are stared into.

The future; in all its shabby, flirting, preening, reticent glory.

With one exception; one he recalls from the last time he made this trip, the previous September at the very start of the academic year.

Stuart remembers cursing his client's timing, just as he is today. He also remembers a young boy on his first day at 'big school', his blazer fully buttoned, hair combed neatly forward; walking away from the security of home – and a junior school where he may have been a big player – and into a jungle.

Clutching a briefcase in one hand.

And in the other, a small teddy bear.

His entire support structure condensed into eight inches of cloth and foam.

A guaranteed bully-magnet.

A fatal error of someone's judgment.

The heart-rending sight had seen Stuart fumbling for

the passenger-side window button, a mercy mission on his mind; only for a hoot from behind to snap him back to a widening gap ahead and the moment was lost in the impatient harrying and manoeuvring of everyday adult life. He'd glanced up and located the boy, a dwindling figure in his rear-view mirror, shuffling to inevitable doom and a major life lesson.

Now here he is again.

Minus the teddy, thank goodness, but otherwise little has changed. He's still isolated and still clutching the handle of that bloody briefcase. The only difference Stuart can discern is that whereas back in September he'd walked with his head held high, a naïf blissfully unaware of the maelstrom he was heading into, now he walks as if leaning into a stiff wind, his gaze fixed on the pavement no more than a few feet ahead, doubtless willing a clear and uneventful passage to the relative safety of the classroom.

Then a foot flicks out and the boy is sent sprawling to the ground. The briefcase slides away loose, and as the boy gets up, its contents are emptied over his head to the amusement of his tormentors. Exercise books flutter. A metal pencil case cracks open on the pavement and spills its contents into the gutter. A plastic lunchbox bounces several times before being picked up and looted.

And a small teddy bear falls to the ground and comes to rest a few feet in front of its master's crouched form. He reaches out but before he can rescue it, a foot connects and sends the bear onto the road and under a car.

And in that moment Stuart feels his heart rend once again and wants nothing more than to stop his car, run over, pick the boy and his belongings up and tell him it'll be okay; wrap him in cotton wool and transport him safely through the years to an adult world where he's allowed to be who he wants to be.

If he was his dad…

But he's not. He's Carl's dad and who's to say he's done any better in the long run?

And this boy's life is not Stuart's to live.

He turns the volume up and loses himself in the flitting, disposable inanities of breakfast radio.

A mile or so on, the lethal cocktail of late-running commuters and the tail end of the school run – not to mention accountants being toyed with by their clients – sees the traffic dawdling both ways along a straight stretch of road; never actually stopping, but rarely getting into double figures; left foot getting tired, brain unable to switch off.

Some way ahead he can see a heavily-laden elderly lady standing on the opposite pavement, clearly wanting to cross. She doesn't appear to be in possession of all her faculties; just all her possessions, judging by the clothing hanging out of the various bulging bags clasped in her hands. Occasionally a car slows and a hand waves her across, only for her to hesitate, look across at the vehicles on the other side of the road and stop the moment she senses any forward movement. By then the driver that first slowed down has run out of patience and accelerates past her with a shake of the head.

Stuart watches this pantomime repeat itself numerous times as he approaches. He slows to a halt and wills one of the cars coming towards him to do the same. They don't, their pilots presumably believing that simply maintaining forward momentum will get them to their destination quicker. Stuart stays put, and gets beeped by a bloke in the convertible behind who feels the world should be moving to his rhythm alone. Which only deepens Stuart's resolve as he waits, the lengthening gap before him an ever-increasing challenge to each oncoming car. Until finally one is shamed to stop and with a few last head jerks from side to side, the woman edges off the pavement and shuffles across the road. As she reaches the dotted white line the other car has already squeezed past, its driver desperate to regain the surrendered twenty yards of tarmac. The woman continues her slow progress until she passes directly in front of him, at which point she stops, lowers her baggage to the ground, turns towards him, brings up her hands as if in prayer, nods her head slightly forward and flashes him a heartfelt smile of gratitude, her eyes glistening with moisture; before picking up the bags and shuffling on towards the kerb.

Stuart summons up a smile too late for her to see, and pausing a few seconds longer than necessary, just to piss off the bloke behind one last time, he moves off. Half a mile on he senses a crack in the dam, knows with a certainty that it will widen into a breach, pulls the car abruptly into a lay-by, turns off the engine… and bursts into tears; lets it all out.

Any steely resolve that his priorities have been reordered for the better by the events that punctuated his journey is severely tested by the bombshell dropped on him amongst the chintz, plump cushions and ornaments: there is to be a changing of the guard; full retirement is confirmed; his useless, parasitic son is taking up the reins; and bringing in with him an old school friend who has recently started up his own accountancy firm.

"You know how it is." *I don't.*

"There's nothing I can do." *Yes, there is; you could tell the waste-of-sperm sponger to fuck off.*

"I've told him he's mad." *No, you haven't.*

"Told him he'll regret it." *They never come back.*

"I'm sure we're only a small client to you anyway." *If only you knew.*

"Thanks for all your help over the years." *That's not enough.*

"The new accountant speaks Ollie's language." *What language would that be? Total shite?*

"I'm sure he'll come running back to you sooner or later." *No, he won't.*

"Maureen and I may well need your advice now and then." *No, you won't.*

In his disorientation he even contemplates begging. Hates himself all the more for it.

That Junior hasn't a fucking clue and will doubtless piss the lot away is scant comfort, given Stuart won't be around to gloat.

He muddles his way through the rest of a meeting that's wasting almost half the working day and stripping him of the privacy to react with honest emotion. Here, in this homage to nouveau riche home decor.

As the car vibrates along the gravel driveway, he resists the temptation to take out one of the procession of decorative terracotta pots that presumably allude to the requisite casa-from-home on the Iberian Peninsula.

He travels back to the office in a trough of resigned despondency, arriving to find a letter waiting for him, the day not done with him just yet.

A firm of lawyers has been kind enough to drop him a line. The envelope is innocuous, the content poison: low on detail, high on implication. They cloak their clumsy threats in the customary veneer of polysyllabic jargon, the mystique that fee-earning professionals rely on to keep their public confused and justify their charges.

Lucy is suing him for sexual harassment and unfair dismissal, trotting out a succession of fictions and fallacies, only five per cent of which would need to be true to leave any employment tribunal convinced of his debauched lechery and corruption of this young innocent. It's all a game of bluff, of course, designed to have him parting with thousands of pounds as gratefully as a drowning man welcomes the lifebuoy thrown to him. It's a haggle he can't avoid and the classic legal double bind. If he says nothing, he'll appear guilty, lending credence to the claim. And the moment he responds, he acknowledges and validates the claim and guarantees some level of compensation. A groundless dispute given substance and enabled by a lawyer guaranteed to profit from its existence.

That evening he drinks himself into a slumber that would have eluded him sober; for once glad that Fiona is away on 'business'.

When he wakes the next morning, the alcohol-infused haze serves as a buffer, shielding him from a tsunami of comprehension – one that could sweep him back under for the day; for many days – and ensuring that the full extent of his lot filters through in manageable dribs and drabs, protecting him from that knock-out reality punch.

He utilises the resulting rationality to come to a resolution, one that leaves him with a clarity of purpose.

Knows this is how it has to be.

Emancipation.

And just two simple questions.

How?

And when?

Plus he has a very important letter to write; the most important of his life; the letter *of* his life.

*

He'd first approached Edward, an old university friend, the previous summer with the idea of maybe helping with an accountancy-related class at the adult night school he ran in the school where he was headmaster. In response to a quizzical look, he'd waffled on about a 'new challenge' and a 'wish to give something back'. His words had sounded unconvincing to his own ears, but if Edward doubted their veracity, or news of Stuart's financial problems had reached him, he'd not let on. "Christ, don't you get enough of that tedium during the day?" he'd laughed. "I'm sure we can find something a little more interesting for you."

And he had, '*An Appreciation of British Literature*', the all-encompassing name of a one-year course he doubted he was qualified to teach, wringing out every drop of value from an A-Level and an upper-second degree in English literature. But it would bring in some additional income and it wasn't accountancy or home.

Fiona had reacted with a 'how nice', the expressed sentiment belied by the horror and scorn he could read in that flaring of nostrils and clenching of teeth; that unconscious and almost imperceptible recoil whenever confronted by something less than acceptable.

He'd overheard her talking about it to some bloke – always the men – at a horrendous dinner party he'd been commanded to attend, presumably because his absence would have been marginally more embarrassing than his presence. "Those who can, do; those who can't, teach," she'd said with a conspiratorial giggle, resting her hand on his forearm for a second or five longer than necessary. He'd hated her for it at the time, but couldn't deny the validity of the sentiment, his own clumsy attempt at *doing* sitting neglected in a drawer.

And here he sits a few weeks before the end of their third term, watching his students file into the room.

This motley band of acolytes, divisible roughly into two. On the one hand, there are the small groups of first-generation immigrants looking to embrace a culture they hope will embrace them back. On the other, there are the middle-aged self-improvers: under-achievers with time on their hands, for whom university had been unattainable, not the norm, and who have seen their own children showered in seemingly unlimited opportunities they never had themselves, accumulating endless qualifications and certificates along the way, not to mention a cockiness and contempt that leaves them, as parents, feeling inadequate. Sick of that look of disappointment on their children's faces. This is their chance at redemption; minus the exam mechanism and its inherent spectre of potential failure.

So here they come every Tuesday evening, to this classroom-by-day that is always slightly too hot or slightly too cold, and such is their communal lack of confidence and self-esteem that they buy into the illusion that this failed-accountant/failed-author/failed-husband is possessed of some elusive mastery over the subject matter that they couldn't easily glean for themselves without his guidance. It's a blind faith that initially gave him room to breathe but has since been a source of nagging concern and self-doubt.

Three terms in and they still nod at whatever he says. They still doubt whatever comes out of their own mouths. They still handle their books like precious treasure maps; keys to some lost world of marvels. And he gets to feel like he still has something to offer and exercise a degree of control and influence so elusive elsewhere.

The one exception to the rule is Adelina, a second-term joiner dragged along by her two girlfriends within weeks of first arriving in the country from Poland. Like them, her English is very good and he could tell very early on that he has little to teach her about literature.

They communicate with each other in a hidden language – hidden to the others at least, with their heads down, trying to sniff out what it is that lifts the dense text to supposed literary heights – of raised eyebrows, suppressed smiles, shared glances and mischievous questions. A flirtation of two minds unwittingly chaperoned by the other students, the artificial setting saving them from the likely-as-not bland monotony of sustained one-on-one discourse. And enough to lift the proceedings above the mundane and several steps removed from having to ask himself any inconvenient questions.

Those have only ever popped up on the very occasional evening when they have stepped out of the classroom as a group for a theatre trip or a quick drink after class. Without the barriers and constraints afforded by the formalised classroom setting, he has had to face up to and deny feelings otherwise conveniently pigeon-holed as harmless academic frisson. Until now, he has done so without difficulty, because he is a married man and the married man he wants to be – needs to be – stays faithful. Otherwise he would be no better than Fiona, and moral superiority is one of the few things he has left to hold on to.

But the internal debate rages.

Deep down he suspects that the head will win. It usually does. After all, soon the only thing that will remain of him is his reputation.

But it's disappointing, for the third week running, that she hasn't turned up.

He muddles through the class without her assistance from the floor, missing their covert communications. He fails to muster more than the occasional statement of the blindingly obvious from the attendees. That leaves him with an awful lot of silence to fill, and a yawning realisation that he doesn't even like *Of Mice and Men*. The trite phrase 'The American Dream' has made repeated appearances and he's fast running out of politically correct ways to refer to Lenny without repeating himself – the perennial scourge of any aspiring author – and failing in that regard on several occasions. "Retard" sounds harsh as it escapes his lips. As he tries to recover lost ground, he's felled by the most perceptive question of the evening: "How is this British literature please?" A valid enquiry that brings Stuart to the point of exhausted and sobbing collapse.

"It's in English," he tries.

"I know, but the pruspec… the prost… the pros…"

"Prospectus."

"Yes. The prospuc… what you said. It said we would be looking at books by British authors?"

There are only so many synonyms for 'context' but he gives them all an airing as he tries to concoct a cogent argument for its inclusion. Only their collective deficiency of self-confidence permits his crumbling construction to stand unchallenged. He takes refuge for the last half hour in the reading out loud of lengthy and entirely random sections, pausing after each for a nod, a look of culturally-enriched smugness and the uttering of a banal "mmm" or "stunning", even an unfortunate "epic".

He intercepts her friends as they make for the door and asks them with forced casualness if everything is all right with Adelina. He tries to ignore the knowing glances flashing between them, but can feel his facial features stiffen as they tell him that a hitherto unmentioned and unconsidered husband has arrived unannounced from Poland.

Stuart has questions, but he can't ask them, so he bids them goodnight.

*

These final days take on a typical shape.

He wakes each morning to the dawning, yawning realisation of the full enormity of what lies ahead, leaving him teetering for a second or two on the edge of an abyss as his brain strives in vain to comprehend the nothingness he is about to become. It's the minutiae that come to the rescue and power him through the day; so much still to do and so little time.

He gets into the office by seven thirty and works hard through to lunchtime, when he takes a leisurely salt and sugar-laden lunch – dietary concerns a thing of the past – in the pub across the road, then spends the afternoon dealing with the technicalities of his death. Typically, there's a phone call with Colin, with whom he's been selectively honest, disclosing the financial and paternity issues but staying quiet about his DIY interventional intentions. Colin will understand. Hopefully.

Later he arrives back at an invariably empty home and pops next door to take the dogs for a walk.

Microwave meals, violin concertos, red wine, tea and cake fuel the evening, which he spends working on the letter to Carl, all thoughts of succinctness long ago abandoned; it will be whatever it needs to be. And when the creative flow stutters, he sticks on a DVD, usually something loud, violent and undemanding that permits him no space for free thought. The routine is altered only by Fiona's occasional presence; he can't afford to give her any clues.

As with first waking, the end of the day is a danger zone of maximum vulnerability. If fear and doubt and panic are to take hold, it's in those unguarded, drifting moments either side of sleep. He occupies himself as best he can and hopes to fall asleep quickly.

Tuesday nights are the exception.

But even that ends tonight with this final lecture of the academic year.

He struggles to hide his disappointment at yet another Adelina no-show; then fails abysmally to hide his elation when she slips into her seat after twenty minutes, his voice rising an octave from soporific drawl to feverish enthusiasm within the confines of a single sentence, one he doesn't even bother finishing. Her friends appear to be as surprised as anyone, judging from the excited whispered exchanges that ensue.

He doesn't immediately notice the slight bruising around her left eye. Then he does; and the way she withdraws into herself in those unguarded moments when she doesn't think she's being observed.

Shamelessly backtracking, Stuart gatecrashes a get-together in a local pub that only hours before he had excused himself from – its main attraction seemingly absent – and makes the expensively grandiose gesture of ordering drinks all around; the price of riding an emotional high unlike anything he's experienced since the early days with Fiona. He slowly navigates a course across the room, his gaze constantly flitting in her direction like a compass needle in twitching search of magnetic north; fixing an interested look on his face as he endures a succession of monotonous polite talk, each intermission a tedious but necessary legitimisation of his presence here.

When he finally arrives at his destination, she flashes him a smile and the travails of his journey are forgotten. They talk easily about everything and nothing and the others leave them to it. He's on the point of pushing his luck when those gorgeous big eyes of hers flicker and fix over his shoulder, the sparkle dissipates, her mouth drops open and the colour drains from her face; like some emotional stroke.

Following her panicked gaze, he turns to find himself the unwitting focal point of a stare of pure vitriol from a man who can only be the husband; a husband built like a brick out-house; a husband doing the mental arithmetic and coming up with far too high a number. And it's abundantly clear who's in the equation upon which his contorted features appear to be cogitating.

Stuart runs through his options as the gap between them closes.

Flight is out of the question. The will is there, but he's scared that if he moves his feet, he'll fall over. Which leaves him with nothing more than a facial expression to arm himself with. But which one? He experiments, a process that in itself is sufficiently off-putting to induce hesitation and a glimmer of puzzlement in his potential assailant. Stuart opts for a welcoming smile, one so confused and conflicted that it serves only to convey guilt.

"You teacher?"

"Yes, I am *a* teacher," answers Stuart, happy to be fed an easy question for openers, and a grammatically incorrect one at that, permitting him the chance for a helpful correction that sounds almost conversational.

"What the *fuck* you smiling at mister teacher?"

"We were just…"

"I know what you been doing."

"Doing? I've done nothing…"

He asks Adelina a question in Polish and they both glance at Stuart.

"Emil…" she starts, only to be interrupted by Emil repeating the question. "Tahk," she says with a resigned sigh so damning that it has Stuart wondering if he's significantly underestimated what's passed between them during the previous months.

The husband's English may not be as accomplished as his wife's, but he has little trouble in communicating to all assembled precisely what he thinks has been going on. How his wife has been corrupted by this 'pervert'. How she came to study. How they put their faith in the British education system and this is what they get: some creep who drools all over his students and blinds them with his fancy language. Who doesn't want to teach. Just sleep with them.

"You married?" he concludes.

"Technically," mumbles Stuart.

"*Technically,*" he mimics effectively. "Yes or no?"

"Yes."

"Children?"

"One. A son."

"They know what Daddy do when they not around? They know what slimy fuck you are? Maybe we get them and see what they think of Daddy with his eyes and hands all over my wife. Should we? *Should we*?"

Stuart shakes his head, unable to think of anything to say that will put an end to the tirade. He looks down at his feet and waits for the storm to pass.

Emil grabs Adelina by the arm and shoves her roughly towards the door.

"You stay away or trouble. Yeah?" comes the final threat.

For a second, Stuart considers some heroic gesture. Grasp this one last chance to interject.

But of course, he doesn't.

An awkward silence descends.

He offers an insipid smile that convinces no one, especially himself, before making his excuses and sloping off.

It's not until the next day that he gets angry and indignant; starts to feed off those emotions; and that sigh she gave when the husband had asked her that question.

*

The penultimate night of his life, and he's spending it slumped low in the front seat of his car, chomping on a slab of flapjack and juggling a take-away coffee on his knee; trying not to ask himself too many questions or he might just clear off. After all, this isn't putting himself first and wasn't that the golden rule? But this matters; a loose end he feels compelled to tie. The only problem is, it's got messy. Very messy.

Home is no longer an option.

They'll be no emotional conjugal farewell; no last pangs of guilt; no torn loyalties. Emil – that's his name, this bull in Stuart's meticulously organised metaphorical china shop – saw to that when he trumped the pub showdown by turning up at Fiona's studio and giving her the full sordid lowdown, albeit entirely lurid conjecture, on her husband's extra-marital shenanigans: Emil the cheated on, Adelina the vulnerable victim, and Stuart the manipulative sexual predator.

She laid the booby trap on a rare evening in together. The full set-up: candlelit table laid for two, bottle of wine, Sade on the stereo, Fiona actually cooking, brushing against him teasingly as she flounced around the kitchen. He should have guessed what was coming, so out of character was the performance. But he didn't. His gullible male ego saw to that. And she got to deliver her little *coup de grâce* with full impact as he bit into his steak.

Quite the performance, his denials summarily dismissed as the monologue gathered speed and venom.

In the end he had bitten his tongue and permitted this power play of hers; acted the crushed adulterer exposed; played his part in the sham. Because while saying something might have stopped that mouth moving for just a few blissful moments, what he'd have given away would have been far too great a price to pay. The real retaliation would have to wait, and just knowing that had been enough to strengthen his resolve. Although it was all he could do not to smile when she told him that she wanted him out of the house by nine o'clock the next morning. One problem solved.

Adelina runs across the road, throws her two bags into the back seat and climbs in beside him.

"Quick, move, *now*," she says.

She twists in her seat to look back over her shoulder and he glances repeatedly in the rear-view mirror, both looking for signs of pursuit. Satisfied there is no one following, they relax. Stuart concentrates on the road ahead and Adelina stares down at the hands clasped in her lap. He looks across just as she looks up. Their eyes meet and he can feel the last vestiges of tension ebb away, something gives inside and then they're laughing. And he knows that this is exactly what he should be doing and that Adelina is a project worth dedicating a chunk of his last thirty-six hours to.

It's their *Graduate* moment… minus the shared future.

Their immediate past has been a succession of clandestine meetings and snatched moments, none of them sexual; a gradual transformation from pupil/teacher to needing/needing-to-be-needed to victim/saviour and finally to that of co-conspirators, even if their anticipated endgames may differ.

A plan has been formulated, as much from a coincidence of opportunity than any great design, once Adelina had mentioned she had distant relations dotted around the country and that an aunt and two cousins had settled in, of all places, Wrexham. A fresh start for her – he'd made it clear it was never to be *them*, though he sensed she didn't really believe him – and hundreds of miles from *here*. From Emil. And Wrexham wasn't that far out of Stuart's way, as luck would have it.

It's already late in the afternoon and they make it as far as the outskirts of Birmingham before Stuart pulls into the car park of a large upmarket hotel; money no longer a factor in the decision-making process.

He relishes the reassuring anonymity of the large foyer, only to receive a reality check as a very obvious question is posed at the reception desk. It's Adelina who steps up to the mark with a breezy matter-of-factness in stark contrast to Stuart's grappling for the 'right' response. Having established the options, she looks into his eyes, tilts her head slightly to one side, flashes him a smile he can't decipher, and says "Twin, please," to the receptionist.

The elephant that joined their party at the check-in desk is very much still present as Adelina excitedly explores the myriad wonders of a hotel room that is just like any other to Stuart's more world-weary eyes.

"We have towels!" she exclaims.

Stuart smiles.

"Soap! And bubble bath! Look!"

Stuart smiles harder.

"Wow! We have tea *and* coffee *and* biscuits."

Stuart smiles even harder as she brandishes a pad of writing paper and a pen as if they're precious totems.

As she continues on her treasure hunt, he catches sight of himself in the mirror; a defeated, greying middle-aged man past a prime he can't recall ever having had, in a hotel room with a girl young enough to be his daughter, who is acting like a girl young enough to be his granddaughter. With a squeal she bends down to inspect the contents of the mini-bar and has him nurturing very un-fatherlike thoughts. Noble benefactor or dirty old man? The receptionist probably having a laugh about it with her colleagues right now.

"Let's get room service," he says. Away from prying, judging eyes.

Or not.

The young bloke who brings in the trays of food gives Stuart a wink and offers to put the 'Do Not Disturb' sign on the door for them. Stuart summons up a disapproving grimace that fails to communicate anything other than smutty intent, judging by the thumbs-up it receives. He's despairing when Adelina produces a credit card and announces she wants to pay for the meal. Her treat. Stuart is about to explain the concept of the room tab, but she is insistent and anyway, he likes the way it establishes them as equals, challenging this moron's assumptions and bringing a welcome end to the nudge-nudge routine. So he lets it play out.

The food's pretty good, he opens a bottle of wine and starts to relax and enjoy himself again.

He reaches over to pour Adelina another glass of wine, but she places her hand over the glass, shakes her head and announces she's going to have a bath.

The bathroom door closes behind her.

Stuart lies back on his bed, turns on the TV, flicks through the channels and attempts to think about anything but…

"I think I will have that glass of wine after all," comes Adelina's disembodied voice from the bathroom.

Stuart pours the wine, his hand shaking.

"I'll leave it here for when you've finished," he calls out in a tremulous voice, placing the glass on the table by the bathroom door.

"In here, please."

"Oh." Pause. "Okay." He knocks on the door.

"Come in."

"I'm coming in now." He pushes open the door, walks straight to the sink, places the glass down clumsily on the counter, spills some, says "Damn", reaches down and grabs some toilet paper, mops up the spillage, deposits the wad of pink tissue in the toilet, flushes the toilet, turns and heads for the door, gaze anywhere but…

"Stuart?"

"Yes?"

"I can't reach if you leave it there. Over here, please."

"Right," he replies steadfastly, moving towards the glass before pausing again.

"It's okay. I have bubbles."

"Excellent." The word sounds stupid on its own, so he throws in some more for company. "Yes indeedy. Glass of red for the lady. Here we go. Lovely jubbly. Ah yes, bubbles. Lots of bubbles."

He's both relieved and disappointed to note that Adelina is fully covered from the tops of her shoulders downwards, save for a troublesome knee poking out.

"Thank you." Her words snapping him away from that isle of suggestion.

"No problem," he says and turns to leave. Her hand darts out and grabs him by the arm. They both look at it, then she lets go.

"I'm sorry," she says. "I've made you all wet."

"No problem." The vibrato back again.

"Stuart, would you soap me, please." And in the time it takes his mind to ponder the full implications and send his eyebrows skywards, Adelina has sat up and is offering him a bar of soap. He takes it, stares at the bubbles sliding down the slope of her breasts, looks at the soap, then back to her breasts, senses the dim and distant voice of his conscience shouting something, and…

They're about half an hour away from Wrexham when Adelina places her right hand on his left thigh, leans towards him and whispers in his ear.

"One more time?"

"Here?"

"No, not by road. I don't want people to see. Out of sight."

They soon spot a left-hand turn down little more than a track that promises privacy as it winds out of sight into a patch of forest. He turns off, guides the car between the potholes and ridges of dried mud and eventually they pull to a halt in a small clearing.

The next five minutes are a frantic and far-from-coordinated blur of hands and tongues and saliva and seat adjustments and fumbling with buttons and zips and elastic and hastily removed or manoeuvred articles of clothing and muttered swear words and panicked rummaging for a condom and ferocious ripping apart of the foil wrapper and too many slippery fingers rolling it on and Stuart trying to think of anything but this gorgeous, fragrant bundle of lithe curves and smooth flesh writhing in his hands and crouching above him as his scrambled brain seeks anti-coital imagery and he stiffens and strains and positively welcomes a sudden bout of cramp that she thinks is him coming too soon but is actually the one thing stopping that and he tells her what it is and buys himself a short intermission in which to edge back from the precipice only for her to halt that respite with a nibble of his earlobe and a breathy X-rated whispering in his ear that sees the lactic acid bid a hasty retreat from his calf as she slides him into her and sits up as much as the car roof will permit and squirms on his lap and he cedes to the inevitable and can feel that tidal wave begin to swell and then…

…everything erupts.

There's a brief period of utter disorientation as his brain attempts to reverse out of the one-way street of their climactic surge and comprehend the sudden commotion.

Adelina has collapsed against him, her hair in his mouth, her chest heaving against his. His hand has protectively reached up to cradle the back of her head. His ears are ringing from Adelina's scream and what he thinks, as he replays the last few seconds, may have been several almighty bangs that shook the car. His head is stinging from a clash of foreheads as she lunged forwards and there's a sharp pain where her fingernails have dug into his left shoulder. Something glints. There are crystals in her hair. No, not crystals. Glass. Then he sees the windscreen, or what remains of it: a warped mosaic punctured in a couple of places. An indistinguishable shadow moves in front of the car and he's about to call out when there's a rush of cool air and Adelina's body lurches with a squeal out of the now-open passenger door.

"What the…" Stuart mutters as he pulls himself into a sitting position and twists to look outside.

A half-naked Adelina is being dragged by her hair, screaming and fighting, to the far edge of the clearing. She loses her footing and falls to the ground, only to be yanked back up into a flailing stagger by the irresistible force that is Emil.

Stuart stumbles out of the car and summons up a "Hey."

Emil pushes Adelina to the ground and turns slowly to face Stuart with an air of extreme menace, only enhanced by the large wrench he's hefting in his left hand.

Stuart responds by sticking out his chest and chin, in bluffing contrast to the churning in his stomach and the shakiness consuming his legs. A waft of wind has him looking down to where his shrivelled and partially latex-coated penis dangles out of his open fly, like some depressed earthworm trying to shrug off a mac. Even now, as he messily unsheathes and hastily tucks himself away, his fragile male ego can't suppress a twinge of embarrassment.

Emil bends down and screams something in Polish into Adelina's ear, pointing at Stuart and laughing hysterically. In case the message is lost, he repeats in English for Stuart's benefit. "You fuck that?" Another contemptuous laugh. "Bitch," he adds and brings the wrench down on the back of her shoulder.

"No," Stuart screams.

"What? What you gonna do about it. Fuck me?" replies Emil, before landing another blow on Adelina's back.

Stuart instinctively takes a few steps forward. Emil straightens up again, throws away the wrench and reaches behind his back.

So incongruous is what he produces, that Stuart finds himself smiling.

A mistake, it appears.

"You think this funny?"

"No. Of course not. It's just… hey, come on. What are you doing with that?"

"Making you shut the fuck up is what. Now sit down." Stuart sits down. "This the man you are?"

"Actually no, it isn't," Stuart answers, truthfully.

"No wonder your wife leave you. Maybe when this done, I go fuck her. Not in a car like this. Maybe in your bed. Then I go find that boy of yours and I fuck him up."

That snaps Stuart out of his self-pity and clears his brain to start working more logically again. But it also gives him away.

"Ah, you not like that? You fuck my wife. I fuck yours. And your boy. Fair, no?"

"No," answers Stuart with a forcefulness at odds with the utter helplessness of his situation. "I didn't know she was married," is the best he can muster.

"You knew today, though. No? And it did not stop you."

A valid point, but Stuart needs to maintain eye contact and keep him talking and distracted because in his peripheral vision he can sense the crumpled heap behind Emil that is Adelina flinch and slowly uncurl. He so wants to look, but he can't or all will be lost. "When I met her, I mean. I really didn't know. I wasn't looking for anything. Nothing happened before you arrived, I promise. In fact, nothing happened before last… before today. Look, I don't know what your history is together, but all I saw was this scared woman, scared of you, and I just wanted to help and I thought that maybe if she could get away somewhere and start afresh that…"

And as the bullshit flows, Adelina rises shakily to her feet and sends the wrench in her hand arcing through the air and crashing into the side of Emil's head. He staggers, goes down on one knee, puts his left hand to his head, brings it round and stares uncomprehendingly at the blood-smeared fingers. The sight appears to jolt him out of his daze and Stuart realises, all too late, that he's down but most definitely not out, and that a window of opportunity has been allowed to close unutilised. Adelina too has hesitated, but now comes in for a second attack. Her arm bends back but before she can bring it down there's a deafening crack and a red rose sprouts on her chest. She takes two steps back, then goes down like a felled tree. Her body jerks hideously several times. And then is still.

Stuart can't move. He just sits and stares at Adelina's body, hoping she'll sit up and then this won't have happened. He feels cold and light-headed and nauseous. His throat is dry.

Emil has fallen back onto the ground, but now reacts first. Groaning with each movement, he turns onto his side and then his front; his laboured progress drawing Stuart's gaze away from Adelina. In time to see a still-drowsy Emil effortfully focusing on a right hand no longer in possession of the gun.

Then the sparks start to fly between recovering synapses and the thought process quickens.

The gun?

Emil looks around and sees it lying on the ground between them.

His eyes flicker up and meet Stuart's.

For the briefest of moments, they hold each other's gaze and both know what the other is thinking.

They also both know who will win, so much greater is the distance Stuart has to cover.

Stuart feels his shoulders slump, conceding defeat.

Emil can't suppress a smile, his complacency opening the door a fraction.

Stuart propels himself off the ground and into a run.

Emil gets hold of the gun but fumbles as he turns it in his hands. Stuart arrives just in time and delivers a drop kick that sends the gun spiralling into the undergrowth.

Clutching his wrist, Emil starts to get to his feet and Stuart knows this isn't over. He bends down and picks up the wrench. Emil charges at him and Stuart brings the wrench down as hard as he can on his head. Then the red mist descends and Stuart rains blow after blow on the body now lying at his feet.

When he no longer possesses the strength to raise his arm, he staggers back, falls to his knees and surveys his handiwork with numbed dispassion. Then feels the warm and sticky wetness of the wrench in his hand; and vomits; the spasms gripping his chest until he falls on his side and curls into himself.

Then the tears come.

What the fuck?

Stuart sits with his legs pulled up, chin resting on his knees. Once more he crunches his eyes shut, breathes in and out deeply and then opens his eyes again… only to find the same scene of carnage before him. The two battered and bloodied bodies haven't moved; won't move; however much he might will one of them to.

He's lost track of time, but it must have been a while judging by the stiffness in his knees and back as he gets to his feet and walks over to check for pulses.

Corpses, both of them.

He screams.

Lets it all out.

"Why can't anything be fucking simple?" he asks the assembled dead, but he's on his own now, with nothing but the tattered remnants of plans for company; those best laid plans that have for so long been his salvation.

His cherished companions, gone.

And with it, all purpose.

Not quite.

He wanders across to the side of the clearing and searches through the undergrowth. It doesn't take long to find what he's after. He walks back and kneels by Adelina's body. He leans over, tenderly pushes her matted hair back and kisses her on the forehead.

Then he brings the gun up, digs it into his temple, squeezes his eyes shut and pulls the trigger.

"Mind if I sit here?"

Shit. Where did he come from? The inner disquiet

manifests itself in a mumble. Pete prods half a sausage with his fork, nudging it through a grease-slicked orange puddle and up against a coiled heap of discarded bacon rind.

"I know they say revenge is a dish best served cold, but you didn't have to actually eat it."

The corners of his mouth twitch, but Pete catches himself. "I don't know what you mean."

"Course not. Silly me." Ron takes a seat and rests his forearms on the table, palms flat down.

A silence ensues as Pete counteracts the urge to resume his gloating contemplation – needing to confirm for himself what he'd caught on a TV local news bulletin – and stares down at the congealed remains of his cooked breakfast; a guilty and celebratory pleasure very much at odds with the rest of his diet. He eventually glances up and into eyes that flit to their right, dragging his gaze back to what he's come here to relish.

"So, what do you make of that, then?" asks this intruder in his reverie.

"What?"

"Oh, let's see. Could it be that red car parked over there? The closing-down sale at the furniture shop? An interesting cloud formation? Or maybe, just maybe, I mean that blackened and still smouldering heap of rubble across the way there. What do you reckon? Or hadn't you noticed?"

"I reckon someone's in for a big insurance payout," Pete posits, nowhere left to go but to attack.

"An enlightening observation, Peter."

"Don't use my name. We don't know each other."

"Cut the crap, son. And maybe then we can have a long-overdue adult conversation, don't you think?" Pete grunts. "I have to ask. Just between you and me, like. That your handiwork over there?"

Pete follows the nod and the implication hits him hard. "*No!*" he near shouts.

"But you're not unhappy about it?"

"No."

"In fact, you're fucking elated, aren't you?"

"Let's just say I'm amused."

"Amused? There's an interesting choice of word. Very interesting. Sharon, love. Couple of teas over here, please, and my usual."

"No, I need to…"

"Come on. Spare me a few minutes. And if nothing else, you can admire the view. It's what you came for, after all."

Pete sinks back into his chair. They share an awkward silence, a confrontation in itself. And one that, annoyingly, he feels he's losing. He offers a weak smile as two mugs and a plate of buttered toast are deposited on the table. Tells himself to be strong.

"My dear departed father opened that shop in 1962, a year after the government first legalised betting shops," Ron starts, heaping sugar into his tea. "It was his life. Been mine as well. I've been working there in one capacity or another since I was thirteen. Never been easy, whatever people say about bookies raking it in, particularly in the last ten or so years. The big boys make it bloody hard with their non-stop marketing and shops full of all mod cons. The independents just can't compete with that. Forced me to keep it old school. If you can't beat 'em, be as different as possible from 'em." Pete gives him his unimpressed look and pretends to suppress a yawn. "Boring you, am I? The real hard man. No sympathy coming my way, I see. Though what about the locals who spend their afternoons having a punt and a spot of banter in the warm? What about the links we have with other local businesses? The sponsorship and charity work we're involved in? And what about the members of staff who no longer have a job? In particular, what about your mate Kevin? What do you reckon he'd make of that smug grin on your face?"

"Kev will be all right. He can do better than a pisspot local bookies. The bloke's a maths genius. Maybe this is just the kick up the arse he needs. We all know he's wasted with some underpaying bully."

"That'd be me, I guess."

"That'd be you," says Pete, warming to the task in hand.

"And what about you?"

"Me?"

"Yeah. What'll you do with yourself, now that your little crusade is at an end?"

"Wha..." The question dies in his throat as the realisation of his own transparency hits home and throws him off balance.

"How did I know? You think you're that fucking clever? I've been on to you from day one, son. So, what next for Hertfordshire's own Robin Hood? How you going to fill your time now?"

"I'll be fine," fights back Pete, struggling to recover lost ground. "This was one mug you couldn't beat. I ended up nicely ahead and I'll let you off the rest. It's enough to know you've lost. I'd call that a victory."

"Better men than me would be tempted to knock that smirk off your face."

Pete tries to turn a reactive leaning back out of reach into a casual stretch, reaching his hands behind his head, only for a flex of Ron's jaw and shoulders to see them whip back down across his exposed stomach.

Ron smiles. "Don't worry, lad. I've far too much respect for your parents to stoop that low."

"My *parents*? How dare you. *Respect?* After what you did?" spits out Pete, now gripping the edge of the table.

"And what is it you think I did?"

"There's no think about it. I was there, remember. I saw it all."

"You saw what you saw, but that doesn't mean you know everything."

"Fuck you. Telling me I don't know."

"Peter, sit down."

"I don't need this shit."

"And I do? *Sit.*" His voice raised for the first time, and enough to halt Pete's intended exit. "Take a look out there, big man. Take a good look. That's my bloody shop smoking away. My livelihood. The business my dad built from scratch. And from where I'm standing, there's one bloke very much in the frame. Maybe I should give the Old Bill a call. Ask them to pop over and give 'em a recap of our little conversation. Maybe tell them how fucking deee-lighted you are. How much you hate me. What do you reckon? Sound like a plan? Or do you think maybe we could sit down like adults and have a frank and equal exchange of views."

Pete can appreciate a certain logic to sitting down, so he does; effecting as much nonchalance as his churning interior permits.

"Now then, why don't we start with the gospel according to Peter, seeing as how you're the fucking expert and all that?"

"You know full well what you did." His voice modulating as thoughts and emotions clatter against each other. "You knew full well he had a gambling problem and yet you kept taking those bets. He worked forty years for a bloody carriage clock, a shit pension and ten grand of savings that you took off him pound by fucking pound. You left him with nothing. No money. No self-esteem. Nothing. He died a broken man and it sure as hell finished off Mum. Drove her to drink and…

well, we know where that sent her. So yes, I do blame you, for everything. For reducing my dad to the pathetic specimen he was when he keeled over. For taking every drop of dignity they ever had. For making my mum an alcoholic. For ruining my childhood, while you lord it over your little empire, ripping off Kevin, who's worth ten of you by the way, and I am so fucking pleased you've crashed and burned. Literally, eh? And I'm going to sit here all day and I'm going to have a big fat smile on my face. That clear enough for you?"

Ron's tongue pushes at the inside of his lips. He stares out of the window, his gaze following the wisps of smoke dissipating above the rooftops.

"You done?" he asks, eventually.

"I think I just about covered everything. Unless you want more, that is, because…"

"Enough."

"Enough? You can give it but you can't take it. Is that it? Unless it's money, of course. You can take that all bloody day, can't you? And who cares where it comes from, as long as it's in your bank account."

"I met your dad…"

"Don't you dare. You were a parasite and you sucked him dry. You were never anything but that. So don't…"

"*Enough*, I said. You've had your say. Made yourself very clear. But I said an exchange of views, not a fucking monologue. And I've sat here and taken my medicine. Now please return the compliment and suspend the vitriol for a few minutes. Okay?" Pete can't bring himself to nod as he endeavours to keep down the magma of suppressed emotion, so his head just vibrates. "I'll take that as a yes. Right. My turn. You've based your life around a set of facts that paint you as the victim and me as the villain. It leaves your parents blameless, excuses their weaknesses and then justifies this crusade of yours.

Well, let me give you another side of the story, shall I?"

"*Story*. You make it sound like something I made up. I lived that *story*, as you call it."

"I know that."

"Really?"

"If you'd shut up and listen, maybe you'd find out. Five minutes. That's all I ask. Then you can walk out of here and go and dance around in the ashes for all I care."

It's a fair offer. "Five minutes."

"Right. Thank you."

"Four minutes and fifty-five seconds."

"Listen to yourself. All this self-pitying crap. You're not interested in the truth. The truth scares you shitless. You'd rather wallow in being *poor old Pete* who the world's shat upon, *poor old Pete* with the dead dad and the alcoholic mum and the bum deal. On his mission. How's that bird of yours Kevin's been telling me about? She seen this side to you?"

"She'll understand."

"Ah, the future tense."

"When she knows the full facts."

"Which you don't have." Pete flounders for a response.

"And how would she feel watching your gloating performance today? That the kind of guy she's going to want to spend more time with? Or do you think maybe she might start wondering where all that hate and bitterness you've stored up is going to be directed now your pet hate is vanquished. Because it won't just go away, you know. And it's going to poison you and every relationship you ever have. But hey, what do I know? If it was me on fire over there, you wouldn't even cross the road to piss on me. So have a lovely and very lonely life, young man, you and that cancerous growth of yours. And good luck finding the next person to blame. Keep the change. Add it to the plus column."

A five-pound note flutters down onto the table as the door bangs shut.

Pete is aware that all eyes are on him. Heat prickles his face and he wants nothing more than to escape. But male pride demands he put on a show of casual indifference – a farce of lip wriggles, neck stretches and forensic inspections of fingernails; even a silent whistle – before sloping off into the comparative freshness of the smoke-imbued street.

It's only as he walks away that an internal switch flicks and a circuit is completed, as he recalls a brief late-night conversation with Andrew; and succumbs to a cold surge of dread.

*

They spend an idle hour or so wandering round Dolgellau; conversation stilted, Emma pensive and distracted. He's about to suggest they go for a coffee, when Emma abruptly announces "Time to go."

"Where to?"

"Last-chance saloon."

Emma parks up in the same place as the previous day.

"I see what you meant now," offers Carl, if only to break the silence.

"What?"

"The last-chance saloon. Clever, though technically it's a bit late for them."

"It's not them I was referring to. Come on." And reaching round to grab a bag from the rear seat, she opens her door and climbs out.

He follows orders and traipses after Emma as she strides towards the ruin of what he now realises must have once been a chapel or tiny church.

They make their way through gaps in walls and enter the small graveyard. This time she walks up the slope to the top, crouches down by the dry-stone wall and prods at the grass in a patch of dappled sunlight.

"This will do," she announces, and starts to rummage around in her bag. "Take a seat. The ground's dry."

"Picnic?"

"More of a last supper. Here, take this." She hands him an iPod and a set of headphones. "I don't want any smart-arse comments. I just want you to do one thing for me. Sit down there with your back against the wall." He does. "Get yourself comfortable." He shifts around. "I'm going to leave you here for a while. What I need you to do is put these headphones on and press *play*. You don't get up. You don't look at the track listing. You don't skip anything. You just sit here and you listen. Can you do that for me?"

"Emma…"

"*Promise me.*"

"I promise."

"Good. I'll be back when it's finished. Just press *play*."

He does so, and as Emma heads down the slope and out of sight, a low drum roll and a short burst of woodwind herald the mournful sound of a violin that soars, is briefly joined by the orchestra, and then soars again. There's something about the music that tugs at him, brings goosebumps to his skin; or maybe it's just the gentle breeze. He can feel himself relax, and for the first time looks up and properly takes in his surroundings. The sweep of Cadair Idris to his right, set against the vivid blue of the sky; the rest of his panoramic view a spread of distant hilltops and the rippling green of trees bathed in sunshine. Not a person or car or building in sight. A wave of tranquility washes over him. Thinks he may have heard this before. Can't quite place it. Then gets a flashback.

Standing in a doorway looking into a room lit only by a desk lamp, saying goodnight to Dad, who is sitting at his desk in front of a computer screen. He turns, his face tired but content, and asks for a hug. Carl runs over to him and they embrace. Carl asks him what he's doing and Dad says he's just playing with words. Carl asks if he can read it. Dad says one day, maybe, but not now. It's late and time for bed.

Carl smiles to himself and rubs at his eyes with the back of his index fingers.

The violin piece ends and another track starts. This time some opera. A male duet. It's a nice piece he doesn't know. More than nice. As the singing builds and dies and then builds again, he closes his eyes and as he does so, can feel an unsettling internal shifting tugging him out of kilter. Bloody hangover, he thinks.

He recognises the next song, with its simple guitar refrain and spare, imploring lyrics repeated time and again. Now he knows why he's here. What this is. The song escalates and Carl can feel a slight pressure starting to accumulate behind his eyes and in his temples.

It's released when the opening guitar riff kicks in on the next track, one Carl loves, and he nods away as it implores him to *remember me;* although the lyrics exert a melancholic tug he's not experienced before.

A voice comes in. A Welsh lilt that is faintly familiar. Words he hasn't heard for ages. *The House at Pooh Corner.* Transporting him back to bedtimes many years ago; when his dad was alive; when they were a family.

The reader pauses for a loud sniff, before ploughing on, and it suddenly hits Carl that it's his grandfather reading. Questions clamour for answers; the incongruity of these words from that mouth; the emotional wavering in a voice he'd always recalled as strident and strong. The memories of those many times having them read to him. Then come the final words and the effect on Carl is profound and emotionally debilitating. That pressure is rising. He swipes at his eyes and cheeks, seeking refuge from an onslaught of emotions. What he could really do with is something bland and innocuous. A refuge.

What he gets is Portishead and 'The Road', a song of utter desolation; Beth Orton's plaintive voice, haunting and melancholic, swirling around him suffocatingly.

Pulling him under.

He's momentarily reprieved by the familiarity of the next track. A hymn: *Lord of All Hopefulness*. Sung by a Welsh male-voice choir. Carl finds himself abstractedly mouthing some of the words, unsure of where he's dredged them up from, but in doing so having to face up to their heft.

And there's that pressure again. He pushes his thumbs into his temples to try and suppress it, but it seems to be spreading down the back of his throat. He grits his teeth and resolves not to give in. But he's wavering and is mightily relieved when the hymn finishes.

As the next track gets under way, it appears that at least there are no words in this one to taunt him. Just plenty of strings instead. Cellos? There's a rock sensibility he latches onto. Nothing too much about this to loosen his faltering grip on equanimity.

But as the tune builds, and the cellos drive it on, so does that pressure in his head and that stinging in his eyes and there's a burning constriction in his throat and a churning in his gut. And still the music continues to swell, coming at him on ever heightening surges, battering away at his flimsy fortifications. And this time he is definitely not in control. There are forces that will have their say. And suddenly he feels something rip deep inside and whatever barricades his psyche has constructed are breached and he surrenders to a flood of naked emotion that sends tears running down his cheeks. He leans forward and hugs his sides as his whole torso convulses with wave upon wave of sobs as the anger and the sadness and the regret and the impotence and the love and the loss overwhelm him. And he has no choice but to let all that poison out.

And as this disintegration consumes him, he is dimly aware of movement to his right. A hand on his shoulder. He needs contact and he needs to be held and he keels over and feels arms around him, holding him tight and secure, and he clings to this rock in the storm that threatens to engulf him because if he doesn't he knows he's going to be swept away, and somewhere in all this turmoil he can dimly hear a voice telling him that "it's okay", and even though it doesn't feel like it can ever be, there's something in her tone that persuades him that it just might be; that he can be like this and it will still be fine; that he can survive in one piece. The sobs start to intensify once more, resonating through his body.

*

Pete finally gets an answer early in the afternoon.

"At last. I've been ringing all day. Why can't you carry round a mobile like everyone else? Where you been?"

"School reunion."

"What?"

"The new me. Or should I say the new unemployed me."

"You've heard then."

"That's where I've been since I got back."

"How are you feeling?"

"Cut the fake empathy. Ron said you'd popped by earlier to pay your respects."

"I just… fair comment. But it was never you I had it in for."

"That's all right, then. Careful though, or I'll start to think you had something to do with it."

"*What*? No. How could you think that? I didn't... of course not... not directly, anyway... though maybe indirectly... or something... oh, I don't know."

"That's all clear then."

"Look, I wanted it. Okay, I'm not denying that. But I'd never actually do anything like that. You know that."

"Good to hear."

"But..."

"Go on."

"I may have wished for it."

"Pete, what *are* you going on about?"

"You remember Andrew kept asking us what we'd want if we didn't have to keep to all those rules. You know, who we'd most like to stuff it to? And none of us ever said anything. Well, I stayed behind one Monday after poker and we had a little chat."

"What kind of chat?"

"Things."

"You'll have to be a bit more specific."

"I told him. You know. About Ron and my dad and what he did to him and how it led to my mum... you know..."

"Yes, Pete. Everyone knows. But it's a bit of a leap to get from that to full-blown arson."

"It's not just that."

"Go on."

"I... I told him about Ron not having insurance."

"You *what*? I told you that in confidence."

"I know. But I thought it was just a bit of harmless fantasy. You know, a *what if* type thing. I'd won the poker that night and was on a bit of a high. It was just a bit of a laugh."

"And what could be funnier than burning down a

building, maybe with a few people inside. Put a bloke out of business. Hilarious."

"There wasn't anyone inside," says Pete, just about making a panicked question sound like a statement.

"That's not the point."

"Look," Pete replies, pausing to recover. "I'm just saying it's a bit of a coincidence, don't you think? I mention it and then hey presto, it happens?" He waits for an answer, but there's only silence. "Kevin? You still there?"

"Have you spoken to Andrew about it?"

"That's the odd thing. I went to the club this afternoon. He's normally in on Sundays, but he wasn't there. Some other bloke was, counting stock. *For the new owner,* he said."

"What?"

"That's what I said. But he just said he wasn't permitted to disclose that sort of confidential information."

"Maybe we should drop round and see him at home."

"Tried that already. *For Let* sign up and when I looked through the windows, it was empty. What do you think's happening?"

"Christ knows."

The line goes quiet.

"Kev?"

"Sorry, I just thought of something."

"What?"

"It's nothing, probably. I need to check something. Come over to my place in an hour's time."

Pete's response drowns in the disconnected tone.

*

"Come on in," says Kevin, waving Pete in through the door.

"Why did it need me to…? What the hell's he doing here?" He turns to walk back out, but the door is closed and Kevin is leaning against it.

"I asked him here," Kevin says with an atypical assurance that cows any contradictory response.

"Thanks, *mate*."

"A pleasure. But I've listened to and watched the way you carry on for years now and I'm sick of it. We all are. So as your friend, it finishes now. I'm going to take a book and sit on the stairs outside that door and I don't want to see either of you until you've sorted out this shit."

Speech over, he departs.

"Who the hell was that?" asks Pete, as the front door closes.

Ron smiles. "I hardly recognise him. It's either an alien invasion or there's a girl involved somewhere."

"A girl? Kevin?"

"Why not? They say there's someone for everyone" – the slightest of pauses – "and Kevin's better than most."

"I know, but…" He fades into silence.

It's Ron who fills it.

"Funny how things aren't always what they seem."

"Yeah," says Pete, still coming to terms with Kev and a girl in the same sentence.

"Like me and your parents, for example. Now hear me out. If nothing else, tell yourself you're doing it for Kevin." Pete pouts, folds his arms and begrudgingly nods at Ron to continue.

"Strange as it may sound, given what you'd like to do to me, if it wasn't for your dad, I wouldn't be here today. I was a bit of a lad in my twenties. My father still ran things at the bookies and I always had a few quid in my pocket. A lot of the blokes from the factory used to come into the shop and I got to knowing a few of them. We used to meet up for snooker on Thursdays and then in the local pubs on Friday and Saturday nights. Your dad often tagged along, though he was a bit older than most of us; a kind of older brother really, always at the edge looking in, if you know what I mean. Anyway, I liked a drink back then. More than liked. I had a bit of a problem. A lot of a problem. Once I started, I couldn't stop, and I used to end up shooting my mouth off and more often than not I'd end up in a scrap. Got barred from a few places and it was a miracle I didn't get into serious trouble. And that miracle was your dad.

"There was this one time when I'd had a few, as per usual, and I got lippy with a few squaddies from the NATO base. They weren't in uniform, so I didn't know that's what they were, but there you go, everyone else did and tried to shut me up, but I had to have my say. The booze did that to me. I was a decent pool player, even after a skinful, but just winning was never enough, nor taking their money. I had to give it the big verbals as well; rub their faces in it. Three of them jumped me in the car park and started laying into me pretty bad. I don't know how he did it, let alone why, as God knows I probably deserved a kicking, but your dad put himself in the firing line, took a few hits himself but kept on trying to get them to stop until they pulled back and cleared off. Then he called me a taxi. I was all for buggering off home, but something about me got him concerned and just as we were about to leave, he jumped in and told the driver to take me straight to the hospital. Bloody good job he did. Turned out I'd ruptured my spleen. If I'd keeled over and passed out at home later on, I'd have been a goner. Like I said, he saved my life that night.

"And that wasn't all. He came to visit me in hospital the next day and I hadn't even got a 'thank you' out before he gave it to me straight. An intervention, I reckon you'd call it. Told me what a bloody idiot I was being and how the first step was me admitting I had a problem with the booze. I didn't like that one bit, but he was right of course. I just didn't want to see it. Called him all the names under the sun, but he kept coming back until I agreed I'd go to an AA meeting. I was just saying it to get him off my back. But he only went and picked me up and drove me there and sat outside the whole time to make sure that even if I didn't want to be there, I was. I sat through those first few meetings with a sneer on my face, listening to the others whine on and thinking I was better than them. But eventually it hit home, and I haven't touched a drop since. The girls weren't as pretty, I didn't feel as irresistible and the jokes were never as funny in the pub, but the tongue stopped getting me into trouble, I buckled down at the shop and my life started making a bit more sense.

"Anyways, your mum. How did she fit into all this? Like I said, there was this local social scene going on and she used to be part of that. She liked to have a good time and went out with a few of the lads, though never for that long. She disappeared for a while – no idea where – but then came back and things carried on much as before. A few got married, sometimes within the group, sometimes outside, and didn't make it out quite as often, but we all kept in touch. Something happened to your mum at her work. I never found out the full details but I think she made some kind of claim against her employer and it ended up at a tribunal. Way I heard it, everyone knew she had a case, but the employer wouldn't admit it and chucked a load of crap back at her, raking up all kinds of stuff about her private life and childhood and making her out to be some kind of nutcase. She lost the case and it almost finished her. She was never the same as before. Like she was damaged goods. If I'm honest, the rest of us kept our distance a bit, but your dad saw something and stepped in. He was probably just what she needed: someone reliable and dependable who wouldn't let her down or be scared away by what she'd been through. I'm not saying they didn't love each other or anything – they did – but it felt more like a father and daughter thing. Don't look at me like that, there's plenty of relationships like that around; both getting something they need from the other, something they maybe haven't had enough of in the past. And there was always something of the Good Samaritan about your dad. She'd had the stuffing knocked out of her by that tribunal thing and despite the age gap, your dad was the best thing that could have happened to her at the time. Then they got married, which surprised us all, and you came along.

"I didn't see much of your parents for a while, until your dad came into the shop and asked to have a word. My father had passed away by then, so I was the boss and doing very nicely for myself. No such thing as a poor bookmaker, they say, and it was certainly true then, though those days are long gone what with the offshore, online firms grabbing most of the business and the exchanges setting punters off against each other while taking a cut without ever even having to take a stance themselves. Spineless chances. Sorry, I'm digressing. Bit of a hobby horse of mine. Not that you care, and I'm not after anyone's sympathy, especially yours. Where was I? Oh yeah, your dad coming in that day."

This time the delay is more marked, and Ron's gaze is inward. Pete knows this is where they head off-piste; and wonders if his much-nurtured resentment will survive the unchartered terrain.

"He wanted to talk about your mother."

"Go on," says Pete, sensing he needs to give the go-ahead.

"She was the gambler. It was never your dad."

"Bollocks. I was there."

"I know that, lad, but hear me out. As I tried to tell

you yesterday, you saw what you saw, but that doesn't mean it's how it was. And you said you'd hear me out. Right?" Pete grunts. "He told me it was as if she was switched to self-destruct mode. She'd always liked a flutter, but it hadn't been a problem the first few years, when she'd got pregnant and was the centre of attention, and then you were born and she had her hands full. The problem came when you went off to school and she had some time to herself, and I guess the inner demons came calling. I hate to think what she'd have got up to had it been like now, when you can piss away fortunes on the lottery or online without ever having to get off your sofa, while convincing yourself it's charity or sociable or just a bit of fun. But back then it was different. Unless you had a phone account and a credit line or a runner, it was walking into a betting shop or no bet. And your mum was old school. She wanted to bet real bad, but she wouldn't be seen dead in a betting shop. Women just didn't do that and no one she knew was going to see her in one. Something to do with shame. You can shake your head, and I don't blame you. That's exactly how I used to think back then. But I was wrong.

"I didn't get it until I read this book a while ago. Yeah, I know, me and a book. Surprise, surprise. There was this woman in it who'd been an SS guard in a concentration camp during the war and been involved in some horrendous stuff. She'd been made to pick prisoners to be sent to the gas chamber and this one time had to transport a load of prisoners with some other guards. They'd locked them in a church overnight and the church caught fire by accident and a load of prisoners died because the guards chose not to unlock the doors, rather than face the repercussions from the serious nutcases at the top if they let even one of them escape. Then years later, a survivor brings a law case against the guards and a Germany that didn't want to look in the mirror and ask some uncomfortable questions of itself can't wait to stick them in the dock and pour all that venom on them. Like they were from a completely different country or something. And there's this written report by the guards to their bosses that explains what happened and the court has it, and the other guards gang up to say that it was this one woman who'd written it and how that proved it was her who'd taken the lead and made the decision not to unlock the door. Anyway, it couldn't have been her, because she couldn't read or write. But rather than admit that to the court, this woman said nothing and just took the shit and she gets life, while the others get just a few years. And when we discussed the book – look, you got me: it was at a poxy book club, right; yeah, I know, but you can end up doing some weird shit when there's a woman involved – and we were discussing this book and I thought this was my big chance to look all literary and clever and stuff, so I launched off on one, giving it all that about how I didn't believe in the character – like I was Melvyn fucking Bragg or something – and why the hell didn't she just tell the court she couldn't read or write and how it made no sense and was one huge gaping plot hole; like I'd just solved some great mystery. I was sitting back enjoying the nods of approval when this quiet woman pipes up and suggests, in that way clever people do when they already know the answer but don't want to rub your nose in it, but which still leaves you feeling stupid, that wasn't it all about the shame she felt at who she was and how that was so fundamental and to her core that she'd rather take the full hit of the court than face up to that shame, and through that, what she'd been part of. Or something like that. She put it a whole lot better and all I can remember thinking was what did it say about me that the one I fancied was the one who said that Harry Potter was her favourite book. But that other woman had a point there and the more I thought about it, the more I got it.

"And what I'm trying to say is that your mum couldn't go into a betting shop because that would mean facing up to a whole load of shit. It was like a finger in the dyke – there's a joke in there somewhere; shut up, Ron – keeping all that shit from pouring out. I don't know what that stuff was, though I heard rumours. Some serious shit may have been done to her when she was a kid and we never got to the bottom of those years she went missing. But rather than face up to it, she gambled. And she didn't need to go in any betting shops because she had a runner. She had your dad. I don't know how much he knew when he married her, but knowing him I'm guessing that if he did, he believed he'd be able to keep the demons at bay. But shit like that never goes away. It just festers and eventually it comes to the surface. Always does. And when it did, he had a choice: he could walk away or he could challenge her on it. But he was no quitter and no shrink so, rightly or wrongly, he decided to try and manage the situation. Looking back, maybe he should have walked. It might have worked out better for everyone. But he was a good man and he meant well. He loved your mum, and he loved you too much to give up.

"Problem with an addiction is that it's like an itch. There's this brief moment of bliss when you scratch it, even though you know it's going to come back and you can see your skin is getting red and sore. And in that moment of bliss, you don't think any more long term than the second you're inhabiting at the time. I know. I've been there. And what I'm just trying to explain is that no one's blaming your mum here, because she was the victim, not the cause. Problem was, there was never any telling her. She wouldn't listen. It was always about damage limitation with her. And you had to be sneaky. She couldn't be in on anything or it was bound to fail. You had to tiptoe around and let her think she was always in control. To begin with, anyway. That was why your dad came to me. If he couldn't stop it, the least he could do was keep it in the family, so to speak. If the money had to go to a bookie, it might as well have been me."

"Very noble of you, I'm sure. Do you want a pat on the back?"

"Hear me out."

"I saw."

"I'm not disputing that, but you don't know what happened after your dad came in the shop."

"You took their money, that's what."

"Are you going to let me finish?" Pete can't bear to cede anything, so the most he can offer is a petulant shrug of his shoulders. "The stuff you saw was a charade designed to keep you away from the reality your dad was living every day. Make it into a game for you; a bit of fun. Your dad's harmless little hobby rather than your mum's nasty big addiction. I doubt she even got any enjoyment out of what she was doing. She certainly wasn't any good at it. No love for the game. It was just a means to an end, and that end was the hit she needed. So apart from keeping you ignorant, he needed a plan, and that was where I came in. It was kind of neat, really. Your dad would come along with your mum's bets on a bit of paper and I'd sit on them. If they won, I paid out – had to or she'd have known – and if they didn't, as was usually the case, who knew? Meanwhile, your dad was depositing bits and pieces of money with me, roughly in line with the losing bets; getting it out of harm's way. His biggest fear was what would happen if he wasn't around to keep a lid on things, and worst of all, the house was in her name. He was beside himself with worry, so I had a word with a lawyer pal of mine and he came up with the idea of the loan. I loaned your parents ten grand, which was a lot of money in those days, and of course most of it ended up being deposited back in the bank of Ron. Just in case, we put a legal agreement in place that whacked a load of interest on the loan and secured it against the house. Your mum didn't bother reading anything before she signed. All she saw was the next big fix coming her way. Good job we did really, because after your dad died, she just went to pieces, as you know better than anyone. I had to cut off her supply and when she couldn't bet, something else had to fill the void, so she went the way of her dad, from what I heard, and hit the booze.

"Believe me, I wanted to explain things to you. Let you know why things had to be as they were. But you were still just a kid, for Christ's sake. I just kept to the plan, exactly as I promised your dad, and if that made me public enemy number one as far as you were concerned, so be it. I've got broad shoulders. Doesn't mean I didn't come close to saying *fuck this* a few times, but I owed him. Don't for one moment think I enjoyed patting you on the head that one time and telling you politely to fuck off. But what else could I do? And then your dad died, and I was powerless to do anything. I couldn't step in and take over. You had family to do that. And who the hell was I? What would you have said if I'd turned up one day and said to come with me? No, all I could do was sit back and keep to the plan, even if it meant being the villain of the piece; the evil bookie who ripped your parents off, took their house off them and turfed a poor widow onto the street."

"You played that part pretty well," says Pete. "You took the lot. She had nothing when he died. No house. No money. If what you say is true, you were meant to be looking after her. It was her money, not yours."

"And what would she have done with it?"

"I don't know. Maybe she *would* have blown the lot. But that was her choice to make, not yours."

"You're living in cloud cuckoo land, son. She needed protecting from herself. I'm not judging her there, just saying it how it was. Much as you might want to paint it different, with all due respect, you didn't see half of the shit that was going on; what she did to herself; to your dad; what he had to put up with."

He runs out of steam. Knows what's coming.

The big unspoken question: where did all the money go? Knows Pete badly wants to ask, but also knows that Pete fears the answer.

But credit to the lad. He asks anyway.

"Where's the money, then?"

"You're living in most of it."

"*What?*"

"Come on. Where did you think it came from?"

"The trust fund."

"And what trust fund might that be?"

"Uncle Ern… oh shit."

"Yep."

"Please… no."

"Say hello to Uncle Ernie."

"You're kidding."

"You seriously saying you hadn't twigged."

"No."

"You'd rather believe in some mysterious, but totally unfeasible, benefactor than stop just for one second and see a side to things that wasn't based entirely on my being a complete and utter bastard."

"You could have told me ages ago."

"I shouldn't be telling you now. I promised I wouldn't. Your dad worried about some of Uncle Ernest's greedier relations coming sniffing around. This was his gift to you, not them."

"What about the monthly standing order?"

"What do *you* think? Me and my offshore friends."

"Shit."

"Well, thanks to you and all."

"I don't get it. Their house wasn't worth that much."

"Nice try, but you're not going to get figures out of me. There's a whole lot more you don't know about and never will. Whatever you may think of me, I'm not a complete mug. Nor was your dad. That's all I'm going to say."

But Pete has drifted into a world of inner contemplation.

Of redefinition.

Losing his grip on all that righteous indignation.

In need of breathing space.

"Can you leave now?"

"Look, Peter…"

"*Can… you… just… please… go… now.*" No longer a question.

Ron does as requested, giving Kevin a resigned shrug as he passes him in the corridor.

Peter rises unsteadily to his feet, cricks his neck as if it's some inner reset mechanism and stares out of the window as Ron gets in his car and heads off.

Kevin comes back into the room and silently takes a seat on the sofa.

"So how much of that did you already know?" asks Pete.

"None of the detail. Just that he wasn't the total wanker you thought he was."

"And you didn't say anything?"

"Like you'd have listened."

"I might have."

"Yeah, right."

"Feels like you sided with him."

"Grow up, Pete. That business was his life. It's been part of this community for well over forty years. He took it over from his dad. How's it going to feel for Ron to see it burnt to the ground on his watch. Then you turn up to gloat. Most people would have punched your lights out or had you down the police station, yet here you are, still expecting everyone to feel sorry for you."

"Still?"

"Come on, Pete, wake up and smell the coffee. You've been lapping it up for years now. It's been your poison of choice ever since I met you. But we all got bored of listening years ago."

"Thanks." His voice betraying the hurt.

"Hardly your finest hour, was it? Laughing about having no insurance?" Each question further dismantling Pete's bravado. "Wishing you'd been more careful about what you wished for?"

"I could be fucked here, couldn't I? I mean Ron's going to be totally out of pocket and if he thinks I know who might have done it… *shit…*"

"Which all makes it a bit of a relief that the bloody thing *was* insured."

"*What?*"

"Always has been."

"But…"

"Like I said. He's got an image to maintain: the impoverished bookie cutting corners to get by was good for business. I even believed it to begin with. He didn't so much tell anyone as let the rumours keep circulating. You know what punters are like; all those gaps between races to fill. Ron may be many things, but he's no idiot. Doesn't do anything without a reason."

"That's something, at least," says Pete, smiling with nervous relief as he momentarily forgets himself.

"Wouldn't count your chickens just yet," continues Kevin. "Ron expects there to be loss adjusters crawling all over it, and if they get a whiff of an inside job they may not pay up, in which case Ron's as screwed as if he had no policy in the first place. Worse, actually, as they could try and do him for fraud."

"Thanks for that. I feel a whole lot better." Pete scrunches his eyes shut, scratches at his forehead and then runs a hand through his hair. "Aargh. Kev, did I cause this?"

"I think there's a chance we might have," Kevin replies after a few moments' thought.

"We?"

"You weren't the only one who had a private little chat with Andrew."

"When?"

"A while back."

"What about?"

"A load of stuff that happened years ago. Back at school."

"What kind of *stuff*?"

"There was some serious shit going on at school that I thought had been dealt with, but then recently discovered hadn't. I was fuming, so when I had a few minutes with Andrew in the kitchen one Monday, I had a moan and opened up. Told him exactly what I'd like to be done and to whom if we didn't have the rules. I felt safe doing it. It was a pressure release. I may have mentioned some names."

"And?"

"I don't know for sure, but something may have happened. I went to a school reunion over the weekend to confront a couple of teachers. They should have been there, but they weren't. I couldn't find out for sure, but from what I did hear, one had had an *accident* and was off for a while and the other was on some kind of *leave*. I'm sitting here having a go at you for feeling smug about Ron, but how am I any better? I'd be lying if I said I hadn't wished the worst on them."

"And you think Andrew had something to do with it?"

"Too much of a coincidence."

"It's all right for you. At least you're totally removed from anything he's done. I'm looking like the prime suspect in a fire that could still cost Ron a fucking fortune. He's going to screw me if it does, isn't he?"

"I'm not so sure. He seems remarkably calm. I told him you wouldn't have anything directly to do with it and that the worst you possibly did was mention it to someone else."

"And?"

"To begin with, he was well pissed off with you, but then I told him who and he lightened up."

"You saying he knew Andrew?"

"Knew *of* him more like. Seems there was a bit more to Andrew than we realised. Rumour has it that our friend the mild-mannered, poker-playing snooker club owner, was actually – and apologies if I sound like I'm delivering the advertising blurb for the sequel to *The Long Good Friday* – a Northern Irish ex-paramilitary turned pseudo-Mafiosa who's been keeping out of the firing line in Watford and laundering crime proceeds through the snooker club. Allegedly."

Kevin takes a well-earned rest, pleased to have trotted out most of what Ron told him in a remotely intelligible order. Not that Pete's looking overly elucidated.

"Shit," is his considered conclusion.

"Shit indeed." Their heads bob up and down in the wake of such profundities. "And it explains why Ron isn't angrier at you and worried about the loss adjuster. If he reckons this is Andrew doing you some kind of favour, there wouldn't be any point if it could come back on you, so he'd have made damn sure it looked like an accident. It would have been a professional job."

"Who'd have thought?" says Pete.

"What?"

"Andrew. A bloody arsonist."

"No, Pete. Not Andrew."

"But you said…"

"Pete. Switch your brain on. Blokes like Andrew don't do stuff like that. They know people who do it for them."

*

"This had better be bloody good," he mutters to himself as the Jag's tyres surf across the driveway gravel. On the back seat – stupid tiny fucking boot – his golf clubs clink and clank noisily, their clatter and chatter a taunting reminder of what he's had to leave behind, only serving to intensify his irritation.

He'd been on the seventeenth green when the call came through. *Get home now*, Jason had said. *It's urgent.* He'd told him to sod off and ended the call. But the cheeky sod had rung back immediately. *Dad, seriously. Get the fuck back home now. We need you here.* Made him miss a put. Cost him a pony. Have to have a word with him about that later on. Show some fucking respect. No one talks to him like that, not even his eldest.

He gets out of the car, leaving the roof open. Thinks of taking in the clubs, but no one's going to take them, not with ten-foot electric gates between them and the outside world. Well worth the money, they were. Keep the fucking riff-raff out. He relishes the quality thunk of the car door as it closes. Pats the car on the bonnet as he walks past, noting that the only other car is Barry Junior's. Must have come together. No sign of Chantelle's Cayenne. She's probably off spending his money on more shite they don't need or another stupid fucking fitness class – Zumba or some such bollocks; not that any of them ever seem to improve that wobbly, fat arse of hers.

He bounds up the stone steps and lets himself in. There's a piece of paper on the floor of the hall; 'In the pool room' scrawled on it. He shakes his head, thinks about changing just to make them wait, but decides to get it over with, maybe pop back to the club after.

He walks through to the kitchen, throws his car keys on the table, grabs himself a beer, opens it and takes a long swig. Burping loudly, he places the bottle on the counter, wanders along the corridor and down the stairs. Hears the low hum of the pool machinery. Pushes open the doors to the pool and for a few seconds is blinded by the sunlight reflecting off the water.

"Right, you sponging gits. This had better be f…"

The word arrests in his throat as the full import of the scene before him manifests itself and each new detail presents itself. The four boys – *his* four boys – sitting in a row on the far side of the pool; arms and ankles tied to chairs; gags in their mouths; stifled voices vainly striving to communicate.

Not just that.

There's claret.

"What the…" He stops, as for the first time he sees the bloke standing behind Darren. The fucker's smiling. The sunlight glints off whatever he's got in his hand. A blade of some sort; a big one at that, and enough to tell him he's safer this side of the pool. "What do you want?" he asks, hearing his own fear.

"Hullo dare, Barry," comes the reply.

Jesus, a fucking Paddy, and a fat old one at that. Fleetingly emboldened, he tries again.

"Look, mate, you're trespassing. You seem to know me, but I don't know you, so no harm done. Just leave right now and we'll forget this ever happened. You've got my word on that. How about it?"

"Can't be doing dat, Barry."

Remembers his phone and pulls it out.

"I'm calling the police unless you get out now." He prods at the screen, but before he can press any numbers a sharp pain shoots through his right elbow, sending him to his knees and the phone skittering across the tiles and into the pool with a plop.

He staggers to his feet and turns to find a second man standing in front of the doors he's just come through. How had he missed him? Must be nearing sixty, with a great big gut on him. For a brief moment Barry fancies his chances, but there's something about this bugger that warns him to be wary. Recognises the type. This is one mean bastard, and he knows there would only ever be one winner.

Letting out an audible sigh, he shouts back over his shoulder. "What do you want? How much?"

He hears the laughter and fears the worst.

Several minutes later, he too is trussed up in a chair, the front legs of which rest on the edge of the pool. The boot of the second man rests beside his right ear on the back of the chair; the threat abundantly clear.

All the while, on the far side of the pool, the main man has been setting down on a table a succession of metal tools and knives – seriously scary-looking shit – each clunk on the table triggering a fresh bout of panicked shaking and muffled shrieking from his palsied offspring, their eyes wide with terror.

After some final repositioning of his instruments, the man steps back, throws his arms out wide and smiles.

"Now den, Barry," he says with a chilling, empty smile. "Let's play a wee game, shall we. I get da choose an instrument… and you get da choose a son."

*

When Carl finally collects himself together, pushes off and heads for the surface, it's Emma's face he looks up into. She smiles back with a warmth he knows he doesn't deserve, and for a few moments her kindness is overwhelming and he's drowning again.

"Hey, it's all right," she says softly.

"Is it?"

"It will be. Just give it time."

He responds with a sniff, and daubs at his eyes.

"Come on, let's get out of here."

"Where to?"

"Nowhere. Somewhere. Does it matter?"

And off she sets, striding down the slope, her purposefulness the antithesis of how he's feeling.

He takes a last look around, mutters "Bye, Dad" and heads after her.

Stuart's first reaction when his finger had met resistance had been to press harder, so committed was he in the pursuit of release. When that hadn't worked, he'd lowered his arm and stared disbelievingly at the gun; one moment so ruinous, the next so impotent.

"Useless bloody…" he'd spat out and hurled the gun away, only for the shock of an explosive discharge to assail his eardrum and send him scampering on all fours for cover.

"*Fuck*," he'd shrieked, before rationalising the detonation and slumping back against the reassuring solidity of a tree trunk; starting to laugh manically; then dissolving into sobs.

Helplessly, hopelessly adrift. He looks around for something to grab on to; anything. But it's all too much. He needs to break it down into manageable pieces.

"Little steps," he mutters to himself. "Little steps."

Start with what he knows.

In less than twenty-four hours, Stuart Evans will – Stuart Evans *must* – die in the manner and the place of his own choosing. And that place is not here; not like this.

He must leave.

Looks around.

Sees his car; the windscreen a twisted mess.

Needs another plan.

Finds Emil's car, a white Fiesta, parked up on the verge a hundred yards back up the track.

Returns to the carnage grimly adorning the clearing, but he can't think clearly out here. Not with those bodies screaming for attention; the flies now joining the party, their ceaseless whining another mocking taunt. He needs a refuge.

Sinking into the passenger seat of his car, he pulls the door shut with a comforting clunk.

Slowly inhaling and exhaling, he stares into the shattered windscreen and tries to clear his mind. He follows lines through the crazy paving of cracked glass, but wherever they lead him, he's always trapped in the same maze of dead ends, false horizons and impossibilities.

It's only when one of the lines comes to an abrupt end at a wrench-created hole, and he's staring instead at a patch of sun-dappled foliage, that he hears the chirping of the birds and the rustle of the leaves in the gentle breeze. The fog starts to disperse and a simple truth presents itself: this need change nothing. He's been wasting that most precious of commodities – his time – dwelling on what has happened, what he cannot change, instead of what he can control.

Strangely, scenes from various films and books play on the blank canvas of his liberated mind: digging graves in *Shallow Grave;* Bruce Campbell wielding a chainsaw; assorted zombies. Then Liam Neeson cuts through the montage and growls "*but what I do have are a very particular set of skills; skills I have acquired over a very long career.*" There he was, thinking he needed Winston Wolfe, when this has always been just an A-to-B logic problem.

And who better to solve one of those than an accountant.

A chartered accountant.

Make that a maverick chartered accountant.

Bring it on.

When Stuart opens the door and climbs out to resume his acquaintance with Emil and Adelina, his predicament hasn't altered, just his mindset.

Now it's a game.

And he likes games.

Whilst sitting in the car, part of a song had played in the back of his mind. A British Sea Power track that halfway through breaks down into discordancy, interspersed with moments of tuneful respite. And throughout the chaos plays a simple repeated refrain on the higher notes of a piano, barely discernible at times, but always there; a glimmer of clarity in the feedback-laden turmoil; something to latch on to.

And a plan had presented itself, a thread of logic he could follow out of his labyrinthine despondency. It may not be cunning – more like borderline insane – but it's a plan nonetheless. He must leave and he knows he can't use his own car. He has that covered, so it's what he leaves behind that now needs to be dealt with. He could just drive away, but then what? His death is all about the time, the place and, much later, the note; without these it's meaningless and he can't leave this behind as it is; can't be associated with it, or at least not that obviously. And although, deep down, he knows it's unavoidable that he will be, there's a challenge here – to wipe out his presence; or worst case leave more questions than answers – and it's with renewed purpose that he sets about his task.

First of all, he establishes his escape route, heading off to collect Emil's car. It's locked. A few choice expletives and he's walking back, tentatively prodding at Emil's pockets until he locates the keys, then returning to collect the car and drive it into the clearing.

He sets about looting the cars and bodies for personal belongings and anything of potential use, then stands back to take stock of his bounty: a green plastic container two thirds full of petrol; a first aid kit; a large car blanket; a roll of gaffer tape; a thermos flask; his own coat; Emil's jumper; two road atlases; the gun; the wrench; a rattling box of bullets; two cans of de-icer; a box of tissues; a packet of cigarettes and a lighter; assorted sweets, coins and general car detritus; Adelina's holdall and small suitcase bulging with possibilities, kindling for a new life; his pathetic, limp rucksack, the last dregs of a life all it needs to support; Emil's wallet, containing forty pounds in notes and a few coins, which he pockets; and most poignant of all, Adelina's shoes, recovered from the footwell of his car, one of them now stuffed with her crumpled, discarded pants.

The process also reveals a logbook and some household bills stuffed into the glove compartment that suggest this is not Emil's car, as do the three fluffy-haired trolls stuck to the top of the dashboard.

Stuart gets to work, trusting in frantic activity to quell the doubts.

He gets in his own car, puts on his seat belt, starts the

engine, reverses to the edge of the clearing, slips it into first gear, brings his left arm up across his face and slams down the accelerator pedal. It's only a short journey to the tree trunk, but he picks up enough speed to ensure a satisfyingly crunching impact that triggers the air bag.

He emerges from the wreckage with just a sore neck and takes it as a providential sign; the relative success of step one serving to reinforce the viability of the madness to follow and spur him on.

Spreading the blanket out on the ground, and with as much tenderness as the gruesome task permits, he shoves and rolls Adelina's body until she lies diagonally across it. Opting for a fajita wrap, he grabs the free corner and drags her dead weight across the dusty ground to the pleasingly steaming car, playing its role to perfection. He retches as he uncovers her body and the pungent aromas assault his nostrils. He notes for the first time that her eyes are wide open and a shudder runs through him. Can't bring himself to close them. Recomposing himself, he takes a deep breath and with considerable difficulty completes the task of lifting and pushing her into the passenger seat. He staggers back, fights a wave of nausea and drinks deep of the unpolluted air.

Next comes Emil, who gets kicked onto the blanket. The back of his head is pulp and the smell of piss and shit is overwhelming, coated with the cloying sweetness of fermenting flesh. Swiss roll for this one. He's a lot heavier and Stuart takes it a few feet at a time, pausing regularly to step away and clear his airways noisily. When he does finally reach the car and prop the bundle against the open driver's side door, he realises that he should have done Emil first. It would have been easier to pull him in from inside, but that's a non-starter unless he fancies moving Adelina again; which he doesn't.

It takes another ten minutes of huffing and puffing

and retching and exasperating experimentation before the bundled corpse is stuffed behind the steering wheel. Stuart hasn't the stomach to unwrap him, and in any case the blanket's job isn't done.

He's on the point of congratulating himself when he realises with a gasp of anguish that he's forgotten a key ingredient in this demented dog's dinner of a plan. He deliberates a while, but he's too attached to the concept to let it go now, so he grits his teeth, draws in his lips and pulls and probes the blanket at arms' length until, with pyrrhic relief, he uncovers a blood-smeared forehead.

Emil's not looking too good. The blanket forms a fetching cowl, but what it's framing is truly grotesque.

What Stuart has endured so far is as nothing compared to the ghoulish task he now commences. Several approaches are abandoned just before contact, almost as if he expects to be bitten. His hands flutter uselessly in front of Emil's lips as he ponders the best angle of attack, before finally committing, his face contorting in grim anticipation. They're like two bloated earthworms. With near-paralysing apprehension Stuart inserts two fingertips and hits teeth. Another couple of fingers join the party, tentatively peel back the lips and attempt to prise apart the two rows of teeth. They meet resistance, so he increases the pressure slightly and with an unearthly squelch, the teeth part. There's a faint hiss of escaping gas – a final breath? – a fetid stench assaults his nostrils and his eyes widen with sickened astonishment as a thick, brownish-red gunge oozes out of Emil's mouth and drools, lava-like, down his chin.

Stuart gags, brings a hand up to cover his mouth… and smears whatever saliva/blood goulash they are coated in all over his own lips. The tip of his tongue is too slow to react and tingles with a bitter metallicity. His brain catches up and he doubles over, retching nosily, only bile left to dredge up.

When the spasms have relented, he backs away, pulls a handful of leaves off the nearest bush and dabs them frantically at his mouth and chin, pausing only to spit and hack.

Then back to business, Emil looking like some prosthetic mask on a horror film set and giving off a cluster bomb of odours, none of them pleasing.

The next stage of the plan has pretty much dictated everything else. It owes very little to a cogent thought process, but given he won't be around to face the consequences, he might as well leave the world a puzzle.

He jams his fingers between Emil's lips and forces open the teeth. Reaching into his pocket he pulls out a handful of bullets and feeds them into Emil's mouth. Goes back for the few his first scoop failed to gather and in they go. He withdraws his left hand, shakes it clear of a string of sanguine slaver and wipes what remains on the headrest.

Using the corner flap of the blanket, he dabs at Emil's swollen, blood-smeared face until it's as dry as possible. He fetches down the roll of gaffer tape from the roof of the car and tugs loose a stretch, presses it against Emil's mouth, clasping the lips together as he does so, and pulls the roll to release more. Emil's head lolls, following the tug, and for a sickening moment it feels like it's no longer attached to his body. But Stuart persists and succeeds in one circumnavigation. One more and he feels able to remove his left hand and place it on the top of Emil's head, only letting go to allow the tape to pass each revolution.

Round and round it goes, until the cranial mummification is complete. It looks like a metal coconut. Stuart gives Emil a congratulatory pat on the tuft of matted hair that has escaped incarceration and then wraps him in the blanket once more.

Fetching the petrol can, he empties half of it over the trussed Emil until the blanket is sodden. The rest he splashes around the interior, giving Adelina an irrationally respectful wide berth.

It doesn't feel sufficient, so he gets the two cans of de-icer and liberally sprays Emil, the upholstery and the dashboard; unclear as to the chemistry, but surely it can only help.

Standing back, he studies his pyre.

And in that moment of reflection the doubts creep forward. How combustible are car seats these days? Is de-icer even flammable? Will the bullets explode? What if all he achieves is a smoking car with localised burning and containing two readily identifiable corpses, one of them in a woollen straitjacket and with a mouthful of live ammunition?

Fuck it, he thinks, his lips corrupting into a sneer. At the very least he can leave the CSI boffins a challenge or two; throw in as many possible narratives as possible. Better an intriguing enigma than a known failure.

Conclusion? This car needs to blow-up big time.

Rushing over to Adelina's suitcase, he opens it and rummages around until he finds a towel. Pulling and tearing at it with teeth and fingers, he attempts to rip off the hem. Getting nowhere, he spies her wash bag and fishes out a pair of nail scissors. They're next to useless, but with sheer weight of effort they eventually generate enough of a nick in the material for brute force to be able to take over and do the rest. With a final tug he has in his hand what is basically a frayed piece of string.

It's not enough to guarantee success, so he sets about the towel with scissors, teeth and brawn and, several minutes of effing and blinding and straining later, he has the other hem and the two edges coiled on the ground at his feet. He separates it into four lengths; two long and two short. He twists the two long ones round each other, before tying a knot at one end. Does the same with the shorter lengths and then ties the two loose ends together. He surveys his handiwork with some satisfaction; now more rope than string, definitely long enough, and hopefully possessive of sufficient integrity to carry a flame.

He walks over to the car, removes the petrol cap and starts to feed in his makeshift fuse. It's only as he does so that he recognises an essential design fault and chides himself profanely for having used up all the petrol in the can. He pulls out the rope and is pleased to see that at least the final foot or so is sodden with petrol. He lays it out on the ground and looks around for inspiration.

The next few moments are not his finest, as he coats the remaining section of still-dry material with whatever potentially flammable substances he can locate: the last drips from the petrol can, the smeared contents of three small bottles of nail varnish, some fizzing dregs of de-icer, hairspray and roll-on deodorant are all applied. He even pops Emil's bonnet, pulls out the dipstick a few times and smears on what oil comes with it, then wipes the cord against any surface of the engine that looks even remotely dirty.

Only then does his inner voice of rationality posit a rather obvious thought.

Stuart stomps over to the car, reinserts the cord, only this time the other way round, pauses for a while and then withdraws it. He now has about eighteen inches of dry material. That'll do, he hopes. It will have to. He feeds one end carefully back into the fuel tank, leaving the other hanging down to the ground.

Then he starts shuttle runs between stockpile and car, throwing everything onto the back seat. He can't be bothered to repack Adelina's suitcase, so he lifts the spilled contents en masse and throws them into the car. As he withdraws his hand, his watch snags on something and comes clear trailing the cord from a dressing gown; just the kind of thing one might wish to use as a…

"For fuck's sake," Stuart screams, life continuing to mock him at every turn.

He's about to close the door when his eyes fix on the gun and he recognises with a weary sigh that another opportunity has gone begging for the want of some calm reflection and the application of his supposed occupational skill set.

He fetches it out and eventually succeeds in opening the barrel, though not without painfully trapping the side of his finger and drawing blood. Three bullets. He stands and contemplates the car.

Now what?

If this was a film, he'd simply offload a bullet into the fuel tank – or is it the engine? – and the car would explode into a gratifying fireball. No harm in trying, he thinks, and is steadying himself for the shot when he's struck by an image of nothing happening but the petrol emptying out into a useless puddle under the car, leaving his homemade fuse hanging redundantly high and drying. Then what? Ignite the pool of petrol? What would that do? And the noise of a gun discharge might attract attention. Come to think of it, that ship has already sailed, a realisation that hurries him along. He resolves that it's plan A he has to stick to and the gun goes back.

Pulling out Emil's lighter from a back pocket, he takes one last look at its former owner and is reminded of a candle a six-year-old Carl once brought away with misplaced pride from a handicraft class in Porthmadog. Hopefully Emil will burn a little longer and a lot more heartily. He presses the lighter and holds the flame against the sodden blanket. It ignites and immediately spreads encouragingly, forcing him to step back. He slams the door shut and hastily sets the cord alight.

There's nothing else to do, so he walks away, effecting nonchalance. In his imagination, the music builds and the camera, positioned just the other side of Emil's car, catches his assured and unconcerned stroll in slow motion as his own car explodes in the background, precisely when and as he knew it would, his body haloed magnificently in a ball of roiling flame as the soundtrack kicks into overdrive.

A worrying creak and hiss snap him out of his filmic reverie and send him into a far from casual jog. Jumping in the car, he fumbles the key into the ignition, starts the engine and accelerates away, bouncing over the rutted track. As he turns back onto the road, he hears an explosion, then another more muted one and, casting a last look back, he's reassured to see a healthy glow filtering through the trees.

Job well done, Stuart thinks with no objective justification whatsoever, and not only smiles but punches the steering wheel in ludicrous celebration of his own genius. Turns up the radio and forces himself to sing along.

It's not long before reality rips at the comfort blanket of self-delusion. For a start, he smells: a hybrid of sweat, blood, urine and petrol. His shirt is torn and looks like a used artist's palette for some painting of an autumnal scene. His trousers are similarly smeared, as is the face that looks back at him with dismay from the rear-view mirror.

He turns into a large lay-by; empty save for a small closed-up shed on which the letters 'TINAS' are daubed large in red paint. He sniffs away the absent apostrophe, but the sight of the roadside café this box presumably transforms into on busier days brings on a wave of hunger and thirst. No wonder he hasn't been thinking straight; he's exhausted and still in a state of shock. His body needs refuelling.

But before he can contemplate a public appearance, he gets out and performs a full self-inspection. The clothes have to go. There's no styling out this look. He knows what he'll find, but looks in his rucksack anyway, as though it might magic up something extra. Sure enough, the only clothes it contains are a tightly-packed cagoule, a pair of dark green cargo trousers – of the kind he more or less lived in during all those north Wales holidays – a T-shirt, a thin fleece top and a change of underwear.

Needs must. But first, he has to clean himself up. Get the dirt off his face, hands and arms. Do something about this fetid, cloying stench.

He looks around. His options are limited. A brown pool of stagnant liquid winks at him from the far side of the field that stretches away from the road, but he's not that desperate.

Yet.

Getting back in the car, he drives on in search of private washing facilities.

A while later he pulls to a halt in a sparsely-populated car park situated at the start of a scenic walk heralded – unsuccessfully it appears – by the succession of brown road signs he's been following. Having checked the other cars are empty, Stuart grabs his bag from the back seat, gets out and trots across the tarmac to the toilet block.

He's seen better. It stinks of urine and he's not sitting on that toilet seat for anything, although what does he care any more about a germ or two? Not where he's heading.

The floor is sticky and filthy, puddles of liquid with no

obvious source, and there are no hooks or other hanging places, so he wedges the bag between his ankles an inch or two off the floor, pulls off his jumper and T-shirt and clasps them between his knees. He starts by scrubbing away at his hands, which are a swirling mass of black, red and purple smears. Once applied, the opaque gunk that dribbles out of the soap dispenser clings greasily to his skin and takes little of the dirt with it when he does finally succeed in releasing its stubborn grip. He uses it more sparingly on his face and shoulders and opts for just water on his hair, the exercise made all the more difficult by the metal basin having no plug and taps that turn off the moment he withdraws his hands.

Shuffling over to the hand dryer, he presses the button and dipping, bending and twisting, he passes various body parts under its feeble stream of warm air, before giving up and using the relatively untainted patches of his T-shirt to rub away any residual moisture as best he can.

He had planned to change his trousers as well, but can't face the requisite contortionism, so does it on the back seat in the car. He contemplates putting the dirty jumper, T-shirt and trousers in a bin, but decides there's no point in leaving clues to a mystery he doesn't want solved, so he pushes them under the passenger seat, only to be engulfed by a wave of panic. He pulls out the trousers and searches the pockets, then runs back to the toilet block just in case.

End result: no wallet. It must have fallen out. Too late to go back.

Emil's generous, if involuntary, forty-pound bequest soon dwindles to just under ten of loose change after the petrol warning light comes on and he stops at a garage for as little petrol as he dares, some chocolate and several bags of crisps.

It's late afternoon by the time he pulls off the Barmouth road and into a familiar guest-house car park. Taking with him only what he'll need, he locks the car and trudges over to the house. It's been how long? Five years?

"Been a while," echoes Megan when she opens the door.

"It has."

"You look like shit."

"Thank you. It's been a long day."

"No, really, you look terrible."

"It's shabby chic."

"Bullshit. You look like a hobo."

"Nothing like a charm offensive to bring in those repeat bookings."

"You're here, aren't you?"

"That I am."

"Suppose you'd better come in."

He follows her in. "Everything looks the same."

"Me or the house?"

"Both."

"Liar."

"How are you keeping?"

"Better than you, by the look of it."

"Hope you treat the other guests better."

"I do the regulars."

"Thought that's what I was."

"*Was* being the operative word. Couple of times a year for almost twenty years and then nothing. Did we do something to offend you?"

"No. Life just got a bit… messy."

"How's Carl?"

"He's fine. Working for some big telecom company as a financial analyst."

"Chip off the old block, then."

"That wasn't the idea, but he sort of drifted into it."

"Future partner?"

"No chance. Last thing I'd want," he replies, but with the slightest of hesitations that does not go unnoticed.

"Never mind. And Fiona?"

This time the delay is more pronounced. He settles on "Again, messy," and a wordless conversation of glances held or avoided is played out. In the end she takes pity.

"Anyway, you're here. Would a cup of tea and some bara brith simplify things for you?"

"That'd be perfect. Am I forgiven?"

"What for?"

"Not keeping in touch."

"Why would you? I'm the woman who runs a guest house where you used to stay for a few weeks each year. You see your postman more than you see me. You owe me nothing. Not even the rent. It's a rare guest who pays so far in advance."

"You sounded so dubious on the phone, so I felt I needed to make a gesture. Show some commitment."

"I'll stick the kettle on. You're in room three; as usual. The key's in the lock. Why don't you go and freshen up? Maybe have a shower or a soak in the bath."

"Is that a hint?"

"It's an order. Do you want to get the rest of your bags in?"

"This is it," he says, riding her enquiring look; relieved when she lets it go.

"Will you be eating here tonight?"

"No, I th…" Then remembers his petty cash crisis. "Yes please, that'd be great. But any chance you could put it by for me and I'll eat it a bit later? I wanted to walk along to The George and catch the sunset with a pint. I won't be late."

"It'll still be there tomorrow, you know, and you do look knackered."

"It's just something I have to… want to do."

"You sound like you're in a rush."
"I am and then again, I'm not."
"Suit yourself."

It's not until he's sitting on the wall outside The George – pint in his hand; collar turned up against the early evening chill; serenaded by the intermittent percussive rumble of car tyres on the toll bridge – that he starts to breathe easily and relax. Regain his balance. He's made it. The end is in sight; the route there now clear and uncluttered.

He stares across the estuary, up and to his right, and locates the spot.

And he can't wait, he recognises with a rush of relief that brings tears to his eyes and a smile to his lips.

Downing the last inch of his pint, he gets up and heads inside for another, wondering if his meagre cash resources will stretch to a packet of peanuts.

*

Megan surprises him as he's leaving the next morning, his stomach comforted by a full Welsh breakfast. She's sitting, for no obvious reason, on the obligatory piece of rusting farm machinery that seems to pass as garden ornamentation around here.

"You off?" she asks, staring past him into the distance as if she's forgotten the question immediately it left her lips.

"Thought I'd take a walk."

"You don't have to, you know."

"What?"

"Go."

"It's just a walk."

"If you say so."

He's about to turn away when she rises to her feet,

walks over to him and plants the lightest of kisses on his cheek.

"What's that for?" he asks.

"Just in case. Hope the view's what you're after," she says, and with a rueful smile and a slow shake of her head she turns and walks back into the house.

Dead man walking.

Dead man travelling light, a half-full rucksack slung over his shoulder.

Dead man on a one-way journey to oblivion.

Dead man negotiates a stile, skirts round a lake and heads up the steep path that climbs through the pine forest.

Dead man stops for a rest.

Dead man takes in the natural beauty, the peace and the solitude.

Dead man might start to believe in a world that still has something to offer him… if dead man wasn't so committed to his cause.

Dead man continues on his long ascent.

Dead man is not as fit as he thought he was.

Dead man clambers over another stile and turns left, breathing heavily.

Dead man walks past a derelict building and across a footbridge spanning a tiny stream rattling inconsequentially in a steep-sided valley that hints at former glories.

Dead man sees a parallel and smiles ruefully to himself.

Dead man turns left through a gap in the dry-stone wall just after another shell of a building.

Dead man climbs up the side of a hillock and along its summit.

Dead man finds a place; a favourite place. A rocky

outcrop that will multitask as a screen from passers-by, a backrest and then as his first tombstone.

Dead man experiments with seating positions. The most comfortable proves to be a small cushion of spongy grass beneath a curved section at one end. The two rocks slightly below had initially put him off, but they prove to be more than useful. By jamming his left foot against one rock and resting his right calf on the other, he can achieve far more comfort than he'd expected. He has to twist slightly to ensure his head has support and that turns him towards Dolgellau and away from the Mawddach Estuary's majestic sweep seawards. But dead men can't be choosers and it's too perfect a fit to relinquish.

Dead man remembers a time, a naive time, when he thought the worst that could happen – did happen – in his life was not having Carl for willing company on these trips.

Dead man opens his rucksack and starts to empty it.

Dead man folds the cagoule and places it under his backside to stem the encroaching dampness.

Dead man inflates the travel pillow and alternates it between head and lower back before opting for the latter.

Dead man wishes he'd brought something else for his head; tells himself not to be so soft.

Dead man knows that bar this intervention, the only way would inevitably be down; that his grip on the things he holds most dear would gradually and unavoidably be loosened until that moment when his time would come; whether that be on some dirty pavement lying at the feet of strangers; or straining on a toilet; or shouting at the TV; or lifting some heavy object. And, if he's unlucky, before consciousness fades, it will grant him a brief and tortured moment for the bitter regret and pain of lost opportunity; of things left undone and unsaid. Or else the life will slowly leak out of him in a drawn-out haze of pain, incontinence and medication, lying in a semi-vegetative state in some hospital bed, doubting the motives of the few who sit by his bed and deposit fruit and flowers, trying not to look bored while furtively looking at their watches and making polite talk to bridge the inconvenient and uncomfortable period before they make their break for freedom and a life to be lived.

Dead man is tired. So very tired.

Dead man doesn't want to fight any more.

Dead man has put his affairs in order. Said all that needs to be said to the few who matter; and no longer cares about the many who don't.

Dead man fetches out and opens the two small bottles.

Dead man alternates between them, popping pills into his mouth and swishing them down hastily, before any second thoughts can snare him. Then downs the rest of the water and belches loudly. The deed done.

Dead man reaches into his pocket, pulls out the *traffic light* lollipop, peels off the cellophane and pops it in his mouth.

Dead man puts on the headphones and fiddles with the iPod, selecting the 'Exit music' playlist and setting it in motion.

Dead man leans back against the moss-covered stone and gets comfortable enough.

Dead man sucks on the lollipop and savours the saccharine hit. Sugar-coat the medicine.

Dead man opens his eyes and drinks in the view one last time. Not a bad one to go out on.

Dead man closes his eyes as Uto Ughi hits his stride. Allows the soaring violin to wash over him.

Bring it on.

This time Emma doesn't ask him for directions.

She takes the same turn off the Barmouth road as yesterday, but with a confidence that suggests to Carl that she's been playing him all along. They make the serpentine climb and cross the cattle grid. A little way on, she slows as they approach a rough track off to the left, rising between the trees to nowhere obvious. Carl doubts it's been used in years, so he's surprised when Emma turns onto it. They jolt and jar over its uneven surface for a while, until it becomes more pothole than road, at which point she pulls over to the side just short of the brow of the slope, cuts the engine and gets out, slamming the door on his question.

"What are we doing here?" he asks again as he gets out.

"Going for a little walk. A voyage of discovery," she throws back over her shoulder.

"Discover what?"

"I'm not sure. Right now, I don't know any more than you do."

"Shit. You must *really* hate that."

If she hears, she doesn't acknowledge it, and he trudges off after her.

They negotiate a mile or so of rises, drops and turns in silence. Just as Carl is despairing of any discernible destination, they breast the crest of yet another rutted incline and come to a halt. No more than a hundred feet ahead lies a cluster of old and neglected farm buildings. Hearing running water, he looks around and locates a stream running through the trees to their left. Then realises it's not just water he can hear. There's another babble somewhere ahead competing with the passage of the water. People talking? Can't be; they're miles from anywhere and there isn't another vehicle in sight, just the ubiquitous sheep and their perpetual foraging.

"It appears we're late," Emma says, setting off again.

"What for?"

She doesn't answer and by the time he catches up with her they're almost upon the first building. They pass a piece of wood nailed to the trunk of a tree; the word 'Limbo' crudely painted on it. What had initially been an indistinct murmur is now more defined and he can make out different voices, a laugh here and there, even a cheer. Garden-party-next-door vibe.

They round a corner into a courtyard area to find a small gathering of maybe thirty people standing in loose groups, chatting and laughing. Carl pulls to a halt, but Emma says softly "It's all right, we're expected," and gives him a gentle nudge before he can say anything. There's little, if any, reaction to their arrival and Carl assumes them to be strangers; Emma's hand resting on the small of his back his only certainty.

Their arrival has not gone unnoticed, although collectively the assembled are doing a pretty good job of not making it a big thing. He feels ignored, yet observed. There are glances in his direction; nods; smiles; but never more than that and always with an edge. Discomfort? Awkwardness? Sympathy? Pity? No one holds his gaze for longer than a second or two. He feels like Mia Farrow taking that walk in *Rosemary's Baby*. There's a group dynamic in play here and he can't work out if it's for or against him, which makes him feel exposed. Examined. Claustrophobic. And it's all too much to take in. He can't focus on anyone long enough to establish a connection to grab hold of and use to drag himself from this stifling fug of confusion.

A loud whistle sees all heads turn and snaps Carl from his spiralling bewilderment.

"Always wanted to do that," says Colin McLeod, looking a lot less like a lawyer, standing in the doorway of an outbuilding that's little more than an aggregation of rectangular stones and a sagging roof littered with patches of tarpaulin weighed down with rocks. "Despite the complete informality of the occasion, I'd like to formally welcome Carl to our annual gathering." Greetings are murmured, Carl unsure how to react. "Emma, I'm assuming from the look of confusion on Carl's face that you've not given him any advance warning." Emma nods. "Well, let me explain then. Everyone here has one thing in common, Carl. Your father. Or rather our fondness and respect for him and a shared belief that the person we knew him to be, and whose loss we mourned, got overlooked and forgotten in the unfortunate confusion and bitterness that followed. So, each year, a few of us get together to toast his memory on the anniversary of his untimely death."

"I'd forgotten," Carl whispers in horror, turning to Emma. She knows. He sees that. Must have been like hitting her head against a brick wall. But there's no reproof in her expression. She simply offers him a smile and squeezes his hand gently. And he loves her for it.

Then feels like a lost little child.

"That's all there is to it, really. No big deal. Help yourself to drinks and food, settle in and I'm sure everyone will make you feel welcome. And maybe along the way you'll get a different perspective on your father. As indeed may we. Most of us here today attended Stuart's funeral and I think I speak for everyone when I say the Stuart *we* knew wasn't represented. So I was pleased to learn recently that the format it took was very different to what Stuart had intended. It's only by sharing that we can keep the real Stuart alive. I'll leave it at that."

Initially Carl clings to Emma – and a bottle of lager – for support, but gradually they are separated as a succession of people come up to him and make themselves known, each a faint echo from the past; individually of little consequence, mere snippets of jogged memories, but collectively they start to accumulate. And before long he's enjoying it, in spite of himself.

Then through the crowd he catches sight of Emma on her haunches, chin resting in her hands, staring into the distance and being comforted, it appears, by an older woman who looks faintly familiar. He walks over.

"Hello, Carl," says the woman warmly. Emma looks up. Her face is ghostly pale.

"You okay?" he asks.

"I'm fine," she replies, looking anything but fine.

"Do you want me to stay?" the woman asks Emma.

"I started this. I should finish it."

"We'll speak again later," says the woman.

"Thanks," says Emma, and a brief look flickers between them that he can't even begin to access.

The woman gives Carl a nod and a tight-lipped but friendly smile as she turns and walks away.

Emma offers him a silent look that appears to presage more than he wants to deal with right now, so he dives for cover.

"Who was that?"

"Apparently you stayed at her guest house every year."

"Shit. Of course. She looks a bit older than I remember."

"Funny that."

Silence descends. He looks around at the small groupings dotted about the courtyard, lost in animated and congenial conversation. Others have moved inside the main building, judging by the chatter and clatter of voices and glasses emanating from within.

"What did you mean about finishing what you started?" he asks.

Her mouth opens to reply, then closes, apparently

stuck for words. Very un-Emma-like. When she looks back up at him, it's with moist eyes and an expression he cannot begin to fathom.

"Your Grandad would like a word."

For a moment he's thrown by a word that sounds alien. "Grumpy? He's here?"

"Of course. Why wouldn't he be?"

"I don't know. I just… Where is he?"

"Over there," she replies, pointing over his shoulder. He turns and sees the dishevelled form of his grandfather standing awkwardly under the branches of a tree on the far side of the courtyard.

The day can't get any more peculiar. "You coming?"

"No. It's you he wants to speak to."

Carl wanders across the courtyard.

"Hi," he ventures.

"Hello, Carl," comes the gruff response. Their first dialogue in ages. They hadn't even spoken at the funeral.

Then something very strange happens. He reaches out a large and calloused hand to roughly squeeze Carl's upper arm, while his facial muscles contrive to form a rare smile – of sorts anyway – that hints at a future at odds with their substantially unshared past. But there's something else lurking there. Just like with Emma. Sheepish. Almost apologetic. But for what? Before he can ask, and set up their longest conversation in over fifteen years, he's received a nod of the head that announces this exchange is all but over. "I'll be heading back then," he concludes.

As he passes, he gives Carl's arm another reassuring squeeze and nods back over his shoulder and through the trees that lead down to the river.

*

"Can I come in?" asks Pete.

"I buzzed you up, didn't I?"

That's all she can manage; all those mental dress rehearsals discarded in that initial meeting of gazes. She can't bring herself to do anything but spin on her heels and escape to a haven.

This is all so confusing.

She's angry he hasn't called; needs him to convince her he's had good reason not to.

She's been worried about him after the way they parted and deeply regrets letting him go that day.

Disappointed at herself for not feeling able to meet a need she sensed in him, but also irritated at his failure to rise above his past; his coasting unquestioningly through a life of pointless and petty revenge. And she resents his playing on – more than that, his active encouragement of – an image of the shrewd, calculating and successful punter. That smug self-satisfaction. Annoyed at herself for falling for it; for finding it appealing.

But worst of all, she's more than aware that she's a hypocrite.

And that she's missed him terribly.

She heads for the lounge, curls herself into a ball on the armchair and pulls her fringe forwards, letting it hang down over her eyes.

Defences raised.

Abdicating all responsibility, she leaves it to him to deal the cards and dictate how this plays out. Whether they rise together or fall apart.

She can hear him enter and rock to and fro on his feet, unable to decide where to go. She offers him nothing but silence; can't help herself.

"Sorry I haven't been in touch the last few days, but a load of stuff's happened and I needed to think things through." He pauses, presumably for a response; which he doesn't get. "I want to be honest with you, and I have to admit I was a bit put out the other day. I told you things that were very personal, and the least I expected was your understanding and support. It took a lot to tell you those things and I think that's vital if we… you know… are going to… er… it's vital that we don't have secrets. That we can tell each other things."

She's heard enough. Can't bear this maudlin self-pity any longer.

"Honesty?" she snaps.

"Yes," he replies, with the cautious dread of someone who knows that whatever logic train he's misguidedly boarded is now out of his control and heading towards the buffers, picking up speed.

"No secrets?" With real venom.

"None." Managing to draw out the one syllable, as if the sound alone can save him from collision.

"Right. If that's what you want. Let's start with sexual partners. Wouldn't want those skeletons to stay in the cupboard. Let 'em *all* out. I've had a few. Does that bother you? Although that depends on how you define a few. What do you reckon?"

He thinks of a number. Winces at it. Takes one off. Sounds better. But surely too high? Goes with it anyway, adding the one back just in case. Surprise her with his knowing worldliness. "I don't know. Ten?" Almost sounding casual.

She snorts and he inwardly recoils at the contempt in that dismissive sneer. "Before university, maybe, but I really found my wings when I got there. Played the field, I guess you'd call it. Though I tended to go for the more artistic, less conventional types. Maybe it was because they were more in love with themselves and that meant I felt less on show, less observed. But basically, they were just a bit more interesting than the good-looking ones, and it meant I had less competition." She hesitates, then thrusts. "Apart from Carl, that is. He was the one exception." Pause for effect. Achieved. She observes the realisation ripple and twitch its way through the muscles of his face. "Oh, didn't you know we both went to Exeter? With the others it was just a couple of shags – more if they were any good – before I got bored and moved on. But with Carl it was different. I really liked him. I'd have swopped the lot for him, but that was never his style; at least not then. I had to make do with what I could get, not that I didn't experiment myself. I guess he'd have called us *fuck-buddies*." Another mischievous pause. "I always believed that if I just hung around and didn't ask for too much, that he'd see sense and maybe we could be an item. I wanted that. You know, all that rubbish about letting them go so they realise what they're missing.

"When we first got together, I'd just formed this indie music society. Not the soft-as-shit, piss-poor excuse for indie you get these days, but the proper stuff from the late eighties and early nineties. I'd been into it for ages, but he still hadn't grown out of heavy metal and thought my stuff was either mumbling or a mess. Took a lot of persuading to get him to come along one night, and even then, it was probably just because he was on a promise. Anyway, he did come along and you could tell it was a real eye-opener. He was hooked the moment he heard his first Hüsker Dü track. He sort of hijacked it from then on, which did grate a bit, but it meant we stayed in regular contact, so I wasn't really complaining. Then he started playing guitar in this university heavy metal band and it was all the usual AC/DC and Iron Maiden guff. He loved playing, but used to moan about them never doing anything different. I said why didn't he try and persuade them to play some of our – make that my – stuff, but he said they'd just laugh at him. But I kept on nagging and when they had a get-together in the new year before term began, I gave him a tape to take along. And sure enough, they gradually saw the light and became this indie/metal hybrid. Quite a cult following. They played this Pixies song called 'Tame' that went down really well, but they kept cocking up the bit where Black Francis and Kim Deal make these moaning sounds, a bit like they're having sex. It never sounded right when Dan, the lead singer, grunted away. They let the bassist have a go but he was even worse. He just sounded like he was having a painful dump. I suggested they get me up on stage to do that bit and we could extend and ham it up a bit. They went for it, and even though I pretended like I was reluctantly doing them a favour, truth was I was chuffed to bits; a dream come true. I couldn't wait.

"It was all set, then I went down with a stomach bug. I thought they'd just wait until the next gig, but it turned out that my *friend* went along and did it for me. Rather well, in fact. Bless her. Pretty much came on stage. Made it her own. Her name was Emma. Yes, *that* Emma. They became inseparable and I was cast well and truly onto the scrapheap. Not sure I got more than a few words from Carl after that. Why do you think he used you to give me that package? I even got off with the bassist – creepy little bloke who was far too grateful – to try and get Carl's attention, but he and Emma were smitten and that was that. They both jettisoned me. Not that I blamed Carl, of course. Emma was lovely and clever and I… I was just some comfort lay when there was nothing better on offer. Hardly the settling-down-with type. Obviously I still see Emma a fair bit for work reasons, but that's more of a mutually-beneficial business arrangement and I doubt she'd see me at all if I didn't make her some money every now and then." She attacks the side of a thumbnail with her teeth and stares into the distance; her hand shaking slightly. "Maybe that's how I like it anyway; casual and uncommitted. Makes you and I look like an anomaly, and let's be honest with each other, this really isn't going to work, is it? You'd be mad to put all your eggs in this particular basket. Can't imagine group gatherings going smoothly, what with the whole me and Carl backdrop, can you? How many times will that come up and cause problems, I wonder? You couldn't deal with it and I'd get bored hearing you banging on about it.

"What I'm trying to say, Pete, is that I'm trouble. It can't possibly work, so why don't you just tootle off and leave me well alone. Find yourself a nice, normal girl who'll flatter your fragile ego and play along with all that self-pity. Say *poor little Pete* whenever you need her to. Congratulate you for being the moral avenger you clearly see yourself to be, rather than the spoilt little fake we both know you are. So, let's call it a day, shall we? You were an interesting enough diversion for a while, but you're just going to be too high maintenance and I'm already bored with it all. Please. Just go."

Pete opens his mouth but no words escape.

"I'm asking you to leave, please. *Go*."

He turns slowly, then pauses.

"For fuck's sake. I'm going in the other room and when I come back you had better be gone. At least do that for me, will you?"

She makes her exit into the spare bedroom, albeit a room without a bed. It's her refuge; her inner sanctum. A burrow for when she needs to escape; to forget; to eliminate thought.

Like now.

Flicking the light switch washes the room in turquoise light; the dimpled sound-proofing material lining all four windowless walls and ceiling a treat to herself – and the neighbours – to ensure a guilt-free ambience. The room's only contents are a stereo system sitting in a corner, several tall racks of CDs, four large free-standing speakers and a recliner chair, which she pushes across the wooden floor to beside the stereo as the light gradually makes its way through purple to a deep and resonant red. The chair won't be needed for this particular cleansing process.

She knows precisely what is required and quickly locates the jewel case. She takes out the compilation CD, slides it in, removes her glasses, pulls off her jumper and hairband, shakes her hair loose, makes sure the volume is set high and presses play.

'Glider' for starters. Not the ten-minute EP version; three minutes is more than enough to generate the buffer between reality and the state she wants to attain; the simple repeated refrain, if you can call it that, grinding and boring its way into her mind as she closes her eyes and lolls her head loosely on her shoulders. Eases out the emotional wrinkles; gives her mental *Etch-a-Sketch* a gentle shake.

Aural lobotomy achieved, MBV double up, cutting straight into 'You Made Me Realise', the sudden injection of a discernible tune enough to release her arms and activate her feet. A forty-second insertion of industrial noise – the nearest thing to having a helicopter landing on your head, as someone once described it – brings a smile to her face. This is *her* CD. *Her* music. *Her* therapy. Everyone else can fuck right off – that's the point, after all – and if 'Glider' hasn't sent them running for cover, this sure as hell will.

Alienation.

Now for the release.

She shakes her limbs loose as Kim Gordon mumbles and the rest of the band fiddle around with their instruments for a while. Then 'Teen Age Riot' kicks off and so does she, her body spinning, twisting, convulsing; piloted by whatever primitive, instinctual force she's succeeded in awakening from its lair deep within her psyche and dragging to the surface; giving it free rein, untethered by the constraints of conscious concerns.

Her essentiality unleashed.

'Teen Age Riot' makes way for 'Silver Rocket', its natural successor, bedfellows she's never seen fit to separate. Then on to an even greater opening salvo… *the* greatest: the mighty 'Debaser' and 'Tame'; any Carl-tinged negative association with the latter track immediately dwarfed by the joy in reclaiming what was always hers. Quiet-loud-quiet-loud…

Her body twists and turns; arms flailing, damp hair swirling and the sweat running down her face and the small of her back.

And on she drives in delirious abandon.

She emerges, chest heaving, into a living room devoid of Pete and heads off for a shower.

*

They've each thrown several stones into the water before Carl breaks the silence.

"An hour ago, I said goodbye to you on a graveyard in the middle of nowhere." Gets the words out. Just.

"You found it then. Although that was a different me. One I said goodbye to a while ago."

Carl looks directly at him for the first time.

"You're telling me. Great look, by the way. I'm getting Robin Williams in *Jumanji*. Or maybe Tom Hanks in *Castaway*. It's a nice disguise." He picks up another stone, but this time doesn't throw it. Finds the feel of it in his palm reassuring; a fixed reference point in a spinning world. "Is that what it is? A disguise?"

"More a side effect. I don't need a disguise. No one's looking for me. Until Emma, that is. A very resourceful young lady. Are you and…"

"No."

"Pity."

"She has herself a good-looking air ambulance pilot."

"Ouch."

"Yep. Not that I can blame her." The stone now warm in his hand. He stares down at it. Slowly shakes his head. And suddenly it's all too much to keep contained. "I'm sorry," he says, hurling the stone into the trees on the far side of the stream.

"It's all right, Carl."

"No, it's not." The tears now in full flow.

"Come here." Arms envelop him and his face is pulled down into the angle between shoulder and heavily bearded cheek. His whole body shakes uncontrollably. "It's okay."

"I'm sorry," he repeats.

"For what?"

"Not looking. It should have been me, shouldn't it? But I never even thought to… not once."

"Why would you? I was dead as far as you knew."

"Didn't stop Emma though, did it? She always thought something wasn't quite right and she never gave up. But I…"

"Carl, it doesn't matter. I didn't want you to. Don't you see? It wasn't a challenge. You read the letter. I wasn't testing you. I didn't want to be saved or stopped. I was ready and happy to go. Do you hear me? I wanted to."

"I should have tried."

They retreat into silence.

"I hated you," blurts out Carl.

"I can take that."

"For doing that to Mum and me. Leaving us with all the shit to deal with. For dying on us. On me."

"I'm sorry. I really am. But it was something I knew I had to do and when it didn't work out as planned, the next best thing was to act like it had. Most of it came easy. But not you. Losing you all over again was the hardest part of all. I did write that letter though."

"Great. Pity I had to wait so long to read it."

"Trust me, there were very good reasons for that."

Carl shakes his head and the silence descends again.

"What happened?"

"On the day? A total shit storm is what happened."

"Not you in the car then."

"Obviously not."

"Who was it?"

"The husband of the girl… the woman I was giving a lift to."

Carl rubs at his temples, his mind bombarded by a succession of questions clamouring for precedence.

"Your girlfriend?" Get that one over with.

"No. Not really."

"But she meant something to you?"

"I was fond of her. Don't look at me like that. You have no idea what it was like. Don't judge me for something you know nothing about."

"Where were you taking her?" asks Carl, steering into calmer waters.

"Away from him. He was a nasty piece of work and no good for her. She was intelligent and articulate and funny and…"

"Twenty-six."

"Yes, Carl, I know that. She had a lifetime of potential ahead of her and he was going to destroy it. I just wanted to give her a clean break. And I was heading up this way to… and she had some relatives near Wrexham, so it seemed to make a lot of sense. Thought we'd got away from him as well, but something went wrong. She used her credit card in the hotel. Maybe made a phone call to a friend. Either way, he tracked us down and must have followed us from the hotel when we left the next morning."

"So how did he get in the car?"

Stuart smiles to himself. "That's a long story for another time."

"And you weren't going with her?"

"No. Just drop her off and head on up here. Stay the night and take a load of pills the following day. End it."

"Why didn't you?"

"I did. Swallowed the lot. Never been surer of anything in my life. I was done."

Not-dead-yet man is confused when the playlist concludes with Chopin's *Funeral March* sonata. It had seemed like a dryly amusing idea when he'd put the list together; a self-service funeral as his corpse lay on a mountainside. Now it seems a bit silly. He doesn't know how long the tablets should have taken to kick in, but this can't be right. He doesn't even feel woozy yet. Nothing for it but to set the playlist going again and wait.

He's about to do so when he hears something move over to his right. Leaning forward and peering round the outcrop, he sees a man sitting on a small hummock sporting an air of serene nonchalance and an inane grin, both very much at odds with Stuart's state of mind.

"Hello?" asks Stuart, with undisguised irritation.

"*Bore da*," comes a breezy response. Stuart glares. "Oh, I see what that was. Not so much a greeting, as a sod off."

Stuart looks away and across the estuary, in the hope that this moronic intruder will take the hint.

Dares to think he may have.

"Lovely day." Clearly not.

"Is it?" Stuart asks, with a sigh.

"For round here, it's not half bad."

"Look. Much as it's nice to chew the cud and all that, I was hoping for a bit of privacy. It's a big fucking hill, you know."

"Oh, don't mind me."

"Well, I do mind and right now I'd really like to be alone, so please can you just *go away*?"

"Sorry. I can't be doing that. Strict orders."

"What *are* you on about?"

"If it was up to me, I'd leave you to it."

"Why don't you then?"

"Ask a lot of questions, don't you?"

"I'll stop when you start making sense."

"Just pretend I'm not here, why don't you, Stuart?"

That throws him.

"Sorry, do I know you?"

"Oops."

Stuart repeats the question.

"Nope."

"But you know my name?"

"Lucky guess?"

"You know my name."

"Appears so."

"How?"

"A mutual friend."

"We don't have a mutual friend."

"Isn't that the way of things? All those one-way streets. All those unrequited feelings."

"What the hell are you on about?"

A shake of the head. "Someone I think very highly of clearly thinks enough of you to send me up here on the off chance that you might be contemplating doing yourself some harm, and here we are. Not that it's any skin off my nose what you choose to do to yourself. Your business entirely. But that certain someone feels differently and I made a promise, so I'm afraid I can't be fucking off. Sorry," he adds with a shrug of his shoulders and a smile that only add to Stuart's intensifying exasperation.

He grabs the hair on top of his own head, scrunches his eyes shut and shouts "*Fuck.*" Looks back up and the fool is still there, now with a strange look of amused puzzlement.

"*What?*"

"I'm just wondering how long to give it."

"How long?"

"Before I step in."

"What *are* you on about?" asks Stuart.

"Those pills you've swallowed."

"Too late. It's done now. We're miles from anywhere. And you can fuck right off if you think you're going to try and stick your fingers down my throat."

"Whoa. Hold your horses. I'm not going near your throat. I'm just a little disappointed, that's all. I thought it might be a bit more entertaining."

"Entertaining?"

"Yeah. Bit ghoulish, I guess. But I am intrigued."

"*Intrigued?*" he echoes, again.

"You're not going to die, you know."

"You're wrong there." Hears the panic in his own voice. "That's exactly what I'm going to do. I'd just rather I didn't have a sodding audience."

"What do you think you've swallowed?"

"Sleeping pills. A load of them."

"Nope."

"What?"

"We swapped them this morning while you were at breakfast. Megan's idea. She sussed you out pretty quick yesterday. *Not yourself* was how she put it. She took a little look through your things while you were having your bath, and a longer one while you were having your pint and a half and peanuts. No wallet, no change of clothes, a load of sleeping pills, not your car – nice troll collection, by the way – and some disturbingly stained clothes hidden under a seat. Then she checked the news. Shit, man. If that was you, what the fuck? Anyway, she rang muggins here, well after the shops had closed of course, gave me a couple of the pills and I pulled a few strings until I found someone willing to flout their Hippocratic Oath for the greater good."

"What the hell have I taken?"

"They had to all look just about the same for it to have any chance of working; and remember we had two bottles to fill."

"Tell me."

"A mixture of placebos left over from some drug trial, so you're all right there, and…"

"What?"

"Let's just say there's a fair few looking for dramatic weight loss around here."

"Great."

"And a few blokes who aren't quite what they used to be, if you know what I mean. I slipped those in for good measure."

So much for taking control, reflects Stuart, squatting down behind a gorse bush small enough to leave his head and shoulders exposed, as the liquefied contents of his bowels void themselves messily on the ground, while this fuckwit who is taking him to Christ knows where loiters close nearby whistling 'Always Look on the Bright Side of Life' very badly. And all under the beady eye of a bobbing and insistent erection that will not go away.

"How's it going behind there?"

"Fuck you. I wish I was dead."

"Nice one. Hang on. Sshh. Someone's coming."

"Shit." Stuart hunkers down even further and duck-walks as close to the bush as he dares. Feels a pang of pain, lets out a barely suppressed yelp and looks down to observe a gorse needle impaled in the tip of his penis.

"Only kidding. Just having a laugh."

"Aaarrrgghh. Ha, *bloody* ha." Stuart eases back, attempts a reverse waddle and loses his balance. With one hand holding his trousers and pants out of harm's way, the other shoots back to help maintain his balance. The resulting shaky configuration just about maintains its structural integrity as Stuart establishes what has gone where and lets out an exasperated sigh. He's sorely tempted just to sit down, roll into a ball and cry.

"You done yet?"

"Piss off. Don't suppose you've got a tissue or something there?"

"Let's have a look," he replies and half-heartedly rummages around in his pockets. "Nah, sorry. Could you not use a bit of grass or a leaf or something? Oh, hang on. Here you go." A fluttering white ball flaps erratically through the air and lands a foot or so out of Stuart's comfortable reach. It's clearly been used before. Stuart purses his lips. Looks up at his tormentor. Shakes his head.

"None of this would be happening if it wasn't for you."

"We've got a deal, remember."

"Why on earth should I trust you?"

"Because that's one thing you can do. I may be a lot of things, but I'm true to my word. Give me these twenty-four hours and if you still want to top yourself, I'll gladly feed you the pills myself. Might even have a bottle of whisky somewhere to wash them down."

"You won't change my mind."

"Maybe I will, maybe I won't. No skin off my nose. But I've promised to try. And I really think we're bonding here. The name's Rhodri by the way."

"You know what, Rhodri?"

"What?"

"You are a complete and utter *cunt*."

It takes them the best part of an hour to travel from well-fertilised gorse bush to chez Rhodri, a collection of seemingly derelict buildings in the middle of nowhere.

"Welcome to my humble abode." Stuart takes in this latest slap to the face. "It may not be much, but 'tis my own," adds Rhodri, continuing to exhibit an uncanny ability to irritate.

"It's a shithole."

"Ah, but it's my shithole. Well, when I say 'my', I mean in a possessive sense. I'm relying on the nine tenths protection that commands, plus a degree of goodwill."

"I doubt you'll have much competition."

"Fair comment. Let me give you the grand tour."

It doesn't take long and it isn't grand. In a former lifetime, it would have been a functioning farmhouse and three outbuildings arranged in a loose square around a courtyard. The structures remain, but in some disarray. The outbuildings have imploded under the weight of neglect and the passage of time, their roofs collapsing, daylight visible through walls in places. The main building doesn't look much better to Stuart's eyes as they approach and Rhodri pushes open the front door.

"Don't you lock it?"

"What's the point?"

He's right. It's barely habitable and virtually devoid of creature comforts. Downstairs comprises a large open-plan, flagstone-floored room dominated by an inglenook fireplace at one end, in front of which are clustered an armchair, a tattered sofa and a low table. The rest of the room is bare, save for a floor-to-ceiling bookcase healthily stocked with books and CDs, a simple wooden kitchen table – on which sits a CD/radio and a pile of magazines – and chairs, a camping stove connected to a gas cylinder and some shelves bowing under an assortment of cans, cartons and basic kitchenware. There's a kettle and a single light bulb hanging limply from the ceiling above the table. He sources an alternating rattling and humming to what appears to be a small fridge lurking behind the gas canister.

"You've got electricity then?"

"Most of the time. Though I doubt what I've rigged up would pass any safety standards."

"Water?"

"Listen."

Stuart frowns, hears the nearby stream and nods. "Lovely."

"I've set up a pipe line that draws off water. Runs to a tap out in one of the other buildings. Even set up a basic shower."

"Must be nice in winter."

"You get used to it."

"Maybe I *have* died after all and this is purgatory and I'm being punished for all my sins. I suppose the luxury bathroom, games room and home cinema are upstairs?"

"Nice one. Cup of tea?"

"The solution to everything. You can run to that?"

"I can try. You play chess?"

"What?"

"Chess. Do you play?"

"A bit."

"There's a set on top of the bookcase. Why don't you set it up while I conjure us up a brew? Help pass the time. And stick a CD on. I'll let you choose."

He wakes the next morning to a sore back, a throbbing headache and the sight of a worryingly self-assured rodent ambling across the floor, pausing briefly in a shaft of sunlight otherwise populated by a myriad of dancing motes.

Beside him he finds a bottle of amber liquid, a carton of milk, a glass half-full with pills and a handwritten note that says: *Have a good trip. Your choice of conveyance.* It's signed *Dr Feelgood.*

"I couldn't do it."

"What changed?"

"I beat him. He wasn't very good. Kept trying these stupid attacks." Carl frowns. "The thing was, it didn't seem to bother him at all. He just started setting up the pieces again and made his first move. And I beat him again. So we played another. And another. And the more we played, the closer the games got and the greater my dread of losing, and I realised that I might be winning but he was having by far the better time. I don't know; it's difficult to explain. But I guess I started to enjoy *what* we were doing, the process itself. Then he beat me, and the world didn't end. Game on, not game over. I was lost in a moment and everything I needed was suddenly there, stuck in some glorified outbuilding in the middle of nowhere.

"Anyway, he kept his side of the bargain and sure enough, when I woke the next morning, he'd left me everything I needed to finish the job I'd come up here for. But all I wanted was more of *that* moment. I walked down the stairs, ate a surprisingly decent fry-up and challenged him to a rematch. And I'm still in that moment."

"But up until then?"

"Never a doubt in my mind. But my narcissistic bubble burst that day and I realised life outside of it is more meaningful and honest and that I'm not alone any more. And I got out-thought by Megan. Have you spoken to her yet?"

"Briefly. And Megan is…"

"It's complicated."

"Isn't everything?"

"You're right there."

"Do you think you chose her guest house because unconsciously you wanted her to stop you?"

"I've thought about that a lot since. If I did, it was buried very deep. At the time I was one hundred per cent committed to the cause. Until Rhodri came along."

"Is he *complicated*?"

"Rhodri?" He chuckles to himself. "He's far from that. In fact, I'd go as far as to say he's the most irritating bloke I've met. And without doubt the best friend I've ever had. In this life or the last. But basically, things didn't go to plan and ultimately, female intuition and a game of chess did for me."

"So where do you live?"

"Here, believe it or not. We're pretty much off the grid. It's amazing how little you really need. We've no hot water. I have the odd bath at Megan's, but otherwise it's just the most basic of amenities. We make do."

"You're not… you know…"

Stuart laughs. "No, but he's good company. Over two years of bickering, platonic bliss. I do get out. There are pubs and shops I can go to without any worries. I have some very influential friends round here. I'm known, but not known, if you get my drift. But to all intents and purposes, I don't exist."

"But what do you do all day?"

"Play a lot of chess. Most of it with Rhodri, but also

online; the computer is our main luxury. Funnily enough, I play against Emma's nephew quite a bit. Anonymously, of course."

"Michael?"

"I met him a few times. Remember? We talked and he said he loved playing chess, so I set him up on the site. Thought nothing of it until I entered this mini-tournament a couple of years back and recognised the name. He's quite a player. Left me behind long ago."

"I know. Hang on, you're not the one pretending to be his dad, are you?"

"Is that what he thinks? Explains a lot. He's very chatty."

"*Michael*?"

"We talk all the time, if you can call typing in boxes that. About all sorts of stuff."

"And you say you're his dad?"

"Of course not. That's never come up. It's not like that. We just chat about stuff. If he wants to make it into something more to help himself come to terms with things, that's up to him. I've not encouraged it."

"That all you do here? Play chess?"

"We listen to and argue about music a lot. Rarely agree, but that's the fun of it. Same with DVDs; we have a small TV, but no licence. I walk. A lot. We're spoilt for choice on that front. Actually, I spend most of my time writing."

Carl gives a sympathetic half smile. Shares his pain. Knows exactly how it feels. A connection established. "Just because it doesn't go anywhere doesn't mean it isn't hugely enjoyable. The process, I mean. I can spend hours messing around with a paragraph, looking for a precise turn of phrase, and get huge satisfaction from it. People don't get that. They think that unless you get something published, it has no worth."

"But you do get published. Every month."

"You know about that?"

"I may be dead, but I'm not disinterested." Brings a grimace; which Carl forces into a smile; and struggles to hold under his father's gaze; and looks away. "Though I'm guessing they're not giving you any genuine satisfaction." That one hits home.

"Aarrgh. I'm stuck," says Carl, burying his head in his hands. "My novel's at the same bloody place I was when you… when you went away. I have one lousy *fucking* chapter. Well, three actually; I keep splitting it in a pathetic attempt to fool myself into thinking I might be making progress. I'm forever rewriting the same forty pages, but I can't move it on. And all the while I hear people talking about me as someone who's writing a novel and I just let them. I say nothing. I'm a fraud, happier taking the plaudits as Carl the novelist-in-waiting than actually writing something, because I'm scared stiff that if I do and it's no good, I'm not anything anymore; just Carl who wrote that crap book."

"Have you thought that maybe deep down you didn't want to outdo me; to achieve something I never could? That writing was something we shared – some way in which you could still keep a bit of me alive – and what little respect and fondness you had salvaged for me might disappear if you achieved something I never could?"

"Maybe." He laughs to himself. "Although saying that does conveniently avoid the distinct possibility that I lack the ability in the first place."

"It's funny. When it mattered more than anything else, it was so constricting and debilitating if no one was interested. But when it didn't matter, it was like a knot untied. I didn't have to think of anyone but me. I just started again. Same basic outline, but without any constraints. Just me writing for me."

"And how did that work out?" A low blow.

"That's the point. It doesn't matter." Carl can't prevent a derisory snort escaping. "But as you're asking, it worked out fine."

"How do you mean?" Fears what's coming.

"I'm coming to the end of my fifth."

"*Fifth?*"

"Like I said, it freed me up."

"Aren't you tempted to try and get them published? I'm sure you could send them off anonymously through someone else. Hey, we…"

"Carl."

"No, I'm serious. We could ask Emma's company to look at them. And if that doesn't work, you should self-publish. I know that costs, but I'm sure we could work something out."

"Carl," repeats Stuart, and this time gets Carl to look at him. "They're already published. Well, three of them anyway. The other two are flying a holding pattern in the literary sky, waiting to land in the next couple of years." Carl juggles a jumble of emotions, none of them magnanimous, then blushes at this recognition. "Nothing special. A small publishing house willing to take a chance, and people seem to like them."

"Another thing I didn't notice."

"Once again, why on earth would you? We didn't use my name, for obvious reasons."

"We?"

"Colin helped out. We did it through his firm and used a pseudonym: Philip David. I'd rewritten the first book from scratch, but just in case anyone remembered reading the first draft, we concocted a cover story. Total baloney, but needs must."

"Have you made any money from them?"

"I have a loyal following, particularly this side of the

border. There's even talk of S4C making a TV series."

"So why the hell are you still living here… like this?"

"Carl, you're not listening. This is my *choice*. The money isn't important. It's just the way of keeping score in a world I'm no longer part of."

"More money for the bloody lawyer."

"No, you get it. Eventually. Who else? Contrary to what some may have had you believe, I was never a complete fool."

"But…"

"But how? When? That was the whole reason for leaving it two years before you got the letter. We needed to make sure we could get any money to you without your mother getting involved and turning your head."

"What's to stop me giving her some later on?"

"Nothing. But at least this way it will be an informed decision."

"You know she had to go through shit when you died, don't you?" Old loyalties dying hard.

"Maybe, but she was never in any real financial difficulty and certainly didn't lack for willing benefactors. And it's not as if she hasn't done all right for herself. She was, don't forget, the first in the family to get published."

"But…"

"Look, Carl, I loved your mother. I really did. Maybe I still do, a little. But I was only ever a safe pair of hands. And the harder I tried, the more pathetic and needy I must have seemed to her. I would wish her happiness, but I suspect that will always be a fleeting concept for her."

"She's getting married again."

"I hope he's better equipped than I was."

"Who knows?" replies Carl, but that's not what's on his mind. He takes a couple of deep breaths, then dives in. "It was because of me that you got married."

"You may have been the reason she married me, but

you were *not* the cause of our problems. We screwed up in spite of you, not because of you. So don't waste your time and energy blaming yourself. Self-pity is the worst of emotions. You were the best thing by a mile that we ever did together."

"I couldn't even give you the funeral you wanted."

"That ego trip. What was I thinking?"

"But it was what you wanted."

"Not me. Him. My former self. Carl, you're not getting it. Don't you see? That list of songs came from a different person, someone who doesn't exist anymore. It would have been the longest and most self-indulgent funeral ever. It was the same with the letter I wrote you. I should have titled it 'The Narcissist's Lament'. I was desperate for validation, still trying to prove I was worth something. But you can never be everything to everyone. Why would you want to be? That's just controlling and more about yourself than them. And when perfection is the only thing that is acceptable, you're destined to always be disappointed, then more desperate, then more disappointed and so on. And the only escape from the vicious circle is to have a collapse; a fall, if you will.

"And for me… well, you know what that meant. And when it didn't go as planned, I had a choice. I could come back fighting and try and show the world they were wrong, like some phoenix rising from the ashes. But that way I would have learned nothing. It could only ever have led to failure, another rise, another fall, and never any release. This may not be much, but it's blissfully free of all the crap that brought me down before and that's good enough for me. And everything else? What I had – what I thought I had – before? Good riddance. Present company excepted, of course."

"What about what you said up here on that walk years ago?"

"That ridiculous speech before you went away to school?"

"I kind of liked it. One of the better memories."

"Okay, it had its moments, but don't you see? Too much of it was about appearance. How to *act*, not how to *be*. What *was* I thinking? That stuff will imprison you, it really will. Maybe it already has."

They both fall silent as they take emotional stock.

"What now?" says Stuart, after a while.

"I don't know. It's a lot to take in."

Stuart laughs.

"You and me both. How about we take it slowly. No plans. No expectations. The future is just a succession of todays, and I never plan for tomorrow. Let's just see how it goes."

"All right," replies Carl, still floundering.

"Come on. Let's get back."

"Talking of world reordering, what's with Grumpy? For a start, he actually spoke to me. And I thought you hated him."

"I stopped despising him and guess what, he's a real person."

They start to make their way through the trees when Carl comes to an abrupt halt.

"Can I ask you a question?"

"Of course."

"We went for this walk once. In the woods. I was fifteen or sixteen, I think. You probably won't remember, but one moment you were walking with me, and the next I looked back and you were standing in front of some trees just staring up at them. I called over, but it was like you were in a trance. Then you shook your head, snapped out of it, caught up with me and walked on as if nothing had happened."

"And?"

"It's stayed with me for some reason. Can you remember what you were thinking? It was windy and I've always told myself it was the creaking noise they were making, but… I don't know… it had to be more than that, surely?"

"I know the trees you mean. I used to stop and look at them all the time. It was the way they lent against each other and then grew apart further up. I just thought they represented us. The way we'd been. The way we were heading."

"Me being the smaller one?"

"No, the other way round, more often than not. That was the point. All those years of being so close and there you were, starting to not need me. Getting stronger all the time. And what was left for me but to shrivel away. Live in your shadow. Of course, I know that's the way it goes for all parents, but seeing it represented like that brought it home. Got me thinking every time I walked past. Different days I identified with a different one, depending on how I was feeling about life."

"I don't feel like the bigger tree. Never have. Even more so since you… disappeared. And that funny little egg pod thing on the top of that building near Kings Cross?"

He laughs. "Blimey. You remember some odd things. I know exactly what you mean, though. That one was much simpler. All about me. Whenever I looked up at it, I wanted nothing more than to find a hatch and crawl inside. Close the door. Lock myself away from the world. Shut it all out. Maybe that's what I've found here."

*

It's not until Seph's leaning over the coffee table, looking for a literature-less gap big enough to take a mug of coffee, that she finds the note. She picks it up tentatively and falls back into the comforting hug of the sofa; sensing she'll need it. She realises she's never seen his handwriting before and a ripple of sadness washes over her. She angrily shakes the unwelcome sentimentality away. Knows she should do the same with this sheet of paper, but persuades herself to read on.

Dear Seph

Sorry, but words are not really my thing. I struggle to find the right thing to say at the best of times, so the worst are always going to leave me lost. What you heard before you told me to go was a waffling preamble while I plucked up courage. I've done a lot of thinking over the past few days. What I had come to say, and would have got round to eventually had you let me get a word in (!) is that I'm a prat. My mother was an alcoholic and a compulsive gambler who would have needed to marry a cross between a saint and a psychoanalyst to have had any chance of escaping her dependencies, or at least getting to grips with whatever lay behind them. Instead she got a well-meaning, decent bloke who I don't think she ever loved other than as some kind of surrogate father figure and who was totally out of his depth. He did his best and died trying. But when you're that age your mum and dad are your heroes. They can do no wrong. And I tried everything possible to protect that status and keep them innocent parties in the mess that followed. I needed a villain and Ron fitted the bill. That was okay for a young child, even a teenager. But not for an adult. And this adult has been a pathetic, self-pitying fake conning himself into believing that he could control the world by reducing it to facts and probabilities and that winning back an arbitrary amount of money might in some way bring back a mum and dad who didn't then leave him and he could have a proper family. I know I needed to work this all out for myself, so I'm glad what happened did happen, even though that didn't mean I enjoyed being told. I threw my toys out of my pram and did what I always do when faced with reality. I ran. And nowhere in that process did I consider you. For which I am ashamed.

You and me shouldn't work. We make no sense. And yet we do. Did? But it's clear that whatever we had was based on a me that doesn't exist, not the self-deceiving hypocrite you've unmasked. But then again had I had any self-awareness would we have got together in the first place? I'm sure there's a clever move here that might rescue the day but I don't seem to do clever moves. I'm too busy playing the percentages to let myself go. It scares the shit out of me to be honest. You scare the shit out of me. You always have, but in a good way I think. I've read all those books you recommended but I'm so afraid of sounding foolish in front of you, of messing up whatever it is you see… or saw in me, that I'd rather pretend I haven't and play dumb. As you can see there's a lot that scares me. But nothing scares me more than being me without you.

I'm going to go now, not because I want to but because it's what you want and I owe you that. I just wish I'd played this hand better.

Love
Pete

P.S. Love your dancing by the way. Sorry, I peeked. Crazy… but in a very sexy way!

The word 'love' appears to have been crammed in between lines. An afterthought? No, that implies casualness and she doubts it came easily. Knows what it took.

"Well, there you go," she says to herself out loud, aware of the waver in her voice. Pretty amateurish really: poor punctuation, needs more paragraph breaks, a little repetitive and no real style. And did it grab its audience?

She squeezes her eyes tightly shut, massages them with her thumbs… and knows the levee is about to break.

*

Carl and Emma sit together two thirds of the way up the staircase, observing the ongoing merriment below; a part of the gathering, yet necessarily apart as they come to terms with this reality shift. Occasionally one of them offers up a fresh interpretation of prior events, but most of the time they just stare and repair.

Stuart stands leaning against the table, very much the eye of this social storm. Happy to let others do most of the talking, the smile on his face one of contentment and ease. Comfortable in his own skin and this much-filtered company. Living in a *now* of his own defining. By his side stands Megan, every now and then resting a hand briefly against his arm or leaning in to make some private remark; the subtext clear, or at least it would be were it not for the intermittent presence of Rhodri and the obvious fondness the three of them have for each other.

"What is it with those three?" says Carl, voicing what they're both thinking.

"I don't know," she replies, in that way of hers that usually means she thinks she does. And sure enough, "I'd say it's honesty and mutual respect. I think they're just doing the best they can."

Carl nods as if he understands, which he doesn't really; and tentatively changes the subject.

“What about us?”

“Don’t, Carl. I know where you’re going and we’ve been though that so many times.”

“But doesn’t all this…” He gestures at the chattering congregation below.

“Change anything? Between us?” She sighs. “You’re persistent, I’ll give you that.” He senses a chink and offers her his most endearing smile. Playing his trump card. “That wasn’t a compliment and that look doesn’t work anymore. I don’t want a little boy to mother. It changes nothing. I’ve done my bit getting you here and I’ll drive you home tomorrow. But that’s it. Then we’re done. Over to you. Just take some bloody responsibility, for fuck’s sake.”

And there he sits, once more searching for the words that might make a difference.

EPILOGUE

Carl rebuilds his chip stack, running out of patience with a game being played at his expense, the effort of sustaining a facade of ambivalence taking its toll. And his face is itching like crazy. He gives up, sends the chips flying and addresses the room.

"All right. Very funny. You got me. Don't you want to know?" Blank faces stare back, the bluff maintained. "Well, fuck off, the lot of you."

Kevin takes pity and permits a smile that quickly proves contagious.

"Go on then, tell us what happened," he says.

The release sends Carl's hand up to his face, where it probes gently at the bruising, then scratches tentatively at its edges.

"Box populi is what happened. Last week."

"That smug look tells us you think you've just been very clever. I'm guessing there was a witty pun in there somewhere, but I'm afraid you've lost us."

"It appears that some people have taken exception to my light-hearted little commentaries on the vagaries of the world."

"Is that what you call them?"

"They're just banter."

"Ah, banter," comes in Seph. "That very masculine word used to excuse being casually rude, racist, misogynistic or homophobic."

"It's all harmless stuff."

"To you, maybe," says Pete. "But banter can only really exist between people who know each other's boundaries, and that's not what your articles are. They're just you taking the piss. And you wonder why people take exception now and then?"

Carl bridles at this new-look loved-up Pete, complete with tag team partner, but ploughs on. "It appears I upset some readers with one particular article I wrote."

"*Really*? Which one?" asks Kevin, and Carl can't help but smile.

"The one about that day I spent driving round spotting all the crap motorists. But I was stitched up by the magazine. The initial draft I submitted had all the full car registrations in. I knew they couldn't be published, but it made me feel more like an investigative journalist if I forced them to censure me. Anyway, I was told they'd take out enough letters and numbers to protect the anonymity of the idiots involved, while still giving enough so that they'd know who they were; or more to the point, people who knew them would. I just left them to it. The official story, if you believe it, is that a regrettable administrative error led to a first batch of magazines going out with the full detail still intact. It was spotted after a flurry of calls complaining and the offending copies were recalled immediately, though not before the press had picked up on it. Made a few of the tabloids."

"But you don't believe that?"

"No, of course not. They're far too savvy for that. No publicity is bad publicity and they got a shed load of it. The whole thing was managed for maximum impact at minimum cost. They just needed a fall guy and that's where I came in. Not that I was bothered. I got some serious journalistic kudos, and I liked the thought of some of those morons having to face the music. Sort of the point of the article in the first place."

"And?"

"There was one bloke I gave a special mention to. Driving like a total nutter on the M25, weaving in and out of lanes going way too fast. Turns out that he was on a last warning from Daddy, who'd said that if he ever drove like that again in a car with his company's name all over it, he'd lose the car and would get taken off sales and stuck in a back office on half pay. My article did for him, particularly when journalists turned up asking his dad for a reaction. Serves him right of course, and a big hurrah for parental consistency, but the son thought differently."

"How do you know all this?"

"He told me last night; breathed it in my face in a cloud of cheap aftershave and second-hand alcohol as I lay winded after he'd knocked me to the ground with a sucker punch and his mates held me down. Apparently, Daddy was true to his word, plus his girlfriend chucked him when he couldn't ferry her round any more or afford to take her out. He'd taken it all quite badly, poor chap, and needed someone to take it out on."

"Report him to the police," says Pete, and can't help but glance at David, who raises his hands to say *don't look at me*.

"Ah, might have a problem there," replies Carl. "It was made very clear to me what would happen if I did. It appears it's not just him and a few other piss-poor selfish drivers. There was another article I wrote that upset a few people."

"Who?"

"Mini drivers, BMW drivers, golfers, cigar smokers, people who wear hats in cars, blokes who say 'mate' or 'buddy' a lot or call women 'love'… let me see."

"How did you manage to offend *all* of them?" asks Pete.

"It was a subtle piece. A quiz actually. Called *Are you a Cock?*"

"Nice."

"Not my choice. I wanted to use another four-letter word beginning with 'c'. It was a load of questions for the readers to answer and then they got to see what band they fell into. A self-help piece, basically. One single 'yes' was enough for there to be a rebuttable presumption of cock-ness, so it was all encompassing. Just a bit of harmless fun."

"But not for them, maybe."

"No sense of humour. Matey-boy got in touch with a few owners' clubs, cigar-smoking websites and so on; it didn't take much to whip them all into a frenzy. He says he's the tip of an iceberg I don't want to be messing with."

"He sounds very eloquent," says Charlotte.

"My words. His were a bit cruder and to the point. He let me know that this was a message from the lot of them. They'll be more to follow if I don't take my medicine like a good little boy. Then they gave me a couple more kicks and they were off."

"Mmm. Methinks there might be a moral lurking in that little cautionary tale."

"You reckon I got what I deserved."

"I reckon you've had a charmed life, that's all," says Kevin. "I don't support what those idiots did. But you've been dishing it out like you're untouchable for years now, and sooner or later someone was going to bite back. I'm just surprised it took this long."

Carl retreats into silence, before changing tack.

"If this bruising doesn't die down, I'm going to get a lot of dodgy looks this weekend."

"The chess competition?" asks Kevin.

"Bit more than that. England trials."

"Does the kid know he's doing it vicariously for Uncle

Carl? Or that he's a pawn in your never-ending mission to win back his auntie?"

"Bloody hell, Kevin. What the fuck? Girlfriend, long words, pseudo-insight and a pun to top it all off. The new world order really has arrived. Well, you're wrong. I'm just finishing something I started. And I want his mum to see how good he is."

"She's going as well?"

"I'm working on it." And in reply to Kevin's quizzical look, adds "Don't even go there."

"Talking of children, how are the little additions to the family?"

"What's this?" asks Pete.

"Carl has come into an interesting inheritance."

"How much?"

"Nine K," replies Kevin, warming to his task and heading into punning overdrive. "Or should that be K-nine."

"Very good, Kev. No, really, sensational stuff," says Carl.

"Not to be sniffed at," offers Pete supportively.

"Oh, I don't know. Definitely to be sniffed at, eh, Carl?"

"Careful, Kev, or you'll give yourself a nosebleed. What Kevin is hinting at oh so subtly is that my elderly next-door neighbour died recently and left me her two delinquent dogs in her will."

"Shit. Bum deal. You could refuse though, couldn't you?"

"I suppose I could."

Kevin moves all in.

He has Carl covered.

Pete still to bet, hands placed behind his stack like he's ready to shove.

Means nothing, of course, but…

All eyes on Carl. Who is struggling. Has been all evening, if he's honest with himself. And not liking how it feels. Looking for explanations; excuses. Thinking maybe it's David – or *Dave*, as Carl insists on calling him; can see he hates it – still learning; the classic poker free radical disrupting with the randomness of his dabbles in hands? Or it could be these disconcerting women, so uninterested in him. Or it's wondering where the old Peter and Kevin have gone; who are these insouciant strangers playing, it pains him to admit, with a degree of imagination and creativity? And then there's the chiding of himself for inviting Darren – an inevitable casualty in the PFN cull, the rationale for his position proving even more evasive than Carl's, and now retraining as a social worker – slouching there beside him wearing sunglasses, oversized headphones leaking the nagging thump and hiss of some misogynistic rap bollocks, the peak of his baseball cap pulled down low; new cliché, same twat. Not even in the hand, and still performing.

Or maybe it's that he's pot-committed and facing the ignominy of being first to fall and on kitchen duty, with all this dead money swilling around just begging to be mopped up.

"Is it just me, or does no one have a bloody clue where they are in this hand?"

ACKNOWLEDGEMENTS

My heartfelt thanks to the following, who endured drafts of this and its companion piece in various guises and offered me their feedback and encouragement:

Jayne, Jack, Joe, Jude, Richard Pipe, Paul Hanson, Antony Durrant, Paul James, Dr Stephen Carver, Martin Ouvry and finally, Andy Lawton, who first suggested a way to divide a behemoth into two more digestible portions.

Matador